Cindi Myers is the author of more than fifty novels. When she's not plotting new romance story lines, she enjoys skiing, gardening, cooking, crafting and daydreaming. A lover of small-town life, she lives with her husband and two spoiled dogs in the Colorado mountains.

New York Times and *USA TODAY* bestselling author **Caridad Piñeiro** is a Jersey girl who just wants to write and is the author of nearly fifty novels and novellas. She loves romance novels, superheroes, TV and cooking. For more information on Caridad and her dark, sexy romantic suspense and paranormal romances, please visit caridad.com

Also by Cindi Myers

Eagle Mountain Cliffhanger
Canyon Kidnapping
Disappearance at Dakota Ridge
Conspiracy in the Rockies
Missing at Full Moon Mine
Grizzly Creek Standoff
Investigation in Black Canyon
Mountain of Evidence
Mountain Investigation
Presumed Deadly

Also by Caridad Piñeiro

Lost in Little Havana
Cold Case Reopened
Trapping a Terrorist
Decoy Training

Discover more at millsandboon.co.uk

MOUNTAIN TERROR

CINDI MYERS

BRICKELL AVENUE AMBUSH

CARIDAD PIÑEIRO

MILLS & BOON

First Published in Great Britain 2022
by Mills & Boon, an imprint of HarperCollins*Publishers* Ltd
1 London Bridge Street, London, SE1 9GF

www.harpercollins.co.uk

HarperCollins*Publishers*
Macken House, 39/40 Mayor Street Upper,
Dublin 1, D01 C9W8

Mountain Terror © 2022 Cynthia Myers
Brickell Avenue Ambush © 2022 Caridad Piñeiro Scordato

ISBN: 978-0-263-30370-4

1222

MOUNTAIN TERROR

CINDI MYERS

Chapter One

The school bus lay on its side halfway down the canyon, its path from the roadway marked by the torn limbs of trees and deep groove marks in the layer of snow over the rocky surface. As Ryan Welch and the other members of Eagle Mountain Search and Rescue made their way down to the wreck, the terrified screams of children rose above the roar of rushing waters from the creek below. An involuntary shiver raced up Ryan's spine, and he picked up the pace, half skidding down the incline, his boots sinking into the snow with every step, the vacuum mattress strapped to his back bouncing against his pack.

"We've got to secure the vehicle before we can go inside," SAR Captain Tony Meisner ordered. He directed a trio of volunteers—Ted Carruthers, Eldon Ramsey and Austen Morrissey—to affix lines to the vehicle and chock the wheels, while the others waited in an anxious huddle just up the slope.

The screaming in the vehicle rose to a fever pitch, and several children stuck their heads out the open windows of the bus. "Help!" they screamed, and waved their hands, frantic. "Our teacher is hurt and I think the bus driver is dead!" one girl shouted.

"Remain calm!" Tony, a tall, bearded man in his late

thirties, instructed through a handheld hailer. "Help is on the way."

"That bus isn't going anywhere now." Ted Carruthers, tall and wiry, with thick gray hair and a gray goatee, reported to Tony. "It's wedged against some good-sized boulders, and we've secured all the lines."

Tony nodded and studied the vehicle. "Let's see if we can get those back emergency doors open and go in that way," he said. "If not, we'll climb on top."

Tony led the way to the bus. "Can someone open the emergency exit?" he shouted.

"I'll try," a voice called from inside. Ryan couldn't tell if the speaker was an adult, or an older child. The person who had called in the accident hadn't been able to tell the dispatcher how many people were on the bus, only that it was full of middle school students and their chaperones, on their way home to Eagle Mountain, Colorado, from a drama competition on the other side of the pass.

The back door of the bus popped open and children began to spill out. "Stop!" Tony shouted. "Nobody move!"

Everyone froze. One boy had one foot on top of a boulder beside the bus, the other still inside the vehicle, but he stilled and looked expectantly at the SAR commander. "You're going to exit one at a time," Tony instructed. "A volunteer will help each of you and check you out to make sure you're okay. Then another volunteer will escort you to the road. If you're hurt, remain inside the bus until one of us can help you. Understood?"

Choruses of "Yes," and "Okay" and "Yes, sir," rose from the bus.

Things moved quickly after that. Sheriff's deputies and fire department personnel moved in to assist the children who hadn't been injured. As soon as they were out of the way, Ryan, along with paramedic Hannah Richards and nurse Danny Irwin, climbed into the bus, scrambling awkwardly over the seats to reach the huddle of people near the middle.

While Hannah and Danny focused on a child who was screaming and clutching her arm, Ryan moved toward a woman who sat slumped against the roof of the sideways bus. Blood poured from a gash on her head. Twentysomething, with honey-brown hair now soaked in blood, she wore a stick-on name badge that identified her as Ms. Traynor. "Ma'am?" Ryan touched her cheek, which was soft and reassuringly warm, in spite of the chill that had seeped into the bus. "Ma'am, can you hear me?"

The woman's eyelids fluttered, then she looked up at him with green-blue eyes. Beautiful eyes, which should have been full of distress, considering her situation. Instead, she began to giggle.

Ryan sat back on his heels. "Deni! You're supposed to be seriously injured. You're not supposed to laugh."

"I know!" She choked back a fresh wave of laughter, and tried to sit up a little straighter against the sloping roof. "It just sounds so funny when you call me *ma'am*."

"Could you just get back in character, please?"

She assumed a sober expression. "Of course. Where were we?"

"I'm trying to assess if you're conscious or not."

"Right." She closed her eyes and rested her head back against the bus once more. The high school student who had volunteered to do the makeup for this training exercise had done a phenomenal job, making Deni's injuries look real. The only thing missing, he realized, was the metallic smell of blood. Instead, the aroma was slightly sweet. He forced his thoughts back to the task at hand. His job was to assess Deni's status.

But as soon as he touched her shoulder, she opened

her eyes again. "Am I conscious or not?" she asked. "I can't remember."

Before he could answer, Danny leaned over Ryan's shoulder. "What have we got here?" he asked.

Ryan decided to skip ahead in the script. "We have a young woman with a head injury. She's conscious, pupils evenly dilated and responsive to light, vision tracking." He reached up and gently felt the back of her head. "No depression of the skull." He caught and held Deni's gaze. "Have you vomited?"

She wrinkled her nose. "No!"

Ryan shifted his hand to her neck. "Pulse is strong and regular," he said, ignoring the flutter of awareness at the feel of her warm, silken skin against his fingers. "Are you hurt anywhere else?" he asked.

"No. I was in my seat, with the seat belt fastened, when the bus went off the road, and I was slammed against the side of the bus and hit my head." She touched the gash on her forehead and winced, convincingly, then stared at her hand, now red and sticky with fake blood.

"Let's get her in a cervical collar and on the litter for transport to the ambulance," Danny said.

"What am I supposed to do now?" Deni whispered after Danny had left them.

"Whatever we tell you," Ryan said.

"That could get pretty interesting," she said. The words—and the flirtatious look that accompanied them—sent a rush of heat through him. Maybe she really had hit her head—this was a side of Deni he hadn't seen before in their frequent encounters at the local coffee shop where they both stopped before work most mornings. Not that he knew her well, but he had definitely noticed her. He looked forward to seeing her. He had even been thinking about working up the nerve to ask her out.

Tony and Eldon moved in with the litter and the three of them set about the awkward task of balancing it over the bus seats and helping Deni into it. She played the part of a disoriented injured person well, complete with being uncooperative and unable to follow directions. "You don't have to be quite this realistic," Ryan whispered to her ten minutes into the ordeal. "We have other patients to see to."

"Sorry," she mumbled, and meekly hoisted herself onto the litter.

He left Eldon and Tony to transport her to the roadway, while he moved on to the next "victim," a thirteen-year-old boy who sported an impressive network of cuts on his face, as well as bruises indicating a broken nose. He moaned dramatically as Ryan touched him. "Am I going to be scarred for life?" he asked.

"It's amazing what plastic surgery can do," Ryan said. "Can you tell me where it hurts?"

"My back hurts."

"Your back?" Maybe the dramatic makeup job on the kid's face was designed to throw him off. "Where exactly, does it hurt?"

The boy started to sit up, but Ryan pushed him down. "It's very important for you to lie still. If you try to move, you could injure yourself further. Just tell me where the pain is."

"It's in the middle of my back," the boy said.

Ryan prodded the boy's ankle. "Can you feel that?" Each victim had been coached ahead of time as to what symptoms they should display, but the first responders had been kept in the dark about what to expect.

"I can feel you fine." The boy sat up. "I just ended up laying on something and it's poking me."

Ryan reached back and retrieved a red aluminum

water bottle. The boy's face lit up. "Hey, I've been looking for that."

"Great," Ryan said. "Now could you lie back down
and let me treat you?"

The boy grinned. "Sure." He lay back down and let out
another moan. "My face! My modeling career is ruined!"

DENI, FREED FROM the litter, some of the corn-syrup-and-
food-coloring fake blood wiped away, sat on a boulder
just past the ambulance, her hands wrapped around a mug
of coffee. The trip up from the canyon, strapped to the
litter, had been more frightening than she had thought it
would be, though the search and rescue volunteers had
assured her they knew what they were doing and wouldn't
drop her. Still, the sensation of having to rely totally on
other people for her safety had been unsettling.

Those few minutes with Ryan in the bus had been
fun, though. She smiled, remembering. After weeks of
exchanging hellos and comments about the weather with
the good-looking man who always stopped for coffee
about the same time she did, it had been nice to get a little
more up-close and personal, as it were. Careful questioning of friends who kept track of that kind of thing had
revealed that Ryan Welch was twenty-four, worked for
the Ride Brothers, a local manufacturer of snowboards
and skateboards, and was not, as far as anyone knew,
seriously dating.

As it so happened, neither was she. So the challenge
became how to arrange for the two of them to go out
together. She could simply ask, she supposed, but if he
turned her down it would be too embarrassing. So her
plan was to let him know she was interested and take it
from there.

"More coffee?" Iris Desmet, owner of the Cake Walk Café, approached, a large insulated carafe in one hand.

"I'm good." Deni smiled. "Thanks for providing refreshments."

"It's the least I can do. Would you like a cookie?" Iris slipped her hand into the pocket of her apron and pulled out a large cookie wrapped in Cling Wrap. "Chocolate chip."

"Wow. Thank you." Deni accepted the cookie, which she knew from previous experience was as close to perfect as a cookie could get.

"How's your dad?" Iris asked. "He usually comes in a few times a week, and I haven't seen him for a while."

"Oh, he's fine. Just busy, I guess." She struggled to keep her smile in place, and tried to ignore the sudden cramping in her stomach. The truth was, she hadn't seen her dad in several days, either. She had spoken to him on the phone, once, when he called to tell her he was going to be working on something for the next few weeks and it would be better if she didn't come around. He had refused to elaborate and had ended up hanging up on her. Her father had always had his quirks, but this secretiveness was new, and worried her.

"Well, when you see Mike, you tell him to stop in soon." Iris moved on to the next volunteer.

A cheer rose from the crowd by the roadside and Deni looked up to see the search and rescue crew, their bright blue parkas and yellow climbing helmets standing out against the gray and white of snow and rock, climbing out of the canyon. The county's emergency management director, Sam Olsen, shook SAR Captain Tony Meisner's hand as Tammy Patterson from the *Eagle Mountain Examiner* snapped a photo. "Great exercise," Sam said. A young man with a long blond ponytail, Sam was a familiar figure in town. He had visited Deni's eighth grade classroom earlier that year to talk about outdoor safety to kids for whom hiking, skiing and camping were as much a part of daily life as riding public transportation might be for city kids.

"Thanks, everyone, for all your help," Tony said, addressing the gathered volunteers. Several of the students, still sporting their "victim" makeup, stood with their parents, grinning broadly. Tanner Vincent, who had played the part of someone cut up by windshield glass, raised two thumbs up. "These kinds of exercises help us learn the best ways to respond to a real emergency," Tony continued. "Though let's hope none of what we pretended today ever becomes a reality."

Another cheer rose, though a shiver ran down Deni's spine. As much as no one ever wanted to deal with a tragedy like a school bus crash, the treacherous mountain passes and harsh winter weather around Eagle Mountain meant they were only one icy spot on the highway from a scenario very like what they had playacted today.

She finished her coffee and stood to go. "Hey, Deni!"

Her heart beat faster as she turned to see Ryan striding toward her. He had removed his helmet, leaving his dark hair ruffled, and his cheeks were reddened by wind and cold. The effect was to make him look even heartier and more rugged. Or maybe she just thought that because she had been nursing a crush on him for weeks now. "It was good to see you today," he said, stopping in front of her.

She put up a hand to brush her hair back from her cheek and felt the stickiness of the fake blood. She must look horrible, with most of the makeup still in place that portrayed her as having hit her head. She guessed it was a good sign that that wasn't putting him off. "It's good to see you, too," she said.

"How did you end up volunteering for this?"

"When Sam came to recruit kids from my class, he asked if I'd like to participate, too." She shrugged. "It sounded like a fun way to spend a Saturday morning."

He chuckled. "If you say so."

"We can't all moonlight as superheroes," she teased, and felt the spark of heat from the look he gave her in response.

"Listen," he said. "I—"

But she didn't get to hear what he would have said next, as Sheriff Travis Walker interrupted with an announcement over the speakers in his SUV. "Everyone needs to leave the area immediately," he said. "Please return to your vehicles and leave now!"

"What's going on?" Ryan asked one of the deputies who was hurrying past.

"There's a suspicious object attached to the piling of the bridge." He pointed downhill, toward the highway bridge over Grizzly Creek, approximately one hundred yards from where Ryan and Deni stood.

"What kind of object?" Deni asked.

The deputy shook his head. "We don't know for sure, but it might be a bomb. We need to get everyone out of here, just to be safe."

A bomb. The word hit Deni like a punch in the gut. She swayed, suddenly dizzy. *No. This really can't be happening.*

Chapter Two

All the color had drained from Deni's face behind the garish makeup, and she looked as if she might faint. Alarmed, Ryan took her arm. "Hey, are you okay?" he asked.

"Just a little…shook up." She swallowed hard, and her eyes met his, terror making the pupils huge.

"Come on," he said. "Where's your car?"

"Back at the school," she said. "Another bus dropped us all off this morning." She looked around. "I think it was supposed to pick us up."

"I don't see it," Ryan said. "You can come with me."

She looked toward the bridge. The sheriff and three deputies stood on the edge of the road, looking down into the creek. "I should stay," she whispered, so softly he almost didn't hear her.

"We have to leave," Ryan said. He tugged her toward the parking area.

She didn't resist, but let him lead her toward his battered Tundra. He spotted Tony in the parking area, along with paramedic Hannah Richards. "How did they find this supposed bomb?" Ryan asked.

"Jake and Shane hiked down to the creek to make sure no debris from the wrecked bus had washed into the water and saw it," Hannah said. She was dating Deputy Jake Gwynn, and Deputy Shane Ellis was his best friend.

"What did they see?" Deni asked. She didn't look as dazed as she had at first, though she was still pale, and her voice shook.

"Jake said it looked like a bundle of highway flares," Hannah said. "I don't know any more than that."

"Or it could be dynamite," Tony said.

"Lots of people knew we were doing this mock bus crash today," Ryan observed. "Maybe this is someone's idea of a joke."

"Sick joke," Tony said. He took his keys from his pocket. "Anyway, we'd better get out of here and let the cops do their job. Good work today." He nodded to Deni. "You, too."

Deni slid into the passenger seat of the Tundra and Ryan joined the caravan of vehicles headed back into Eagle Mountain. She remained silent until they were almost back to town, then she pulled out her cell phone. She punched in a number, then listened to the phone ring and ring. She stabbed the button to end the call and pocketed the phone again. "Everything okay?" Ryan asked.

"I was trying to call my dad," she said. "But he isn't answering."

"I doubt he could have heard about this already," Ryan replied. "I bet the sheriff didn't broadcast something like this on the scanner."

"I, um, I just promised to call him when the mock crash was over," she said.

"Your dad is Mike Traynor, right?" Ryan asked. "He lives in that off-grid cabin up Tennyson's Gulch?"

Her eyes flashed with something like alarm. "How did you know that?"

"I drove up there this fall to look at those cliffs for

possible climbing," he said. "A buddy and I met your dad. He told us he thought the rock there was too brittle for climbing, and he was right. He introduced himself as Mike Traynor, so I figured, right age, same last name..."

She nodded. "That's him."

"Cool place he has, though I imagine it can be rough up there in winter. The county doesn't plow that road, does it?"

"Dad has a tractor and he keeps it clear," she said. "Or he uses his snowmobile. He says he likes the privacy."

"He's got that. Did you grow up there?"

She shook her head. "No. I grew up in Amarillo, Texas. Dad was a truck driver and my mother was a teacher."

"Like you."

"Yeah. Like me."

He wondered if he had said the wrong thing. She looked like she might be about to cry. He was really out of practice talking to women, or at least, talking to women he was attracted to. He searched for something else to say, to lighten the mood, but before he could think of anything, she said, "Mom died of cancer about a year and a half ago, about nine months after I moved to Eagle Mountain."

"I'm sorry," he said. "That must have been rough." His own parents were living happily in Albuquerque and though he didn't see them that often, he couldn't imagine not having them in his life.

"It was." She sighed. "Hard for me, but harder for Dad. I worried about him, in that big house by himself. When he said he had decided to move here, I was so happy."

She didn't sound happy now. "Why do I sense a *but* at the end of that sentence?" he asked.

"I thought he meant he'd get a condo in town, or a little

house—not that he would move up into the mountains and live like...like some hermit."

He thought about what he could say to reassure her. She was still obviously upset, though he wasn't sure if she was worried about the supposed bomb, or her father or both. He probably shouldn't even get involved, but it tore at him, seeing her so distressed. "I can see how you would worry about him, living so remotely, and alone," he said. "But he seems like he's in good shape, and he's not that old, is he?"

She shook her head. "He's 55, and healthy. It's just..." She didn't finish the sentence, merely shook her head again.

They were almost to the school now. "My car is around back," she told him. "In the employee lot."

He slowed, but instead of turning into the lot, he said, "I don't like leaving you by yourself when you're still so upset. Do you want to go somewhere for a cup of coffee? Or something to eat?"

"I wouldn't be very good company right now," she observed.

"I'm not asking you to entertain me," he said. "I just want to make sure you're okay."

She straightened her shoulders, and looked him in the eye for the first time since she'd gotten into his car. "I'll be fine. I'm sorry I overreacted. The idea that we were so close to a bomb, with the children and everything... it was so unexpected."

"Of course it was." Her fear made more sense now— it showed how seriously she took her responsibilities toward her students. That made him like her even more. It made him want to take a risk and get to know her better. "Are you sure you don't want that coffee?"

She smiled, a genuine smile that warmed him deep

inside. "Can I take a rain check? I have some things I have to do at home."

"You bet." He glanced in the rearview mirror and saw a car approaching, so he turned into the lot. "Maybe we can meet up one day after school."

"I'd like that."

He dropped her at her car, then drove to search and rescue headquarters. The metal building with three bays with roll-up garage doors was perched on the side of a mountain above town, convenient to both Caspar Canyon and Dixon Pass, as well as most of the trailheads leading into the high mountains, all locations of frequent callouts for the squad. Most of the other volunteers were already there, unpacking and inventorying gear, re-coiling ropes, restocking medical supplies and getting everything ready for the next emergency.

"How was it out there for you today?" Tony asked as Ryan passed him on the way to help with the climbing gear.

"Good." Ryan resisted the urge to rub the arm he had injured last month. Today's training exercise had been his first time to suit up as part of the team since the accident.

"No weakness in the arm?" Tony asked.

Ryan's first impulse was to lie and say he was fine— a hundred percent. But Tony and the other members of the team would depend on him in tough situations. If he wasn't up to the task, he needed to be truthful. "A little," he admitted. "But I'm getting a lot stronger."

Tony nodded. "You've come a long way. We'll keep you a light-duty until you're back full strength. Don't overdo it."

"I won't," Ryan said, though the temptation was always there. When Charlie Cutler, a convicted serial killer who was running from the law, had shoved him off the side of Mount Baker, he had been sure he would die. Thick snow had saved him from fatal injury, but after he had awakened from surgery to piece together his damaged arm, he had feared the life he loved, which revolved around climbing, and search and rescue, had ended. Hours of therapy and work were bringing him back, but he worried he would never be the person his fellow team members would trust to bear his share of the load.

It was bad enough knowing that if they knew about his past, they probably wouldn't trust him ever again. He couldn't help thinking he had to work harder than other people to prove he was worthy of their faith in him. He pushed away these thoughts and moved to help the others. "Any more news on that bomb?" he asked as he helped rookie Austen Morrissey and Training Officer Sheri Stevens hang up coils of climbing rope.

"It was a real bomb, all right," Austen said. "The sheriff's department had to call in an explosives team from Junction to disarm the thing. I heard one of them say if it had detonated, it would have taken out the whole bridge and probably shut down the highway for months."

"Who would do something like that?" Sheri asked.

"A terrorist," Austen said.

"In Eagle Mountain?" Sheri shook her head. "Who cares what happens here?"

"They just finished that bridge last fall," Ryan added. "Didn't it win some kind of design award?"

"So maybe the designer's rival blew it up, jealous that he or she didn't win instead?" Sheri looked skeptical.

"More likely, it's just some crank trying to make trouble," Ryan speculated.

"The world is full of those," Austen said.

But Eagle Mountain wasn't, Ryan thought. Or at least, it hadn't been. Sure, bad things happened here—murders and robberies and natural disasters. But terrorism seemed pretty extreme for a small town in the middle of nowhere. And why try to take out a bridge that the bomber had to know would just be built again?

He didn't like to think about anyone trying to destroy the beauty and peace of this place. Eagle Mountain was his safe place. He had built a good life here after a bunch of big mistakes. He would rather focus on folks like Deni, who was so concerned about her students that even the prospect of danger to them upset her. She was the kind of person he wanted to be around.

The kind of person he wanted to know better.

AFTER TRYING UNSUCCESSFULLY to reach her father on his cell phone all Saturday, Deni got up early Sunday morning and decided to drive up to her father's place. Never mind that he had told her to stay away. She was his daughter and she had a right to see him. Not to mention, what if he wasn't answering her calls because he was sick or hurt? Who else but her would care enough to check on him?

Though Mike Traynor's cabin was only about ten miles from Deni's house in town, it took her almost forty-five minutes to reach the remote dwelling, the last half hour on a road that was little more than a narrow Jeep trail. She coaxed her Outback through snow-packed ruts that must have been made by her father's four-wheel drive truck, until she reached the gate where he usually parked in the winter. His truck, with its cab-over camper, wasn't there, and neither was the snowmobile he kept chained to a nearby aspen.

Ignoring the sick feeling in the pit of her stomach, Deni strapped on the snowshoes she'd brought with her, slipped on a pack and headed up the path through the bare aspens for the last half mile. The day was cold, but clear, and she hadn't gone very far before she stopped to peel off her parka. The sun beat down and ice crystals sparkled on every surface. If she hadn't been so worried, the effect would have been magical.

She followed the snowmobile's tracks, which told her her father had probably traveled this way to his parked truck. Had he loaded the snowmobile onto a trailer to pull behind the truck? Maybe he'd decided to go play on the snowmobile for the day. That was probably why he hadn't answered her calls—he was out of cell range.

If that was the case, she didn't need to be concerned. She began to feel a little better. That was probably it. As much as she worried about her father, he was a grown man, in good health. He had always liked being in nature and after a lifetime on the plains of Texas, he had fallen in love with these mountains just as Deni had.

Yes, he was grieving the loss of his wife, but maybe living in this remote location, surrounded by nature, was healing for him. Maybe he wasn't retreating from life so much as immersing himself in it. He had been excited when he first told her about the cabin. "There's nobody up there to bother me," he had said. She had argued that it wasn't good for him to be so alone but maybe that was what he had needed.

By the time she was in sight of the cabin, she had convinced herself she was worrying for nothing. The same way she had overreacted to news of that bomb at the bridge. Ever since her mother's death, her emotions had been so close to the surface, like exposed nerves sensitive to the slightest stimulus. No one told you that about grief—how it stripped you of so much, and just when you were sure you were getting better, something happened to rip off the scab and expose all your pain again.

Her father's cabin, built two decades ago as a summer retreat for a family from Houston, Texas, was a one-room structure with a sleeping loft and a deep front porch sided with slabs of rough cedar, protected from the elements by a rusting metal roof with deep eaves. Water came from a spring up above the structure, and an outhouse sat in a grove of aspen a hundred yards behind the house. Her father had added a three-sided shed where he kept his truck and the snowmobile, a workbench and an assortment of tools. The truck and snowmobile were gone from the shed, she noted. At the bottom of the porch steps she kicked off her snowshoes and mounted the steps to the porch. The door was in deep shadow, so she didn't see the big padlock until she was right on it. The lock was dull brass, as large as her fist with a hasp as big around as her finger. She had never seen it before. Then again, she had never been here when her father wasn't home.

She stared at the lock a long moment, then moved to the window beside the door and peered in. Dark drapes had been pulled over the window so she couldn't see inside. A shiver washed over her, and she hugged her arms across her chest as she paced the length of the porch. A neat stack of firewood sat at one end, a wooden bench her father had constructed of half logs at the other. Snow had blown in to dust the surface of the bench. It added to the abandoned atmosphere of the place, as if the person who lived here had left for good.

She was letting her imagination run away from her again. Resolutely, she pulled out her phone, intending to call her father again and let him know she had stopped by. Her father had installed a cell booster that allowed him to make and receive calls. She punched in her dad's number and was surprised when, this time, the call went straight to voice mail. A robotic voice recited her father's number—no name or instruction to leave a message and he would return her call. Her father had told her this was because he didn't want to hear from anyone, or return any calls, though he had agreed to make an exception for her.

"Dad, it's Deni. I drove up to the cabin to see you. I see the snowmobile isn't here, so I guess you're out riding it somewhere. Call me when you get back. Let's have dinner sometime. My…my Outback is making a funny noise and I'd like you to listen to it and tell me what you think."

That last was an afterthought, and a complete fabrication. Her Outback was running fine, but, while her father was as likely to turn down a dinner invitation as to accept it, he felt an obligation to keep her car running well and make minor repairs at her home. "There's no need to waste your money hiring someone who probably doesn't even know what he's doing," he would say. He had spent his lifetime repairing everything from cars to well pumps to small appliances. He didn't trust anyone else to do the job right.

She ended the call and started to tuck the phone into her pocket once more when it vibrated in her hand. Startled, she checked the screen and saw an unfamiliar local number. "Hello?" she answered.

"Deni, it's Ryan. I called to see how you were doing this morning."

Butterflies rustled in her stomach. "Hi, Ryan. I'm good. How are you?"

"I'm good. Um… I wondered if you had time for lunch today?"

She checked the time—just a little after ten. "That would be nice."

"Want to meet at Mo's at noon? Or we could go someplace else, if you like."

"Mo's is fine." She had plenty of time to get back to her house and change.

"I guess you heard that was a real bomb they found," he said. "Though it was defective or something. The explosives team from Junction said it couldn't have detonated, the way it was wired."

The butterflies had all died, replaced by a sick heaviness. "Do they have any idea who put it there?" she asked.

"I don't think so. I'm sure they're looking. Hey, I've got another call coming in. Don't go away."

Before she could tell him goodbye, that she'd see him at noon, he was gone, leaving her on Hold. She couldn't hang up now, so she held the phone in one hand and put on her snowshoes, awkwardly fastening the clips with one hand.

"Sorry about that," Ryan came back on the line. "And I'm sorry I'm going to have to cancel our lunch. That was Tony. Search and rescue got a callout."

"Oh no," she said. "What is it? I mean, are you allowed to say?"

"An injured climber in Caspar Canyon."

"I hope they're okay," she said.

"Me, too. I've got to go. Talk to you later."

"I'll look forward to that."

She ended the call and tucked the phone away, a little shaky with relief. Not that there was anything good about an injured climber, but at least it hadn't been another bomb.

She glanced toward the shed, and the workbench inside. She was tempted to go in there and look around—but what was she looking for? Her father had told her he had purchased dynamite to blast out a dam of ice that was blocking the spring. Why shouldn't she believe him? She had trusted her father her whole life.

It felt wrong not to trust him now. He had changed since her mother's death, but so had she. Loss changed people. Did she seriously believe her dad—her father—had been building bombs? Just because he had complained a lot lately about the cost of progress and development—just because he had said someone should "do something to slow all this down"—that didn't mean he had turned into a terrorist.

Chapter Three

Some search and rescue callouts were almost peaceful—
long hikes in beautiful country to retrieve an injured
hiker. A sense of urgency drove every action, but the
scene was controlled and orderly. Everyone had a job to
do and performed each task with choreographed grace.

Then there were the calls like this one to Caspar Canyon—a peaceful Sunday morning shattered by chaos.
Ryan and five other search and rescue volunteers drove
into the canyon past police barricades, fire trucks, ambulances and even a camera crew from a Junction television station. Crowds of people milled around outside
an area cordoned off with yellow caution tape, and the
air was thick with smoke.

Only it wasn't smoke, Ryan realized as they exited the
specially outfitted Jeep they had dubbed the Beast. The
air in the canyon was hazy with dust. Voices drifted from
the haze—shouts for help, screams of pain and voices
demanding order.

"Is that a helicopter?" fellow volunteer Eldon Ramsey
asked.

Ryan followed Eldon's gaze up toward the throbbing
sound that was, indeed, a blue-and-white helicopter hovering over the canyon.

"Focus on the job, guys," Tony reminded them. He

opened the back doors of the Beast and began unloading gear.

"What are we dealing with here?" Ryan asked as he helped maneuver a litter from atop the vehicle.

"The call said an injured climber in Caspar Canyon," Tony said. "No details."

"This is bigger than one climber who misjudged a move," Ryan said.

"The man you want is at the far end of the canyon." Sergeant Gage Walker with the Rayford County Sheriff's Department joined them. "There's at least one climber trapped under some fallen boulders," he said. "There are half a dozen other injured people, but EMS is seeing to them."

"What happened?" Tony asked. "Dispatch didn't provide any details."

Ryan had always thought of Gage as easygoing, a bit of a joker, even. Today, he looked grim. "We're not certain of all the details," he said. "But from what we've been able to determine so far, someone set off a bomb."

The words jolted through Ryan. He steadied himself with one hand on the side of the vehicle. "Was anyone killed?" he asked.

"Not yet," Gage said. "The ambulance transported Perry Dysert. I don't know any more than that."

Ryan knew Perry. The climbing community was a tight group and everyone knew everyone else. If that murderer hadn't thrown Ryan off the side of a mountain a little over a month ago, he would have been here this morning, too. A dozen questions half formed in his head, but before he could ask them, Eldon clapped a hand on his shoulder. "Come on," he said. "Let's take care of this guy who's trapped."

The trapped guy turned out to be Garrett Stokes,

an experienced climber many of the younger rock rats looked up to. His handsome, normally ruddy face was pasty white and aged by pain as he lay half-buried in a tumble of rock. "You're supposed to climb over the boulders, not under them," Ryan said, as he dropped his gear bag nearby. On closer inspection, Garrett's lower body proved to be pinned by a jagged block of black rock the size of a small SUV.

Garrett called Ryan a foul name, but with no malice behind the words. RN Danny Irwin moved in to examine him, while the others studied the rock pinning him. "We need a crane to lift that off," Eldon put in.

"The canyon is too narrow in this spot to bring in anything bigger than a garden tractor," Tony said.

"Hydraulic jacks and a winch it is, then," Eldon stated.

"If they make a jack big enough to lift that, I don't think there's one in the county," Ted said.

"Maybe we could break the rock into pieces," Ryan suggested.

"Not without risking further injury to Garrett," Tony added.

Danny joined their huddle by the rock. "We're going to run an IV to get some fluids and pain meds into him," he said, keeping his voice low. "I'm worried about him going into shock. He's in a lot of pain, but there's no telling the extent of his injuries until he's out from under there. I expect there's broken bones, and maybe some internal injuries."

Ryan looked up at the waterfall of rock that had collapsed into the canyon. He thought this was the location of a route named McKenzie's Wall. It had featured a twenty foot slab of almost sheer, vertical rock that Ryan had never attempted. "Was he up there when the bomb exploded?" he asked.

"Looks like it," Eldon said.

"How is Garrett?" Sheriff Travis Walker, Gage's brother, joined them. He wore jeans and a black parka with a shearling collar, his badge clipped to his belt. Ryan wondered if he had been working at his ranch when the call had come in about the explosion. He didn't know the sheriff well, and preferred to steer clear of law enforcement, but Travis seemed like a good guy. If he knew about Ryan's past, he had never said anything.

"We need to get him out from under that rock," Danny said. "Sooner rather than later."

"We need to dig him out," Ted concluded.

The others turned to him. At sixty, Ted was the oldest member of Eagle Mountain Search and Rescue, a sometimes prickly personality who bristled at anything he took as an implication that he wasn't up to the job. But Ted was smart, and he had experience on his side. "We have to dig a trench and make room to slide him out from under the boulder," he said. "We'll have to be careful and dig it by hand, but if we can keep the rock from sinking lower as we dig, we should be able to free him."

"What tools do you need?" Travis asked.

Within ten minutes they had assembled an assortment of small shovels and one pickax, some lumber to shore up beneath the rock and several volunteers. They began excavating a trench around and beneath Garrett, who was mostly silent as they worked, numbed by the medication dripping into the line in his arm. Danny and paramedic Hannah Richards monitored the injured man as the others worked.

Ryan dug until sweat beaded on his forehead and his right arm, five-and-a-half-weeks postsurgery to insert a metal bar and seven screws, began to throb. "That's enough for you," Tony said, and relieved him of his shovel.

Reluctantly, Ryan stepped back to assume the role of spectator. "How much longer before they have him out?" a man standing next to Ryan asked. Compact and muscular, he wore a black jacket with an Explosives patch on the shoulder.

"Soon, we hope," Ryan said. "Any idea what happened?"

"The story we got was there was an explosion and the whole side of the canyon came down." The man eyed the debris critically. "My guess is the charge was set about halfway up, probably along a natural fault. It wouldn't take a huge charge to collapse one section of rock."

"Who would do something like that?" Ryan asked.

"Someone who doesn't like climbers. Or crowds in the canyon." The man met Ryan's gaze, a hardness there Ryan found unnerving. "Or maybe they did it just to prove they could."

"Stand back. We're going to try to move him now."

With one group of volunteers monitoring the rock for movement, and another prepared to shift Garrett an inch at a time, Danny gave the signal to begin. They shouted encouragement and directions to one another and two minutes later, Garrett was free. A cheer rose up from the crowd as Garrett was carried toward the waiting ambulance.

Ryan joined the others in collecting their gear. The explosives team took over the area, ordering everyone else away. "What do they expect to find in that mess?" Austen asked, looking over his shoulder at the men already sifting through the rock and gravel.

"They're hoping to find something to lead back to the bomber," Deputy Jake Gwynn said. He was also a trainee volunteer with search and rescue, and had been one of the group working to free Garrett.

"Do you think it's the same person who planted the

bomb by the highway bridge?" Ryan wondered. Jake had shown him the photo he had taken of the sticks of dynamite wired to the bridge support. It had looked exactly like the bomb in cartoons, minus a ticking alarm clock.

"We don't know," Jake said. "We've been interviewing everyone we can find who was here this morning. We're hoping someone saw someone acting suspiciously at this end of the canyon, but there's a good chance the bomber planted the device late last night or early this morning, when no one else was around."

"It has to be the same person who planted that bomb by the highway bridge," Austen conjectured. "How many bombers could you have in one little county?"

"Even one is too many," Jake said. "We need to find him before someone else gets hurt."

Ryan and Austen made their way back to the Beast, arriving just as the ambulance with Garrett aboard pulled out. "Garrett is stable," Danny said before anyone could ask. "He was lucky the dirt where he fell was soft enough to allow him to sink in a little. He has a fractured ankle, torn ligaments in his right knee, some cracked ribs, a broken finger and bruised kidneys. Hopefully nothing worse, though they'll do scans and X-rays at the hospital."

Ryan flashed back to his own arrival at the hospital after being transported from a scree field by an army helicopter. Though his recall was fogged by all the painkillers he had been floating on, he had memories of many machines and people hovering over him.

"He was unlucky enough to have been up there on those rocks when a bomb exploded," Danny said. "But lucky enough to live to tell about it."

Someone had said the same about Ryan, though as he recuperated from his injuries, unable to compete in the annual ice-climbing festival and restricted from so many activities for weeks, he hadn't felt very lucky. He saw things differently now, and was grateful his fellow search and rescue members hadn't been tasked with retrieving his remains from that scree field.

"Ryan!"

He looked over his shoulder and was startled to see Deni pushing her way past a clot of spectators. "I just heard!" she said as she skidded to a stop in front of him, out of breath. "I saw the ambulance. Who was hurt?"

"Garrett Stokes," Ryan said. "Do you know him?"

"A little. Is he going to be okay?"

"We hope so," Ryan said. "He's pretty banged up. How much did you hear?"

"Someone said a bomb exploded and a bunch of people were hurt in Caspar Canyon." She looked past him toward the chaos in the canyon, and her fair skin blanched the color of aspen bark. "Is it true? Was it really a bomb?"

"The explosives guys are here from Junction," Ryan said. "So I guess so."

She swayed and he put a hand on her shoulder to steady her.

She leaned her weight against him. "Thanks," she whispered.

Everyone else was distracted by the work of reloading the Beast, so Ryan took Deni's arm and led her a little away from the others. "What's wrong?" he asked. "I know this kind of thing is upsetting, but what else is going on?" She hadn't struck him as the type to overreact, yet this—and the bomb they had found at the bridge yesterday—had her terrified to a level he couldn't account for.

"Oh, Ryan." She met his gaze, her eyes shiny with tears. "I'm so afraid."

He put his arm around her and held her close. She was trembling. "What are you so afraid of?" he asked.

"I think I know who the bomber is." She wet her lips. "Who it might be. I don't have proof, but…"

Her voice trailed away, and she stared at the ground. "Who?" he asked. "Who do you think did this? If you know, you have to tell."

"It's too awful." She shook her head and pushed away from him, but she didn't run away, as he half feared. Instead, she met his gaze full-on, her terror raw in her eyes. "I think… I think it might be my dad."

Chapter Four

As soon as the words were out of her mouth, Deni wanted to take them back. What would Ryan think? She was as good as accusing her father of being a terrorist. An attempted murderer. She put a hand to her mouth. "Please tell me no one died today," she said. She looked past him, into the canyon shrouded in a gray mist, bright yellow emergency tape snapping in the breeze that funneled through the area, hard-hatted emergency workers everywhere.

"No one has died yet, though some people have serious injuries," Ryan said. His voice was tight. She risked a glance and saw him watching her, concern tightening the vertical line between his eyebrows. "Why do you think your father did this?" he asked.

"He's been acting so strange lately. And he's said some things that didn't alarm me at the time, but when I think about them now…" She shrugged, helpless to explain her mixed-up feelings.

Ryan took a step back, his gaze fixed on her. "You need to tell the sheriff."

"I don't know anything," she said. "I only…suspect."

"Then tell him what you suspect. If you don't, you could end up in a lot of trouble yourself."

He was still staring at her. He didn't look angry, exactly. More afraid. "I haven't done anything wrong," she said.

He looked away, and she wondered if he would leave altogether, but after a moment in which he seemed to be struggling with something, his gaze met hers again, and a new calm showed in his eyes. "You could help a lot of people by telling the sheriff everything," he said. "Maybe especially, your father."

Would she be helping her dad by sharing her suspicions with the sheriff? Maybe she was wrong and her father really was off on a snowmobile trip and he had nothing to do with trying to kill people and destroy property. If she set law enforcement on him, he might never speak to her again.

But what if he was behind this? If he was really responsible for planting those two bombs, maybe he was past helping. The idea made her want to double over in pain.

She might not be able to help him, but she could prevent other people from being hurt and possibly dying. She had to try to save them, didn't she? "Would you come with me?" she asked. "To talk to the sheriff?"

Ryan blinked, and she was sure he was going to refuse. She started to apologize. After all, they scarcely knew each other. Why should he get involved in this mess with her dad?

"Come on." He took her arm and guided her past a group unloading wooden barricades from the back of a truck. "I think I saw Travis over this way."

Ryan didn't ask what she knew, or why her father would do such a terrible thing. She was grateful for that. She didn't have any answers to give him. She only knew that as soon as she had heard about the bomb at the bridge, a lot of things began to make sense. A horrible sense, but it explained a lot about her father's behavior in the last year, and especially in the past few weeks.

Ryan kept hold of her arm and led her back toward the search and rescue crew. He was probably afraid if he let go, she'd run away. She was a little afraid of that too, and was grateful for his strong fingers anchoring her.

"I need to help Deni with something," he told the SAR commander, Tony Meisner. "I'll get a ride back to town with her."

Tony didn't even glance at her, his body halfway into the back of the vehicle. "Okay. Thanks for your hard work today."

They found the sheriff standing just inside the yellow plastic tape that cordoned off the blast site. Travis stood with his arms crossed, watching a group of men who wore dark jackets with EXPLOSIVES stenciled across the back. "Sheriff?" Ryan asked.

Travis turned, his gaze assessing them both. "What do you need?"

"Deni has some information," he said. "About the bomber."

Travis said nothing, merely looked at her, waiting.

"My father…" Her voice faltered, and she tried again. "My father, Mike Traynor, has been acting oddly the past few weeks. He's said and done things… I thought it was just talk at the time. An unhappy man venting his frustrations. But now I'm worried he could have had something to do with this."

Still the sheriff said nothing. He looked at her steadily, as if weighing her words. "Could you come to the sheriff's department and give us a formal statement?" he asked after a long moment.

"Yes," she said. "Of course. And then what will happen?"

"We'll probably want to talk to your father."

"I don't know where he is," she said. "He isn't answering his phone, and I went up to his cabin this morning and he wasn't there. His truck and his snowmobile are gone and there's a padlock on the door."

Travis nodded. "We may need to search the place, but let's start with your statement." He turned to Ryan. "Could both of you meet me at the sheriff's department in fifteen minutes?"

"Yes, sir," Ryan said.

"You don't have to come if you don't want to," Deni said as they moved away, back toward the parking area. "I feel terrible about involving you in any of this." She had thought having him with her would make things easier, but now she felt guilty. And embarrassed. So much for thinking he would see her as someone he'd like to go out with. She would be lucky if he didn't avoid her the next time he saw her on the street. The missed opportunity to get to know him better might be one of the things she regretted most about this whole ugly situation.

"It's okay," he said. "And you heard the sheriff. He's expecting me to be there."

"Oh. Right." She fought back a wave of nausea at what she might be about to face. She didn't want to face it alone. "If you don't mind, it would be good to have a friend with me," she added.

He took her hand in his again, so warm and gentle. He looked a little less tense now. "Then I want to be there," he said.

Though she had passed the Rayford County Sheriff's Department countless times in her two years in Eagle Mountain, Deni had never been inside. The single-story brick building was unremarkable in its blandness, which she supposed was a benefit. No one greeted them when they stepped inside. "I guess we just wait here for Travis," Ryan said.

She sat in one of two straight-backed chairs by the door and studied the photographs on the wall of men and women in uniform, including a formal portrait of the sheriff, as handsome as a movie star, dark hair and dark eyes and sculpted cheekbones. His detractors liked to grouse that he had won election on looks alone, but most people she knew were fans of his no-nonsense approach to law enforcement, and the skilled group of deputies he had built to support him.

"I've never been in here before," Ryan said as he took the seat beside her.

"I guess that's a good thing," she mused. "I've never been here, either."

The front door opened and Travis walked in. "Come back with me," he said, and punched in a code that opened the door leading away from the reception area to a hall lined with offices. He led them to what she assumed was an interrogation room—gray walls, a single table with chairs and a camera situated overhead. "I want to record what you have to say," Travis said, as he flicked switches on another control panel inside the room.

Deni's stomach churned with nerves, but she took deep breaths and tried to remain calm. She sat in one of the chairs, Ryan next to her, and Travis recited the date and the name of everyone present, then settled opposite her. "Okay," he said. "Tell me everything you know that might relate to the bomb that detonated today at Caspar Canyon."

The first thing she knew was that whatever was going on had started long before today. "My father was a truck driver in Amarillo, Texas," she began. "It's what he did my whole life. He owned his own truck and contracted to various shippers. He said he liked being his own boss. He used to complain about regulations, and about bigger companies horning in and making it more difficult for independent operators like him to compete, but it was the same things his friends complained about, and I never felt like he meant anything by it."

She fell silent, not sure how to continue. Maybe the sheriff didn't want to know any of this. He probably wanted facts, but did she have any?

"When do you think that changed?" Travis asked.

She tried to pinpoint when her father had begun to act differently. "My mother died of cancer 18 months ago," she said. "Of course Dad was devastated. They had been married 32 years. Not long after that, he decided to sell his truck and quit the business."

"Did that surprise you?" Travis asked.

"Yes, but he assured me he had been saving his money and that, with Mom's life insurance, he would be fine. When he told me he wanted to move to Eagle Mountain to be closer to me, I was thrilled."

"He has a place off-grid, right?" Travis clarified.

"Yes. In Tennyson's Gulch. That choice surprised me. I was hoping he would find a place here in town. Maybe even a part-time job, or at least some activity that would allow him to make friends. But he said all those years he spent on the road alone made him value solitude, and he really liked that cabin location."

"So your father had been acting a little differently for a while," Travis said. "Why do you think he might be connected to the bombs?"

He probably thought she was wasting his time, telling him the story of her life. She was trying to tell him about her father, but everything was so complicated. "Dad has never been the biggest fan of progress," she said. "But after he moved here, he complained a lot more about any changes. It was like, he thought he had found the perfect place to live and he didn't want anything to happen to change that. When they talked about putting in a traffic light at the highway intersection, he wrote letters to the editor of the paper and showed up at county commissioner's meetings to complain. So did other people—it's not like he was the only one."

Except with her dad, his protests had been different. Angrier. "He said someone needed to stop people from ruining the world," she said. "And…one time he told me he thought the only way to get through to some people was violence. That shocked me. I said, 'Dad, you don't really mean that.' He looked right at me and said, 'Have you ever known me to say anything I don't mean?'"

She shivered. Ryan put a hand on her back—just resting it there lightly, the heat of his palm seeping through her shirt. Comforting.

"Did Mike say anything specific about bombs or explosions?" Travis asked.

"No. But he has a workbench up at his place and he's always tinkering with things. He's very mechanically minded. He can fix just about anything. And…and a couple of weeks ago I was up there and I saw some dynamite on the workbench. It alarmed me, really. I asked him about it and he told me not to worry—he was going to use it to dynamite an ice dam that was choking off the spring that provides his water."

"And you believed him?"

She felt miserable. "He's my father. He doesn't usually lie to me." But what if he had been lying this time?

Travis got up and retrieved a bottle of water from a cooler in the corner and pushed it toward her. "Drink some of this, then we'll go on."

She uncapped the bottle and drank, the cold of the water shocking, making the muscles of her throat clench. She replaced the cap but still held the bottle, grateful for something to do with her hands. "Last week, Dad called and said I wouldn't see him for a few days. He had a new project he was involved in and he didn't want me coming around. He wouldn't give me any details, and he told me not to ask any more questions. He also told me—no, he ordered me—not to come up to his cabin for the next two weeks."

"Did he say anything else?"

"He told me not to worry and that I would understand everything soon enough."

"Why do you think your father is connected to the bomb at Caspar Canyon?" Travis asked. "Had he ever mentioned anything about that particular location?"

"When the ice-climbing festival was going on last month, he was so upset," she said. "He complained about the festival bringing all these tourists into town, about the climbers driving metal stakes into the rocks and stringing rope everywhere and not leaving nature alone. I tried to joke with him about it, but he was so upset. Really out of proportion, I thought at the time."

"Did he make any specific threats?"

"Not exactly. But he said if those climbers realized how dangerous their little hobby was, there wouldn't be so many of them. I didn't think anything of it at the time, but…"

Travis nodded. "Anything else you want to tell us?"

Deni sighed. She didn't want to tell him any of this, but she knew she had to. "The bomb at the highway bridge—the one that didn't go off. I wondered if he might have planted that one, too."

"Why is that?" Travis asked.

"He hated that bridge. I mentioned one day that I thought it was beautiful, and that it had won a design award, and he said expanding that new bridge had brought too many new people into town, that the next thing we knew they would be expanding the highway to four lanes and this beautiful little corner of paradise was being destroyed." She leaned across the table toward the sheriff, hoping she could make him understand. "That isn't like my father. It isn't the man I grew up with. Before, he always wanted to help people, not hurt them. He was the person everyone called to pull their car out of a ditch or fix a broken appliance. Something is really wrong with him for him to be so angry and…and mean."

"What did you find when you visited his cabin this morning?" Travis asked.

"His truck and his snowmobile were both gone, so I thought maybe he had decided to go riding—maybe camping, too. The truck has a camper on it. There was a padlock on the door—it looked new. I don't think he bothered to lock the cabin before. The drapes were pulled over the window so I couldn't see in. I've tried and tried to call his cell phone and he doesn't answer. The calls go straight to voice mail."

"What is your father's cell number?" Travis asked.

She recited the number and the sheriff made a note of it. "What about friends?" Travis asked. "Someone he might be with or have gone to visit?"

"He isn't close to anyone around here that I know of," she said. "He has coffee with Rouster Wilson pretty regularly, but mostly he kept to himself. He said he liked being alone."

"Is there anything else you think might be helpful?" he asked.

She shook her head. "I hope I'm wrong. I hope you find him and that he had nothing to do with any of this."

"You were right to come forward with your suspicions," he told her. "Thank you." He glanced at Ryan. "Do you have anything to add?"

"No, sir," Ryan said. "I'm just here to support Deni."

Travis stood, so they did also. "What are you going to do about my dad?" Deni asked.

"We'll try to get in touch with him," Travis responded. "We'll stop by his cabin. Try not to worry."

She almost laughed. Of all the useless advice people gave, "try not to worry" had to be at the top of the list.

They left the sheriff's office and returned to Ryan's truck. "Please take me home," she said. "Or to my car. I guess I need to get it."

"If you give me your keys, I'll get a friend to help me retrieve it," he said. "You look exhausted. Did you sleep at all last night?"

"Not really." She had been too worried about her father.

"Maybe you can get some rest this afternoon. Where do you live?"

She gave him directions to the small Victorian that had once probably served as a guest house or mother-in-law residence, but had been divided from the main house at some point and sold as a starter home. Deni thought it looked like a doll's house, painted pale gray and trimmed in dark blue, with a front porch just big enough for two chairs and a small table, and a single bedroom squeezed upstairs under the sloping roof, a half bath in what had once been a closet up there and a full bath downstairs in what might have been a back porch in the distant past.

"Thank you for bringing me home," she said when

Ryan pulled into the driveway. "And thank you for staying with me. It was a little easier with you there."

"I'm not ready to leave you alone just yet," he said. "No offense, but you don't look well. When was the last time you ate?"

"I had coffee at breakfast." The thought of food made her stomach churn.

"That's what I thought." He switched off the truck engine. "It's late and I'm starving, so let me come in and make something for both of us."

She didn't have the strength to fight him, so she unlocked the door and let him inside. Her cat, a long-hair tortoiseshell named Cookie, yowled an angry complaint from her perch on the front windowsill, then jumped down and raced up the stairs. "That was Cookie," Deni said. "She's probably gone to hide under the bed. She doesn't approve of strangers."

"She'll learn I'm no one to be afraid of," he replied. "I like cats. And dogs. All animals, really. Better than a lot of people. Now, which way is the kitchen?"

"It's just through here." She started toward the back of the house, but he put a hand on her shoulder.

"You sit and rest," he said. "If you trust me to rummage in your cabinets, I'll find something for us to eat."

"I trust you." He already knew her worst secrets—what difference did it make if he discovered the sad state of her refrigerator or her love of cinnamon toaster pastries?

She sank onto the sofa, leaned her head back and closed her eyes, her interview with the sheriff replaying in her mind. She had no clue if Travis believed her or not. She only hoped they found her father, soon.

She might have dozed—the next thing she knew Ryan called her to the table. She roused herself, smoothed back her hair and shuffled into the kitchen. "I found some chicken noodle soup," he said, as he set a bowl on the table. "No crackers, so I made cheese toast."

She tried to remember how old that can of soup must have been. Maybe she had bought it last fall, when she had been fighting a cold. That wasn't too old, was it?

She sat and studied the food in front of her—a steaming bowl of soup with noodles floating in it, and two triangles of golden cheese toast on a saucer beside the bowl. She tasted the soup and her eyes widened. "This doesn't taste like any canned soup I ever had," she said.

"I found a bottle of sherry way back in the cabinet and added a little of that," he said. "And some fried onions."

She took another spoonful. "It's delicious. Is it a family recipe?"

He laughed. "My mother always said her favorite thing to make for dinner is reservations, and my father believes in paying other people to do things like prepare meals."

"So where did you learn to cook?" She sampled the cheese toast. It was also perfect, the buttery cheese warm and velvety.

"I worked six months at a pretty high-end restaurant in Boulder," he said. "I was hired to wash dishes, but when the chef discovered I knew the difference between a shallot and a leek, he promoted me to sous chef."

"I'm impressed."

He shook his head. "Don't be. It just means I chopped a lot of vegetables and stirred a lot of pots. But I picked up a few useful ideas along the way."

"Tell me more about your family," she said. After all, he knew more than she wanted most people to know about hers.

"My mother and my father are both lawyers—corporate real estate law and contracts," he said. "My sister is also a lawyer, married to a lawyer. I'm the black sheep of the family."

At first, she thought he was kidding, then realized he wasn't. "Your parents aren't happy that you didn't choose law as a career?" she asked.

He looked away. "Let's just say they've accepted that's never going to happen."

Silence stretched between them, awkward and cold. She searched for something to get the conversation back on track. "You work for the Ride Brothers, don't you?" she asked.

He shifted, the chair creaking beneath him. "Yes. And I volunteer for search and rescue, serve on the Ice Festival planning committee, and when I'm not recovering from surgery, I climb. A lot. I'm happy." He sounded more grim than content. He obviously wasn't the type to volunteer much about himself, but she wanted to keep him talking.

"I heard about your accident," she said. "When that escaped killer pushed you off Mount Baker. You were hurt pretty bad, weren't you?"

He made a face. "I had to have a couple of surgeries but I'm almost as good as new. Another few weeks and I'll be able to climb again."

He reached over and collected her empty bowl. "I'll do the dishes."

"No!" she protested. "You've already done so much."

"I insist."

In the end, they did the dishes together. When everything was washed and dried and put away, she realized she had drawn out their time together as long as possible. "I'd better let you go now," she said. "Thanks for staying. And for the soup."

"It was your soup," he countered.

"But you made it special."

His gaze met hers, searching. "Are you sure you'll be all right?"

"I'm sure." It was a lie, but one she needed to tell him, and herself. "Goodbye."

She walked him to the door, where he pulled on his coat, then bent to kiss her cheek.

Except she turned her head, and caught his lips; what had been intended as a brief caress transformed into more—a delicious meeting of their mouths that proved cooking was not his only talent.

He pulled back first, cheeks flushed, looking a little stunned. "Um, I'd better go," he said, and before she could object, he turned and left.

She moved to the window and watched him go. He was definitely an intriguing guy. He spent much of his spare time helping others, many of them people he didn't even know. He was good-looking and friendly, but he also held himself a little apart. This reserve had surprised her, but it also made her want to find a way to break past it. Not because she didn't respect his privacy, but because she thought Ryan Welch was a man worth knowing better.

Chapter Five

Going home with Deni had been a bad idea. Ryan knew it, yet he had done it anyway, which proved he hadn't learned all that much in the past six years.

That wasn't right. He had learned how easily he could be led astray. Especially when his normal instincts to want to help someone in trouble overruled his common sense. Yes, Deni was a really nice woman, at least on the surface. And yes, he was attracted to her. But when he learned her father might be some kind of domestic terrorist, he should have run away and never looked back.

The entire time they were sitting in the sheriff's department, he had been waiting for Travis to ask him how he was involved in all this. Had he known about the dynamite and bombs? He was a climber—had he helped plant that bomb in Caspar Canyon? Because guilt by association was a real thing, wasn't it?

And by that time, Travis could have said, "We know about your prison record. So it wouldn't surprise us at all if you were in trouble again."

He stood in the shower, the hot water cascading over him, and tried to wash away the old fear and anger. This was the kind of thing he appreciated now—the ability to take a shower as long as he wanted. Alone. With the water as hot as he wanted. He hadn't been able to do that in prison.

He shut off the water and slicked back his hair, then reached for a towel and blotted water from his eyes. Two years and twenty-nine days he had spent in a Colorado prison, all because he had fallen for the wrong woman. Tracy had known just what to say to persuade him to help her. He had known what he was doing was wrong, but had done it anyway. Because she needed him.

~~Because~~ Because he thought he was in love.

He finished drying off and pulled on jeans and a T-shirt. His injured arm ached worse than usual, so he swallowed some ibuprofen, then lay on his bed and stared at the ceiling.

It wasn't fair. Not big news, but he had to acknowledge his resentment over this fact, all the same. For the first time since getting out of prison three years before, he had decided to risk asking someone out. If he let Deni get to know him, maybe she wouldn't hold his record against him.

But the last thing he needed was any association, however tangential, to criminal activity. Especially something like these bombs.

He closed his eyes, and saw Deni's face again—hurt, confused, trusting him to help her. He remembered the feel of her lips on his, the taste of her. He had wanted her so badly in that moment. He still felt the ache.

He ought to be used to that by now. His life these days was as much about what he couldn't have as what he could. He had told himself walking around free with a job he enjoyed and volunteer work that mattered was enough.

But then he had met Deni, and he realized he had been lying to himself all along.

DENI DIDN'T HEAR from anyone for the next two days—not her father, or the sheriff. Not even from Ryan. The barista at the coffee shop said he had told her he was going out of town for a couple of days, so that was probably the reason for his silence.

She tried to put her worries about her father out of her mind. She told herself not to obsess over things she couldn't control. But she continued to call her father's number several times a day, leaving messages that all sounded the same: "Dad, I'm worried. Please call me," until a recorded voice informed her that "The recipient's voice mailbox is full. Please try again later."

At school, she put on her usual pleasant expression for her students. Eighth grade was a tough year for so many of them—they were too old to be little kids, and too young to be grown. Hormones, awkward growth spurts, shifting friendships, desperate crushes and academic challenges made for plenty of crises for Deni to address and wounds to soothe. With her own emotions so raw, she sympathized even more with her students.

Tuesday evening, she was on her way home from a yoga class when she saw Ryan headed into Mo's Pub. She thought about stopping and going in after him. She could pretend to be surprised to see him. Maybe they would end up having dinner together. Instead, she drove on. She liked Ryan a lot—liked him too much to drag him into her current drama. He might argue that he was already well into it, having sat through her interview with the sheriff—not anyone's idea of a good first date. He already knew how bad her father might be and that hadn't put him off.

But she had a feeling things might get worse before they got better. Her father was bound to turn up soon, and even if he had nothing to do with those bombs, questions would be raised. Relationships were difficult enough to launch without adding in family problems.

Wednesday morning, she still hadn't thought of a good way to explain to Ryan that she needed to pull back, so she skipped stopping for coffee. She was being a coward, not to mention really rude, blowing off a nice guy this way. She would talk to him and explain everything—soon. She just couldn't deal with it right this minute.

For one thing, she had come up with a plan to try to track down her dad. Wednesday evening, the town council was meeting to discuss a variance request by the people who had converted a historic building downtown into a hotel. Though the Nugget Hotel had been open less than a year, the owners were proposing to triple its size. The council had indicated that they were in favor of the proposal, but loud protests from a number of locals, including her father, had led them to schedule one more public forum to discuss the issue. After tonight's public comment session, the council would cast its vote.

Deni had little interest in the issue, but she remembered how upset her father had been about the proposed expansion, and how he had rejoiced over the delay in the vote. He wouldn't miss the opportunity to have one more say about the matter. If he was anywhere nearby, Deni felt sure he would show up for the meeting.

Seven o'clock found her in the crowded meeting room upstairs at the county courthouse. She took one of the last vacant seats and scanned the crowd. People filled the ranks of folding chairs and stood along the wall. She saw plenty of familiar faces—the school principal nodded to her and several parents waved. But her father was nowhere in sight.

Council chair Mac Rodriguez stood and banged a wooden gavel. A slight man with a hawk nose and thick silver hair, Mac had a sonorous voice that surprised Deni every time she heard it. "I call this meeting of the Eagle Mountain Town Council to order," he intoned. The four council members flanked him behind the long table on the dais. They stared out at the crowded room with the expressions of guests at a shotgun wedding—everyone agreed this meeting had to happen, but no one really wanted to be there.

People continued to arrive as the first items on the agenda were checked off—approval of the minutes from the last meeting, a report from the town planner on the purchase of a new riding lawn mower and recognition of a high school student who won a national essay-writing contest. The door at the back of the room creaked loudly when anyone opened it, and every time, Deni turned around to see who had entered.

The third time she turned, a man with a bushy white moustache, a white Stetson pulled low over his eyes, stepped in. He wore starched Wrangler jeans and a blue-and-white-striped Western shirt and no jacket, despite temperatures in the twenties. Her dad was like that. "I'm not going to put on a coat to walk from my truck to the restaurant," he would say. She tried to get a better look at the man, but he had already been swallowed up by a new group entering the room. Something about him was familiar. Was he a friend of her father? Should she ask him if he had seen her dad recently?

"Now we will open the floor for public comment on the variance request from Nugget Hotel," Mac said. "Speakers who have signed in will have no more than five minutes to state their case. When your name is called, please come up to the microphone at the front of the room." He glanced at the clipboard on the table before him. "Glenda Nassib, you're first."

While Glenda, a tall, angular woman with close-cropped white hair, made her way from the back of the room, Deni tried to figure out where she knew the guy with the moustache.

"I know that growth is important to any economy," Glenda said. "But there is a right way and a wrong way to handle that growth, and I don't think allowing the Nugget to add two more floors and a new annex that will take up half a block downtown is the way to go. It's going to look as out of place in Eagle Mountain as a dress shirt on a sheep."

The shirt! Deni sat upright. That blue-and-white Western shirt was identical to one she had given her dad for Father's Day last year. Or his birthday. She jumped up. Mac banged his gavel. "Ma'am, do you wish to be recognized?"

"Oh! No, I, um, no." She sat back down to mild laughter from those around her, and wished someone would trip the fire alarm, or provide some other distraction. She waited until Glenda started speaking again before she turned to look back to where the man with the white moustache had been standing, but all she could see was the top of his Stetson.

The door at the back of the room opened, squeaking loudly, and Deni turned again to see the hat—and the broad shoulders covered in the blue-and-white cotton—disappearing into the hall. She would have recognized that back anywhere, having followed it so many places over the years.

She jumped up and, mumbling apologies, pushed her way down the row to the aisle. Once clear of other people's feet and knees, she hurried to the door, hoping everyone would assume she had remembered something she had to do, and no one would feel compelled to come after her.

She burst into the hall in time to see the man she was after disappearing through the exit door at the far end. "Dad!" she shouted. "Wait!"

She ran, the hard soles of her boots echoing on the polished wood floor. She was almost to the exit when she collided, hard, with a man in a black leather duster. "Deni! Are you all right?" Ryan gripped her shoulders firmly.

She looked past him, to the now closed door. "I thought I saw my dad," she said. "In the council meeting. I was trying to catch him."

Ryan followed her gaze to the door, then took her hand and pulled her forward. "Come on. If we hurry, maybe we can catch up with him."

They ran onto the sidewalk and scanned the cars parked along the curb, then hurried to do the same on both sides of the courthouse. "He's not here," Deni said, disappointment heavy in her stomach.

"You're sure it was your father?" Ryan asked. "I came in just now and the only person I saw was some cowboy in a white hat with a Sam Elliott moustache."

"That was him," she said. "Or at least, I'm pretty sure that was him."

"I didn't know your dad had a moustache."

"He doesn't. And he doesn't wear a Stetson. I think he was trying to disguise himself. But he was wearing the shirt I gave him for Father's Day last year. And when he left the room, I recognized his back. It was him." She pulled out her phone and hit the speed dial for her father's number. It rang and rang, then disconnected. "What am I going to do now?" she moaned.

"Let's get some coffee and talk about it," he said.

Now that she wasn't so focused on following her father, she realized how close they were standing. She caught the scent of mint on his breath, and cold leather from his jacket, and remembered his hands gripping her shoulders, steadying her. "I don't want to keep you from the meeting," she said—though really, that was exactly what she wanted, now that he was here.

"I didn't come in here for the meeting," he said. "I came in to pay my water bill." He nodded toward a slot for depositing payment after hours. "Then I saw you and thought maybe something was wrong."

My father might be planting bombs around town. Isn't that wrong enough? But she didn't say it. Instead, she zipped up her parka. "Coffee sounds good."

THE ONLY PLACE to buy coffee after seven at night was the ice cream shop next to the post office, where the bored teenager behind the counter had to be persuaded to brew a fresh pot. "No one ever orders coffee this late," he said. "Or almost never."

"We want coffee," Ryan insisted. He put a dollar in the tip cup.

"Suit yourself," the student said, and turned to dump beans in the grinder.

Ryan returned to the table where Deni waited. Hair windblown and cheeks flushed from the cold, she made a particularly attractive picture—except for the pinched look around her eyes and the dark circles that told of sleepless nights. He had been forcing himself not to contact her, but he hadn't been able to turn away after she had literally run into him. "I guess your dad is one of the people who is against the hotel expansion," he said. "So you thought he'd be at the council meeting?"

"Yes. And he was there. When he saw me, he left. Why is he avoiding me?"

"Maybe he doesn't want to get you into trouble," Ryan supplied. "If he is involved somehow in these bombs, he could be trying to protect you."

"I don't want to be protected," she said. "I want him to stop trying to kill people."

The teenager working there dropped a spoon or something, and Deni flushed a deeper pink and lowered her voice. "If I could talk to him, maybe I could find out where he's been, and if he had anything to do with those bombs."

"I know he's your dad, but maybe you should leave finding him to the cops," Ryan said. "I mean, if he is involved with this, maybe it's because he's had some kind of mental breakdown or something."

"It has to be something like that," she observed. "My dad wouldn't hurt anyone."

"Coffee's ready!" the teenager called, and Ryan went to get it. He set one cup, along with two creamers and two sugars, in front of Deni.

A smile broke through some of her worry. "You remembered how I like my coffee," she said.

"I've been paying attention." He added a packet of sugar to his own cup. "I've been trying to work up the nerve to ask you out for a while."

The smile faded a little. "And I turn out to have a father who could be on the sheriff's department's Most Wanted list."

"Yeah, well, not ideal." Way to state the obvious, he thought.

"I really like you," she said. "But my life is such a mess right now." She met his gaze. "I could use a friend, even though you're not exactly seeing me at my best."

What he saw was a beautiful, hurting woman who was as alone in the world as he was. The look she gave him then made him feel ten feet tall and unbreakable. "I could be your friend," he said, even while part of his brain was screaming *No!*

"Thanks." She lifted her cup to her lips. "I heard you were out of town for a couple of days," she noted after she drank. Was she changing the subject because she sensed his uneasiness? Or maybe she just wanted to focus on something besides her own troubles.

"I went to see Garrett Stokes," he said. "He was transferred to Anschutz Medical Campus."

"He was one of the climbers hurt in the bombing, wasn't he?" she asked. "How is he doing?"

Some of the lightness left Ryan as he remembered his visit with his friend. "He's probably going to lose his leg above the knee," he said. "There's too much damage to repair."

She pressed her hand over her mouth, her eyes wide and glistening. "I'm so sorry," she whispered.

"Hey, it's not your fault. And Garrett is going to be okay. He's already talking about getting a special prosthesis for climbing. I heard Perry is doing good, too. Word is he'll get to come home in just a few more days."

She nodded. "I heard that, too. But I haven't heard anything from the sheriff—or from my dad."

"Maybe Mike has a new girlfriend and he's afraid you won't approve. Or…a boyfriend?"

That surprised a laugh from her. "Either way—I might be surprised, but I wouldn't disapprove," she said. "I want Dad to be happy. It would be a relief to know he had found someone. And he should know that. We've always been close."

He envied her that. His dad was not an especially

warm person and from a young age Ryan had been aware that he was not the son his father would have wanted. But there was no sense dwelling on that.

"I was thinking about going back up to my dad's place on Sunday," she said.

"Maybe you should leave that to the sheriff," he said.

"I called today and it sounded like they haven't done anything," she said. "I can't sit here and do nothing. If I can get inside his cabin, maybe I'll find something to tell me where he is."

"There's been a lot of snow up there," Ryan said. "You shouldn't go by yourself."

"I'll be okay." She sipped her coffee. "But if you don't hear from me, you might check to make sure I'm not stuck in a snowdrift."

She said the words as if she was kidding, but he had been on enough search and rescue calls to know traveling those mountain roads in winter was a real risk. "I have to teach an avalanche class on Saturday, but I could go with you Sunday," he said. "That is, if you haven't heard from him by then."

"You don't have to do that," she said.

"I'll worry about you if I don't." If she got hurt up there by herself, he would feel responsible.

"Do you have a key so we can get inside?" he asked.

"No. There's a big new padlock on the door."

"Is there another way in? A window, maybe?"

"Maybe. At least we could try." She smiled—just a brief upturn of her lips and warming of her eyes. Enough to make him feel good again. "Thanks. At least I'd be doing something, instead of calling his phone repeatedly and worrying."

"Garrett told me he never saw the bomb—no one did," Ryan said. "It must have been planted way down in the rock. And the explosives expert I talked to at Caspar Canyon that day said whoever did it knew just where to put the bomb to bring down that wall. That sounds to me like an expert—not a man who worked all his life as a truck driver."

"You're right," Deni said. "But that doesn't mean Dad couldn't have studied the matter and learned. He has a knack for figuring out engines and things like that."

"Explosives aren't like a car," Ryan explained. "And the sheriff's office hasn't questioned you anymore. I think that means your dad isn't their top suspect."

"I guess I hadn't thought of it that way." She met his gaze again. "Do you think our parents worried about us this much, when we were growing up?"

"I know I gave mine plenty to worry about," he said. "I still do, I imagine."

"I'm beginning to think I didn't worry mine enough," she added. "Maybe he wouldn't be doing this to me now."

"You've got me on the case now," he said. "Between the two of us, we'll track him down." Every word was pure bravado. He didn't know the first thing about finding a man who wanted to stay missing. But he wanted Deni to feel better, and seeing the way her expression lightened a little at this comment, he determined to do everything in his power to locate Mike Traynor—and then give him a lecture on how lucky he was to have a daughter like Deni in his life. Ryan hadn't known her that long, but he was smart enough to have already figured out that she was special.

Chapter Six

Ryan had volunteered to teach this avalanche safety course with search and rescue commander Tony Meisner shortly before the accident that put him in the hospital. He had insisted on keeping the commitment even in the early days, when his prognosis was less clear. "If there's anything too physical for me to handle—though there won't be—you can do it," he had told Tony. "All I have to do is talk, and there's nothing keeping me from that."

Now that the day of the course had arrived, Ryan felt stronger than ever, though his doctor had cautioned he wouldn't be at full strength for a few more months yet. No worries about that today. This was a beginner's course, focused on the correct use of an avalanche beacon, techniques for reading snow conditions and avoiding a slide, and what to do if you or a companion was caught in an avalanche.

The class convened at the parking area in Galloway Basin, a popular backcountry ski area. The lot was almost full of cars by the time Ryan and Tony pulled in. They exchanged greetings with several skiers who were heading out, then went in search of their students. Today's class consisted of six people: two couples, a single man and Deputy Jake Gwynn, a new search and rescue trainee who was here to fulfill part of his training requirements.

Jake met them at the back of Tony's SUV and helped unload the gear while the others huddled at the edge of the lot, talking amongst themselves. "Any news about that bomb that went off in Caspar Canyon?" Tony asked the question that was tops in Ryan's mind.

"We haven't found the bomber," Jake said.

"Is it the same guy who planted that bomb at the highway bridge?" Tony asked.

"Maybe."

Jake clearly didn't want to discuss this, but Tony pressed. "Well, is it or isn't? What's the big secret?"

"The materials used in both bombs were the same, as far as we can tell," Jake said. "That's all I can say."

"So, any suspects?" Tony asked.

Jake glanced at Ryan, who figured he had probably read the transcript of the interview with Deni. "We've got a couple of people we're looking at, but nothing very solid."

A couple of people. So Mike Traynor wasn't the only possible bomber on their radar. Deni would be relieved to hear that.

The three of them quickly transformed a corner of the parking lot into an outdoor classroom. Everyone introduced themselves and Ryan launched into the first lecture, using a whiteboard on an easel to illustrate points as necessary. They had a discussion about different types of terrain and snow condition, using their surroundings as examples.

Then it was Tony's turn. He set up a device like the ones used in some ski resort backcountry gateways and a few popular remote rural areas and showed everyone how to test their beacons using the device. Then everyone paired off to practice using their beacons in send and receive mode.

After a break, they moved out onto the slopes for instruction on testing the quality of the snow, hazards to look for, best practices when skiing in an area with heightened avalanche danger and who to contact for information on that day's conditions. "You're skiing for free in some amazing terrain," Tony said. "But it's up to you to do your homework and be prepared for the worst. If something happens, search and rescue will respond and try to save you, but the truth is, most avalanche rescues are body retrievals by the time we arrive."

Ryan watched the faces of everyone present as this information sank in. No one set out on a beautiful winter morning thinking about the possibility that they could die that day, but part of this training was to have them do so, and to take all the precautions they could to prevent that from happening. "Backcountry skiing is risky," he said. "But there are ways to mitigate the risks. Taking this course today is one of them. Implementing what we teach you—every time you set out—is another."

The rest of the day was spent practicing what they had learned—taking samples of the snow, probing terrain, reading a slope and avoiding the most unstable conditions and finally, using the beacons to locate one another—on top of the snow. They shared tips on what to do if caught in an avalanche that might provide that little extra cushion that would allow you to survive until your friends could find you and dig you out. Though Tony and Ryan had both had the unpleasant task of digging out the bodies of people who had died in avalanches, they had rescued survivors, too. It wasn't impossible to come out alive, and even uninjured, but it did require good equipment, good technique and a lot of luck.

By two in the afternoon they were packing up to leave. Jake helped haul their gear back to Tony's SUV. When everything was loaded in, Ryan pulled him aside. "I know there are probably things you aren't supposed to tell me," he said. "I just want to know if you've had any luck locating Mike Traynor? Deni is really worried about him."

"I'm sorry. We haven't heard anything from him. We put out a bulletin saying we wanted to talk to him in connection with a case, with his description and information about his truck, but nothing has come up. Sergeant Walker went up to his cabin, but didn't find anything outside, and we don't have a warrant to go inside. He's not answering his phone, either."

"He won't return Deni's calls, which she says is unusual."

"It's possible he went somewhere on that snowmobile and had an accident," Jake said. "Depending on where he was and how badly he was hurt, he might not be found until spring."

Jake meant Mike's body might not be found until spring—or ever. People went missing in these mountains every year. Some of them were never found. "Deni thinks she saw her dad at the town council meeting Wednesday evening," Ryan said. "He was one of the people who spoke out against the hotel expansion before. She attended the meeting, thinking he might show up."

"No one else said anything about this," Jake said. "I wasn't at the meeting, but Deputy Douglas and her husband, Nate, were there. They would have been watching for him, too."

"Deni says Mike was wearing a disguise—a big white moustache and a Stetson pulled down low over his eyes. She didn't recognize him at first, but he was wearing a shirt like the one she had given her father as a gift."

Jake looked doubtful. "Lots of people probably have the same shirt."

"Deni was sure this was her dad."

"Did she speak to him?"

"No. When he saw her, he left in a hurry. She went after him—we both did. But he was gone."

"Do you think this man was Mike Traynor?" Jake asked.

"I never saw him. And I only ever spoke to Mike once, so I'm not sure I'd recognize him if he looked at all different. But Deni was sure it was him, and it does seem odd that someone would come to the meeting and leave before the first speaker had finished."

"You can tell Deni we're still looking for her father," Jake said. "And if she sees him again, call us right away."

"She was talking about going up to his cabin tomorrow and trying to get inside," Ryan said.

Jake frowned. "I can't stop her from doing that, but tell her to be careful. If she finds anything suspicious, don't touch it. Leave and call us to come take a look. If Mike is involved in this somehow, she doesn't want to compromise any evidence."

"I'll tell her," Ryan said. He didn't want the sheriff's office to know he had agreed to go with Deni.

"Tell her we haven't found anything linking her father to the bombs," Jake said. "We're still looking, but right now we're focused on a man who used to work for the highway department. Apparently he had a lot of experience with explosives and was upset because he had been fired for using some state equipment to do some work at his house without permission."

"She'll be relieved to hear that. Thanks."

"You didn't get it from me," Jake said.

"Understood."

Ryan told himself he should wait until tomorrow to talk to Deni, but instead of heading to his apartment over the art gallery, he drove to her house. Maybe hearing Jake's update on the search for her father would change her mind about going up to his cabin. She answered the door wearing pink leggings and an oversize sweatshirt, a pink bandana tied over her hair. "I was cleaning house," she said, and looked down at the rag in her hand.

"I have some news," he told her. "Not much, but it might cheer you up."

"Come in." She held the door open wider. A vacuum cleaner stood in the entry, and the furniture was pulled out from the walls. He caught a glimpse of the cat on the stairs before it vanished into another room. Deni tossed the rag onto the coffee table and sank onto the sofa. "So, what's the news?"

He sat beside her. "Deputy Jake Gwynn was one of the students in the avalanche safety class I taught this morning," he said. "I asked him if they had been able to locate your father. He said no, but that they hadn't found anything connecting Mike to the bombs. In fact, they have another suspect—a disgruntled highway department employee who is supposedly experienced with explosives."

Her lip trembled, and she leaned back against the cushions. "Really?"

"That's what he said. He also told me not to pass it on to anyone else. I'm sure they don't want the information getting back to their suspect. But he said it was okay to tell you. They're still looking for your father, but they don't think he had anything to do with those bombs." Those weren't Jake's exact words, but they were what Ryan had taken away from their conversation.

Deni grabbed his hand. "Thanks for telling me. It's a huge relief—though I'm still worried about Dad."

"Maybe the sheriff will find him soon."

"I've been thinking, and I'm pretty sure we can get

in the back window at Dad's cabin," she said. "If I have to, I'll break a windowpane and undo the lock. Dad can argue about it with me later."

"So you're still determined to go up there."

"Yes. I'm feeling more positive about checking out the place now that you've agreed to go with me."

Here was his chance to back out. He could make up some excuse about having forgotten another commitment. But he couldn't do it.

He stood. "I'll let you get back to your cleaning. See you at nine in the morning?"

She stood and walked with him to the door. "Thank you for talking to Jake about my dad. You can't imagine how much better I feel."

She looked up at him, eyes shining. He wanted to kiss her—his gaze flickered to her lips. But the last thing he needed was to get any more involved with her. His mind knew that, even if his body didn't agree.

Then she slid her hand around the back of his neck and pulled his head down to her. There wasn't any hesitation in her kiss, and there was more passion behind the gesture than he would have expected for a simple thank-you. He wrapped his arms around her and pulled her against him, enjoying the feel of her body close to his. She was soft and warm and smelled like flowers and vanilla. Irresistible.

She pulled away, still smiling. "See you tomorrow," she said.

If she had intended for him to spend the next fifteen hours thinking about her, that kiss had guaranteed she would figure prominently in his dream. So much for keeping his distance.

DENI WOKE FEELING better than she had in a week, but her good mood scarcely lasted past her first cup of coffee.

The sheriff's department didn't think her father was the man who had planted those bombs, so neither should she. But if he wasn't hiding because he had done something wrong, where was he?

Had he gone somewhere on his snowmobile and been injured? But if that was the case, he wouldn't have been at the council meeting Wednesday, and she was positive the man she had seen had been him. He had been wearing a disguise and hadn't wanted her to see him. Why? Nothing about this situation made sense.

By the time Ryan arrived with a bag of muffins from the bakery, she had worked her stomach into knots again. He said hello, then studied her, picking up on her agitation. "Are you having second thoughts about going to your dad's place?" he asked.

She shook her head. "I've just been thinking about seeing Dad at the courthouse Wednesday. Why was he avoiding me?"

"Maybe he doesn't want to involve you in whatever he's doing," Ryan said. "That could be a good thing."

"Whatever he's up to, I need to know," she said. "I'm strong enough to deal with the truth." Though she didn't feel very strong right now.

Ryan offered to drive, and his truck seemed better equipped for heavy snow than her Subaru. The snow on the forest service road leading into Tennyson Gulch had thinned, exposing gravel in places. Ryan's Tundra bounced over the ruts and through soft spots with ease. Sun shone down through dark green ponderosa pines and burnished the bare white trunks of aspen. "It's been a long time since I've been up here," Ryan said. "How did your dad ever find this place?"

"It was listed with a local real estate agent," she said. "I think the family who owned it used it as a summer getaway and had had it for years and years. I was shocked when he told me he planned to live here year-round. I thought he spent so many years in Texas because he hated snow. But he told me he enjoyed the challenge, and for a while it seemed to make him happy, fixing up the place." She had been glad to see him focus on something positive, emerging from the grief that had engulfed him after her mother's death.

"The turnoff is just up here." She pointed to the right. "There's a parking area. We'll have to snowshoe in from there."

They parked and she got out of the truck and studied the tire tracks in the flat, cleared off area beside the trail that led to her father's cabin. "What are you looking for?" Ryan asked.

"I don't know." Did she really think she could recognize her father's tire treads in all these tracks? "I guess these tracks are from the sheriff's deputies," she said. "They weren't here when I stopped by the other day."

They strapped on snowshoes and headed down the path through the trees to the cabin. When they emerged into the clearing in front of the structure, she paused to look around. "Nothing looks any different than when I was here last Sunday," she said.

"What's over there?" Ryan asked. He nodded toward the open shed to the left of the cabin.

"Dad parks his truck and snowmobile in there," she replied. "And there's a workbench and some tools and stuff."

"Let's have a look." He led the way to the shed, which was mostly empty, save for a couple of gas cans, some gardening tools and a chainsaw. Ryan examined the hand tools scattered across the workbench. "Nothing suspicious here," he said. "Did you say your dad had some dynamite?"

"It was in a box on the workbench when I stopped by to see him a couple of weeks ago," she said. "It's not here now. He said he was going to use it to get rid of an ice dam that was blocking his spring."

He nodded. "Are you ready to try the house?"

"I am—and I'm not." She sighed. "I'm afraid of what I'll find—or what I won't find. But there's no sense putting it off any longer." She led the way past the front door, the big brass padlock still intact, around the side of the cabin, to a big window. "This opens into the bedroom," she said, pointing up. The ground fell away sharply from the wall of the cabin, so that the window was five feet over their heads. "It's big enough to crawl through, and it's up high enough I suspect Dad didn't keep it locked, but I don't know how we're going to get up there."

"Wait a sec." Ryan hurried back toward the front of the cabin. She stuffed her hands in the pockets of her parka and studied the window, nothing visible through the glass from this angle.

Ryan returned a few moments later, carrying an aluminum ladder. "This was behind the shed," he said. "I figured your dad probably had one around." He extended the ladder and propped it against the side of the house, wedging the bottom of it in the snow. The top reached just below the window. Then he stepped back. "You should go first," he directed. "It's your dad's house."

She hesitated.

"What's the matter?" he asked. "Are you afraid of heights?"

"It's not that." She looked up again. She wasn't going to tell him the thought that had popped into her head. What if her dad was up there, dead? But that was ridiculous. He wouldn't be in the house with that big padlock on the front door. "Hold the ladder," she said, and put her foot on the bottom rung.

RYAN WATCHED DENI climb the ladder, distracted as much by the grim expression on her face as the sight of her shapely backside as she ascended. Maybe he should have offered to do this for her, but it hadn't felt right, essentially breaking into the home of a man he scarcely knew.

She reached the third-to-last rung of the ladder and steadied herself with her hands against the window. "Everything looks okay in there," she said. "Normal."

"Can you open the window?" he called up.

She shoved up, but the window didn't move. "I might need something to pry it," she said.

"Stay still," he offered. "I'll get something from the shed."

He ran to the shed and returned half a minute later with a pry bar that had hung above the workbench. "Climb down and get this," he said. "I don't think two of us on the ladder would be safe."

She climbed down a few steps, until she could reach the pry bar he held up to her. Then she hurried back to the window, and fit the narrow end of the bar under the sash. The ladder shifted as she pried at the window and he steadied it with both hands. "Careful!"

With a wrenching sound, the sash rose a couple of inches. Deni tossed down the bar and shoved the window the rest of the way up. There was no screen, so she was able to lean into the room. Then she was up and over the sill, disappearing from sight.

Seconds later, she stuck her head out and called down to him. "Do you want to come up, too?"

Not really. But it didn't seem right to have come this

far only to leave her to search alone. He began climbing. He reached the top and swung his leg over the window-sill and stepped into the room. The small space—maybe eight feet by ten feet—had the stale air of a room that had been closed up and unoccupied for a while, but otherwise looked normal. A green wool blanket was pulled up over the pillow on the double bed in the corner, while a pair of jeans and a shirt were draped over the single straight-backed chair by the door. A hairbrush, coffee mug and some papers were scattered on top of a wooden dresser against the far wall. "Do you see anything unusual or out of place?" he asked.

"No, it pretty much always looks like this." She picked up a paperback book from the table beside the bed and examined it, then laid it back down. "Dad isn't much of a housekeeper."

He followed her through the open door into a larger room across the front of the cabin. A table and two chairs sat by another window on one side of the room, while two recliners, a woodstove and a lamp filled most of the rest of the space. A large braided rug, its colors mostly obscured by age or grime, covered most of the floor.

Ryan followed Deni around the room as she flipped through stacks of magazines by one of the recliners, and shuffled through another pile of papers on one end of the table. They looked like old newspapers to Ryan. "I don't know why Dad saves all this junk," she said, and picked up one of the newspapers.

"Maybe there are articles he's saving to read." He looked over her shoulder and saw the paper was folded back to a story about the ice festival, dated two weeks ago. The hair on the back of his neck rose. Jake had seemed pretty certain that Mike Traynor wasn't linked to the bomb at Caspar Canyon, but why had Mike saved an article about the festival?

Deni moved on, but Ryan flipped through the rest of the papers in the pile. Each one was folded back to an article about some new development in the county—the Nugget Hotel expansion request, the award for the highway bridge, new mining developments, new businesses that catered to tourists. If Mike was a suspect in the bombings, would these be considered evidence that he had been researching potential targets?

Deni had moved on to examining what looked like a stack of mail on the small table between the recliners. Ryan studied the rest of the room. Mike had a fondness for detective novels and spy thrillers, judging by the titles in the single bookcase against one wall. The only artwork on his walls was a watercolor of horses grazing in a meadow, mountains rising in the distance; and a shadowbox that contained a portrait of a young man in uniform; and an assortment of medals and combat patches. "Is this your dad?" he asked, studying the photo.

Deni joined him in front of the keepsake. "Yes. He was in the army during the Gulf War."

"What are the medals for?" He tilted his head, trying to read the inscriptions.

"There's a purple heart where he was wounded by shrapnel," she said. "He has a scar on his shoulder from the explosion, but he always said it was no big deal."

"This one is for marksmanship." Ryan indicated a gold shield with the image of a target. He leaned in closer to read the patch beside it. His voice trailed off, his pulse hammering in his throat as the significance of the design registered.

"What is it?" Deni leaned in beside him. "It looks like a crab."

The badge depicted a bomb over crossed lightning bolts, over two curving branches of laurel leaves. Ryan swallowed, and cleared his throat. "I'm not positive," he said. "But it says something about explosives." He looked at her, trying to gauge if the meaning behind those words had registered yet. "You said your father didn't know anything about explosives," he said. "But I think this badge says he did—that he was good enough to be awarded for his expertise."

She wet her lips. "You're saying Dad probably did know how to build a bomb?"

"Maybe." He looked at the badge again. "Maybe that's what he did in the military. Did he say?"

"No. He didn't talk about his service, and I never asked." She looked crestfallen.

"Maybe we should find out," he said.

Her eyes met his, dark and troubled. "It still doesn't prove anything."

"Of course it doesn't," he agreed. Except that her father was familiar with the places that had been targeted so far, and he may have had the skill to build a bomb. It didn't make him guilty, but they weren't finding anything to prove his innocence, either. "But I think we need to tell the sheriff about this."

"They don't think Dad did anything wrong."

"Maybe not, but they'll want to hear about this." And he couldn't in good conscience keep it a secret, now that he knew. He put his arm around her. "If you tell the sheriff's office, they can figure out if this means anything or not. If you keep the information to yourself, you could end up worrying for nothing. Or in serious trouble with the law."

"You're right." She looked around the room. "Let's go. I've seen enough."

They left, neither of them speaking on the way back to his truck. The silence continued, a heaviness in the air around them as they drove toward town. As he turned off the forest service road onto the highway, Ryan glanced at her. "Are you okay?" he asked.

She shifted toward him. "I wasn't completely honest when I said I didn't see anything out of place back there," she said.

"Oh?" He tensed. "What did you see?"

She made a fist and brought it to her mouth, as if trying to keep back the words. "Dad had a trunk in his bedroom—at the foot of his bed. The trunk isn't there."

"What was in the trunk—do you know?"

She nodded. "I don't know everything, but I do know he kept his guns there."

"What kind of guns?"

"A couple of pistols and at least one rifle. Maybe more. I didn't want to know about them, so I didn't ask. But he wouldn't have taken that trunk if he was just going out to ride his snowmobile." She let out a ragged breath. "I'm really worried. Whatever is going on with Dad, I don't think it's anything good."

Chapter Seven

For the second time in a week, Ryan found himself back at the Rayford County Sheriff's Department with Deni. Deputy Dwight Prentice was the only officer on duty when Deni and Ryan arrived Sunday afternoon. "I need to talk to someone about my father," Deni said after he met them in the front lobby. "We've just come from his cabin and I found some things the sheriff needs to know about. It may be nothing, but I think he should know."

"Come back here and tell me," Dwight said. "I'll pass it on to the sheriff."

He led them to a crowded office, cleared off two chairs for them, then listened as Deni told him about visiting her dad's cabin. "I noticed right away the trunk that usually sat at the end of his bed was missing," she said. "I was hoping he had moved it to some other part of the house, but we didn't find it."

"What about that trunk worries you?" Dwight asked.

"I know my dad kept guns in that trunk. He showed me once—there were two pistols and a rifle in there, and some ammunition and other things. I wasn't interested, so I didn't pay close attention."

"I'll pass this along to the sheriff," Dwight said. He didn't sound alarmed but then, he probably had a lot of practice not giving anything away.

"That isn't the only thing we found," she said.

"What else?" Dwight asked.

Deni looked to Ryan, who nodded in a way he hoped was encouraging. "Dad has this shadowbox on the wall, with a picture of him from when he was in the army, and some medals and stuff," she said. "My mom made it and gave it to him for Christmas one year. He's had it for years and though I've looked at it a hundred times, I never really noticed—" She glanced at Ryan. "Ryan is the one who spotted the badge in there—apparently my dad was some kind of explosives expert in the military."

Dwight tensed. "What makes you say that?"

Ryan described the badge. "I'm pretty sure it's for service in some special explosives unit," he said.

Dwight swiveled his chair to face the computer on his desk and began typing. A few moments later, he angled the screen to face them. "Is this what you saw?" he asked.

The image was of the same bomb over crossed lightning bolts, over a swag of laurel. "Yes." Deni looked from the image on the screen to Dwight. "Do you know what it is?"

"It's an explosive ordnance specialist patch," Dwight said. "If your father has this, it means he was trained to deal with the disarmament and disposal, and construction and deployment of explosives."

"I didn't know." Deni shook her head, looking stunned. "When the sheriff asked me if my dad knew about explosives, I told him he didn't. Dad was a truck driver. But I guess I was wrong. Dad never talked about his time in the army, and I never asked."

"Do you know where he served?" Dwight asked.

"He was in the Gulf War. Desert Storm?"

Dwight nodded. "We'll look into this. Will you give

us permission to cut the lock on the cabin door and do a more thorough search?"

"Yes. Do you think it will help you find my father?"

"It might."

"We didn't see anything to indicate that Mike had done anything wrong," Ryan said.

Dwight nodded. "We need to check it out." He typed into the computer again, then stood and retrieved a print-out from a computer nearby. "You'll need to sign this," he said, laying the single sheet of paper in front of Deni. "It gives us permission to remove the lock and search the cabin."

She signed where he indicated. "Dad is going to be really angry when he finds out I did this," she said.

"You're a loving daughter who's concerned about her father," Dwight reassured. "Let's make this more official. How long has your dad been gone now?"

"Since Wednesday before last. That's the last time I talked to him on the phone."

"Would you like to file a missing persons report on him?" Dwight asked.

Her expression brightened. "Yes!"

Dwight filled out another report and printed it for Deni to sign. "This will add resources to our search for your father," he said.

"Thank you." She stood. "You'll let me know if you find anything?"

He nodded, but Ryan wondered how much the sheriff's department would reveal, if they found anything that indicated Mike Traynor had participated in a crime. They probably wouldn't want Deni passing on that information to her father.

They left the sheriff's department. "Do you want to get coffee or something to eat?" he asked.

"I just want to go home." She gave him an apologetic look. "I'm sorry. I'm terrible company right now."

"You don't have to be any particular way with me." He unlocked the Tundra and they climbed in and drove to her house in silence. He sensed her weariness and her sadness and wished he could do something to help her.

At her house, he walked her to her door. "Thank you for coming with me today," she said.

"Are you sure you'll be all right?" he asked.

She leaned into him and his arms automatically went around her. She felt so right, close to him this way. "I don't know. I... Dad is a grown man. He can do what he wants. But..."

"But he's your father and you love him and you're worried about him," he supplied.

"Yes."

"Call me if you need anything," he said. "Or if you just need to talk." He started to step away, but she held on to him, and pressed her lips to his. The kiss had a fierce, desperate quality, as if she was trying to blot out her pain with passion. But he responded with equal fervor, willing to give comfort any way he could, and enjoying the way she made him feel. The heat of her curves against him aroused him, and he pulled her closer, savoring the taste of her, inhaling the perfume of her hair and smoothing his hand along the curve of her hip.

When at last she pulled away, he reluctantly let her go. "I'd better go," she said, and turned and ducked into the house.

He stood for a moment on the step, letting his breathing return to normal and reining in his frustration. He had prided himself on living a simple life, free of complications and any hint of trouble. But there was nothing simple about Deni or her life. Nothing simple about her missing father, who might or might not be terrorizing locals with homemade bombs. Ryan knew all the bad ways this could play out, but he couldn't stay away from her. He couldn't abandon her when she needed him. He was a strong man, but he wasn't strong enough for that.

Deni felt important, worth facing a lot of trouble for. She had shifted something inside him, something surprising, a little frightening, yet with the potential to be wonderful. As long as she would let him, he intended to stick around, to see what happened next.

MONDAY, DENI'S CLASS was scheduled to take a field trip to the Zenith Gold Mine, and she arrived at school to the chaos of excited children and anxious parents. She met up with seventh grade teacher Mallory Rush, whose class would also be part of the outing, in the gymnasium.

"Want to take bets on how many kids get carsick on the bus and who freaks out when we get down in the mine tunnel?" Mallory asked as they surveyed the milling children.

"I might freak out in the mine tunnel," Deni said. "Whose idea was this particular field trip? No one asked me."

"Zenith Gold Mine reached out to the school and offered to host classes," Mallory said. "All part of their efforts to be good local citizens. Some people weren't happy with them reopening the mine. There were concerns about traffic and the environmental impact. I guess this is their response. Besides, it meshes well with our natural science and local history curriculum." Mallory sipped her coffee. "I think it'll be interesting."

Deni tasted her own coffee—she had had just enough time to say hi and bye to Ryan as she dashed in to grab her usual latte on the way to work. But the memory of that brief exchange, pleasant as it was, wasn't enough to counter the queasiness in her stomach at the memory of her father's participation in the protests over the mine's reopening. His photo had been printed in the paper as part of a group shot taken of people picketing at the entrance to the mine. They hadn't broken any laws, but what if her father had decided to take his dislike of progress further?

"Ms. Traynor, Drake says we have to hold our breath when we get underground at the mine or we'll use up all the oxygen." Kendra Richardson, the beads on the ends of her braids rattling, skidded to a stop in front of Deni. "That's not true, is it? It can't be true."

"It's not true," Deni said. "People work in that mine all day and they certainly don't hold their breath while they're there. There's plenty of oxygen in the tunnels." She hoped. "I'm sure they pipe it in or something."

Kendra nodded, though she didn't look very relieved. Deni looked around for Drake. She suspected the boy, who had a reputation for stirring up trouble, had a crush on Kendra and was trying to impress her. Most boys his age didn't seem to grasp that the way to a girl's heart did not lie in frightening her or grossing her out.

"Our bus is here!" someone shouted, which started a mass push toward the exit.

"Everyone line up!" Mallory called.

"Eighth graders, over here by me," Deni called. "Adam, that means you, too," she added as Adam Escovar veered off toward the back exit.

When she was sure everyone was ushered safely onto the bus, she took a seat beside Marsha Edmonds at the front of the vehicle. Marsha's daughter Sadie was one of six children, and Marsha volunteered with all their classes, so that she spent as much time at the school as some of the teachers. "How are you doing, Marsha?" Deni asked as the bus moved forward.

"I'm good. I'm sorry to hear about your dad, though."

"My dad?" Deni didn't try to hide her alarm.

"I heard he was missing. I saw a notice on the bulletin board at the post office."

Deni immediately felt guilty. The sheriff's department must have posted the notice, but why hadn't she thought of that? Should she print posters with her dad's picture to hand out? It was what people did for missing children and dogs, but did it apply to a fifty-five-year-old who may have left of his own accord?

Marsha was still looking at her, so she forced a response. "Thanks. He's probably fine, but it's not really like him to go off without saying anything to me."

"I saw him in the hardware store week before last," Marsha said. "He was buying a bunch of wire, I guess for some electrical work at his cabin. You can run everything off solar these days, can't you?"

"I guess so," Deni said. Dad had never mentioned any work on the cabin to her. She thought she knew everything about his life—how wrong she had been.

As the bus drove onto the bridge across Grizzly Creek she shuddered, remembering the mock rescue. There had been the same kind of excitement as today in the run-up to that exercise. Getting made up to look injured and practicing what they would say and do had been fun.

Then the rescue workers had found the bomb wired to the bridge and she had been hit with the realization of how close they had been to true danger.

A few minutes later the bus stopped at the entrance to the Zenith Gold Mine. A man in a hard hat came out from a guardhouse and climbed onto the bus. "Welcome to Zenith Mines," he said in a hearty voice. "Today you're going to see how a modern-day gold mine works. You'll see some things most people never get to see."

"If we find some gold, can we keep it?" one of the seventh graders asked.

"That depends on where you find it," the man said. "After lunch, you can try your hand at panning for gold in the creek, just like the pioneers did. You can keep any gold you find then."

A flurry of excited conversation drowned out whatever he was going to say next. Deni rose and faced the rest of the bus. "We're going to stay on this bus until everyone is quiet," she said.

The silence wasn't instant, but things did quiet down considerably. The man in the hard hat—who introduced himself as Kent—continued.

"The Zenith was founded in 1887 by Philemon Cass, a speculator from Boston who came to these mountains looking for gold. Where a lot of people who had the same idea failed, Phil succeeded, and discovered the rich vein of gold and other precious metals that we are still harvesting from today."

Kent shared a little more of the history of the mine as the children fidgeted. Deni, who had sat again, sent him a look meant to signal he should move things along before boredom overcame manners and the students started talking over him again.

Thankfully, he wrapped up his spiel about history and said, "Are you ready to go down into the mine?"

"Yes!" rang out a chorus of voices.

"No!" added several more.

"How will we get there?" someone asked.

"You'll ride a train." Kent grinned as several children responded with excited whoops. He looked to Deni. "Are you ready?"

She nodded and stood once more. "All right. Everyone off the bus in an orderly fashion. Stay together and follow Kent's instructions."

"As you exit the bus each one of you will be given a hard hat and a yellow slicker," Kent said. "Put these on, then follow Ben, who will have a hard hat like mine." He pointed to the yellow safety helmet he was wearing. "He'll lead you to the train."

They managed to get everyone off the bus and outfitted with hard hats and slickers, including all the adults. "What's the raincoat for?" Sadie Edmonds asked.

"It can be wet down in the mine," Kent explained.

The train that would convey them into the mine consisted of three open cars attached to an electric tractor. Kent ran through safety precautions, including "keep your hands and heads inside the car at all times" which at least half a dozen boys immediately ignored.

But at last they were off, traveling from daylight into darkness—but only briefly, as bright lights banished every shadow from the rest of the tunnel. "You can't even tell we're really underground," one girl observed, and Deni had to agree—they might have been inside any windowless museum, except that the walls, ceilings and floors of this place were all made of gray rock.

The company had obviously put a lot of thought into this tour. The tram stopped briefly in a large space set up to look like a historical mine, complete with mannequins in old-fashioned clothing holding pickaxes and sticks of what she hoped was fake dynamite. Kent explained how early miners used the dynamite to break rock loose from the sides of the tunnels, then hauled the rock in handcarts to the surface, to be sorted for transport to the mill, where the valuable minerals could be extracted. He answered the children's questions about the process, though Abigail Murphy flummoxed him when she asked why all the mannequins had funny moustaches.

"That's so they can strain their soup!" Drake called, sending the group of boys around him into gales of laughter, while the girls rolled their eyes.

The tram started up again and they moved into a more modern section of the mine, with pneumatic lines running along the ceiling, safety posters on the wall and men and machinery all around. Kent rattled off statistics about the amount of ore taken from the mine daily and projected earnings, but the children seemed content to watch the men—and as far as Deni could tell, they were all men—work.

Deni sat back, feeling more relaxed now. Her father would have loved this, she thought, both the historical aspect and the glimpse of the modern operation. He had always loved learning things, and he and her mother had passed that love on to her. Had that aspect of his personality really changed?

She estimated they had been in the mine about an hour and a half when Kent announced they would head back up top. "You can have lunch in our outdoor pavilion, then pan for gold in the creek. How does that sound?"

The students'—and possibly some of the parents'—cheers echoed off the stone walls. The train started backward down the tunnel. Kent leaned over Deni's seat and whispered. "Don't worry—we salt the creek with flakes of real gold for the kids to find," he said. "And a lot of chunks of iron pyrite, which most of them seem to like just as much."

"You've done a wonderful job with the tour," she said. "Thank you so much."

Their exit was much faster than the trip down, the tram traveling surprisingly fast through the tunnel. Deni felt a little dizzy, but welcomed the idea that they would soon be back up top in the open air.

She could see the entrance up ahead, an oval of light past the brief stretch of unlit tunnel. She was focused on this, and mentally running through the procedure for distributing sack lunches to the students, when the tram lurched.

"What was that?" a girl asked.

"These old trams are balky sometimes," Kent said. He turned, as if to address Ben, who was driving the tractor.

Later, Deni couldn't remember the order in which everything happened. In her memory, the darkness descended first, then the explosion and dust. She was falling, the tram cars tossed onto their sides, and screaming filled the air. Not the overly dramatic wails of the mock rescue, but true cries of terror, both her own and those of the children. Children who were hurt and needed her help.

Chapter Eight

Ryan was at work when he received the text from search and rescue. The words on the screen sent a shock wave through him: Explosion at Zenith Mine. A number of children and adults trapped/injured. Urgent.

His boss's eyes widened when Ryan showed him the text. "Kids? What were they doing up at the mine?"

"I don't know," Ryan said. "But I need to go. They'll need everyone they can get on this rescue."

"Of course," he said. He made a shooing motion. "Go!"

Ryan kept his gear in his truck. He pulled on his parka as he drove, and fell into a line of vehicles headed toward the mine—sheriff's and fire department vehicles and ambulances, the cars of other first responders and probably media and concerned or curious civilians. He tried to envision what he might find at the mine.

But his imagination didn't prepare him for the chaos he drove into just past the entrance gates. A sheriff's department vehicle blocked the road a quarter mile from the gate, but waved Ryan through when he saw the search and rescue parka. Ryan left his truck behind Sheri Stevens's Jeep, grabbed his pack and jogged to the Beast, where the rest of the search and rescue team was gathering.

Tony, grim-faced, stood with a man in a yellow hard

hat. "This is Peter Grayson, with Zenith Mines," Tony said. "He's going to give us a rundown on the situation."

Grayson, his face the color of paste, nodded. "The tram with the kids was at the entrance to the mine when the explosion occurred," he said. "One car was mostly out of the tunnel, but the explosion twisted the tram tracks and threw the cars over onto their sides. Some of the kids and adults were able to walk away, but we know others are trapped under the tram cars or under rock that fell as a result of the explosion."

"How many kids and adults?" Tony asked.

"Forty-seven total," Grayson said. "We don't know how many made it out and how many are still trapped. There are two mine employees with them. We were able to evacuate the rest of our employees through emergency exits."

"Why were the kids there?" Sheri asked.

"Field trip, from Eagle Mountain Middle School," Grayson said.

Ryan's heart stopped for half a second, then began beating so hard it hurt. "What classes?" he asked. "What grade?"

"Seventh and eighth," Grayson said.

"Do we know the cause of the explosion?" Ted, who was standing just behind Ryan, asked.

"No," Grayson said.

"Some buildup of gas in the mine or something like that?" Eldon asked.

"No." Grayson shook his head. "That can't happen. Not with the ventilation system we have. And not at the mine entrance."

"Sabotage?" Danny asked.

"We're not going to speculate at this time," Grayson said.

"That's not our concern," Tony said. He stepped forward and began assigning jobs and distributing gear.

The team headed toward the mine entrance. As they drew nearer they could see the tram car on its side amid a tumble of rock, other emergency personnel already working to shift rock and tend to the injured. Paramedics, including some SAR volunteers, worked on the injured, while Ryan and others began the search for more survivors, and for those who had not been so lucky.

"Deni Traynor is here somewhere," he said to no one in particular. "Let me know if you find her."

Soon all his attention was focused on freeing a little girl from beneath the tram. Miraculously, she was wedged in a gap between two boulders and other than a scrape on one arm and a terrible fright, was unharmed. He sent her off in the care of a female firefighter and turned his attention to an adult, who proved to be the seventh-grade teacher, Mallory Rush. Mallory had twisted her knee, but was calm. "Who is the other teacher with you?" Ryan asked as he and Ted shifted the rocks around her. He already knew the answer, but he wanted confirmation.

"Deni Traynor," Mallory said. "She's in the first car. The one farthest in the mine." She bit her lip, which had begun to tremble.

A front-end loader rumbled up, a man in coveralls and a hard hat at the controls. "We need to shift the rock blocking the entrance to get at the others," he shouted over the rumble of the diesel engine.

Grayson jogged up to them. "We've established radio contact with one of the workers inside," he said. "They've got some injured kids and one adult who was hit in the head by a rock and unconscious, but the car protected them from most of the rock fall."

"Who is the adult?" Ryan asked. He had a horrible image of Deni lying among the rock, senseless.

Grayson shook his head. "I don't know. A woman."

Ryan felt sick, but pushed the nausea aside. He retreated with the other volunteers while the front-end loader operator and other mine workers began the slow process of carefully shifting the cascade of rock and debris.

It took over an hour to move most of the rock. Meanwhile, they evacuated the children and adults in the first tram car. Three people had to be transported by ambulance with broken bones, but all of the injured were expected to recover.

As the pile of debris blocking the mine tunnel diminished, the rescuers waiting outside could hear sobs and cries from those trapped inside. Ryan bit the inside of his cheek to keep from shouting Deni's name. Even if she could hear him, he wouldn't be able to help her. Not yet.

"A little different from that mock rescue, huh?" Eldon said.

Ryan nodded. No training exercise could prepare you for the reality of an actual event, in which people were seriously injured or possibly dying. And no one talked much about the feeling of helplessness that flooded him now, as they waited for someone else to make it possible to do the jobs they had trained for.

At last, the machinery and men cleared a pathway into the mine. Rescuers swarmed into the tunnel, like soldiers charging into battle.

Ryan headed toward the front of the tram. "Hello!" he shouted. "I'm with search and rescue. Who's here?"

A chorus of voices answered. "We're in the tram car," said a strong male voice.

Rescuers had to climb on top of the car and squeeze between the rock wall of the tunnels and the edge of the open tram car. Ryan dropped down into a scene eerily reminiscent of the mock bus crash—a vehicle on its side, children and adults clustered in twos and threes in an upside-down world.

Except that this scene was dark, save for dim emergency lights on the tram and the puddles of light from the rescuers' headlamps, and the blood that smeared children's faces and bodies was real, not corn syrup and food coloring.

"We need to move everyone to the end of the car," a fireman instructed Ryan. "We've got a torch to cut away the side of the tram car to make evacuating everyone a little easier."

Ryan found Deni in the crush at the end of the car. She had a streak of dirt or grease across her cheek, but seemed otherwise unharmed. "Are you okay?" he asked, examining her face for any sign of pain.

"I'm fine," she said.

"They told us a woman had a head injury and was unconscious," he said. "I was so afraid it was you."

"One of the chaperones, Marsha Edmonds." She turned to look at where nurse Danny Irwin was examining a brunette in jeans and a blue sweater. "I hope she's okay."

Ryan put his arm around Deni and held her as the whine of the torch drowned out further conversation. A few moments later a shout went up and light from a powerful work lamp bathed the space.

Ted stood up and took charge. "Everyone who can walk unaided, line up and follow Deputy Douglas here."

Deputy Jamie Douglas waved from the new opening. "Come on, everybody," she said. "Let's get out of here."

"I should go with my students," Deni said, and moved out of Ryan's arms.

He nodded. He had work of his own to do here. Now

that he knew she was safe, he felt lighter, more focused on the job at hand.

Ryan lost track of how long he and the other rescuers worked, performing triage, stabilizing limbs, preparing patients for transport and searching for anyone who might have been left behind. By the time they received the message to stand down and emerged from the tunnel, he was surprised to see the light was fading.

Much of the crowd that had been in the area earlier had dispersed. Parents had long since come to claim children, the ambulances had transported the more seriously injured, and only a few sheriff's deputies and firefighters remained, along with a contingent of mine workers.

The search and rescue team convened once more at the Beast to load in equipment and review the operation. "The forty-seven people on the tram were all accounted for," Tony said, consulting the notes he had made on a tablet. "Twelve children with minor injuries. One adult with a concussion, admitted to the hospital for observation. Five children with broken bones, two with cuts severe enough to require stitches, one crushed finger which I'm told should heal." He looked up. "The fact that they were all wearing hard hats, and that they were at the mine entrance when the explosion occurred, saved a lot of lives today."

"What caused the explosion?" Ted asked. "Was it another bomb, like the one at Caspar Canyon?"

"The sheriff's department and mine officials aren't saying anything yet," Tony said.

Ted grunted.

"Good job today," Tony said. "Let's get back to headquarters and put away the gear, then go home and get some rest."

Ryan started toward his truck. He was surprised to

find Deputy Jake Gwynn waiting for him. "Have you spoken with Deni today?" Jake asked before Ryan could ask him what he wanted.

"I saw her in the mine, briefly." Ryan took out his keys and pressed the button on the fob to unlock the truck. "She was in the first car, but she's okay. Why?"

"We're wondering if she's heard anything from her father."

"She would have told the sheriff's department if she had." Ryan slipped off his pack and stuffed it into the back of the truck. "What's going on? Was that explosion caused by another bomb?"

Jake looked grim. "I can't say."

"Which makes me believe it was. That, and you're looking for Mike Traynor. If you haven't seen him, Deni hasn't, either."

"He's her father," Jake said. "It would be natural for her to want to protect him."

"She's worried about him and she wants to find him," Ryan countered. "That doesn't mean she's going to condone him doing anything wrong." He faced the deputy, one hand on the door of the truck, a sudden wave of emotion making him shake. "She could have been killed today. Do you think Mike would put his own daughter in danger like that?"

"He probably didn't know about the field trip," Jake said.

"Did you find anything at his cabin?" Ryan asked.

"We were on our way there when we got the call about the explosion," Jake told him.

"Then you don't have anything to tie Mike to this bomb," Ryan said. "And you certainly can't link Deni to it."

"We're not saying Deni is involved," Jake said.

Ryan noticed he didn't try to deny that the explosion had been caused by another bomb. "If you want to talk to Deni, talk to her," he advised. "I don't have anything to tell you that she wouldn't."

Jake stepped back. "Tell Deni if she hears anything, to contact us right away," he said.

"You tell her," Ryan stated. He got in the truck and slammed the door. He needed to stop by SAR headquarters and help with the gear. Then all he wanted was to go back to his place, have a beer and something to eat and try to block out this nightmare of a day with some mindless TV.

But first, he had to see Deni. If he was feeling wrecked by the day, she must feel even worse. And no one should have to go through that alone.

Chapter Nine

"It's a bomb."

"A bomb."

"It must have been a bomb."

Deni heard the conversation around her as she huddled in the overturned tram car with her students, and later, as she waited in the area outside the mine entrance until she was certain all her students were accounted for. Officials refused to confirm these suspicions, but the bombing at Caspar Canyon and the attempt to destroy the Grizzly Creek bridge had everyone convinced that a terrorist was targeting their little community.

All Deni could think of was her father protesting the reopening of the mine. And him buying electrical wire at the hardware store shortly before he disappeared. *That doesn't prove anything*, she told herself. But it didn't make him appear innocent either, did it?

She had been home about an hour and had just stepped out of the shower when her doorbell rang. She hurried to finish drying off and pulled on her robe, then, in bare feet, went to see who was calling.

Ryan stood on the front porch, still in his SAR parka. She pulled open the door. "Ryan?"

His gaze flicked over her, heat behind the look, and she was conscious of being naked beneath the robe—

even though it was an ankle-length plush model that revealed nothing save a triangle of damp skin at the base of her throat and her bare toes.

"Can I come in?" he asked.

"Sure." She stepped back and he moved past her into the front room. He smelled like fresh air and woodsmoke and the faintest hint of aftershave, a combination that struck her as sexy, though maybe it wasn't the scent so much as the man himself.

She shut the door and he turned to her. "You look like you're feeling a little better," he said. "At least you're not as pale."

She tucked a lock of damp hair behind one ear. "I was terrified," she said. "It was bad enough going into that mine and being underground, but being trapped in that overturned tram car, not knowing if we were buried under tons of rock, or if there would be more explosions…" She hugged her arms across her stomach, queasy at the memory. "The only thing that helped me keep it together was knowing the kids needed me." She met his gaze again. "No one was seriously hurt, were they? I was told everybody would be okay, but I wasn't sure if they had found everyone at that point."

"There are a couple of broken bones, and a parent with a concussion, but they should all recover." He touched her shoulder lightly. "Let's sit down."

"Marsha Edmonds's hard hat must have come off when the tram car overturned," Deni said as he steered her toward the sofa. "She was sitting right next to me. At first, I didn't know where she was or what had happened to her. I didn't know where anyone was. Then someone switched on some emergency lighting in the tram car. It was still dim, but when I saw all the blood and she wouldn't answer me, I was so afraid she was going to die."

"She's in the hospital but the word we got is that she's going to be okay."

They sat and Ryan took her hand. "Do you want to talk about what happened, or would you rather not?"

"The tour was almost over. I could see the mine entrance up ahead. Then everything went crazy. I can't... I can't even explain. One minute we were riding in the car and the next we were lying sort of under it. There were loud noises and smoke and darkness, children screaming, blood..." She shuddered. "I thought we were all going to die."

He pulled her close and she laid her head on his shoulder and closed her eyes. This was what she needed, just to be held.

"You're okay now," he said, his voice soft and soothing.

"It was the oddest sensation." She opened her eyes, but didn't lift her head from his shoulder. "All day I had flashes of having been through this before—déjà vu. I think it was the mock bus wreck I participated in the week before. The scenario had so many similarities. Was it like that for you, too?"

"We knew going in that the bus wreck wasn't real, even though we tried hard to act as if it was." He smoothed his hand down her shoulder. "It's so different in a real emergency. It was dark, and there was a lot of debris. We weren't sure where everyone was, and we had to wait a long time for mine personnel and machinery to dig out the tunnel so we could reach the injured."

"I only saw one small part of the whole scene," she said. "And that was terrifying enough."

"At first it looked much worse than it turned out to

be," Ryan added. "Someone said that the fact you were all wearing hard hats probably saved lives, and when the cars were thrown over on their sides, they shielded you from the worst of the blast."

"Right away I heard people say it was a bomb." The thought made her feel sick. "I guess with what happened in Caspar Canyon and at the Grizzly Creek bridge, that was on everyone's mind."

"No one is saying yet exactly what caused the explosion," Ryan said. "They probably don't know yet. Mines still use explosives to get at the ore, don't they? And there could be pockets of gas trapped underground, I think."

She sat up straighter and stared at him. "Do you mean it might not be a bomb at all?"

"I don't know," he said.

The sob that escaped her startled her. She covered her mouth with both hands, trying to stifle it, but the tears flowed freely. Ryan put his arm around her again. "It's okay," he soothed.

She shook her head. It—whatever "it" was—was not okay, but she appreciated him wanting to comfort her. Her feelings were in such turmoil. "I want to believe my dad doesn't have anything to do with any of these explosions," she said. "But I keep remembering things or hearing things that seem incriminating—even though I know they may not mean anything."

"What kind of things?" he asked.

She plucked at the lapel of the robe, a nervous gesture. "Marsha and I were talking and she told me she had seen my dad at the hardware store about two weeks ago. She said he was buying electrical wire. But why would he do that? His cabin doesn't have electricity. So I thought, maybe bombs need electrical wire for something."

Ryan frowned. "The only explosives I've been around

are the ones the highway department uses to trigger avalanches to keep the roads clear. They use charges that explode on impact, so, like grenades or rockets. No electrical wire." He shrugged. "I guess you could look it up online."

"I don't think I want that on my browsing history," she said.

"Your dad was probably just doing some work for a friend or something," Ryan said.

But what friend? How terrible was it that she didn't even know who he socialized with when he wasn't with her.

"What else are you worried about?" he asked.

"Dad hated that they reopened the Zenith Mine," she said. "He was one of the people who tried to block the opening. They filed papers in court and when that didn't work they picketed the site and tried to block work on the mine."

"I remember people were worried about environmental damage," Ryan said. "But so far I take it the mining company is doing a good job."

"They seem to be," she said. "When we were on the tour today, I remember thinking that Dad would have really enjoyed it. They had a section on the history of the mine, and the demonstration of the extraction methods they use today was really interesting."

"It seemed to me there was a lot of security at the mine," Ryan said. "I don't see how anyone who didn't work there could possibly get into the mine to plant a bomb."

She stared at him. "I hadn't thought of that."

"I don't see how your father could have anything to do with what happened at the mine," Ryan said. "And no matter what he thought about the mine, surely he wouldn't put you and a bunch of students in danger."

"He didn't know about the field trip," she said. "Or at least, he and I never talked about it. We didn't talk about my work much."

"He wasn't interested?" Ryan asked.

"It wasn't that. But my mom was a teacher and hearing about my job was just one more reminder she isn't around anymore." She swallowed a fresh knot of tears and took a deep breath. "But you're right. He wouldn't have wanted to hurt me, or children." Surely, he wouldn't. She leaned against him once more. "All this worrying is exhausting. I wish I knew what the sheriff's department found at Dad's cabin. You and I didn't really see anything, but do you think they found something suspicious?"

"I ran into Deputy Jake Gwynn at the mine site this afternoon," Ryan said. "He told me they were on their way to search Mike's cabin when they got the call about the explosion at the mine. So I guess they haven't gotten up there yet."

She sighed. "So we wait a little longer."

"Jake told me to tell you to contact them if you heard from your dad."

"Does he think I won't?"

He looked pained. "You need to know that whenever someone is suspected of a crime like this, law enforcement looks at all the people around them, friends and family. If your father has done something wrong and authorities think you helped him, you could end up in trouble, too."

"But I haven't done anything wrong." She stared at him, heart racing. "You believe me, don't you?"

He squeezed her hand. "I believe you. I'm just telling you how law enforcement works, so you can be prepared."

"How do you know this?"

He looked down at their clasped hands. "I've known people who have had to deal with this kind of thing."

"This whole situation is so bizarre," she said.

"It is. And I don't want to see you hurt."

"I need to talk to Dad," she said. "I'm sure he could explain everything."

"I think it would be better if you let law enforcement handle this," Ryan said.

"He's my father. I can't abandon him."

He released her hand and sat back. "Okay. But if you're going to find your dad, you have to be smart about it. You said you last spoke to your dad Wednesday almost two weeks ago, right? And you saw him at the town council meeting last Wednesday."

"Then you do believe it was him I saw?"

"Of course." He said it so matter-of-factly, but relief flooded her. She had been worried that he would think she was overreacting, seeing her father in places where he wasn't.

"Anyway," he continued. "That means wherever he's hiding, he's not that far away. He has his truck with the camper, his snowmobile on a trailer and probably other stuff."

A trunk of guns, she thought, but said nothing.

"To me, that suggests he's camping, probably in the mountains," Ryan said.

She nodded. "He liked to camp. Even in winter. But the sheriff's department will have figured this out, too, won't they? They're probably looking for him."

"I'm not so sure they are. They said Mike wasn't very high on their suspect list, and even though you filed a missing persons report, Rayford County has a small force. With the bombs, and now the explosion at the Zenith Mine, they don't have the time or personnel to do a very widespread search."

"So what do you suggest?" she asked.

He hesitated. "The two of us could drive around some. We can visit some likely camping locations and see if we can find any indication that your dad has been there. Maybe we'd get really lucky and even find him."

She tried to tamp down the hope that soared at his words, but the idea of doing something—anything—to help her father made her feel lighter.

"That's a fabulous idea." She slipped her arms around him and hugged him close. He returned the embrace, his gaze dropping to where her robe had spread a little farther apart, revealing the curve of her breasts. Once more, she was aware of how little she was wearing, but she didn't pull away.

Instead, she slid one hand up, fingers twining in his hair, and urged his face down toward hers.

They kissed slowly, as if they had all the time in the world to explore the sensation of warm lips meeting, mouths open, tongues tangling. He broke the kiss. "Maybe we shouldn't be doing this," he said.

"Why not?" She angled toward him, letting the robe fall open a little wider. "I really like you," she said. "And I really want you."

She sighed as he cupped her breast. "Yeah. I want you, too." He dragged one thumb across her hardened nipple.

She squirmed, bringing him closer still. The robe was all the way open now, and she brought her right leg up to drape her thigh across his. A draft swept across her crotch, and she thought of Ryan touching her there, and bit back a moan.

He was caressing her bare bottom now, stroking down and around to her thigh, fingertips tantalizingly close to her sex, his lips trailing kisses along her jaw, then down the side of her neck. She tilted her head to provide him better access, as he reached down to unfasten his belt.

The sound of the doorbell pierced her like a jolt of electricity. She stared up at Ryan, confused, as it sounded again.

He swore and withdrew his hands from beneath her robe. "Are you expecting someone?"

"No." The bell sounded again, followed by a hard knocking.

"You'd better answer it," Ryan said.

She stood and cinched the robe tighter, then walked to the door, Ryan right behind her.

Two men she didn't recognize stood in the yellow glow of the porch light. Ryan looked at her. She shook her head. "I've never seen them before," she whispered.

"Ms. Traynor, open the door please," one of the men said. "We need to talk to you."

"Who are you?" she asked.

"We're with the United States Bureau of Alcohol, Tobacco, Firearms and Explosives. We need to talk to you about your father."

Chapter Ten

Ryan took an immediate dislike to the two men who strode into Deni's living room, partly because they had interrupted his make-out session with her, and partly because of the way the taller of the two looked Deni up and down, the way a hungry dog might size up a steak. "Sorry to interrupt your evening," the man said, in a voice that made it clear he wasn't sorry at all.

"Who are you?" Ryan asked. They had flashed a couple of official-looking badges on the front porch, but he had no idea what those badges had said.

"Who are you?" the shorter man, with buzz-cut blond hair and a cocky swagger, demanded.

While the feds glared at Ryan, Deni stepped forward. "I'd like to see those IDs again," she said.

With exaggerated slowness, the tall man—slicked back hair and cowboy boots with pointed toes—fished a wallet from the inside pocket of his black overcoat and opened it. "Agent Olivera, United States Bureau of Alcohol, Tobacco, Firearms and Explosives," he said.

"Agent Ferris." The blond offered his own wallet.

Deni nodded. "You can wait here while I get dressed," she said.

"Ma'am, you need to stay here where we can see you," Olivera instructed.

Deni lifted her chin and sent him a look that should have had frost forming on his eyebrows. "I'm not going to talk to you until I'm dressed." Not waiting for an answer, she turned and left the room.

Ferris made a move as if to follow, but Ryan blocked his path. "She didn't have to let you in," Ryan said. "You can wait a few more minutes."

Instead of answering, Ferris turned and began examining the room.

"What's your relationship to Ms. Traynor?" Olivera asked.

"A friend," Ryan said.

"Your name?"

"Ryan Welch."

"Do you know Mike Traynor?" Olivera asked.

"No."

Ferris picked up a framed photograph of Deni with her father. The two of them were standing on a mountain summit against a backdrop of clear blue sky. They had their arms around each other and grinned into the camera. They both looked so happy. "Yet you're friends with his daughter," Ferris said.

"She's not sixteen. She doesn't need her dad's permission to socialize with anyone."

"When was the last time you saw Mike Traynor?" Olivera asked.

"I didn't."

For the next long minute the two held a staring contest. Ryan refused to be intimidated by this stranger, and held his gaze until Deni returned. She entered the room on a wave of vanilla-and-spice perfume. She had not only dressed in slacks and a soft-looking cream-colored sweater, she had dried her hair and darkened her lashes and lips. She looked less fragile than she had before.

"What can I do for you?" she asked.

"We need to ask you about your father," Olivera said.

"Why are you interested in my father?"

"Let's sit down." Olivera nodded to the sofa.

Deni sat on the sofa. Ryan settled in next to her, resisting the urge to take her hand. Gone was the weeping woman of earlier. Now she projected the dignity and strength of someone who didn't need to lean on anyone.

Olivera took the only other chair in the room, leaving Ferris to carry in a chair from the kitchen table. "We're investigating the explosion at the Zenith Mine," Olivera said.

Deni said nothing, letting the silence fill the room like poison gas.

Olivera frowned. "When was the last time you spoke to your father?" he asked.

"Have you spoken with the sheriff's department?" she asked.

"I don't think that's relevant," Olivera said.

"If you had spoken to them, you would know I haven't heard from my father since Wednesday, March 10," she said. "I reported him missing."

"You also indicated you suspected your father might have had something to do with the bombs placed at the Grizzly Creek bridge and in the Caspar Canyon ice-climbing area," Olivera said.

So they had spoken to the sheriff, if they knew that.

"I don't know where my father is or what he's done," Deni said. "If you've read my statement to the sheriff, then you know everything I have to say."

"You were at the mine today," Ferris said.

Her gaze flickered to him. "Yes. I was there with my class of eighth graders for a field trip."

"Did your father give you anything to take with you?"

Olivera asked. "Maybe he asked you to leave a package near the mine entrance."

Ryan sat forward, fists clenched on his knees. This is what he had warned her about. She had fallen under suspicion simply because she was Mike Traynor's daughter.

"I haven't seen or spoken to my father in almost two weeks," she said. "He didn't know about the field trip. And the idea that you think I would in any way endanger children—not to mention myself—is absurd."

The two agents exchanged looks Ryan couldn't interpret.

"Can you tell us anything about the explosion at the mine?" Olivera asked.

"It was terrifying," she said. "I thought we were all going to die." Her voice trembled on the last words.

"You told the sheriff your father's guns are missing," Olivera said. "What kinds of guns?"

She repeated what she had told Deputy Prentice—that she didn't know what kind of guns.

Olivera and Ferris took turns peppering her with questions. Why had she gone to her father's cabin? What did she expect to find there? Had her father ever made threats toward the mine?

"Not threats," she said. "He protested against the mine reopening, but that was always peacefully."

"How did he protest?" Ferris asked.

"He spoke out against the reopening of the mine at a public meeting. He picketed outside the mine gates. He carried a sign with the word *reopening* in a red circle with a line drawn through it."

"Did he have any friends who worked at the mine?" Olivera asked.

"I don't know."

She didn't know where her father had gone. She

thought he had bought the dynamite to get rid of a dam in the spring above his house. She hadn't known he had been trained to handle explosives in the army. She didn't know his friends.

"Were you aware your father had a criminal record?" Olivera asked.

Ryan felt the shock wave pass through Deni. Her eyes widened. "No! That isn't true."

"It's true," Ferris said, sounding smug.

Deni looked to Olivera. "What did he do? When?"

"In 1992 he was convicted of assault for beating a man in a fight in a bar. He served three months in the county jail."

"That was before I was born."

"It shows he's capable of violence," Olivera said.

"You probably carry a gun," Deni said. "I imagine you're capable of violence, too."

Olivera didn't flinch. "What about you?" he asked. "Are you capable of violence?"

To Ryan, she looked angry enough to strike the agent at the moment, but she only said, "No. I teach children for a living. I'm trying to make the world better for them, not more violent."

"So you don't have any idea what your father's plans are?"

She stood. Ryan rose also. "You're repeating yourself now," she said. "I've had an exhausting day. You can go now."

Olivera and Ferris both stood. "We're not done yet," Olivera said.

"But I am." She turned and left the room.

The muscles in Olivera's jaw bunched. "You need to tell your girlfriend she could land in serious trouble for failing to cooperate with federal authorities," he said.

"You tell her," Ryan said.

Ferris took a step toward him. Ryan tensed. He didn't relish fighting this man, but he was prepared to defend himself, and to defend Deni.

"We'll be talking to you both again," Olivera said.

The two agents walked to the door. As soon as they were gone, Ryan locked it behind them, then went in search of Deni.

DENI SAT ON the side of her bed, hands clasped between her knees, trying to stop shaking.

A knock sounded on the bedroom door. "They're gone," Ryan said. "Is it okay if I come in?"

"Please."

He came and sat beside her. "They think my father had something to do with the bomb at the mine," she said. "They think I helped them." The implication in their questions had been clear.

"They were fishing, trying to unsettle you," Ryan explained.

"I wish I had never said anything to the sheriff."

"You did the right thing," he said.

She leaned against him, and he put his arm around her shoulder. She wanted this day to be over, for none of this—not the bombs, not her father disappearing, not federal agents questioning her—to have ever happened. She knew that wasn't possible, but maybe it would be possible for just a little while to forget. To focus on something else.

She turned toward him and kissed him, intent on recapturing the passion that had flared between them before Agents Olivera and Ferris had interrupted them.

"You've had a terrible day," Ryan said. "You don't have to do this just because it's what I want."

"It's what I want," she said. "It's what I need." She

crawled into his lap, and slid her hands beneath his fleece top. It felt so good to give vent to the storm of emotions swirling inside her, to surrender to good sensations instead of bad ones. He shucked off the fleece and she licked her way across the top of his shoulder, savoring the taste of him. His muscles contracted as she brushed her fingers across the hot skin of his ridged abdomen, and pleasure rippled through her as he stripped off her shirt and bra and shaped his mouth to her breast.

She traced the scar down his arm, ridged white against his skin. "Does it hurt?" she asked.

"Not much."

She dropped her hand lower, down his ribs to his pants, where she lowered the zipper of his jeans and cupped his erection. "How about that?" she murmured.

"That doesn't hurt at all." He put his hand over hers. "Before we go much further, do you have a condom?"

"I do." She hoped that was right. It had been a while since she had needed one. She slid off his lap and hurried into the bathroom. She found the box at the back of the cabinet and fished out a foil packet. She caught sight of herself in the mirror when she shut the cabinet door—cheeks flushed, eyes bright, hair curling around her chin. Not too shabby.

She decided to speed things up a little, and returned to the bedroom holding the condom packet and wearing nothing but a pair of dangling silver earrings. Cool air caressed her skin, but the chill vanished as his heated gaze swept over her.

He undressed and joined her under the covers. His clothing had hidden a lot, she decided. He had a climber's lean body with defined muscles, and he moved with fluid grace. She caressed his shoulder, and smoothed her hand down his arm. "I couldn't stop thinking about you, the first time I saw you," she said.

"Why was that?" he asked.

"You looked different." How could she explain? "Not shy, exactly, but not so, I don't know, sure of yourself. Too many of the guys I meet around here have this attitude like any woman should be thrilled to be noticed by them."

"Most of that attitude is an act," he said. "We're all scared to death of rejection." He grasped her hip and tugged her a little closer. "I noticed you, too. I thought you were out of my league."

A snort of laughter escaped before she could suppress it. "Why would you think that?"

"You were wearing expensive boots and had a nice manicure."

"So you thought I was high-maintenance."

"Nothing wrong with that, but those women usually aren't the type to be interested in a lowly laborer."

"The boots were a gift and I do my own nails." Her hand went to his erection again. "And there's nothing lowly about you."

He grinned, and rolled her onto her back, then reached for the condom.

She pulled him to her and welcomed him in, eager to know every inch of him. It took them a few moments to find a rhythm, the awkwardness smoothed by laughter, then banished by the need to be closer, to feel more.

She loved touching him, and loved the way he touched her. She lost herself in the moment, and when she tensed and bowed in the throes of her climax she shouted for joy that the grief and anguish of the day had, at least momentarily, been banished by so much good.

They clung together for a long time afterward, her face pressed to his chest, breathing in his scent, the steady thud of his heart in her ears. She thought he might have fallen asleep when he stirred and stroked his hand down her shoulder. "You're amazing—you know that?" he said.

"Mmm." She snuggled down closer, hoping to drift off to sleep, but she should have known thoughts of the day wouldn't stay away long. She opened her eyes and shifted until she could see his face. "Did you mean that, about going to look for my dad?"

"Yes. Whenever you want."

"Friday. School is out. Do you have to work?"

"I'll get off."

So there was that to look forward to—or to dread. The shock of learning her dad had been in jail came back to her, though not as terrible now. "I never knew Dad had been in jail," she said.

"I guess it's not the kind of thing a parent tells his kid. But it sounds like he did his time and never stepped out of line again. There are probably a lot of people like that."

"Did you ever get in a fight?" she asked. "Actually hit someone?"

"I think I threatened some guy who ticked me off in a bar once. Both of us had had a few too many beers. Fortunately, my friends had more sense than I did. What about you?"

She laughed. "No. I'm definitely not the fighting type."

"I don't think one bar fight makes your dad a violent man," Ryan said. "And having done time doesn't make him a bad person."

"When they talked about him, it was like they were describing a stranger," she said. "Someone I don't know."

"Our parents are always strangers to us in a way. They lived whole lives before we were ever born, and we can't know that side of them."

"What if they're right and my father did those things?"

she asked. "I don't think he knew about the field trip to the mine, but there are workers there. If he set a bomb, it was with the intent to hurt people."

He sighed, and squeezed her shoulder gently. "If your dad did do that, it doesn't make you a bad person. And it doesn't mean you'll stop loving him."

"It will change how I think about him, and maybe how I feel about him," she said.

"It will be hard," he conceded. "But you'll get through it."

"Will I?"

"You won't be alone." He kissed her and held her close. She lay down beside him once more and told herself she was safe here, but she had felt that before and been wrong.

Chapter Eleven

The meeting at search and rescue headquarters Thursday evening was supposed to be about cleaning out the Beast and brainstorming ways to raise money to purchase a new rescue vehicle. But as team members unloaded supplies from the old Jeep, the main topic of conversation was the two strangers who were staying at Hannah Richards's parents' inn. "I think they're some kind of federal agents," Hannah said as she sorted through a plastic tub of supplies from the Beast. "They paid with a government-issued credit card."

"FBI agents," Danny said. He examined a packet of gauze and tossed it into a bin labeled Expired Supplies.

"Alcohol, Tobacco, and Firearm agents," Ryan said. "And Explosives. They're here to investigate the explosion at the Zenith Mine."

Everyone stopped working to stare at him. "How do you know that?" Austen Morrissey asked. He was crouched in the back of the Beast, charged with fishing out anything that had rolled under the seats.

Ryan silently cursed his inability to keep his mouth shut, but he was in too deep to back out now. "They stopped by Deni's Monday night to talk to her."

"Why did they want to talk to Deni?" Sheri asked.

Ryan tried for a bored expression. "I guess because she was in the mine when the explosion happened."

"You guess?" Ted asked. "Don't you know? You were there, weren't you?"

"How do you know I was there?"

Eldon laughed. "We drove by Deni's last night and saw your truck in the driveway."

"It was still there this morning," Ted said.

Ryan flushed. He had mixed feelings about spending the night with Deni. The sex had been great, but how would she feel when she found out her dad wasn't the only one who had done time in prison? Given how upset she was after Agents Olivera and Ferris had badgered her, he hadn't felt right giving her any more distressing news. Now that the feds were involved, he really should take a step back, but he couldn't.

Watching Olivera and Ferris accuse her of helping her father plant bombs had brought back memories of when had had endured similar questions. Except in his case, he really had broken the law. He might not always be a good judge of other people, but he was pretty sure Deni was innocent.

"How is Deni doing?" Sheri asked. "I can't even imagine how horrible it must have been for her."

"She was pretty shaken up, but she'll be okay," Ryan said.

"Did those agents say if the explosion at the mine was caused by a bomb?" Tony asked.

"They asked a lot of questions, but they didn't offer any information," Ryan said.

"Mom says they don't say much of anything," Hannah reported.

"Where's Jake?" Danny asked. "He could probably tell us."

"Jake is working," Hannah said. "And he wouldn't tell you anything. He doesn't talk about his work."

"But does he tell you?" Danny nudged her. "Then you could tell us."

"I have better things to do with Jake than talk about cop stuff," she said, which prompted shouts of laughter from the others.

"I think it had to have been a bomb," Danny said. "What else would cause that kind of destruction?"

The mood of the room immediately sobered. "What kind of nut is planting all these bombs?" Eldon asked. "It's freaky."

"I heard Mike Traynor was a suspect," Austen said. "After all, didn't he go missing about the time they found that first bomb at Grizzly Creek?"

"Is that why the feds wanted to talk to Deni?" Danny asked.

"They didn't say why they were there," Ryan said. "And it doesn't matter, because Deni doesn't know where her dad is or what he's up to."

"I always liked Mike," Ted observed. "He was kind of quiet, but I always thought he was the kind of guy who lived his beliefs."

"What were his beliefs?" Ryan asked.

"Oh, I don't know," Ted said. "But he didn't like development and using up resources, so he lived off-grid on that mining claim. He certainly didn't use a lot of resources. I don't want to live like that, but I can appreciate the integrity of it."

"Didn't Ted Kaczynski live in a cabin in the woods?" Danny asked.

"Who was Ted Kaczynski?" Hannah asked.

"The Unabomber?" Danny asked. "People probably said he was quiet and kept to himself, too."

"This area is full of people who want to live simply and keep to themselves," Sheri said. "That doesn't make them criminals."

"Well, whoever is planting these bombs, I hope they find him soon," Danny said. "I don't like cleaning up after him. It's bad enough all the people who have been injured, but sooner or later someone is going to be killed. Not to mention the ice-climbing area is a mess. It will probably be closed for the rest of the year."

Ryan let the talk swirl around him, his thoughts in turmoil. What if Deni's dad did those things? How could he be related to someone as good as Deni?

"Maybe you should cool things a little with Deni, in case her dad does turn out to be the bomber," Austen said. "You don't want to be tangled up in something like that."

Ryan's first instinct was to be offended, to protest that this didn't involve Deni. Even if her dad was guilty, she hadn't done anything wrong. But when he was really honest with himself, he could admit shying away from the thought of being associated, however peripherally, with someone who had hurt so many people with such destruction. That would be the sensible thing to do, but his past proved he wasn't always sensible, especially when it came to women.

DENI WAS READY when Ryan arrived at her house Friday morning. "If we're going to figure out what's going on with Dad, we need a plan," she told him. She produced a small spiral-bound notebook. "I figure the sheriff's department and maybe the federal cops have been searching for him, but the sheriff's department as much as said he wasn't at the top of their list, and the feds just got here. Plus, it will take them a while to figure out his habits or talk to the people he knew. I feel foolish, not thinking to do this before."

"You're not foolish," he said. "You were upset and afraid. Human."

"I'm still all that," she added. "But I'm also determined to find Dad and figure out what's going on." She leaned toward Ryan. "I know I told the sheriff Dad's been behaving oddly, and that I was worried he might have had something to do with the bombs. But the more I think about it, the more I believe he would never do something that would hurt other people or put them in danger."

Ryan pursed his lips, considering this. "So, if a bomb destroyed a bridge that wasn't open to traffic or kept a company from ever reopening a mine, you think Mike might do that?"

"Exactly." She sighed. "I know that's still horrible, and a criminal act, but I could almost picture him upset enough to do something like that. I don't think he would ever injure or kill a bunch of random people. Not climbers or motorists or mine workers, and certainly not children."

"You already said your father didn't know about the field trip," Ryan pointed out.

"Maybe this conviction that my father is innocent doesn't make sense," she said. "But this was the man who gave money to the hitchhikers he picked up while he was driving—even though that was against company policy. He was always interested in people's stories. He taught me to pick up litter and keep a clean campsite, to take care of the earth. He cared deeply about history and nature—he wanted to preserve places, not destroy them."

Ryan listened, not interrupting or contradicting her. "Okay," he said when she finally fell silent. "So what's the plan?"

Some of the tension in her chest eased. If Ryan did

think she was wrong about her dad, he at least was still willing to come with her to try and find him. She opened her notebook. "First stop, Rouster's Coffee Roasters."

"Your dad liked Rouster's coffee?"

"He liked Rouster—Rusty Wilson."

"Then let's go."

Rusty "Rouster" Wilson roasted his coffee in a barn-like building in an industrial park on the far edge of Eagle Mountain, a block from the waste transfer station and across the highway from the sewage treatment facility. "Dad came here two or three mornings a week to have coffee with Rouster," Deni said as Ryan pulled his truck into a lot that contained a stack of old pallets and a mud-spattered FJ with green primer on the front right quarter panel.

"I thought the place only sold wholesale coffee beans," Ryan said after they had climbed out of the truck.

"It does. Rouster's Roast is served at restaurants all over Colorado and half of Utah." She walked to the front door and rang the bell. "But Dad didn't know that the first time he came here. He saw the sign that said Coffee and pulled in to buy a cup. Rouster tried to direct him to one of the cafés in town, but Dad wouldn't take no for an answer. Finally, Rouster invited him in and brewed up a fresh pot."

"The next morning he showed up again, this time with muffins from the bakery," a deep voice said. The door opened and a stocky man with a full red beard greeted them. "Where is the old cuss, Deni?" he asked. "I'm almost starting to miss him."

"Hi, Rouster," Deni said. "This is my friend Ryan."

The two men shook hands. "We want to talk to you about Dad," Deni said.

"Come on in." He opened the door wider and led the

way down a short hall, into a room redolent with the aroma of roasting coffee. The space was dominated by a gleaming stainless steel and blue enamel roaster that looked to Deni like a cross between a robot and a giant washing machine. The machine roared softly, radiating heat and the heady scent of roasting coffee. Burlap bags of coffee beans stamped with their country of origin were stacked thigh-high along one wall.

"Have a seat." Rouster motioned to a sagging green sofa, and walked to a silver coffee urn on a nearby counter. "I haven't heard a word out of Mike in over two weeks," Rouster said as he measured ground coffee into the machine. "Have you?"

"No." She sank onto the sofa, which sagged so low her knees were at midchest. She moved to the edge of the seat and sat up straighter. "I'm trying to put together a picture of what he was up to before he disappeared," she said. "When was the last time you saw him?"

Rouster pulled three mugs from a cabinet above the coffee maker. "Monday, March 8. I know because that's my birthday and instead of muffins, Mike brought cupcakes." His voice roughened on the last words and he cleared his throat. "The old cuss never said anything about leaving town."

The coffee maker began to hiss and spit. "Cream and sugar?" Rouster asked.

"Both," she said.

"Black for me," Ryan said.

"Mike drank his coffee black, too," Rouster said. He stared at the coffee maker, his expression glum.

"Did Dad say anything about wanting to change things around here?" Deni asked.

"What do you mean?" Rouster tore his gaze away from the coffee.

"Well, you know he wasn't a big fan of the Zenith Mine reopening."

"Mike didn't like change of any kind." He filled the first mug, steam rising in a cloud around him. "I told him all the time he was too young to be so set in his ways."

"But did he ever say anything about doing anything to stop change from happening?" she asked.

He handed her the mug, along with a ceramic bowl of sugar and creamer packets. "He went to a lot of meetings and protests. He wrote letters. That kind of thing."

"Did he ever talk about bombs?" Ryan's words were an explosion of their own, shattering the calm in the room.

"He never said anything like that." Rouster glared at Deni. "Is that what you think? That Mike is the one who's been blowing up stuff around here?"

"No! Of course not!" She spread her hands wide. "But he's gone, and everyone knows he didn't like the places the bombs have targeted. And he knew about explosives from the military…" Saying all that out loud sounded so bad, but that didn't make her father a bomber.

Rouster shook his head. "I can't believe it. And I'm telling you the truth when I say he never talked about anything like that. We spent hours right there on that couch, talking about everything under the sun. He complained plenty, but he never, ever suggested violence."

"He never said anything like that to me, either," she said. "But I figured he might be different with his friends than he was with me."

"He never advocated violence around me," Rouster said. He took a long drink of coffee, frown lines deep across his forehead. "He was a little 'off' last time I saw him."

"In what way?" Ryan asked.

"Hard to say. Distracted. I asked him what was wrong

and he blew me off, said something like 'nothing important' and changed the subject."

"And he never said anything about wanting to get
away for a while?" Ryan asked. "Maybe take a trip, go
to see old friends, anything like that?"

"No, and if he was going to do something like that, he
would have told Deni." He turned to her. "Your daddy
loves you and he is so proud of you. He said moving here
to be close to you was one of the best things he ever did."

She opened her eyes wide, trying to blink past the
tears, and swallowed the lump in her throat. Ryan sent her
a sympathetic look, then, perhaps to give her a moment
to compose herself, asked, "Can you think of anyone else
we should talk to? Any other friends he hung out with?"

"Mike was pretty much a loner." Rouster set down his
cup and walked over to the coffee roaster and studied the
dial. He made some adjustments, then returned to them.
"There was one guy, Al somebody. Mike brought him
here one morning, but I told him not to bring him back."

"Why is that?"

"I didn't like him," Rouster said. "He used a lot of
foul language and was talking trash about pretty much
everybody. Mike would complain about people, but he
was upset about the things they did. Al referred to one of
the city council members as a communist and said some
really nasty stuff I won't repeat about one of the women
on the council. I don't want anything to do with someone like that and I told Mike so."

"I never heard Dad mention anyone like that," Deni
said. "Did Dad say how they knew each other?"

"I think they met when a bunch of people went up
to the Zenith Mine to protest," Rouster said. "Mike introduced him as 'somebody who thinks a lot like I do,'

but he was wrong. Your dad has never been mean. This guy was."

"Al what?" Ryan asked. "Do you know his last name?"

Rouster shook his head. "I don't think I ever knew."

"Can you remember anything else about him?" Ryan asked. "Where he worked, or where he lived?"

"Mike and him talked like he lived in a cabin off-grid, like Mike. He might even have said they were neighbors." Rouster shook his head. "Sorry I don't remember more. I didn't like the guy, so I didn't want to know anything else about him. But if you can find him, maybe he knows what's up with your dad."

They thanked him for the coffee and information and left. "What now?" Ryan asked.

"I'm trying to think of someone who might know more about Al," she said.

"Your dad never mentioned him?"

"No. And that's a little odd. I mean, I guess I don't know everything about Dad, but when we talked, he often told me what he'd been up to that day, who he had seen, etc. I'm sure he never mentioned anyone named Al. He really never mentioned any friends, except Rouster." She tried to remember conversations with her father, in particular ones where he mentioned names of people he had talked to. She fastened her seat belt. "Do you know where Broken Spur Antiques is?"

"Is that one of the shops on the square?"

"That's the one. A woman named Glenda owns it. She knew Dad. Let's see what she has to say."

Ryan put the truck in gear and headed toward downtown. "How does your dad know Glenda? Were they just friends, or did they date?"

She laughed. "Nothing that close. She organizes a lot of the protests around here and is always lobbying the city council for different environmental and political causes. She got them to set up a recycling program at the transfer station and I'm pretty sure she was one of the leaders of the protest at the Zenith Mine."

Glenda Nassib looked up from behind a desk when Deni and Ryan entered her small antique shop. "May I help you?" she asked, in an accent that carried a hint of the East Coast.

"I'm Deni Traynor. Mike Traynor's daughter."

Glenda stood. "I saw the posters about Mike going missing," she said. "I was so sorry to hear that."

"This is Ryan Welch," Deni said. "We're trying to put together a timeline of what Dad was doing right before he disappeared. I was wondering when you saw him last."

Glenda shook her head. "I haven't seen Mike in a long time. Weeks."

"You helped organize the protest up at the Zenith Mine, didn't you?" Deni asked.

"Yes. And that may have been the last time I saw him. Or, no—the last time was at one of the meetings to oppose the proposed expansion of the Nugget Hotel."

"How did he seem to you then?" Ryan asked.

Glenda shrugged. "The same. He was frustrated that nothing we were doing seemed to be working. We protested, we wrote letters, we voiced our concerns, but it was as if nobody was listening."

"That sounds pretty frustrating," Ryan said.

"It can be, but I try to tell people, it's part of the process. I've been at this a long time, and you learn that there are always more failures than victories, but it's still worth it to make a dissenting view heard, and over time, you can change the way people think. Just the other day over in Lake County, a developer we've argued with for years presented a proposal for a new housing development. Only this time, he included several of the things we've been advocating for over the years—green space, trails, water-wise landscaping. It's progress." She smiled. "But I understand, people get upset when things take so long to change."

"Was Mike upset about the mine?" Ryan asked.

"He was, but not unusually so." She turned to Deni. "Your father is passionate about his desire to maintain the quality of life and natural beauty we all enjoy here. You should be proud of that."

"I am," Deni said. But pride was a poor substitute for having her dad back home. "Do you know anything about a man named Al? Rouster Wilson told us he and Dad were friends, and that they met at the Zenith Mine protest."

"That name isn't familiar to me." She tilted her head. "There was a man named Alex. He was maybe five foot six inches, with a heavy dark beard and horn-rimmed glasses. Could that be him?"

Deni realized they hadn't bothered to ask Rouster what Al looked like. They would have to go back and ask. "I don't know. Do you know his last name?"

"If I did, I've forgotten it," Glenda said. "I really only saw him a couple of times—at the mine, and at that council meeting about the hotel expansion. Come to think of it, he and your dad were there together, it seems. Or at least, they were sitting next to each other."

"What was Alex like?" Ryan asked.

She frowned. "Belligerent. Not a good listener. He interrupted people and had a foul mouth. He said we were wasting our time if we expected anyone to change their minds if money was involved."

"What did he think you should do instead?" Ryan wanted to know.

"He didn't say," Glenda said.

"Do you know where he lived, or if he had a job?" Ryan asked.

"I don't. And like I said, I haven't seen him in a long time, either. Probably since that council meeting."

The sleigh bells attached to the back of the door jangled as two women entered. "I'll let you get back to work," Deni said. "Thanks."

"I hope you find your father," Glenda said. "He can be a bit of curmudgeon, but his heart is in the right place."

They left the store. "We need to ask Rouster what Al looked like," Deni said.

"It's interesting that neither Glenda nor Rouster—if Al and Alex are the same person—have seen him since your dad disappeared," Ryan said. "Do you think they could have left together?"

"I have no idea what to think," Deni admitted.

A sign on the door informed them that Rouster was away for the rest of the day. "What do we do now?" Ryan asked.

"Rouster said he thought Dad and Al might be neighbors," Deni said. "There aren't that many places to live near my dad. It's mostly unoccupied mining claims. Let's see if we can find a neighbor to talk to."

"Al doesn't sound like a very pleasant person," Ryan said.

"No." She leaned over and patted his arm. "That's why I have you along."

"To protect you?"

She grinned. "I figure if things get ugly, you can distract them while I run away."

He attempted to look offended, but ended up laughing with her. It was a good sign, still finding something to laugh about in spite of all the sadness around her.

Chapter Twelve

Ryan headed his truck toward Mike Traynor's cabin, but slowed near the turnoff. "Someone else has been up this way recently," he said, pointing ahead to the tracks in the snow. "Maybe they were headed to another cabin? Maybe we should follow them."

"OK." Deni leaned forward in her seat. "The road doesn't look too bad—like someone cleared it recently."

"That's a good indicator someone is living up this way." Ryan started forward again, moving slowly and trying to stay in the tracks of the person who had gone before them. Though the road had been plowed sometime since the last big storm, the snow was probably soft on the edges and he didn't want to get stuck.

They had traveled about a quarter mile when he caught a flash of pink by the side of the road. "That surveyor's tape looks pretty new," Deni said.

As they drew nearer, they could see the tape was marking the entry into a driveway. Sure enough, the tracks they had been following turned in there. Ryan followed them, hoping he wasn't getting into someplace he couldn't get out of easily.

Unlike Mike Traynor's place, which could be reached only by snowmobile or on foot in winter, this drive was cleared all the way to the dwelling at the end of it—not a cabin, but a yurt, with green canvas sides, smoke puffing from a black pipe protruding from the roof.

Ryan hadn't even shut off the engine of the truck when a man appeared in the door of the yurt. He was stocky, of average height, clean-shaven, with a black watch cap pulled down over his ears. He watched as Ryan and Deni got out of the truck and walked toward him. "Hello," Deni called. "This is a beautiful place you've got here. Do you like living in a yurt?"

"What can I do for you?" The man wasn't unfriendly, but he seemed wary. Or maybe shy.

"I'm Mike Traynor's daughter, Deni." Deni offered a warm smile. "I don't know if you've met my dad, but he's probably your closest neighbor." She gestured in the direction of Mike's cabin. "I was wondering if you've seen him recently."

"I guess I've seen him around, but I don't know him," the man said. "But I pretty much keep to myself."

"When was the last time you saw my dad?" Deni asked.

"Couldn't say."

"What's your name?" Ryan asked. "I'm Ryan, by the way."

The man's expression remained impassive. "My name's not important," he said.

Ryan was taken aback. How could he counter that?

"Dad's been missing a couple of weeks," Deni said. "I'm really worried about him."

"Sorry, I can't help you." The man turned and went back inside, the door closing softly behind him.

Deni and Ryan looked at each other. "I guess we'd better go," he said.

Neither of them said anything until they were in the

truck and out of the driveway. "He certainly wasn't very friendly," Deni said.

"He didn't look like Glenda described Alex," Ryan said.

"We still need to talk to Rouster again about Al." She leaned her head back and closed her eyes. "Let's stop by Dad's on the way out." She didn't say "just in case he's been there" but Ryan thought that was what she meant.

"No problem," he said, and headed back the way they had come.

He parked at the cleared-out space and they hiked up to the house. The path was well packed by now, so they didn't need snowshoes. "Someone else has been here," Deni said, pointing to the packed trail.

"Probably the cops," Ryan said. "They said they would look for your dad, and his house is the best place to start."

"Then why didn't they tell me what they found?" she asked.

He shrugged. She didn't want to hear that law enforcement didn't readily share information with family, especially if the person they were investigating was suspected of a crime.

The ladder still sat under the window, and the same few items lay undisturbed on the workbench. Deni's shoulders slumped. "It doesn't look like Dad is here."

Ryan put his arm around her. "You've done a lot today."

She turned away. "I guess it was foolish to think we could actually find Dad today," she said. "When all the cops looking for him haven't been able to track him down."

"We haven't come up completely dry," Ryan said. "We learned about Al."

"Who also, apparently, has disappeared."

They started back down the path toward the truck. "Maybe Al and your dad ran off together," Ryan said.

She frowned. "I can't really see that, but who knows?" She sighed. "Let's go home."

Back in the truck, he drove down the mountain on the narrow snow-packed forest service road. They were traveling at about twenty-five miles an hour when a roaring sound filled the cab. Ryan looked up to see a large black truck gaining on them. Deni turned to look back. "What is that guy doing, driving that fast on this road?" she asked.

"I don't know, but he's not slowing down." He pumped his brakes and edged over to the side. There was plenty of room to pass if the guy was careful.

But the driver of the black pickup didn't slow down, and he didn't move over. "What the h—?" Ryan didn't get to finish the sentence. The truck driver laid on the horn and the engine revved even louder. Ryan wrenched the steering wheel to the right and felt the tires slip off the road and sink into the soft snow. He wrestled the steering wheel, trying to steer back onto the solid surface, but it was too late, the black truck rocketed past as Ryan's truck tipped, then began to roll.

DENI SCREAMED AS she was thrown against the seat belts. The truck air bag exploded, hard against her forearms, filling the air with a cloud of white. Her head banged against the side of the truck, then the back, and her chest constricted with terror. "Ryan!" she called.

He didn't answer, though she could see him strapped in beside her, his fingers gripping the steering wheel as if he could somehow still control the vehicle.

With a painful jolt, they came to a halt. She was tilted sharply to the right, her body angled down, the seat belt holding her in place, her head pounding. She gripped the side of her seat, heart hammering wildly, and tried to see out, but the window was splintered by dozens of cracks.

"Ryan!" she called again, and looked over at him. He, too, was suspended by his seat belt, his body limp, blood flowing from a gash on his head. "Ryan!" she shouted, louder this time. She tried to reach out and touch him, but couldn't quite close the gap.

Surely the driver of that black truck would see what had happened and would stop to help. She listened for approaching footsteps, but could hear nothing but the ping of the truck engine as it cooled and the creak of the vehicle settling against whatever had stopped its fall. "Help!" she shouted. "Somebody help!"

Ryan moaned, and she turned her attention to him once more. "Ryan! Wake up. Please wake up."

He moaned again, and struggled against the seat belt. "Talk to me," she said. "Tell me you're okay."

His eyelids fluttered, and he groaned louder. At last his eyes opened and he turned his head to look at her. "Are you okay?" he asked.

"I'm fine," she said, her voice shaky with relief. "But you're bleeding."

He touched a hand to the blood on his head and winced. "It's okay," he answered. "Head wounds always bleed a lot."

"That guy didn't even stop to help," she said. "Do you think he ran us off the road on purpose?"

"Maybe. Did you get a good look at him?" Ryan asked.

"No. His windows were tinted, I think. And everything happened so fast."

He fumbled with his seat belt, but it refused to release. "How are we going to get out of here?" she asked. "There's no phone signal here."

"Can you reach the glove box and open it?"

She braced herself against the door and reached out. She had to punch the release button three times, but at last the door to the glove box popped open. "What am I looking for?"

"There's a tool in there with an orange handle."

She spotted bright orange and pulled out a heavy bar and handed it to him. He popped a catch on it and a wicked-looking curved blade was exposed. "Let me cut myself free and I'll help you," he said, and began sawing at the seat belt.

Sweat was beading on his forehead and he was breathing hard by the time he had managed to cut through the belt. Then he had to brace against the steering wheel and turn upright. He leaned across the center console and began sawing at Deni's seat belt. "You're the only person I know who carries something like this in your vehicle," she said.

"I've worked enough rescues where people were trapped in their cars to know I didn't want to be in that situation. One guy hung upside down for six hours before we got to him."

She grimaced. Even though they weren't completely upside down, the position she was in was uncomfortable. Before too much longer, it would probably be painful.

The strap broke and she sagged down, and banged her arm against the door. Still clutching the tool, Ryan crawled back across the console and attacked the driver's side door. At first it refused to budge, but when he threw his body against it, it finally opened, with a wrenching sound that would have been suitable for a horror film. He crawled up and out, then leaned back in to offer a hand to Deni. "We're up against a big tree," he said. "There are a lot of branches and stuff you'll have to fight through."

"I don't care. I want out of this truck." She pulled herself toward the door and he helped her climb out. Then they had to jump to the ground, sinking into the snow, a juniper branch slapping her in the face.

Carefully, they made their way around the truck, holding on to the frame and each other for balance. When they emerged onto the roadway she leaned against him. "Are you sure you're okay?" he asked. "Did you hit your head?"

"I'm fine." She put a hand to your head. "I did bang my head, but it doesn't even hurt."

"Let me see." He ran her hands through her hair, his gentle touch sending a tremor through her. "There's no blood and I can't feel a bump." He looked into her eyes. "Your pupils look okay. How about the rest of you?"

"A few bruises, but that's all." She looked up at him, the sight of all that blood still alarming. "But you look like you're hurt."

"I hit my head pretty hard. I might need stitches. I might even have a concussion. But there's no way to know until we get to someplace where I can be checked out." He pulled out his phone and frowned. "No signal here to call for help."

"Dad has a cell booster," she said. "We can call from there. He probably has a first-aid kit, too."

"Good idea." They were only a few hundred yards from the turnoff to her dad's cabin, but after that they had another quarter mile to walk. By the time they arrived at their destination, she was chilled through. Beside her, she could feel Ryan shaking. "We need to get inside and get a fire going," she said.

The padlock they had seen on the door on their earlier visit was gone, replaced by a lockbox and an official seal

Property of Rayford County Sheriff's Department. They stared at the lock. "That doesn't look good," Ryan said.

Deni shook her head. "We have to get in." She headed for the ladder. "I'll go in the window and come down and unlock the back door. There's a dead bolt on it, but I can open it from the inside."

Ryan looked as if he wanted to object, then nodded and leaned against the porch, his face gray. She prayed he wasn't going to pass out while she was trying to get them in.

She struggled several minutes to force open the window, but at last she was able to raise the sash enough to allow her to climb in. She didn't hesitate, but raced down the stairs from the loft to the ground floor, and to the back door, where she turned all the locks and threw the door open. "Ryan!" she called.

He appeared around the side of the house. At the door, she took his hands and tugged him inside, over to a chair at the table. "Sit here while I start the fire, then we'll see about getting you cleaned up, and we'll call someone to come get us."

He didn't protest that he could help, which told her again how bad he must be feeling. She found split wood and kindling in an old copper wash boiler beside the woodstove, and set about making a fire. Within minutes, a blaze was licking at the wood. It would take a while longer for the cabin to warm, but the fire itself lifted her spirits.

Next, she filled a kettle at the sink, the small electric pump that drew from the reservoir tank outside the cabin humming reassuringly as the slightly rusty water flowed. She lit a burner on the propane stove and set the kettle to heat. "When that is boiling, I'll pour some off to clean up some of that blood."

"A mirror would help me get a better look at it," he said.

"I think there's one in the bedroom. I'll get it in a minute."

He closed his eyes, then opened them again. "I can still see that truck barreling down on us, but I can't picture the driver, or a license plate. I can't even tell you what make of truck it was. It was so unexpected."

"It was terrifying." She dropped into the chair across from him and studied his face. Blood smeared one cheek and matted his hair, but his eyes were focused and clear. "How are you feeling?" she asked.

"I have a headache. I think I hit it against the window." He touched the wound again. "I should be okay. We're lucky that tree was there to stop our fall. But my truck is a wreck."

The kettle began to hiss, so she stood, poured some of the water into a bowl to cool, and went in search of some clean rags and a mirror. She found what she wanted, as well as a first-aid kit with gauze pads and some antibiotic ointment. "This probably isn't going to feel so great, but we need to clean up that blood and get a look at the wound," she said.

He didn't say anything beyond letting out a low hiss at one point when she dabbed at the jagged wound just above his temple. The gash was about two inches long, but not too deep. Once she had cleaned off most of the blood, she handed him the mirror. "Take a look."

He studied his reflection. "Put some of that antibiotic ointment on it, and a gauze pad and I'll be good," he said. "I think I can even get away without stitches."

She did as he asked, then glanced out the window at the fading light. "I'd better call. Do you have a friend who would come get us?"

"Call the sheriff," Ryan said. "We need to report that guy who ran us off the road."

She wanted to protest, but knew he was right. She pulled out the phone and stared at the screen. "It says No Service," she noted. "That can't be right."

She looked around for the cell booster and antennae that usually sat on a shelf above her father's recliner. But the shelf was empty. She drew nearer, but saw no sign of the equipment. "There was a cell booster right here," she said.

"Maybe your dad moved it."

But a quick search of the house revealed no booster. And she couldn't raise a signal no matter where she stood. "I think we should spend the night here and hike out to the road in the morning," she observed. "I'm not comfortable going back to the yurt to ask for help, and it's too late to start walking now. We'll be warm and safe here, and there's food and a place to sleep."

"I was going to suggest the same thing," he said. He looked toward the kitchen. "What does your dad have in the way of food? I'm starving."

"Dad is no gourmet," she said. "But he'll have something."

"Something" proved to be canned chili and boxed macaroni and cheese, but the chili-mac concoction she made was delicious. They ate it all, and were clearing away the dishes when a bright light suddenly shone through the front window, and a voice boomed: "This is the police. Come out with your hands up!"

Chapter Thirteen

Ryan froze, squinting in the bright light that seemed focused right in his eyes. "What is going on?" Deni asked. She stood at his elbow, a water glass in each hand, while he carried a stack of plates and silverware.

"I don't know," he said, as the voice boomed again that they needed to come out.

He set the dishes back on the table. "We'd better do as they say."

She set aside the glasses and followed him to the door. "We're coming out!" he shouted.

"Please don't shoot," Deni said, though not loud enough for anyone outside to hear.

Ryan eased open the door and together they stepped outside, hands in the air. At first he didn't see anyone, then Travis stepped out from behind the woodpile. "You can put your hands down," he said, and holstered his weapon. "We saw the lights and the smoke and didn't know who was in there."

"What are you doing here?" Deni asked.

"We came up to search the place again." He looked behind her to the open door. "What are you doing here?"

"We were driving around, looking for Dad," she said. "Someone ran us off the road. This was the closest place we could come."

Travis walked over to him. Two other deputies emerged from hiding and stood a few feet away. "Looks like you got a little banged up," he said, taking in Ryan's bandaged head. He looked to Deni. "Are you okay?"

"A few bruises, but I'm all right." She hugged her arms around her shoulders, cold without a coat. "The truck is up the road, off the side, up against a tree."

"Let's go inside where it's warmer." Travis nodded toward the door. "I'll send Jake and Dwight to look at the truck."

Deni and Ryan returned to the cabin. A few moments later, the sheriff entered. "Who ran you off the road?" he asked.

"Someone in a black pickup with tinted windows," Ryan said. "They came up behind us, blaring the horn. When I tried to move over to let them pass, my tires slipped into the soft snow on the edge and we rolled."

"We had just been to talk to the guy in the yurt up the road," she said. "We asked him about Dad, but he said he didn't know anything."

Travis frowned. "I know the yurt you're talking about, but I thought it was a summer home. What's the guy's name?"

"He refused to tell us," Ryan said. "He wasn't very friendly. I even wondered if he was the one in the truck."

"Did you get a license plate number?" Travis asked.

Ryan shook his head. "It all happened so fast," Deni said. "It was terrifying."

Ryan took her hand and squeezed it. Her fingers were ice-cold.

"We'll check him out and take a look at his vehicle," Travis said. He looked around the cabin. "Did you find anything to tell you where your dad might be?"

"We haven't even looked," she said. "But we talked to

a couple of people in town who know Dad. They mentioned that he had been hanging out with a new friend named Al or Alex. Rouster Wilson said he was foul-mouthed and negative, and Glenda Nassib described him as belligerent."

"Your dad never mentioned this man to you?" Travis asked.

"No. And it doesn't sound like someone he would want to be around." She shrugged. "Rouster said he thought Al and my dad were neighbors, but Glenda described Alex as having a black beard and horn-rimmed glasses. The man we met at the yurt was clean-shaven and didn't wear glasses."

"It's easy enough to shave and take off a pair of glasses," Travis said. He looked around the room again. "We'd like to come in and look around, but I can have Jake drive you back to town. We'll call for a wrecker to retrieve your truck. Is it okay to take it to O'Brien's garage?"

"That would be great," Ryan said. He didn't even want to think about how much the bill to repair the vehicle would be—if it wasn't a total loss.

While they waited for the deputies to return, Ryan and Deni washed dishes and banked the fire. A knock announced Dwight and Jake's arrival. Travis opened the door for the men and they came in, stamping their feet and rubbing their hands together. "We found the truck," Dwight said. "About a quarter mile up the road. No skid marks. Looks like whoever came up on you didn't even slow down."

"Jake, I'd like you to take Deni and Ryan back to town. Dwight and I are going to question a guy who lives in a yurt down the road. You can meet us back up here to search this place when you're done."

"Do you mean Ed Brubaker's yurt?" Dwight asked.

"You know him?" Deni asked.

"He and his family come for a couple of months every summer and stay in that yurt," Dwight said. "Ed's a big fly fisherman and his wife paints."

"What does he look like?" Ryan asked.

"Tall and skinny. Little gray beard. He's in his seventies now, but he still come up to fish every year. Sometimes one of his boys uses the place, but I've never met them."

"Maybe one of them is in the yurt now," Travis said. "We'll drive down there and see while Jake takes Deni and Ryan home."

Ryan asked Jake to stop by the truck so he could retrieve his pack. He could hardly bear to look too closely at the damage, but what he saw was enough to make his heart sink. He and Deni were lucky they hadn't been hurt worse.

As soon as they were headed out in the sheriff's department SUV, Jake said, "What happened with the guy in the yurt?"

Ryan explained about their visit, and being run off the road by the black pickup shortly afterward. "I've never met Ed Brubaker or his kids, so I can't tell you anything about them," Jake said. "But what reason would one of them have for running you off the road?"

"What reason would anyone have?" Deni asked.

Ryan leaned forward in the seat. "While we've got you here, what do you know about a couple of Alcohol, Tobacco, Firearms and Explosives agents who are in town?"

Jake made a face. "So you've heard about them?"

"They came to my house and started questioning me

Monday evening," Deni said. "They were really rude. They all but accused me of helping my dad plant those bombs."

"Some cops find intimidation an effective interrogation technique," Jake said.

"Well, they're not going to get any information out of me, because I don't know anything." Deni hugged her arms across her chest. "Do they really think Dad is involved in all this, or do they treat everyone that way?"

"You said yourself your dad had been acting strange, and you were worried he might be involved," Jake said.

"Yes, but that was before I really thought about it," she said. "Dad complained a lot about development and changes around here, but he would never hurt people. I'm sure of it."

"Have you heard anything about a man named Al or Alex?" Ryan asked. "He supposedly was involved in some of the protests against the hotel expansion and the mine reopening. We talked to a couple of people who said he and Mike were friends."

"I haven't heard anything about him," Jake said. "And as far as what the feds think—they don't let us locals in on that information. They're here because of the bombs at the mine and in Caspar Canyon. That kind of thing is over the head of a small-town department like ours."

"So you aren't investigating the bombings anymore?" Ryan asked.

"We are assisting the feds with their enquiries," Jake said. "And looking for your dad. Not as a suspect," he added. "But as a missing person." He paused, the silence weighted.

"What aren't you telling me?" Deni asked. She scooted as far forward in the back seat as the seat belt would allow. "There's something, isn't there? What have you found out?"

"We checked your dad's accounts at the local bank," Jake said. "That's standard with a missing adult. We can sometimes track people through their credit or debit card activity. But in your dad's case, there hasn't been any."

"You mean, he hasn't used his credit or debit cards?" Deni asked.

"No. That doesn't mean he isn't just paying for everything in cash. People know about being tracked through their cards now, so someone who is trying to hide will often pay for everything in cash."

"But why would Dad be hiding?" Deni asked. Ryan heard the desperation in her voice. "Especially from me?"

"We're not giving up on finding him," Jake said. "That's why we went up to his cabin today. We're hoping we find something that will give us a clue as to why he left and where he might be."

"His truck, his snowmobile and the trunk where he kept his guns are all missing, right?" Ryan asked her. "Did you notice anything else?"

"No," she said. "But I never went through the closets and everything. Even if I did, I'm not sure I would know what was supposed to be there and what wasn't. He's a private person and I respect that." She shifted. "I mean, do you want to know your father's personal business?"

"No," he said. He couldn't imagine even having a conversation of a personal nature with his father. They didn't have that kind of relationship.

"Just know that we're going to keep looking for him," Jake said. They were nearing town now. "Where should I drop you off?"

"My house," she answered, and gave him the address. "I can take Ryan to his place later." She turned to Ryan. "Or do you want to go to the medical clinic?"

"I'll be fine," he said. "It looked a lot worse than it really was."

Jake had just turned onto Deni's street when his phone rang. He answered and the sheriff asked, "What's your twenty?"

"I'm with Deni and Ryan, just about to drop her off at her house."

"We stopped by the yurt. Someone has been there—we could see tracks where a vehicle, maybe a truck, was parked in back. But there's no one there now. The lock on the door is broken, though."

"Did whoever was there just go to town to run an errand or are they gone for good?" Ryan asked.

"We're going to get in touch with Ed Brubaker and find out," Travis said. "Can you tell us anything more about the truck?"

"Just that it was black and a full-size model." He frowned. "A Chevy or a Ford. A Ram has a different grille, I think."

"And there was no contact between your vehicle and the truck?" Travis asked.

"No, sir. He never hit me—I moved over to try to avoid being hit, and that's when my truck rolled."

"So there's no damage to the other vehicle that we can try to match," Travis said. "Let me know if you remember anything else. In the meantime, keep an eye out for the guy you saw at the yurt. I want to know if you spot him again."

"I will," Ryan said.

Jake pulled into Deni's driveway. "Are you two going to be all right?" he asked.

"We'll be okay," Deni said. "Thanks for the ride."

They got out of the SUV and walked in silence to Deni's door. But once inside, she moved into his arms. "I'm scared," she told him.

He pulled her close. He was afraid for her, but he didn't think saying that would bring her any comfort. "We're going to get through this," he said. "Together."

Chapter Fourteen

Ryan had settled down to watch TV with Deni when the text came in from SAR Captain Tony Meisner. Car off highway at Ruby Falls. "I have to go," he said, standing, the familiar adrenaline rush already firing.

"Are you sure?" she asked. "Your head—"

"It's okay." He touched the bandage. He didn't have any sign of concussion. "I'll be fine. But will you be okay?"

"Of course. What's going on?"

"A car off the road." He started putting on his shoes, then stopped. "I'll have to call someone to give me a ride." That was one aspect of not having his own vehicle that he hadn't thought about.

"Take my car." She got up and fished her keys from her purse. "I'm not going to need it until Monday, really."

"Thanks." He grabbed his jacket and his pack. After a moment's thought, he fished a knitted beanie from the pack and pulled it down low, covering his bandaged head. He didn't feel like answering questions about it right now. Then he headed out toward Ruby Falls.

The scene that greeted the rescuers on their arrival stunned them into momentary silence. The SUV sat upright against the far shore of the icy river, the top partially smashed in, broken glass and pieces of trim scattered among the rocks like party confetti. Some fifty feet from the vehicle two children clung to each other on a boulder, surrounded by icy water. At the sight of the rescuers they began screaming, the terror behind their cries heart-wrenching.

"Don't move!" Tony shouted to them. "Stay right where you are. We'll come to you."

"Mama!" the taller of the two, a girl Ryan thought couldn't be more than six, her long brown hair matted to her head by water or blood or both, gestured toward the SUV. "Mama!"

"We'll take care of your mother," Tony called. "Stay right where you are."

It was easy to see why he kept repeating the admonition—unlike the calmer water where the SUV had landed, the current swept past the boulder on both sides, the water swift and deep enough that it hadn't frozen in this spot. If the children tried to step into that they would be dragged away, to be drowned or frozen within minutes.

"Who's completed swift water rescue training?" Tony searched the group of volunteers who had gathered on the roadside above the place where the car had gone over.

"I have," Ryan said.

"Me, too." Ted stepped forward.

"I've done the training," Eldon said.

Tony eyed Ryan skeptically. "Is your arm up to this?" he asked.

"Yes, sir," Ryan said. Maybe he wasn't up to his preinjury strength yet, but enough time had passed for the soft tissue injury to heal, and those children needed him.

Tony shook his head. "Don't think I don't see that bandage on your head. I heard about what happened up by Mike Traynor's place yesterday. Were you planning to tell me?"

Ryan flushed. "It's not a serious injury," he protested.

"You stay with the crew on shore," Tony said. "I don't think you're up to swift water rescue yet."

"Yes, sir." Ryan knew he had messed up, not telling Tony right away about his head injury, even if he didn't believe it would interfere with his rescue work. All his training had drilled into him that search and rescue wasn't about individual glory, but what was best for the team.

Tony sent Cassie and Jake to see to the mother. "Eldon, you and Ted are with me and Sheri," he said.

Ryan pitched in to assemble the equipment Tony and his group would need. Deputies Jake Gwynn and Jamie Douglas arrived to direct traffic and assist.

The team was setting safety lines when Cassie radioed that the mother had sustained a head injury, was coming in and out of consciousness and was trapped in the partially crushed vehicle. They were going to cut her free with the Jaws of Life. "Then we're going to need Life Flight to get her to the hospital in Junction."

"I'll radio for the chopper." Jamie's voice broke in. "And I've called for a victim's advocate to come be with the children, though if you can find out the name of a local relative who could look after them, that would be even better."

"Thanks," Tony said. "We'll let you know."

The air by the river was even colder than up at the road, the roar of rushing water making it necessary to shout to be heard. The children had stopped crying and crouched on the boulder, the older one's arms wrapped around her younger sibling. Even from his spot on the riverbank, Ryan could see them shivering. The team carried warming packs in their gear, and Sheri had blankets, but would that be enough?

"We're going to cross one at a time," Tony instructed the trio gathered around him. "You'll be clipped in, so if you slip, don't panic. But try not to slip. We don't want to have to treat any of you for hypothermia along with the kids. Eldon, you go first."

Ryan stood by, imagining the shock of the cold water. Eldon grimaced as he waded in, but kept moving. Ryan remembered his training, how the icy liquid seeped through his layers of clothing. Within two steps he could no longer feel his feet. Two more steps and his skin was on fire.

Eldon gripped the safety line, clenched his jaw and kept moving forward, his focus on the kids. Halfway to them, he slipped on an icy rock and landed on his back in the water. The current pulled at him as he struggled to regain his footing. Ryan leaned forward, his body tensed, fighting rising panic as he watched his friend struggle. He hated being stuck here, unable to help. Maybe he wasn't as strong as he should be, but he ought to be able to do something.

The older child let go of her sibling and leaned out from the rock. "No!" Ryan shouted. "Stay there and someone will come to you!"

Eldon managed to crawl out of the water on hands and knees. His teeth chattered and he struggled to open his pack. There was scarcely enough room on the boulder for the two kids, so he was forced to remain half in the water. "Don't send anyone else," he radioed back. "There's nowhere to put them."

He spoke to the children, then wrapped them each in foil emergency blankets from his pack. He radioed back that the children's names were Tamsin and Owen. Tamsin helped wrap her little brother in his blanket, then Eldon tucked warming packs inside their wet clothing.

"Tamsin said she bumped her head, but there's no open wound," Eldon radioed. "They're both very cold and shivering, but no obvious injuries. I want to get them out of here to where they can get warm as soon as possible."

"Bring the smallest child back with you and I'll send Sheri over for the older one," Tony radioed.

"Copy that," Eldon replied. He turned to speak to Tamsin, then gathered Owen into his arms.

Ryan thought he could read the little girl's reply: *I'm scared.*

So am I, Ryan thought. If Eldon fell again on the way back across he might lose hold of the little boy. He hoped Eldon wasn't thinking about that right now.

Eldon knotted the ends of the emergency blanket around Owen's neck and waist to secure it. Then he gathered the child to his chest. The little boy wrapped his arms around Eldon's neck and his legs around his broad chest. He needed both hands free to grip the safety line, and would have to trust the boy not to let go. He grimaced as the icy water lapped at his shins, but focused on moving forward and staying upright. Halfway across, Owen began to wail, a pitiful keening Ryan could hear over the current.

The trip back across the water seemed much faster than the journey across. When Eldon and Owen reached the shore, Ryan took the boy from him and Tony helped Eldon stagger out of the water as Sheri set off toward the little girl. "Get into some dry clothes," Tony said. "That's an order. There's some in the back of the Beast."

Ryan carried Owen, who was silent now, shivering and blue-lipped, up to where an ambulance and two paramedics waited, then hurried back down in time to meet

Sheri coming out of the water with Tamsin. The little girl was in better shape than her brother, able to stand on her own, one hand clutching the emergency blanket wrapped around her. She stared back across the river at the crushed SUV, which the other volunteers were attacking with the Jaws of Life. "Is my mama going to be okay?"

"She hit her head and she needs to go to the hospital," Ryan said. "That's all I know right now."

"When the car landed in the river, my seat belt broke," she said. "I tried to go for help, and thought I should take Owen with me, but we got stuck on this rock."

He shuddered to think of this little girl fighting through that icy current when Eldon had had such a hard time. But he knew from previous rescues that people, even children, could do amazing things when charged with fear and adrenaline.

Tony and Sheri met Ryan on his way back after he had carried Tamsin to meet her brother at the ambulance. "Tamsin told me their grandmother lives in Eagle Mountain," Sheri said. "We're going to call her to come and get them. Later tonight she can take them to see their mother in the hospital."

Another set of rescuers was bringing the children's mother up to road level on a stretcher. The sheriff's deputies had closed off a section of the highway so the medical helicopter could land.

Ryan continued to the riverbank, where he helped Ted coil the ropes and gather the remainder of their gear. "I want to walk down the bank a ways, see if we can spot any big pieces of that SUV," Ted said. "The front right quarter panel and the rear bumper are missing. Something that big gets jammed up in the wrong place, it could cause trouble during melt-off in the spring."

"What are you going to do if you find anything?"

Ryan asked. "You don't want to go into that water to rescue a bumper."

"I'll let the wrecker crew know about it," he said. "They can fish it out when they retrieve the SUV." Ted frowned at him. "You don't have to come with me. Go home and get dry."

"I'll come." A man by himself might slip on the icy bank and drown or freeze before the others realized he was missing.

A hundred yards downstream they spotted the quarter panel wedged against a knot of tree roots against the bank. Ted took a picture with his phone. "Let's go a little farther and see if we spot the bumper," he said.

The bank was steep here and thick with snow. Ryan was cursing his decision to help with what he saw as a pointless search when Ted stopped abruptly in front of him. "That doesn't look good," Ted muttered.

"What is it?" Ryan looked past him, to what at first appeared to be a mass of torn limbs and debris caught in the bend of the river.

"Looks like a truck." Ted dug in his pack and pulled out a pair of binoculars. "There's a license plate. I'll see if I can read it."

Ryan could see the truck now, its front end and grille poking out from a tangle of vines.

"Make note of this, will you?" Ted said. "Type it in on your phone or something."

Ryan pulled out his phone and scrolled to the notes ap. "I'm ready."

"966-XXY." He lowered the binoculars. "Why does that sound familiar?"

"Because it's on those posters all over town," Ryan said. "The ones about Mike Traynor's disappearance." He stared at the truck in disbelief. "That's Mike Traynor's truck."

Chapter Fifteen

Monday morning, Deni stood on the side of the highway with Ryan, watching as the wrecker winched her father's truck up from the riverbank. The process was agonizingly slow, the long boom on the oversize crane pulling the truck up a few inches at a time. She could feel the vibrations of the loud diesel motor through the soles of her boots, and she flinched every time the scrape of metal against rock echoed from the canyon. "Almost there!" the winch operator called, and the nose of the truck appeared at the edge of the roadway, like some bug-eyed prehistoric beast emerging from its den.

Deni turned away and buried her face in Ryan's neck. "I can't look," she whispered.

"Mike isn't in there," Ryan said. "We made sure when we found the truck."

She nodded. But she wouldn't be sure until she saw it for herself. The officers who had come to her house Friday evening to confirm that the truck was her dad's had said they wouldn't be able to examine it closely until they pulled it to the roadway. And that couldn't happen until a special wrecker was available on Monday.

Ryan's arms tightened around her. He didn't say anything, but his embrace was comfort enough. He had been her chief support these past few days. He had showed up at the house while she was talking to the deputies—only then did she learn that it was actually him and another search and rescue volunteer who had spotted the truck while cleaning up after another wreck in the area.

The news had stunned her, and raised more questions than it had answered. She had spent an agonizing weekend, and had taken a personal day from school, wanting to be here when they retrieved the truck, yet also not wanting it.

Deputy Wes Landry spoke with the wrecker driver, who finished winching the truck onto his flatbed, then set about securing it. Wes walked over to Deni and Ryan. "The truck is empty," he said. "We'll go over it more thoroughly, but I didn't see any blood on the seats."

She shivered at the image this brought to mind, but nodded. No blood had to be a good sign, right?

"There also aren't any skid marks at the side of the road, as you would expect if the truck slid off the road in an accident," Wes said.

"Could it have been dumped there?" Ryan asked. "Deliberately pushed over the edge?"

"It's possible," Wes commented. "Mike may have done so to confuse the hunt for him."

"Dad really loved that truck," Deni said. "And if he did deliberately destroy it, how did he get away from here? It doesn't make sense."

"If you think of anything that might help us figure this out, let us know," Wes said. How many times had various law enforcement officers said something similar to her in the past few days? As if she was keeping all kinds of secrets from them.

The wrecker pulled away with the truck. "We may have more questions for you once we've had a chance to examine the truck more closely," Wes added.

She nodded. There were always more questions. If only someone could give her answers.

"I have to get to work," Ryan said when Wes had left them. "Will you be okay?"

"Of course."

She dropped him off at the shop, then drove home and crawled into bed, exhausted, but too agitated for sound sleep. But she must have dozed, because she awoke sometime later, disoriented and aching all over, to the sound of distant music. As awareness returned, she realized the music was from her phone. She groped for it on the bedside table and stared at the unfamiliar number on the screen. "Hello?" she answered.

"Hey, Deni, how are you?" said a cheerful female voice. "This is Tammy Patterson."

Deni blinked. Why would the reporter be calling her? She raked a hand through her hair and tried to come fully awake. "What can I do for you, Tammy?"

"I'm working on a story about your dad's disappearance and wanted to include a comment from you."

The words were as effective as ice water splashed over her. She swung her legs over the side of the bed and sat up straight. Tammy was the sole reporter for the *Eagle Mountain Examiner.* "Didn't you already run a story about Dad going missing?" she asked. She clearly remembered seeing her dad's picture in the paper.

"This is an update," Tammy said. "I heard his truck was found in the canyon past Ruby Falls. Did that surprise you?"

"Yes," Deni said.

"Have you heard anything from your dad?" Tammy asked. "Do you know what he was up to before he disappeared?"

"No," Deni said.

"You must be terribly worried about him."

"Yes." She couldn't seem to manage more than one-word answers.

"So you don't have any idea what he might have been involved in that led him to just disappear?" Tammy asked.

"I don't know that he was involved in anything," Deni said.

"Have agents Olivera and Ferris spoken with you?" Tammy asked.

Another jolt to the senses. "How did you know about them?" she questioned.

Tammy laughed. "This is a small town, and those two stand out, don't you think? So, did they interview you about your dad?"

"They stopped by, but I couldn't tell them anything," Deni said.

"Is it true your dad was an explosives expert in the army?"

"Where did you hear that?" Deni asked.

"Is it true?"

She tried to collect herself. "That was a long time ago. Obviously, before I was born."

"Mike was pretty upset about the Zenith Mine re-opening, wasn't he?" Tammy asked. "And we have on file a letter to the editor he wrote about the ice-climbing festival having a negative environmental impact on Caspar Canyon."

Deni said nothing. The silence between them stretched. "I have to go now," Deni said. "Goodbye."

She hung up before the reporter could say anything further. She tossed the phone aside and debated crawling back under the covers. But she was fully awake now, and too agitated to sit still.

A hot shower and a large cup of coffee later, she was

feeling more human, though her stomach churned whenever she replayed the conversation with Tammy in her head. The reporter had obviously connected her father with the bombings. Well, who wouldn't? On paper, her dad looked guilty.

But how could she ever believe the man she loved so much would do something so horrible?

Better to think about questions she could answer. What was she going to do for the rest of the day? She could clean house or grade papers—perpetual items at the top of every to-do list.

Or she could try to find out more about her dad—the life he lived when she wasn't around.

You might find out things you don't want to know an inner voice warned her.

She ignored the voice, and headed for Rouster's Coffee Roasters. She opted to walk, thinking the exercise would be good for her. Dressed in jeans and boots, and a warm sweater and parka, she could appreciate the brisk winter air. Eagle Mountain's Main Street was busy with a mix of locals and tourists, with a line outside the Cake Walk Café, and a family group emerging from the outdoor shop with rented snowshoes, ready for an outing on a local trail.

The part of town where the coffee roaster was located was quieter. She smelled the rich scent of roasting coffee when she was still a block away, and was relieved to see Rouster's old truck parked in the lot. He raised his eyebrows when he saw her at the door. "Back so soon?" he asked. "Are you planning to take your dad's place as my coffee buddy?"

She followed him into the barnlike space where the coffee roaster gave out a welcome warmth. "I wanted to ask you to describe my dad's friend Al," she said. "I never met him."

"Well, now." Rouster shoved his ball cap farther back on his head. "He was pretty average height and weight. About your dad's age, or maybe a few years younger. He had a bit of a belly on him, but that's not so uncommon." He patted his own modest paunch. "I guess the only thing distinctive about him was he had a big bushy beard. I asked him if he was raising chipmunks in that nest." He chuckled. "I don't think he appreciated the joke."

"Did he wear glasses?" she asked, remembering Glenda's description.

"Yeah, he did. Plastic frames, with a black-and-brown pattern."

"Glenda Nassib described a man like that as attending the protests she organized," Deni said. "Only she said his name was Alex."

Rouster nodded. "Maybe that was his full name, but Mike just called him Al."

"What kind of vehicle did he drive?" she asked, and braced herself to hear Al drove a black pickup.

"I don't know that, either. They came here in your dad's Jeep." He checked some gauges on the coffee roaster and made a few adjustments. "Does that help any?"

"I don't know," she admitted. "I've been trying to find Al, to ask him about my dad, but I haven't been having much luck."

"I'm sorry I couldn't be more helpful," Rouster said.

She walked slowly back toward Main, debating her next step. As long as she was out here talking to people about her father, she felt as if she was doing something to help him. If she went home the worries would close in. The problem was, she couldn't think of anyone else to talk to. She decided to prolong her outing a little longer by stopping in to Mo's for lunch. Their homemade soup sounded good on a cold day like today.

The pub was busy, so she ended up sitting at the bar. When the bartender, an older woman with curly blond hair, topped off her water glass, Deni asked, "Did Mike Traynor come in here much?"

The woman eyed her warily. "Are you a reporter or something?"

"I'm Mike's daughter." She wiped her hand on her napkin and held it out. "Deni Traynor."

"Cherise Rodriguez," the woman said. "And yeah, Mike came in here off and on. Not enough that I'd call him a regular, but maybe once every week or so."

"Did he come in alone or with someone else?" Deni asked.

"Mostly alone." Cherise paused, then added, "The last couple of times I saw him, he was with another man about his age. I didn't know him."

"What did he look like?" Deni leaned forward, as if she might miss something if she didn't focus every sense on Cherise.

"Bearded guy with glasses." Cherise shrugged. "I didn't really pay attention beyond that." She leaned closer over the bar and lowered her voice. "A couple of federal agents came in here yesterday, asking about your dad," she said. "I told them the same thing. Mike came in here for a beer sometimes, but he never stood out. What kind of trouble is he in?"

"I don't know," Deni admitted.

Cherise moved on to wait on another customer and Deni's appetite vanished; she paid for her meal and the tip, then went back out onto the sidewalk. The temperature was dropping, clouds building up overhead. She zipped her parka up to her neck. Was Dad camped out somewhere in this weather, or was he far away from here, perhaps even someplace warm?

She turned her attention from the weather to the buildings around her. Was there anyone else here she should talk to? Anyone who might have information about her father? It sounded as if agents Olivera and Ferris were already doing a thorough job of reaching out to everyone who might have come in contact with Mike. Maybe she should leave them to their job and trust that whatever they found out about her dad would be the truth.

Two doors down, a man stepped from the outdoor store. He turned toward her, a middle-aged man of average height with a black knit cap pulled down to his ears. Their gazes momentarily locked and recognition jolted her. This was the man from the yurt. She started walking faster, but he turned abruptly and strode away, lengthening the distance between them with surprising speed. "Wait!" she called, and began to run.

The man ducked into the alley between a boutique and the Nugget Hotel, but before Deni could go after him, she collided with a man on the sidewalk.

"I'm so sorry," she said, apologizing as she moved away from him and righted herself.

But the man kept hold of her arm. "Where are you going in such a hurry?" Agent Olivera asked, his gaze boring into her.

"I'm going home." She tried to wrench away from him, but he held firm.

"We need to talk to you," Olivera said, though he appeared to be alone at the moment. Maybe he meant *we* in the sense of the whole ATFE. "We have more questions."

"I don't have anything else to tell you," she said.

"We've been talking to people," Olivera informed her.

"They all say you and your father were close. You spent a lot of time together."

She would have said the same thing, before her dad disappeared. She met Agent Olivera's gaze with a direct look of her own. "Do you have any children?" she asked.

"Don't try to change the subject. My personal life is none of your concern."

"I asked because if you did have children, you would know that a parent doesn't tell their child everything. My dad is a loving father to me, but that's the only side of him I really see."

"I don't believe you," he said. "And if we find out you're keeping information from us about your father's whereabouts or illegal activities, we can arrest you as an accessory to his crimes. You and your boyfriend, too."

"Ryan doesn't have anything to do with my dad."

"Are you sure? Maybe the two of them are working together. They could compare notes on their time in prison."

She stared. Nothing this man said made sense.

"You didn't know Ryan Welch had a record did you?" Olivera asked. "We're going to be taking a much closer look at him. You tell him so, the next time you see him."

Ryan? In prison? She couldn't believe it, but would Olivera lie about something like that? She tried to pull away from him, but when he didn't release her she said, softly but firmly, "And as far as I know, neither has my father. You need to let me go before I scream and start making a scene in front of people who know me. They don't know you and they might not appreciate a stranger assaulting a local schoolteacher who was minding her own business on the sidewalk." She wasn't certain of that, but she saw the hesitation in Agent Olivera's eyes.

He released his hold on her and stepped back. "We'll

be talking to you again," he said. "In a more official capacity, where you can't just walk away."

A chill shuddered through her as she turned her back on him and hurried away. Did they have proof that linked her father to the bombs, or only suspicions? And what about Ryan? She had trusted him with all her doubts and fears about her dad, but she realized now he had told her very little about himself. He had never hinted that he had been in trouble with the law. What else was he hiding from her?

AT WORK TUESDAY MORNING, Ryan was cutting blanks for a new batch of longboards. It was a mostly automated process, which left room for his mind to wander. He was waiting to hear from Bud O'Brien about the extent of damage to his truck, but he didn't have hopes of hearing anything good. The truck was so old he had been carrying only liability insurance on it, so he doubted he would get much of anything from his insurance company. For now, he could walk or take his bike to most places he needed to go, but he would have to catch a ride to any search and rescue scenes, and trips into the backcountry were out unless he went with friends who drove.

The last few minutes before the truck rolled kept replaying in his mind. The sight of that black pickup bearing down on him would haunt him for months to come, he was sure, and the feeling of helplessness when the truck went over still made him break out in a cold sweat.

The automated plasma cutter beeped to indicate it had completed the cut and Ryan hit the button to shut it down, removed the completed blank and set it aside, then inserted another piece of fiberglass. Once all the blanks were cut, he or someone else would move on to sanding and shaping them. They would be painted, varnished and then the hardware attached. The result would be a completed longboard, to be sold online and at stores that catered to skateboarders and other outdoor enthusiasts.

Ryan forced his mind away from the truck. He couldn't do anything to change what had happened, and worrying about the future wasn't going to accomplish anything, either. Better to focus on what was going on in his life right now, which meant Deni. In a very short time, she had become a lot more important to him than he would have imagined. The two of them would have probably hit it off no matter what—he had sensed that from the first morning he spotted her in the coffee shop. But the ways the recent bombings had touched both of their lives, as well as the search for her father, had drawn them even closer together.

He hadn't meant for this to happen. After the way his last serious relationship had turned out, he had decided he was better off remaining single. But that was a lonely way to live, and after he had met Deni, he had told himself they could take things slowly. They would get to know each other, then he would tell her about his past. Maybe she would be able to see beyond that to the man he was now.

But there was nothing slow about the way their relationship had progressed. And he could never find the right moment to tell her everything she needed to know. "By the way, I spent two years in prison because I was really stupid" wasn't the easiest conversation opener.

The door to the shop opened and two men in dark overcoats entered.

The business owner, Xander Kellogg, emerged from his office at one side of the workshop. "The workshop isn't open to the public," he said.

"We're not the public." Agent Olivera pulled out his ID and showed it to Xander. "We need to speak to Ryan Welch."

Xander sent Ryan a questioning look. "Is something wrong?" he asked.

"I'm working," Ryan said, and turned back to the plasma cutter. "I don't have time to talk to you now."

Agent Olivera stepped in front of him. "This won't take long." He looked over Ryan's shoulder to Xander. "You can go back to work, sir. We'll only be a moment."

Xander looked as if he wanted to protest, but apparently thought better of it. He went back into his office, but left the door open.

Agent Ferris joined his partner next to the plasma cutter. "We stopped by the garage and got a look at your truck," Ferris said. "You're lucky to walk away from an accident like that."

"How did you know about the accident?" Ryan asked.

"We were up at Mike Traynor's cabin and ran into a couple of sheriff's deputies. They told us what happened," Olivera said. "Do you have any idea who ran you off the road?"

"No. It happened so fast. I didn't get a look at the driver of the truck, or have time to check the license plate."

The two agents exchanged glances. Did they think he wasn't telling the truth? "Did you see any sign of Traynor at his cabin?" Ferris asked.

"No," Ryan answered. "Deni and I went up there, hoping to find some clue as to where her father might be, but we didn't find anything."

"Maybe Traynor didn't like you up there, snooping around," Olivera said. "Maybe he's the one who ran you off the road."

Ryan stared. "Mike's daughter was a passenger in my truck," he said. "Why would Mike want to hurt her?"

"Maybe he didn't know she was in there. Or, more likely, he didn't care."

Ryan shook his head. He didn't know Mike well, but he knew how Deni felt about her father. She would never believe he had tried to harm her. "I saw Mike's truck in the river past Ruby Falls," he said. "It wasn't the vehicle that ran us off the road."

"Maybe he got a new ride," Ferris conjectured.

"He hadn't been at the cabin," Ryan said. "No one had been there in a long time."

"We think he's hanging out somewhere nearby, keeping an eye on the place," Olivera said.

"Do you have any proof of that?" Ryan asked.

Instead of answering, Olivera leaned against the plasma cutter and folded his arms across his chest. "I understand your girlfriend probably wants to protect her father, but she'll be helping him more by telling us what she knows. Keeping secrets is only going to get more people killed."

Anger flared. "Deni isn't keeping secrets," he said. "If she knew where her father was, she would tell the sheriff."

"But you don't tell all your secrets, do you?" Olivera asked.

Ice formed in the pit of Ryan's stomach. "I don't know what you're talking about," he said.

"We know you did two years inside for credit card fraud," Olivera said. "But you didn't tell Deni that, did you?"

He opened his mouth to ask if they had told her, but he never got the words out. The building shuddered as a reverberation like loud thunder blotted out all other sound. Xander staggered out of his office. "What was that?" he asked, wide-eyed.

Agents Olivera and Ferris were already racing for the door. "It's another bomb," one of them called. Then the lights went out, plunging the room into darkness.

Chapter Sixteen

Home again, Deni paced. She replayed the conversation with Agent Olivera over and over in her head, then moved on to reviewing all her interactions with Ryan. He had seemed less shocked than she had by the revelation that her father had a record for a long-ago crime. He had pointed out that having done time didn't make Mike a bad person.

Was this because he didn't want her to think *he* was a bad person? She didn't think that. But failing to tell her this big, important thing about himself didn't exactly make him a good person, either.

She took out her phone, intending to text Ryan, to ask him to come see her when he got off work. But before she could start typing, what she thought at first was thunder shook the house. Then the wail of sirens filled the air. She ran out onto her porch and saw black smoke filling the sky in the direction of Main Street. "It's another bomb!" Her neighbor across the street stood in her front yard, waving her phone.

"No!" Deni gasped. She stared at the smoke pouring into the sky, wondering if she was asleep and this was a nightmare. But you didn't think that in dreams, did you? "Where?" she asked, as the neighbor turned to go back inside.

"Downtown. At the Nugget Hotel."

Deni clutched her stomach, physically ill. Her father had protested the hotel's proposed expansion—but a lot of people had done that. That didn't mean he was responsible for this. She wanted to believe that, but without him here to defend himself, that was getting harder and harder.

She went back inside and stared at her phone. Who could she call to find out what was going on?

She texted Ryan. RU OK? I heard there was another bomb.

He replied almost immediately. She pictured him with his phone in his hand. Maybe he had been about to call her. I'm fine, he texted. SAR responding to scene. Talk later.

She wanted to call him, to hear his voice tell her everything was going to be okay. But he would be busy, trying to help whoever had been injured in the bombing. Another wave of nausea hit her at the thought.

She pulled up Twitter and began scrolling until she found a thread about the bombing. People were tweeting from the scene. *One wall of the hotel is gone!* read one post, followed by a string of responses condemning whoever had done this.

She didn't know how long she stood there, transfixed by the messages scrolling across the screen from people describing the damage and others speculating on the cause. A knock on the door startled her.

Deputy Jamie Douglas stood on the doorstep. Deni had always liked Jamie, who was the only woman on the force. But seeing Jamie now filled her with dread. Reluctantly, she opened the door. "Hello, Deni," Jamie said. "May I come in? I need to ask you some questions."

Deni opened the door wider and led the way into the

living room. "I heard about the bombing," she said. "It's terrible." She sat on the end of the sofa.

Jamie settled into the chair across from her. "Someone said they saw you downtown this morning," she stated.

"Yes."

"What were you doing?"

The question annoyed her. It was a Tuesday morning. She could have been buying groceries or getting coffee with a friend. Jamie must have seen her irritation. "There's a reason I'm asking—I promise," she said.

"I was talking to people who might have known my dad," Deni said. "I'm trying to find out where he's gone and what he was doing in the days leading up to his disappearance."

"You should leave that to law enforcement."

"He's my dad. If it was your father, wouldn't you want to know?"

"Did you learn anything?"

"There's a guy named Al, or Alex, that my dad supposedly hung out with. Rouster Wilson and Cherise, the bartender at Mo's, saw them together. And Glenda Nassib. She says they met at the Zenith Mine protest. The sheriff already knows about this. Except the bartender. I talked to her today."

Jamie nodded and made notes in a small notebook. "Anything else?"

"Agent Olivera stopped me while I was in town today. I mean, he grabbed me and wouldn't let me go. I already told them I don't know where my dad is or what might have led him to leave, but they won't believe me."

"Where was this, that he stopped you?" Jamie asked.

"In front of the boutique on Main."

"That's right by the Nugget Hotel, isn't it?"

Deni blinked. "It is. I hadn't thought of that."

"What were you doing there?"

"I was just walking. I had come from Mo's and I was trying to think where to go to next."

"And Agent Olivera stopped you to talk to you."

"He grabbed me and started accusing me of helping my dad. He all but called me a liar."

Jamie's expression never changed. "Someone said they saw you coming out of the alley next to the hotel," she said.

Who were these people reporting on her movements? "I wasn't in the alley," she said. "I looked down the alley because I thought I saw the man who lived in the yurt near my dad. I wanted to talk to him, but when I called out to him, he ducked down the alley."

"What man are you talking about?" Jamie asked.

"The sheriff knows about him. Yesterday, Ryan and I stopped by his yurt and asked if he had seen my dad. It's just past my dad's cabin, at the next turnoff. He answered the door and wasn't very friendly. He wouldn't tell us his name, and he said he didn't know Dad. The sheriff said the yurt belongs to a man who lives somewhere else and only uses it in the summer."

"Why did you want to talk to him when you saw him in town?" Jamie asked.

"I wanted to ask him about the truck that tried to run us down after we visited the yurt. You know about that, right? Ryan's truck was wrecked and we could have been killed."

Jamie looked at her notebook again. "Can you describe him?"

Even as Deni described him, she realized how vague she sounded—he was average height, clean-shaven, middle-aged, wearing a black knit cap. That description could apply to almost anyone.

"Did you see anyone else near the hotel?" Jamie asked. "Anyone who was acting suspiciously?"

"No."

"Did you see your father anywhere near the hotel this morning?" Jamie questioned.

"No. I haven't seen him at all in weeks. I haven't heard from him. I don't know anything. How many times do I have to keep repeating that?"

"This is a very serious crime."

As if Deni needed anyone to point that out to her. "You're saying you think my father did this."

"I'm saying we would like to talk to him."

"So would I."

Jamie closed the notebook and stood. "Let us know if you think of anything."

That familiar phrase she was growing sick of hearing. She stood also. "What can you tell me about the bomb at the hotel?" she asked as she followed Jamie toward the front door. "Were many people hurt?"

"They were still searching for people when I came here," Jamie said. "Though I know there were already two fatalities."

Jamie left. Deni locked the door after her and leaned against the wall. The sheriff hadn't wasted any time after the bombing, sending someone to question her. People were watching her. Suspecting her. This place where she had always been at home suddenly felt as if she didn't belong.

IN RYAN'S TIME with Eagle Mountain Search and Rescue, he had responded to some terrible emergencies: multiple-car accidents, a gas boiler explosion at a home that had killed three people, and body recoveries on the sides of mountains. But nothing had prepared him for the scene at the Nugget Hotel. Half of the brick building, which had originally been built in the 1890s, had been reduced to rubble, and even before SAR arrived on the scene, people were working to free guests and employees who were trapped in the wreckage.

"This portion of the building held the pool and the gift shop, with a couple of offices over that." Tony briefed them on the sidewalk outside the hotel. "We don't know how many people could be trapped in here, though the manager says less than a dozen—maybe as few as five or six. We know the woman who managed the gift shop was closest to the blast and was killed instantly. A guest who was in the gift shop at the time was blown clear of the blast and died from her injuries. Our priority right now is anyone living. If you find a body, mark it for retrieval later."

"This isn't the kind of urban rescue we train for," Austen said.

"Our job is to assist paramedics and law enforcement," Tony said. "We've got plenty of medical personnel on the scene and the sheriff's department has sent for a couple of search and rescue dogs. The rules are the same as any other rescue—guard your own safety first. The part of the building that hasn't come down could be unstable."

They moved into the scene, joining sheriff's deputies, highway patrol officers, firefighters and others who were combing through the wreckage. At the center of the scene was a large depression Ryan realized was the pool. He started to move away from this when someone shouted they had found a survivor. He and Danny rushed to assist and discovered a boy clinging to the end of a steel girder that extended halfway into the deep end of the pool. "Help! Somebody help!" the boy shouted.

"We're here to help." Ryan lay on his stomach at the

edge of the pool, alongside the girder. Chunks of brick and concrete half filled the pool between him and the boy, an unstable soup of jagged edges. Other sections of roof had collapsed into the pool, leaving only a narrow space above the water in which to maneuver. "I'm Ryan. What's your name?"

"Jameson," the boy said. "Jameson Scoville."

"How old are you, Jameson?" Danny asked.

"I'm nine."

"Are you hurt?" Danny asked.

"No. But I don't know how much longer I can hold on. The water's over my head here."

"Hang on a little longer. We're going to get you out," Ryan said.

"What happened?" the boy asked.

Ryan bent lower, his face right at the water level. Through a gap in the rubble, he could see part of the boy's face—part of his cheek and one eye, wide with fear. "A bomb exploded," Ryan said. "Where were you when that happened?"

"I was in the pool, under water. I was trying to touch the bottom. My sister was with me. Do you know where she is? And my mom! My mom was in a chair on the side of the pool. Is my mom okay?"

"We'll find out for you," Ryan said. "You just hang on." He sat up and looked at Danny. "He's about ten feet from the edge here," he said, lowering his voice so that maybe the boy wouldn't hear. "We need to clear a path to him."

Danny surveyed the area. "We need to get rid of this debris, but we can't risk dislodging this beam. It's what's keeping him up."

"Does anyone know about the mom and sister?" Ryan looked around them.

"Don't know." Danny keyed his radio and called for Tony. The SAR commander answered, and Danny explained the situation. "We need a lot of people over here to start shifting this debris," he said.

Seconds later a dozen volunteers gathered and formed a line to move chunks of concrete and metal out of the water. If a piece of the wreckage was too big to remove, they tried to push it aside. "We don't have to get everything out," Ryan instructed. "We just have to clear a path to get to the boy."

While volunteers worked to clear debris, another group began securing the fallen beam that extended into the water. As soon as it was deemed stable, Ryan looped a coil of rope around his shoulders and crawled out on the edge of the beam. As it dipped beneath his weight, a groan rose up from those gathered around, but after a few inches of movement, the beam stabilized, and he was able to advance toward the boy. "Jameson, how are you doing?" he called.

"I'm scared," a shaky voice answered.

"You're doing great," Ryan said. "I'm headed your way. I'm going to try to move aside some of the stuff that's hanging over your head, so get as low as you can to the water, okay?"

"Okay."

Ryan leaned over and grasped a chuck of concrete twice the size of his head. His injured arm protested at the movement, but he clenched his teeth and ignored it. Even so, he was unable to shift the obstacle.

"Try this." He turned and saw a firefighter, extending a garden hoe toward him. "We've been using this to rake stuff out of the way," the woman said.

Ryan took the hoe and found he could use it to roll and push debris aside. Other volunteers continued to lift out chunks of wreckage. Someone had found a winch and was employing it to haul even larger pieces to the edge of the pool. Fifteen minutes passed, with Ryan periodically calling to Jameson, who sounded more and more frantic. "I can't hold on much longer," he said.

"Just a little longer," Ryan said. But even as he said this, Jameson cried out. There was a splash, like something heavy landing in the water. "Jameson?" Ryan called. "Jameson!"

No answer. Ryan stared at the spot where the boy should be. He could make out patches of clear water now, and through one of them he spied a dark shadow sinking toward the bottom.

He slipped into the water, and immediately scraped his upper arm on a twisted chunk of blackened metal. As he dodged this, a shard of broken glass caught at his shirt. He was forced to dive to avoid the floating debris, and scanned the pool for some sign of the boy.

Movement caught his attention and he realized it was Jameson, legs kicking furiously as he tried to surface, but he had drifted to a part of the pool still clogged with debris. Ryan headed toward him. He tried to catch the boy's attention, but Jameson was too frantic, so Ryan was forced to wrap his arms around the struggling child and drag him back toward the beam. Jameson fought, kicking and scratching, and Ryan's chest ached with the need to breathe. When the beam was in reach, he let go of everything but the boy's hand, and dragged himself onto the beam.

Hands reached out, pulling him up, and the boy with him. Danny and Tony and the firefighter hauled him up and to the edge of the pool, where he lay panting, the boy beside him.

"I'm fine," he protested, and pushed Tony away and

sat up. Danny and Cassie bent over Jameson, who was very still and pale.

"Jamie!" A petite blond woman, her flowered tankini streaked with blood, rushed to them. She held a little girl in a pink swimsuit in her arms.

Just then Jameson coughed, and the paramedics rolled him onto his side in time for him to vomit up a rush of pool water. The woman crouched beside him, the girl balanced on her hip. "Jamie!" she called again, and touched his face.

"I'm okay, Mom," he said, and tried to sit up, but Danny pressed him back down.

"Not so fast, tiger," he said. "Let's check you over and make sure you're okay first."

Ryan thought the boy would be fine. He stood and looked around to see where he could help next. The pool was much clearer now, and he could make out the remains of the tables and chairs that had once dotted this atrium. "You need to have that cut dressed." Tony moved alongside him and began cleaning the wound in question.

"I didn't even feel it," Ryan said, watching as blood dripped onto the cracked tile.

"Adrenaline," Tony said. He finished cleaning the wound and laid on a gauze pad. "I don't think you need stitches. You're up on your tetanus shots, right?"

"Yeah." It was a requirement for search and rescue work.

Sheriff Travis Walker approached. "All the guests and employees of the hotel are accounted for, along with the people in the gift shop," he said. "I'm ordering everyone out of here before someone else gets hurt."

"Do they have any idea who did this?" Tony asked.

Travis shook his head. "There's a good chance it's the

same person who set the other three bombs," he said. "We'll know more once the bomb squad goes over everything."

Do you think it's Mike Traynor? Ryan wanted to ask, but he didn't.

"Whoever is doing this, they had better hope you catch him before someone else does," Austen said. "People are pretty furious about these attacks."

Travis looked grim, but didn't comment. Ryan thought of Deni. What if her dad was guilty? He wanted to be there for her, but how did you help someone through something like this?

DENI CONTINUED TO check the Twitter thread about the bombing, until everyone had been accounted for and the conversation transitioned to speculation about the identity of the bomber. She shut down the app, not wanting to see her father mentioned. She paced the floor, hating this feeling of powerlessness. She couldn't do anything to help the people who had been affected by the bombing, she couldn't stop this from happening again and she couldn't reach her father to find out if he was involved, and if so, why.

She tried to distract herself with work, but concentrating on student essays proved impossible. She tried to remember if any of her students' parents worked at the hotel. She didn't think so, but what if she was overlooking someone? She went online again to pull up the student directory, but while she was waiting for the site to load, a noise outside startled her. It sounded like someone was on the front porch.

Thinking it must be Ryan, she rushed to check the peephole, but couldn't see anything. It was almost full dark outside, so she flipped on the porch light. Still no one in sight, though the noise continued—someone moving about. "Hello?" she called. "Who's there?"

No answer. A chill swept over her. Someone was definitely out there. She grabbed her phone and punched in Ryan's number. "Hey," he answered. "I was just going to call you, see if you wanted some company."

"Then you're not already here?" she asked, even though she already knew the answer.

"No. I'm at my place. I just got out of the shower."

"Someone is outside, on my front porch," she said, keeping her voice low. "I can hear them, but they don't answer when I call out."

"Can you see them?" he asked.

"No. But I heard footsteps, and moving around."

"Hang up and call 911," he said.

"What if it's just an animal? A big dog or a bear? The sheriff's department already thinks I'm lying to them."

"Bears are supposed to be hibernating right now, and a dog doesn't sound like a human moving around. You said you heard footsteps."

"Yes."

"Call 911," he said. "I'll be over as soon as I can." Then he ended the call.

She stared at her phone, then punched in 911. A female voice answered. "What is the nature of your emergency?"

"There's someone on my front porch," she replied. "They don't answer when I call out to them and they're staying where I can't see them."

She waited for the woman to tell her she was probably imagining things, but she merely asked for a name and address and said she would notify the sheriff's department.

Deni returned to the front door and looked through the peephole again. Nothing. But was that a shadow, there on the edge of the reach of the porch light? Her heart pounded and she stepped back and stared at the lock on the door. Would it hold if someone tried to break in?

Headlights illuminated the street in front of her house, and a sheriff's department SUV pulled to the curb. A tall man got out of the vehicle and Sergeant Gage Walker, the sheriff's brother, started up the walk.

Deni opened the door as he mounted the steps to the porch. "Thank you for coming," she said. "I'm sure I heard someone out here."

Gage nodded, and looked to his right. "Looks like someone wanting to stir up trouble," he said. "Did you get a look at them at all?"

"I never saw anyone, just heard them." She stepped onto the porch, the chill air washing over her, and followed his gaze to the wall beside the door. Someone had spray-painted the side of her house in foot-high letters, the color of fresh blood: KILL THE BOMBER.

Chapter Seventeen

"You need to come back to my place," Ryan said, after the shock of seeing the message from the anonymous tagger had subsided. "It's not safe for you here." He had arrived only moments after Gage and had been horrified at what he found.

Deni looked to Gage, who had stepped back and was photographing the graffiti. "Why would someone do this?" she asked.

"People are pretty upset about these bombs," Gage said.

"But I didn't have anything to do with them," she responded.

"No, but some people think your father did." He tucked his phone back into his pocket and took out a notebook. "To them, you're guilty by association."

She frowned, but he had already turned away, his attention focused on the notebook in his hand. "What time did you hear someone on the porch?" he asked.

"Just a few minutes before I called 911," she said.

"Did you see any cars nearby, maybe parked on the street?" Gage asked. "Anyone hanging around, maybe right before then?"

"I wasn't looking outside before then, and I didn't see

any cars or anyone," she said. "Maybe one of my neighbors saw something."

"We'll talk to them," Gage said. He looked around. Snow had started to fall, big flakes drifting through the light from the porch. "This snow is going to cover any tracks your graffiti artist might have made."

She stared at the spray-painted message again. "What am I going to do?"

"The hardware store sells some cleaner that will take off the paint," Gage said. "Though you might have to repaint this part of the house, too." He glanced at Ryan. "In the meantime, it might be a good idea if you went somewhere else for a few days. We'll have a deputy drive by several times each shift to keep an eye on things. Maybe we'll get lucky and catch whoever it was coming back to try again."

Ryan didn't think Gage sounded optimistic. He moved to put his arm around Deni. "There's nothing more you can do tonight," he said. "Why don't you pack a bag and come with me? Cookie can come, too."

Her expression softened. "That's so sweet of you to think of my cat, but Cookie doesn't do well in strange situations. She'll be happier here, as long as I'm not gone too long."

"Will you come to my place, then? At least for the night?"

"Yes. Thanks." She moved away and went inside. When she was gone, Ryan turned to Gage. "Deni hasn't done anything wrong," he said. "She wants to find her dad as much as you do. And she wants these bombings to stop."

"Even if it means arresting her father?" Gage asked.

"At least then more people wouldn't be hurt." He absently rubbed at his arm, which still ached from the afternoon's efforts. "Is Mike Traynor your only suspect?"

"No," Gage said. "We're looking at a lot of people. But Mike is the only one with a background in explosives, and he's the only one who disappeared around the time of the first bombing. That looks suspicious."

"I don't know what to tell you," Ryan said. "Except that Deni hasn't done anything wrong." He stared at the ugly words painted on her house. "She doesn't deserve this."

Gage nodded. "Take her home and keep her safe," he suggested. "We'll keep working things on our end."

Gage called for a team to search the area and question neighbors. Ryan went in search of Deni and found her in her bedroom, a suitcase open on the bed. "I can't think straight," she said. "What should I take with me?"

"Let me help." Together, they assembled clothing and toiletries to last a few days, then collected her student papers and books she needed for her job. By the time they emerged from the house, two deputies were searching the flower beds and yard, though the snow was falling harder now, obscuring everything. Gage nodded to them, then turned back to his officers.

Deni stopped halfway down the walk. "How did you get here?" she asked. "I forgot about your truck."

"I rode my bike." He gestured to the mountain bike leaning against the banked snow at the side of her driveway.

"At least we can take my car now." She hit the key fob to unlock the vehicle and he retrieved his bike, which just fit in the back, with the rear seat folded down.

Ryan lived in an apartment over an art gallery, three blocks from the snowboard and skateboard manufacturer where he worked. "My landlords remodeled this space as a rental a few years back," he explained as he ushered her inside. "I was lucky to get it."

Though small, the apartment had an open, airy feel, with big windows and high ceilings, white-painted walls and blond wood floors. The clock on the microwave in the galley kitchen showed just after ten o'clock when they walked in. "If you're tired, go on to bed," Deni said. "I'm too keyed up to sleep."

"So am I." He moved to the cabinet and opened it. "Why don't I make some coffee and we can talk?"

She settled at the table and watched him move about, adding coffee to the old-fashioned drip machine, getting out mugs and milk. "Are you hungry?" he asked. "I can make toast."

"Just coffee is fine with me," she said. "You eat if you want."

When the coffee was done, he filled two mugs and brought them to the table. "I'll eat in a minute. Tell me about your day."

She stirred sugar and milk into her mug. "I ran into Agent Olivera downtown," she said.

He had been waiting for this, but that didn't make it any easier. He froze, his back to her, gathering the courage to turn around.

"He told me you had been in prison," she said. "Is that true?"

He faced her, every muscle still tensed, trying to read her expression. "It's true," he said.

"Why didn't you tell me?" She pushed the coffee cup away. "Didn't you think it was something I would want to know?"

He moved to the table and sat across from her. Her gaze remained locked on him, hurt radiating. "I didn't tell you because I don't tell anyone," he said. "It's in the past and I don't talk about it."

"No one else knows?"

"Xander knows. You have to tell employers if you have a record. Most of them won't hire you when they find out, but Xander was willing to take a chance on me."

"Does the sheriff know?"

"He probably does now. Olivera probably told him if he wasn't already aware." He wanted to reach out and take her hand. Instead, he laced his fingers together. "I didn't tell you because I didn't want you to look at me the way you are now."

She leaned back. "What way is that?"

"Like I'm a bad person. Someone you can't trust."

"I'm just shocked, that's all. And I don't think you're a bad person. But I wish you'd tell me what happened."

He sighed. "The short answer is, I got involved with the wrong person and was stupid. Remember, I told you I worked at a restaurant? There was a waitress there, Tracy. I was 19. She was 25 or 26. I liked her. I thought she liked me. Turned out she was stealing people's credit card information. When she took the card for them to pay, she would take pictures of the fronts and backs of the cards and use it later to order stuff. She had a friend who resold the stuff. Sometimes she sold the credit card information. I found out what she was doing, but she persuaded me to turn a blind eye. She said it wasn't hurting anyone. Then I found out she had been using my phone to take the pictures of the cards most of the time. I kept the phone in my locker while I was working, but she knew the combination. I never thought to look—until the cops who were onto her scam showed me all the evidence against me. Tracy told them the whole scam was my idea, that she only went along because she was afraid of me."

"Oh, Ryan," Deni whispered.

"Don't feel sorry for me," he said. "I was an adult. I should have known better. As it was, my parents paid for a really expensive, really good lawyer and he persuaded the jury that the prosecutors couldn't prove I was the one who planned everything. He portrayed me as the dupe I really was, so I only had to serve a little over two years."

"What happened to Tracy?"

"I don't know and I don't care."

"I'm sorry you had to go through all of that," she said.

"I got what I deserved and I'm not going to make a mistake like that again."

"I believe you." She put her hand over his. "And I know you're a good person. But I'm glad I know about this, too."

"I was going to tell you," he said. "I just had to work up the nerve."

He turned his hand palm up and laced his fingers with hers. They sat there for a long moment, the silence between them easier. "I want to tell you what happened this morning, before I ran into Agent Olivera," she said.

"I want to hear all about it."

"AFTER YOU LEFT, I couldn't settle down," she said. "I decided to go into town and talk to Rouster again, and anyone else who might have seen my dad with Al. Rouster gave the same description of Al as Glenda gave of Alex, so I think they are the same man. Then I spoke to the bartender at Mo's. She said she had seen Dad in there with Al a few times, but she couldn't tell me any more about him. She said the ATFE agents had been in there, asking about Dad, too."

"They're probably asking about a lot of people," he said.

"Do you really think so?" She shook her head. "Agent

Olivera stopped me on the street after I left Mo's. He grabbed my arm and wouldn't let go. He's convinced I know something that I'm not telling him and he wouldn't take no for an answer. He didn't let me go until I threatened to make a scene, but he threatened to arrest me if he found out I was keeping anything from him."

"He's not finding any solid evidence to tie your dad to the bombings if he's making threats like that," Ryan said.

She sipped the coffee, his reassurance soothing her agitated nerves. "Right before Agent Olivera stopped me, I thought I saw the man we talked to at the yurt," she said. "I called out to him and he ducked down an alley, right by the hotel. I didn't even realize it was by the hotel, but later Deputy Jamie Douglas came to the house to question me. She said someone had seen me right by the hotel not too long before the bomb went off. I tried to tell her about the man in the yurt, but I don't think she believed me."

"Wait a minute," Ryan said. "You were at the hotel? Right before the bomb went off?"

"It was at least a half an hour before the bomb went off, and I was only near the hotel, not even directly in front of it. And I never went inside."

"Was the man from the yurt at the hotel?"

"I don't know," she said. "When I saw him he was walking down the street from that direction. He ducked into the alley. I thought he was trying to get away from me, but maybe he was just taking a shortcut back to wherever he was parked."

"When did Deputy Douglas come to the house?" he asked.

"Right after the bomb went off. Apparently, someone mentioned seeing me at the hotel and the sheriff sent her to talk to me—probably because now I'm a suspect. Maybe they think I planted a bomb for my dad or something."

"It will be easy enough for them to check with Rouster and the bartender at Mo's and confirm that you were talking to them," he said.

"Yes. It's just so…annoying. I keep telling everyone the same things over and over—that I don't know where my father is or what he's doing—but no one is listening."

"I'm listening," he said, and the warmth in his eyes chased away some of the cold fear that had taken up residence inside her these last few days. "What about you?" she asked. "What did you do today?"

"Agents Olivera and Ferris came to see me at work," he said. "Probably after Olivera talked to you."

"Why did they want to talk to you?" she asked.

"I think they were hoping I'd tell him all your secrets about you and your dad. And you're right—they don't listen to anything they don't want to hear. I told Olivera you were telling the truth and that you didn't know anything about your dad's activities. He suggested I should put pressure on you to confess all—even though I told him you don't have anything to confess. And then the bomb went off and the two of them ran out of there." He sat back in his chair. "And I got a text that search and rescue needed me to report to the hotel."

"Oh no," she said. "I didn't even think of that. What could you do at the hotel?"

"Dig people out of the rubble and administer first aid," he said. "Fortunately, not too many people were in the part of the building where the bomb went off. But two people died, and several others were seriously injured."

"I'm sorry," she said. "That must be hard to deal with."

"It can be." He finished the last of his mug of coffee and set it down with a thump. "But today was a good day. We rescued a little boy." He told her about everyone working together to save Jameson.

"Is that how you got this?" She leaned forward and brushed her fingers across the bandage on his upper arm.

"There was a lot of broken glass," he said. "It's just a cut."

She sat back. "This can't keep happening," she responded. "It's terrifying."

"It makes you wonder where the bomber will strike next," he said.

"Do you have some paper we can write on?" she asked. "I want to make a list of everywhere there has already been a bomb, and see if I can see a pattern."

"Sure." He got up and retrieved a spiral notebook from a drawer, along with a couple of pens. He flipped to a blank page in the notebook and slid it toward her. "The sheriff's department is probably already doing this," he said.

"Yes, but if my dad is behind everything, I probably know him better than anyone." The cops were right about that, at least. "Maybe I will see something they don't— some clue as to what he's trying to accomplish."

Ryan gave her a curious look. "So you don't think he's innocent?"

"I do! At least, I want to. I don't know what to think."

He pulled her close. "Whatever happens, it's on your dad," he said. "It's not your fault and it's not on you."

"I know." She took a deep breath and pulled herself together. "But I can't sit here and do nothing, either. So— back to this list."

She drew lines to divide the page into columns, then began writing down what they knew about the site of each bombing, the result of the bomb and her father's connection to each location. "Grizzly Creek bridge, Caspar Canyon Ice Climbing Area, the Zenith Mine and the Nugget Hotel," she read out loud. "Well, we know that my dad had protested development in all those areas, either by writing letters to the editor of the paper or attending town council meetings where development was discussed."

"And the in-person protests at the Zenith Mine," Ryan said.

She nodded and continued to stare at the list. "Do you see anything else?" he asked.

"The bombings are getting worse." She looked at him. "Does that mean the bombs are getting bigger or the bomber is getting better at placing them to do the most damage?"

"Maybe both?" He leaned over her shoulder to study the list. "What else do the sites have in common?"

"I don't know." She clenched her head in her hands, as if that would make it easier to see what she was missing.

"Where else did your dad complain about or protest?"

She closed her eyes. "I can't think. I didn't pay attention, really. Maybe we can ask Glenda. She organized a lot of protests."

"Then let's do that tomorrow." He rubbed her back. "We're both exhausted. Let's get some sleep."

"All right." She brought her hand up to cover his. "And thank you. For letting me stay here and for being here." *For not leaving when you saw that graffiti written on the side of my house.*

"I'm not going to leave you," he said, as if reading her thoughts. "You're too important to me now."

She thought about what he had told her, about the woman he had fallen for. She had betrayed him in the worst way. It was a wonder he had ever let Deni—a woman whose father was a suspected terrorist—get close to him at all. Did he worry he was making another mistake?

She would do her best to prove he wasn't.

Deni slept fitfully and woke early, disoriented by a dream she had had of her father. He had been calling to her, pleading for help. She had stumbled through a snowy ravine, floundering through drifts and scrambling over icy rocks, his voice lost in a howling wind, then coming from another direction entirely.

She woke in a tangle of blankets, cheeks wet with tears, Ryan sleeping soundly beside her. Careful not to wake him, she slipped out of bed and carried her clothes into the bathroom to dress.

The snow had stopped falling and the sun was rising, the scenery outside the window fresh and peaceful. In the kitchen, she made coffee, then studied the list she had left lying on the kitchen table. Last night, she and Ryan had talked about everything the bomb sites had in common, but this morning, a difference stood out to her. While her father had written letters to the editor or participated in organized protests against the bridge, the mine and the hotel expansion, he hadn't done that for Caspar Canyon. Yes, he had complained about the extra traffic, and the damage to the environment that might result from over-use, but he had never suggested anyone close the canyon to climbing, only that the town should better regulate the activities there. Plus, the other three places where bombs had been placed had been man-made structures the bombs had the potential to damage or destroy. The damage in the canyon had been to nature, and to people. Her father had always talked about protecting the natural beauty of this area, not destroying it.

When Ryan came into the kitchen some time later, he found her bent over the notebook, writing furiously. "Good morning," he said. "What's up?"

She looked up, and brushed a fall of hair out of her

eyes. "Hey. I couldn't sleep, so I got up and started studying this list again. I think I figured something out."

He pulled a mug from the cabinet and filled it from the carafe. "What's that?"

She explained about the difference between Caspar Canyon and the other sites. "It's like Glenda said—Dad and the other protesters at the mine and the hotel didn't have anything against the people involved in those projects—they just want to protect the landscape. I think my dad really believed that, too."

Ryan sat across from her and sipped coffee. "That points to your dad not being involved in the bombings, but it doesn't help us find him. And it doesn't give us a clue as to where the next bomb might be."

"I did think of one thing," she said. "Though it's pretty far out there."

He set down his coffee mug. "Let's hear it."

"The town council are the ones who decide on all these projects," she said.

"Right."

She looked at her notebook again. "If you plot the location of the bombs so far, each one is a little closer to downtown. What if that's intentional? What if the bomber's next target is the courthouse, where the council meets?"

Ryan's face registered the shock she had felt when the idea had first occurred to her. "When does the town council meet again?" he asked.

"I checked the town website," she said. "The next meeting is tomorrow night."

"We have to let the sheriff know about this," he said.

"They'll either think I'm imagining things, or they'll believe me and arrest me for having insider knowledge. Or maybe they've already figured this out on their own."

"If I had gone to the police as soon as I figured out what Tracy was up to, I would have saved a lot of people a lot of trouble," he said. "Including myself. Do you want to risk them not knowing, and you being right?"

"No." For the past hour she had wrestled with the question and come to the same conclusion Ryan had. They had to tell the sheriff. After that, it was in his hands.

She stood. "I'm going to take a shower," she said. "I already called the school and took another personal day."

"Were they upset?" he asked.

"No. The principal actually said he thought that would be a good idea. I imagine news about that graffiti on my house is all over town by now." But she wasn't going to think about that.

"I'll go with you to the sheriff's department," Ryan said.

"Don't you have to work?"

"I can go in late. Xander is pretty laid-back and we're not particularly busy right now."

"Thanks." She told herself she didn't need him to go with her, but she would feel better with him there. Through this whole ordeal, he had been the one person she could count on.

ADELAIDE KINKAID, the office manager at the sheriff's department, studied Ryan and Deni over the tops of red-rimmed bifocals. "The sheriff is a very busy man," she said.

"We won't take much of his time, but this is important," Deni stressed.

Adelaide picked up her phone. "One of the deputies can see you," she said.

"It has to be the sheriff." Deni was polite, but it was clear she wasn't going to back down.

Adelaide replaced the phone in its cradle. "Let me talk to him," she said, and left the room.

"Do you think I should have hired a lawyer to come with me?" Deni asked Ryan, her voice just above a whisper.

"Maybe." Probably. But they didn't have time for that. Not if Deni's theory was true.

Adelaide returned a few moments later. "The sheriff can give you a few minutes," she announced.

Travis was waiting for them behind his desk. He didn't stand to greet them, but his tone was gentle. "What did you need to see me about, Deni?" he asked.

Deni sat in the chair in front of the desk and spread out the chart and other notes she had made.

"I've been trying to think where the bomber might strike next," she said. "I still don't think my father is doing this, but I want to help."

Travis looked at Deni, not the paperwork. "What have you figured out?"

She showed him how each bomb target was closer and closer to the center of town. "If this is some kind of protest against development, then why not target the people who made decisions about that development? And the place where they meet?"

"So you think the next bomb will be at the courthouse?" he asked.

"The town council has another meeting there tomorrow night," she said. "I don't know if I'm guessing right, but what if I am?"

"And that's all this is?" Travis asked. "A guess?"

"Yes!"

Ryan rested a hand on her shoulder and felt her trembling. "Maybe you already figured this out and I'm wasting your time," she conceded. "But I wanted to say something, just in case." She gathered her papers and stood.

"Thank you," Travis said. "Are you still sure your father doesn't have anything to do with these bombs?"

"Dad always said he wanted to protect places, not destroy them. And he's not a killer. I can't see it." She shook her head. "But he's my dad, so maybe I don't want to see it. If you're able to catch whoever is responsible, maybe then we'll know."

Travis nodded. "And maybe you've helped. No matter what happens, don't feel bad about that."

"Have you found out any more about the person who ran us off the road?" Ryan asked.

"No," Travis said.

"What about the man we talked to at the yurt?" Ryan asked. "Deni said she saw him in town yesterday, near the hotel."

"We've been looking for him," Travis said. "We contacted the owner of the yurt and he says no one should be there. We stopped by twice and no one was around."

"We really did see him," Deni said. "We didn't make that up."

"I never said you did," Travis replied.

But did he believe that? Ryan wondered. The sheriff was so hard to read, and since Ryan and Deni were the only people who claimed to have seen this mysterious man, he could understand how someone else might think they had made up the story.

"We'll be in touch," Travis said. "Thank you for stopping by." Which was clearly a dismissal.

"What do you want to do now?" Ryan asked when they were on the sidewalk again.

"I want to go back to that yurt," she said. "I want to find the man we talked to and ask him why he ran from me when I saw him Monday. And I want to know what he was doing hanging around the hotel just before that bomb went off."

"If he's involved in this, it might not be safe," Ryan said.

"I'm feeling reckless. Or desperate. At this point, I'm not sure there's much difference between the two." She set off down the sidewalk. Ryan hurried after her. When had he changed from believing he should distance himself from her to knowing he should stick by her? He thought it was probably when Olivera and Ferris had first questioned her. He had been in that position, with no one who believed in him to stand by him. He believed in Deni. He was even beginning to believe in what the two of them could be together.

FRESH SNOW HAD covered the tracks of their previous visit here, and wiped out even the ruts formed by the wrecker that had hauled away Ryan's damaged truck, but someone had traveled this way. They followed a single set of tire tracks up the road. Deni turned her head away from the place where they had been run off the road, fear churning her stomach. She had been half hoping Ryan would try to talk her out of this reckless idea of confronting the man in the yurt, but he hadn't said anything against it, though he had insisted she leave a note for her neighbor, letting her know where they were headed and how the insurance appraiser coming to review the damage to her house might reach her if he stopped by. "With my luck, agents Olivera and Ferris will see the note and decide to come question me again," she had told Ryan.

"It might come in handy to let the man in the yurt know a couple of federal agents are headed his way," Ryan said. "Just in case he turns out to be the man in the black truck who ran us down."

No truck was visible when they pulled into the narrow drive that led to the yurt. No smoke drifted from the stovepipe, and all the windows were shut tight. "It looks deserted," Ryan said, after he had turned Deni's Subaru around and parked with the front of the car facing toward the road.

"Let's get out and look around," Deni said.

Footsteps in the snow led from the front door of the yurt to a cleared area where a vehicle had been parked. "It's a big enough space for a truck," Ryan said.

Deni mounted the steps to the front door and knocked, but there was no answer. "Hello!" she called. "Anybody home?"

"I think he's gone." Ryan joined her on the small front porch. "Remember, the cops said he wasn't here when they tried to talk to him."

"Someone has been here since the snow last night," she said, pointing to the tracks. They were large, a man's lug-soled boots.

"Maybe a cop," Ryan said.

"Let's look around a little, as long as we're here," she said.

She didn't know what she expected to find, but walking through the snowy woods felt better than sitting around doing nothing.

She found more tracks around the back of the yurt, a fainter trail that led into the underbrush. "Maybe that goes to an outhouse," Ryan said.

"Maybe," Deni mused. "But this path heads in the direction of my dad's cabin. Maybe there's a spot where we can look down on Dad's place."

They set off down the path, Deni in front, Ryan on her heels, the underbrush so close on either side they could only travel single file. After fifty yards, the trail ended. Not at an outhouse or any kind of scenic viewpoint.

"Why make a trail through the woods that goes nowhere?" Ryan asked.

Deni turned a complete circle, searching around them. Then she looked up and felt a jolt of surprise. "Not nowhere." She pointed up. "He's got a tree house."

That was the only way to describe what sat overhead, well camouflaged in a large fir to the left of the trail. A little shack was built on a platform in the tree, with wooden sides, shuttered windows and a rusting metal roof.

The two of them walked over and stared up at the little building. "How does he get up there?" Deni asked.

"There must be a ladder." Ryan looked around. "There!" He pointed and Deni followed his gaze to another tree, deeper in the woods, and the wooden ladder propped against its trunk.

"Let's see what's up there," she said, and hurried toward the ladder.

Ryan helped her to haul the ladder to the tree house, where it fitted neatly against two notches in the platform on which the little house was constructed. "This is probably trespassing," Ryan said.

"Probably." Deni put her foot on the bottom rung. "But I'm not going to hurt anything. I just want to see."

She climbed to the platform, ignoring the butterflies in her chest. She had always been the good girl, the one who never broke the rules or stepped out of line. All it had taken was the police to start treating her like a criminal for all her scofflaw tendencies to emerge.

She climbed onto the platform and stood. The door to the little house was to her right—not a flimsy homemade portal, but a solid door like she might see on any home.

She walked the few steps to it and tried the knob, but the door was locked. Feeling a little foolish, she knocked. "Hello!" she called.

A scuffling noise from inside startled her. Heart pounding, she pressed her ear to the door. "Hello?" she called again. "Is someone there?"

"Help!" The word was muffled, but still distinguishable. "Help!" A man's gravelly voice, the voice from her dream.

She raced to the ladder and looked down at Ryan. "Find something to break down this door," she called. "I think we've found my dad!"

Chapter Eighteen

Several hard blows with the tire iron from Deni's car broke the lock on the tree house door. Ryan shoved open the door, brandishing the tire iron. At first, he saw nothing in the dim light, then a voice broke through the stillness.

"Deni!"

"Dad!" Deni started to run to him, then stopped as the bizarre scene before them registered. A thin, white-haired man balanced precariously on a wooden crate on top of a table with only three of its four legs in place. He gripped the noose around his neck with both hands.

Ryan pulled out his phone and switched on the flashlight ap. Mike Traynor stared at them, eyes wide with terror. "Don't just stand there—cut me down!" he croaked.

Ryan rushed forward to grasp Traynor around the knees and hold him up, just as the table tipped and the crate fell. "See if you can find something to cut this rope," Ryan said as the older man's weight sagged against him.

Deni looked frantically around the room which, except for the broken table, was empty. "Break a window," her father said.

Ryan saw now that the windows, though covered with wooden shutters, did indeed have glass panes. "Careful," he said, as Deni picked up the broken table leg and hurled it at the back window. Glass shattered and a few shards fell to the floor. She picked up one, righted the crate and stood on it to saw at the rope with the broken glass. Agonizing minutes passed until the rope began to fray.

With a groan from the rafters, the rope snapped and Mike and Ryan both fell to the floor.

Deni rushed to them and began helping her father loosen the noose around his neck. "Dad, what is going on?" she asked.

"Water," he gasped, and rubbed at his throat, where the rope had chafed an angry red ring.

"There's some in the car," Ryan said, and went to retrieve it. But a note tacked inside the door stopped him. "Deni," he said, in a warning tone.

She looked up. "What is it?"

"You'd better see for yourself."

She joined him in front of the door. The writing was almost illegible, sloping upward on the page. "I'm sorry about the bombs," it read. "I never meant to hurt anyone. I only wanted to stop all this development." It was signed Mike Traynor.

"Al made me write that." Mike staggered to his feet. "He put a gun to my head—one of my own guns, from the trunk he stole from my house. He said he would shoot me if I didn't do as he said. I was ready to let him do it, but then he threatened you, so I gave in."

"Where is Al?" Deni asked.

"I don't know, but he'll probably be back soon," Mike said.

"Then we need to get out of here." Ryan took his arm. "Can you walk to Deni's car?"

Mike nodded. "I may need a little help, but I can do it."

On the way out, Deni stopped and tore the note from the door. She folded it and tucked it into her pocket. "That might be evidence," Ryan said.

"I'll give it to the sheriff," she promised. "I just don't want anyone finding it and thinking it's real before we have a chance to explain."

"I'm sorry about all this," Mike said as he hobbled between them toward the yurt and Deni's car. "I've been really stupid."

"It's okay, Dad," she said. "I'm so glad to see you."

"Just tell us one thing," Ryan said. "Is there another bomb?"

"I think so," Mike said. "I think he intends it to go off during the town council meeting at the courthouse. He wants everyone to think I did it—that I did all of them."

"Al is responsible for all those bombs?" Deni said. "He just framed you for them?"

"We set the first one at the Grizzly Creek bridge," Mike admitted. "It was just a prank, really, to get people's attention. It wouldn't have gone off—I made sure of that. But then Al wanted to make a real one. I refused. That's when he kidnapped me. I thought I had talked him out of the whole plan. He said we were going on a snowmobile outing, and when he got me alone, he tied me up and imprisoned me in that tree house. He stole my guns from the cabin and used the dynamite I'd intended to use on my spring to make more bombs and put them around town. He'd come back and tell me what he had done, and how everyone would believe I was responsible."

The story was incredible. Ryan might not have believed it, except for the way they had found Mike balanced on that table. "He intended to kill you and make it look like suicide," he said.

"Yes," Mike confirmed. "It's a good thing you came along when you did. I don't think I would have lasted much longer."

"What is Al's full name?" Ryan asked. "And what does he look like?"

"His name is Alex Coggins," Mike said. "He used to have a full beard and glasses, but he shaved off the beard and threw away the glasses after he kidnapped me. He was in the Explosives Division like I was. He served in a different part of the country, so I didn't know him back then, but it was one of the things we had in common. I met him at the protest against the Zenith Mine and we hit it off and started hanging out." He looked at Deni. "It was nice to have a friend to do things with. I guess he really played me."

"Is Al the person who ran us off the road when we came up here to look for you?" Deni asked.

"I don't know about that," Mike said. "But it sounds like him. He's ruthless when it comes to getting what he wants."

"We found your truck, wrecked in Grizzly Creek," Deni said. "I was so afraid we would find you with it, dead or injured."

"Al did that to throw off anyone who was looking for me," Mike said. "And maybe to make it harder for me to get away. He said people would think I wrecked the truck on purpose in a suicide attempt."

"Oh, Dad." Deni hugged him close.

"Why is he blowing up everything?" Ryan asked.

"Because he can, I guess," Mike said. "Something isn't right with him. I noticed it pretty early on, but I just told myself everyone has their quirks." He hung his head.

Deni took a firmer hold on his arm. "We're almost to the car, Dad," she said. "You can tell the sheriff what you know. You'll help prevent more people being killed."

Ryan wondered if Deni realized her father could be charged for his part in the first bomb, the one at the Grizzly Creek bridge. He might even be treated as an accessory to the other bombings. He looked across at her, and decided having her dad back and safe meant more than any worries about his future.

They reached the back of the yurt and Mike swayed and made a moaning sound.

"Dad, are you okay?" Deni asked. "What's wrong?"

"Just…don't feel so good." He closed his eyes, his face gray. After all he had been through, was he having a heart attack?

Ryan eased the older man up against the side of the yurt. "Are you in pain?" he asked.

"Just…dizzy." He leaned against the yurt. "Just give me a minute to catch my breath."

Ryan felt at Mike's throat for a pulse. A little rapid but strong. "Are you having any chest pains?" he asked. "Any numbness in your arms?"

"No. Just…weak."

No telling when he had last eaten, or how long he had been straining to balance on his precarious perch upon the uneven table.

"We'll rest here a minute, then get you to the car," Ryan said. Maybe he and Deni could form a chair to carry the older man.

"Someone's coming!" Deni whispered.

Ryan froze, ears straining, then he heard the crunch of tires on snow. He swore and looked around for anywhere they might hide.

"It's Al," Mike said. "He's coming back to see if I'm dead yet."

The underside of the yurt was enclosed, so no hiding place there. They would have to sprint twenty yards to the cover of the woods, through thick snowbanks. Mike would never manage, and the snow would make their retreat obvious. If they retraced their steps to the tree house, Al would find them there.

"My car is parked right out front," Deni whispered. She moved in closer to Ryan. "He'll know we're here."

"Leave me and go," Mike said. "He'll be too distracted by me to go after you. You can circle around to your car and I'll keep him occupied until you get away."

"No," Deni protested. She clung to his arm. "I won't leave you."

Ryan took hold of Mike's other arm. "She's right. We won't leave you."

The vehicle stopped, and a car door slammed. They stood frozen, unable to go anywhere without being seen.

Seconds later, the clean-shaven man in the black knit cap they had first seen here at the yurt came around the side. He carried a large handgun, and focused it on Deni.

"Al, you leave her alone!" Mike struggled, but Deni and Ryan held him firm.

"I'm glad to see you both," Al said to Ryan and Deni. "You've saved me the trouble of looking for you."

"What are you going to do with us?" Deni asked. Ryan wished she hadn't. He didn't really want to know Al's plan, which probably involved the gun in his hand.

"You'll find out soon enough." He jabbed the gun toward her. "But first, we're all going to go back to the tree house. And this time, I promise you won't leave."

AL FORCED THEM at gunpoint to climb into the tree house. Deni climbed behind her father, watching as he took each shaky step. He must be exhausted—and thirsty. They had never made it to the car, and the water he had asked for. Ryan was in front of her father. What did he think about being caught up in such a nightmare?

Al moved right behind her, jabbing her with the pistol

every few steps, as if she needed reminding what was at stake here. When they reached the platform, Al scowled at the broken lock on the door, but said nothing. "Get inside," he ordered.

They filed in. Al turned to Mike. "Get that rope and tie up these two." He gestured with the gun to Deni and Ryan. "Back to back. And do it up tight. I'll check."

Mike shuffled to the noose and picked it up. He looked much older to Deni, and defeated. She would have never thought her father would let anyone order him around this way. Then again, the gun in Al's hand was a powerful persuader. "How do you want me to do it?" Mike asked.

"You two, sit on the floor, arms linked and backs together," Al said.

Ryan met Deni's gaze. He didn't look defeated, more—resigned. He sat, and she lowered herself to the floor also, then sat with her back pressed to his, knees up. "Link arms," Al ordered.

They did as he asked, and her father knelt beside them with the rope. "I'm sorry about this," he muttered.

"It's okay, Dad," she said.

Mike looped the rope around them several times, then double knotted it over Ryan's stomach. Al bent to tug at the rope with one hand, the other keeping the gun focused on Mike. "That should do," he said, and straightened. He looked around the single room. "Where's the suicide note you wrote before?"

Mike blinked at him, looking confused. "I don't know."

Al struck him hard across the face, leaving the red imprint of his hand. Mike staggered back, clutching his face.

"I tore up the note and threw it away," Deni said. "It was all lies."

"We don't need a note," Al said. "It will be clear enough to the authorities when they show up. Mike shot both of you, then put the gun to his own head, after his last bomb destroyed the courthouse and everyone in it."

"You don't have enough dynamite to do that," Mike said.

"I was at the Zenith Mine, remember? The thing about mines is, they have lots of explosives. I was able to help myself to everything I needed. Of course, people will think you stole it, when you planted that second bomb."

He turned to Deni. "You were there, weren't you? Maybe people will think you helped your old man. Like father, like daughter, huh?" He laughed, the sound sending a shiver down Deni's spine. She wanted to fling herself at him, to scratch out his eyes, but the rope bound her so tightly to Ryan she could scarcely draw a deep breath.

"You won't get away with this," Ryan said. "The sheriff's department already knows you were here at this yurt, and Deni told them about seeing you near the hotel shortly before the bomb went off."

"They don't know anything," Al said. "All they have is her word, and she's a terrorist's daughter who won't be around to defend herself." He approached Mike, who stood close to Deni and Ryan, and gestured with the gun. "Kneel down."

"Make me." Mike glared at him, fists clenched at his side. "Kill me if you have to, but I'm not going to let you get away with making it look like suicide."

"I'll make you." Al turned and fired at Deni.

Time slowed down for her. She saw the muzzle of the gun pointed at her, heard the loud report, then felt a burning pain in her shoulder. "The next shot goes right in her heart if you don't do what I say," Al said.

Chapter Nineteen

Ryan felt the impact of the bullet as it pushed Deni sideways. Rage surged through him and he kicked out, striking Al hard in the back of the leg. Al staggered, and turned, the pistol leveled at Ryan, but before he could pull the trigger, Mike wrapped his arm around Al's neck and began choking him. Ryan kicked again, Al's shin hard against his heel, and the gun clattered to the floor.

"This is the sheriff!" a voice boomed. "We have you surrounded. Come out with your hands up."

"Help!" Deni screamed.

"Help!" Ryan echoed.

Scuffling noises sounded outside, and he pictured deputies swarming up the ladder. The door to the tree house burst open and the sheriff, followed by three deputies, crowded in, weapons drawn. They pointed their weapons at Mike. "Let him go," they ordered.

"Al shot me!" Deni cried. "Dad saved me!"

"Let him go," Travis ordered again.

Mike released his hold on Al, who staggered forward, clutching his throat. "He's a maniac," Al said. "I found him up here, those two tied up, the gun in his hand. He shot his own daughter, then went after me."

"That's not what happened," Ryan said.

"Everyone quiet!" Travis ordered. "We're going to

hold you both until we sort this out." He signaled to his deputies and they moved forward and put both men in handcuffs.

Gage Walker knelt next to Ryan and Deni and began cutting them free. "Travis radioed for an ambulance as soon as we heard the gunshot," he said. Together, he and Ryan eased Deni onto her back.

Ryan stripped off his jacket, then tore off his shirt and folded it into a pad and began applying pressure to her wound. "I know it hurts," he said when she cried out. "But we have to stop the bleeding." He told himself a shoulder wound wouldn't be too bad. Al hadn't meant to kill her. But if she lost enough blood it wouldn't matter what his intentions had been.

Travis knelt beside them. "The ambulance should be here soon," he said. "I need you to tell me what happened."

As concisely as he could, Ryan told about returning to the yurt to talk to Al and finding Mike in the tree house. "Al had set it up so that as soon as Mike lost his balance the table would fall over and he would strangle to death in that noose," Ryan said. "We got to him just in time. Then, when we were leaving, Al returned and ordered us up here at gunpoint. He shot Deni when Mike wouldn't kneel down so Al could shoot him. He had a suicide note he forced Mike to write so that you would all think he had shot us, then killed himself."

"I have the note in my pocket," Deni said. She was very pale, but still conscious. Ryan kept the pressure on the wound, and prayed the ambulance would hurry.

"We have security footage of a man with white hair, in a cowboy hat and Western shirt, and a fake moustache like the one Mike wore to the last town council meeting, in the courthouse a little over an hour ago," Travis said.

"It couldn't have been Mike," Ryan said. "He was here then. Al probably dressed up like that to make you think he was Mike. I think he's tried to frame Mike for all the bombings. Apparently Al was an explosives expert in the military, too. His name is Alex Coggins."

"We'll need to interview both of them," Travis said. "We'll figure out the truth."

Ryan nodded, and focused all his attention on Deni. He didn't care about Al, or Mike or anyone but her. Of all the people he had worked to rescue, none had ever meant more.

DENI WOKE TO bright light, the sensation of crisp cotton sheets and a faint beeping noise. As her vision focused, she turned to see Ryan, in a chair beside the bed. He stood and leaned over her. "Hey," he said. "How are you feeling?"

"A little foggy. And numb." The memory of everything that had happened in the tree house rushed back to her and she tried to move her left arm, but it was encased in bandages. She looked around what was clearly a hospital room. "What time is it? How long have I been here?"

"It's about seven, Thursday morning," he said. "You had surgery to remove the bullet in your shoulder. You've got some extra hardware in there now to repair some splintered bone. It will be a while before you're climbing cliffs or doing gymnastics."

"Darn. I was planning to take up both those hobbies next week."

He stroked her hair. "It's good to see you awake."

She tried to calculate how long she had been here, but her mind was still too foggy. A long time, in any case. "Have you been here the whole time?" she asked. Dark smudges shadowed his eyes and the beginnings of a beard dusted his cheeks and jaw.

"Hmmm."

She smiled, then the smile faded, replaced by a look of worry. "What happened with Dad?" She had a vague memory of a deputy putting her father in handcuffs.

"He's going to be okay. The paramedics checked him out. He had quite the ordeal, but he's already recovering. The sheriff is still holding him, but he assured me it's more protective custody."

"And Al?"

"He's in custody, too."

"I don't remember much after Al shot me," she said. "You were there, and the sheriff. What exactly happened?"

"I was so angry when Al shot you that I kicked him. And then your dad got his arm around his neck and strangled him. Then the sheriff and his deputies came in and took charge. They were apparently searching for your father when they came to the yurt, thinking they would talk to whoever was there. They heard the gunshot and rushed to the tree house."

"And they arrested my dad?"

"I guess so. I was too focused on you to pay much attention to them." He squeezed her hand gently. "Hannah, one of the search and rescue volunteers, was one of the paramedics on duty in the ambulance that came for you. She and the others took good care of you."

"You took good care of me." She tightened her hold on him.

A nurse came in and she reluctantly let go of him while the woman checked her vitals and asked about her comfort level, then checked the surgical site. As soon as the nurse left the room, the sheriff stepped in. "Hello, Deni,

Ryan," he said. "The nurse said I could talk to you for a few minutes."

She tried to sit up a little straighter in bed. Ryan leaned over to adjust the pillows at her back, and worked the controls to raise the head of the bed. Travis took Ryan's place beside her. "How are you feeling?" he asked.

"I'm going to be okay," she said. "Where is my dad? Is he all right?"

"Mike is fine. He's in a cell at the sheriff's department, but at this point, it's more for his own protection." He glanced across at Ryan. "The explosives squad from Junction found the bomb at the courthouse before it went off, but by then word that a man who looked like your father had been seen placing it had already spread around town. Until the real story has time to filter out, we thought it might be a good idea to keep Mike safe. And there's the matter of charges for the bomb he admits to having set at the Grizzly Creek bridge."

"What about Al?" she asked. "Where is he?"

"In a cell in Junction," Travis said. "He's been charged with the bombings at Caspar Canyon, the Zenith Mine, and the Nugget Hotel and the attempted bombing of the courthouse, as well as assault, kidnapping and attempted murder."

"Did you find enough evidence to convict Al?" Ryan asked. "Enough to make people believe that Deni and her father weren't involved?"

"I can't tell you everything we found," Travis said. "But when we searched his car at the yurt, we found a shirt that matched the one the suspect in the security footage from the courthouse was wearing, and the fake moustache. Al tried to say Mike had left them there, but we know from your testimony that Mike couldn't have been there. The wound on Mike's neck and tissue samples on the rope confirm that story, also."

"Was Al the person who ran us off the road?" Deni asked.

"He hasn't admitted to that," Travis said.

"He knew we were looking for Mike," Ryan said. "I think he ran us off the road to warn us off."

"Mike told us Al had explosive training from the military, too," Ryan said. "Was that true, or another of Al's lies?"

"It wasn't a lie," Travis said. "And we have other evidence that ties him to those bombs. You'll probably both be asked to testify at the trials."

"Of course," Deni said. Though the thought of reliving their ordeal in the tree house wasn't pleasant, she would do whatever was required to help put Al away for a long time. "What about agents Olivera and Ferris?"

"What about them?" Travis asked.

"Are they satisfied that Al is guilty?" she asked. "Will they leave me alone now?"

"They're the ones who tracked Al to Eagle Mountain," Travis said. "They've had him on their radar for a while, for the bombing of a dam in Ohio. They thought your father was an accomplice, but they had Al pegged as the bomber from the first."

"They never said anything!" Deni's voice shook with outrage.

"It's never a good idea to show your hand when you're dealing with criminals," Travis said.

"I wasn't a criminal, but they treated me like one," she replied.

Travis said nothing. Instead, he stepped back. "I'm glad you're doing well," he said. "Don't worry about your father. He'll be okay."

"He wouldn't say that if it was his father in jail," she observed after Travis had left.

Ryan returned to her side. "Your dad will be okay," he said. "He's tough, like his daughter."

She didn't feel like smiling, but she managed one, for his sake.

"You're tired," he said. "And I have things I need to do. I'll leave for a while, but I promise I'll be back."

"I guess I'm not going anywhere anytime soon."

He bent to kiss her on the cheek, but she turned and caught his lips. "Thank you, for everything," she whispered when the kiss ended. "I've put you through so much."

"You were worth every bit of it." Another, briefer kiss, then he was out of the room. She fell back against the pillows and closed her eyes, intending to replay his words over and over, but she was asleep almost immediately.

RYAN HAD HAD his phone on Silent while he was in the hospital. On the way to his car in the hospital lot, he pulled it out and saw that he had missed a call from his father. He hit the button to return the call.

"Hello, Ryan." His father sounded brisk and alert, what Ryan thought of as his lawyer voice, and he pictured him at his desk, in a dress shirt and tie, his suit jacket hung neatly in the closet of his office. "I have the name of that criminal lawyer you wanted."

"Thanks, Dad. Can you text me the name and number? I don't have anything to write on just now."

"Where are you?"

"I'm just leaving the hospital in Junction." He reached the truck his boss, Xander, had loaned him and hit the key fob to unlock it. "I was with Deni. She's going to be okay." He had poured out the whole story to his father around midnight last night, when he had called to ask for the name of a good criminal attorney who could represent Mike Traynor. It had been the one thing he could think of that he could do to help Deni. To his amazement his father had listened to everything without too much judgment.

"She must be a special woman, to put you to so much trouble," his dad said now.

"She is." His heart felt a little too big for his chest as he said the words.

"But her father needs a criminal attorney. Are you sure this is a good idea, son?"

"He made some bad choices, but he's not a bad guy at all," Ryan said. "He was taken in by a really bad guy."

"Like someone else we know," his father said, but there was no rancor behind the words.

"I've been staying out of trouble," Ryan said. "I learned a hard lesson, but it stuck."

"I believe you. Tell me more about Deni."

"You'd really like her. She's a schoolteacher. A good one."

"Your mother and I would love to meet her sometime."

"I'd like that, too. Maybe you could come here. There's some fly fishing streams I'd like to show you." He and his dad hadn't been fishing together in years.

It was his dad's turn to be speechless. After a moment, he said, "Maybe I could do that. We'll plan on it."

They said goodbye, but Ryan didn't start the truck right away. His dad had texted contact information for a criminal lawyer he said was one of the best, and Ryan needed to get that name and number to Mike. Would they even let Ryan in to see him? Maybe he'd have to leave a message. He should go home and take a shower, and try to get some rest, though he still felt too wired to sleep.

He started the truck. He would head toward Eagle Mountain. By the time he got there, he would have come up with a plan.

Instead of heading to the sheriff's department, Ryan made his first stop at the office of the *Eagle Mountain Examiner.* Inside, he found reporter Tammy Patterson at her desk. She looked up, frowning, then her eyes widened. "Ryan Welch, what happened to you?"

He sat in the chair in front of her desk and leaned toward her, keeping his voice low, not wanting to be overheard by the account reps and other people in the office. "Do you want an exclusive on the dramatic events that led to the arrest of the man behind the bombings that have been terrorizing the town for the last month?"

Tammy grabbed a tape recorder from the in-box at the corner of the desk. "Are you kidding? I heard they arrested some guy from out of town, but the sheriff is, as usual, being really closed-mouthed about it."

"You need to talk to Deni Traynor," Ryan said.

"Deni was involved?"

"She's the whole reason they caught the guy. He shot her and her dad got hold of him and held him until the sheriff could subdue and arrest him. She's in the hospital in Junction, but if you go up there, I'm sure she'll see you." He would call Deni and point out how a positive story in the local paper could help locals see her and her dad in a new light.

"What about you?" Tammy asked. "Were you there?"

"I was there, so I can corroborate anything Deni says, but this is her story." He stood. "You call her."

"You bet I will."

As he walked away, Tammy already had her phone in hand.

At the sheriff's department, Deputy Jake Gwynn led

him downstairs, through two metal detectors to the only occupied cell in the local jail. "You have a visitor, Mike," Jake said.

Mike, dressed in plain khaki pants and shirt, stood at Ryan's approach. "Hey there," he said. "Ryan, isn't it? Have you seen Deni? Is she okay?"

"She's going to be fine. She had surgery to remove the bullet and put some pins in to stabilize some shattered bone. She's awake now and was asking about you."

"Tell her I love her. And I'm sorry. I'd give anything if none of this had happened."

"Don't worry about that now," Ryan said. "I have the name and number of a lawyer you need to call." He took out his phone and scrolled to the text his dad had sent.

"The county said they would appoint me an attorney."

"You need to call this guy. He's an expert criminal attorney out of Denver and he's agreed to defend you for a nominal fee."

Mike laughed. "And why would he do that?"

"Because he's a friend of my dad's. They went to law school together, I think. Anyway, you need to call him. For Deni's sake."

"Give the info to the deputy," Mike said. "I don't seem to have a pen on me."

Jake took the phone from Ryan. "Let me borrow this and I'll write everything down and make sure Mike gets it and makes the call."

He left them and Ryan turned to Mike. "How are you doing?" he asked.

"Better, now that I know Deni is going to be okay, and Al is locked far away from here. When I think of him shooting Deni, I see red." He shook his head. "What a mess."

"The sheriff seems pretty confident of his case,"

Ryan said. "And I guess there are federal charges against him, too."

"So where do you come in?" Mike said. "I never heard Deni mention you."

Ryan sucked in a deep breath. "I love your daughter," he said. "I'm planning on marrying her, if she'll have me."

"That's up to her, but I guess she could do worse." He looked Ryan up and down. "That was quick thinking, kicking Al like that. He didn't see it coming."

"There was no thinking involved," Ryan said. "It was like you said—when he shot Deni, I saw red."

"I guess that's something we have in common, then," Mike said.

Jake returned with the phone. "Here you go."

"I need to get home now," Ryan said. "Take care, Mike."

"You too, son."

Ryan walked out of the sheriff's department feeling drained. He figured he had just about enough left in him to make it back to his place before he crashed.

THE HEADLINE ON the next issue of the *Eagle Mountain Examiner* declared Father-Daughter Duo Bring Down Bomber in inch-high type across all columns. The issue appeared the day after Deni returned home. In her absence, friends had cleaned off the graffiti, and replaced it with a banner that welcomed her home.

"'Ms. Traynor had previously alerted the sheriff's office to her suspicions about Alex Coggins,'" Deni read as she sat on the sofa beside Ryan. "'Fearful for her father's safety, she and friend Ryan Welch tracked Mike Traynor to a yurt in the high country that Coggins had been using as a hideout. Coggins had kidnapped Mr.

Traynor and was keeping him prisoner in a tree house behind the yurt, where Ms. Traynor and Mr. Welch found him and freed him. As they were escaping, they were intercepted by Coggins. Coggins forced Mr. Traynor at gunpoint to tie up Ms. Traynor and Mr. Welch, then shot Ms. Traynor when Mr. Traynor refused to cooperate further. Mr. Traynor was able to subdue Coggins and hold him until the sheriff's department arrived.'"

She lowered the newspaper and looked at Ryan. "She makes us all sound like heroes."

"You are a hero." He put his arm around her. "You never gave up on your father. If you hadn't kept pushing, he wouldn't be alive today."

"And I wouldn't be alive if you hadn't kicked Al." She frowned at the paper. "Tammy left out that part."

"I don't need the glory—your father does."

"Maybe not now that you have that fancy criminal attorney defending him. Dad says they're working out a plea bargain. He's hoping for probation instead of prison time."

"And no more pranks involving bombs, unarmed or otherwise."

"He's learned his lesson—I'm certain of that." She tossed the paper aside and laid her head on his shoulder. "I'm never going to forget the terrible things that happened, but I'm ready to put them behind me."

"Me, too. I think it's a good time for all of us to make a fresh start." He shifted to face her and took her hand. "Xander accepted my offer to buy an interest in the company," he said. "And I'm signing up for business courses at the community college for next semester."

"You're going to be really busy, with a new business and school and search and rescue."

He blew out a breath. "I'm taking a leave from search

and rescue for a while. I probably should have done it before now. I need another surgery on my arm, and certainly I need more therapy."

"We can compare physical therapy notes," she said. She had already started rehabbing from the injury to her shoulder.

"I hope we can do more than that."

Something in his voice forced her attention back to him. "Deni, I love you," he said.

"I know that," she said. "Everything you've done has proved it. And I love you, too."

"Enough to marry me?"

She stared, unable to breathe, wondering if she had heard him correctly.

His face paled. "If it's too soon…"

"No. I mean, yes. Yes, I'll marry you. No, it isn't too soon." She reached her uninjured arm around him and hugged him close. "No way am I letting you get away now. I only wish I'd found the nerve to speak up at the coffee shop months ago. Then again, if you had known what you were in for, you might have run the other way."

"You don't see me running, do you? Except toward you."

He kissed her, and she kissed him back, until they lost track of time, and of everything but each other. As many regrets as Deni had about all that had happened, she could never be sorry that events had brought her and Ryan together. Out of all this pain had come something more wonderful than she ever could have imagined.

* * * * *

BRICKELL AVENUE AMBUSH

CARIDAD PIÑEIRO

Thank you to all my amazing friends at Liberty States Fiction Writers for their support and friendship. It's a pleasure to be able to attend workshops with you and share the trials and tribulations of being a writer, as well as the successes!

Chapter One

The executive's chair suited him well, Ricardo Gonzalez thought as his older brother, Trey, sat at the large wooden partner's desk. The built-ins behind the desk were empty, their content in boxes waiting to be unpacked and displayed on the shelves.

"The suit looks good on you, *mano*," he teased, aware that Trey usually reserved suits and ties for special occasions and funerals. That he was uncomfortable was evidenced by the way Trey slipped a finger beneath the collar of his shirt and tugged as if it was too tight.

"*Caray*, Ricky. When I said I'd join the agency, I didn't realize it meant signing up for this every day," Trey said and jerked at the collar again. He pulled open several drawers as if to check what was in them and where he might put his things.

Ricky laughed and sat on the edge of the desk. "You could always try to convince *papi* to go business casual."

Trey playfully pointed in his direction. "Now that sounds like a plan."

A plan. He wasn't sure his brother had a plan given his rather abrupt decision to join South Beach Security after years of fighting his family's wishes that he do so. But maybe nearly getting killed on his last assignment and finding the love of his life was reason enough. However, Ricky still worried about his brother's decision.

"You're sure you want to do this?" he asked, hoping Trey would be happy with his choice.

Trey narrowed his gaze, his aqua-colored eyes assessing. "Trying to psychoanalyze me, *hermanito*? I'm not one of your patients."

He wasn't, but that didn't mean that Ricky couldn't try to take care of him the way he helped his patients. After all, his brother had been through a traumatic experience recently and could possibly use his expertise.

"I know, but I'm here if you ever want to talk or need my help," he said.

Trey chuckled and shook his head. "You know what I could use help with?"

"What?" Ricky said with a smile.

Trey stood and gestured with his fingers in the direction of boxes and built-ins. "You can help me unpack."

"With pleasure," Ricky said and walked over to one of the containers. He hefted the heavy carton onto the wide ledge of the built-in and it landed with a loud thud from the weight of the contents.

"What do you have in here? Rocks?" he teased.

Trey laughed and shook his head. "Books. You more than most should appreciate that."

Ricky tilted his head in agreement. His older brother had always been an all-action guy while as the youngest he'd been the more studious type. Middle sister, Mia, and their cousin Carolina were the social butterflies in the family, which suited their roles as some of Miami's top social media influencers.

"I do appreciate that," Ricky said as he ripped open the box and emptied the assorted books onto the ledge. There were tomes on cybersecurity, forensic investigations, criminal and civil procedure and insurance fraud, as well as several on military history. No surprise on the latter since all the Gonzalez men, except for him, had served as marines.

While he loaded them onto one of the lower shelves in size, order, symmetry and balance—things Ricky needed in his life—he said, "How are the wedding plans going?"

Trey blew out a rough laugh as he unpacked yet more books from a carton. "Roni, her parents and *mami* are busy planning it like generals directing a military campaign."

Ricky glanced at his brother from the corner of his eye. "Maybe because no one ever expected you to finally settle down. Especially with Roni."

His brother paused his unpacking and a wistful smile slipped over his features. His blue-green gaze glittered with happiness. "Roni," he said with a loving sigh. "I can't believe I was so dense that I didn't see it. Didn't see *her* for so long."

But maybe Trey had seen her now because of the recent death and destruction in his life, which again made Ricky worry if it wasn't all too sudden. "She was always there, Trey. Why now?"

Trey plopped a book onto a shelf and faced him, arms across his broad chest. "Asking as my brother or are you in psychologist mode again?"

It was often hard to shut off his profession from the personal, as much as he tried. "Both, Trey," he finally admitted.

His brother stared at him for a long time, his gaze intense, before he said, "I can't deny it's sudden. But I know in here…" He stopped to tap at a spot above his heart. "I know it's the real thing. She makes me feel like no one ever did before."

Trey's words and their tone were so heartfelt any worries Ricky might have had dissipated like the steam coming off a hot Miami pavement after a summer rain. But they also roused an unwanted emotion in him. He wouldn't call it jealousy. Or loneliness. He didn't know what he'd call it; only as happy as he was for his brother, he was… unsure about his own life.

Ricky had been busy building his practice and support group, as well as helping his family at South Beach Security on occasion. It hadn't left much time for a personal life.

If his very alpha and extreme action brother could come around, he could definitely think about doing something different. Normally he didn't do different but maybe it was time to shake up his very boring and lonely life.

MARIELA HERNANDEZ DIDN'T like confrontation.

She'd had too much of it in her young life, especially during the five years of her tumultuous marriage. She'd hoped the divorce would put an end to that turmoil, but her ex-husband just refused to let go, constantly phoning her or visiting her against her wishes.

"I hope you understand we really can't have this happening here. Many of our women are still fragile because of the abuse they've suffered," her program director, Maggie, said, her voice filled with concern, but also compassion.

Maggie was a sixtysomething woman who could best be described as bohemian with her long, flowing floral tunics and earth-colored maxiskirts whose hems skimmed well-worn Birkenstocks. Her Earth Mother vibe was often a calming influence on the women staying in the halfway house and had soothed Mariela as well when she had first stayed there.

"I understand, Maggie. It won't happen again," she said, although she was unsure of whether or not she'd be able to keep that promise.

Maggie eyed her intently, clearly seeing past the words to what Mariela was thinking. "I know you mean that, only..." Her voice trailed off as Maggie opened her drawer, withdrew a business card and slid it across the surface of the scarred wooden desk.

"This is my good friend Elena Diaz-Gonzalez. She's an attorney who I think can help you. I know your ex-husband has money and is well-connected, but so is Elena. Go see her. Talk to her," Maggie stressed.

Mariela stared at the card but didn't reach for it immediately. She'd had enough of attorneys during her messy divorce proceedings. Even though she'd supposedly had a good one, she'd always gotten the sense that he'd been more interested in the hours on his timesheet than finalizing the divorce proceedings. But he had managed to get her a very favorable settlement that had made her new life possible.

If she could only get her ex to stop bothering her, she might actually be able to get on with her new life.

"Mariela?" Maggie pressed when she didn't take the card.

Knowing her program director wouldn't be appeased, she snatched the card off the desktop and tucked it into the back pocket of her jeans.

"I will call her. Thank you for the information," Mariela said as she stood and headed for the door. She would phone as promised, but not until she'd visited her ex and warned him one last time before she sicced another attorney on him. Especially since using an attorney would eat into the divorce settlement she'd received and which she needed to keep her parents in their assisted living facility as well as pay for her last two college semesters.

Determined to finish out her shift at the halfway house where she volunteered as a way of paying forward how they'd helped her, she returned to the day-care area where she often watched the younger children until their mothers came home from work. She loved spending time with the kids. Their joyful antics after surviving the abuse of their mothers gave her hope that she could one day be free of her nightmares as well.

The first of the moms returned and little by little the children filtered out of day care, heading to their private areas in the house as well as the common kitchen and living spaces.

She shot a quick glance at her watch. If she hurried, she might be able to catch her ex—Jorge—at his office where there would be other people around in case things went south.

Her car was in the shop for repairs, so she called a car service for the trip from the halfway house in Little Havana to the office building on Brickell Avenue where Jorge had his office. She hated doing that since being around unknown people, especially men, made her fearful, but it was too far to walk.

Barely ten minutes later, the driver dropped her off on Brickell and she hurried into the lobby of the office building where she badged herself through security. Her ex hadn't deactivated her card, clearly still in denial mode about the end of their marriage, which was why he continued to chase after her despite her many requests that he leave her alone.

There was no way she was going back to a marriage filled with both physical and emotional abuse. A marriage where she had lost herself and her dignity until she'd found the courage to stand up for herself.

Rushing off the elevator on his floor, she walked to the door of his company's business and was surprised to see that no one was at the reception desk. Even though it was just past five, Jorge often met with clients after hours and insisted on having someone in reception to greet them.

She entered the office to striking silence.

The office was totally empty, with none of the usual

collection of salespeople and project developers who used to fill the space when she and Jorge had been married.

Weird, she thought and forged ahead to Jorge's corner office. There was a small anteroom where her ex's administrative assistant normally sat, but as with the rest of the office, his assistant wasn't at her desk.

The door to Jorge's office was ajar and she went to enter, but heard him speaking, his voice agitated.

She snuck a peek and realized he was on his cell phone, pacing back and forth as he spoke to whoever was on the other end of the line.

"You don't understand. This project has to go forward," he said and raked his fingers through his thick, dark hair.

A pause followed his words and then he said, "I don't care how dangerous it is. Tell me how much you want."

How much you want? As in money? Mariela thought and stepped back so Jorge couldn't see her, but she continued to listen in, worried that something bad was going on.

"Are you crazy!" Jorge almost shouted into the phone.

A pause again, shorter as he jumped in with, "I know you're taking a big risk. So am I. You've made good money with me in the past—"

Apparently cut off by the other party, Jorge shut up and sighed. Peering through the crack of the doorframe and the edge of the door, she saw him standing there, his face mottled with rage. His hand fisted at his side. The tension in his body evident.

She recognized the stance well. It was how he would look before his rage exploded and he'd start whaling on her with his fists.

"No, you listen to me. You do this and you'll get your blood money," he yelled and swiped to end the call.

She muttered a curse and stepped back, afraid that Jorge would realize that she'd heard the conversation he obviously didn't want anyone to hear. That might explain why the office was empty.

Rushing back out of his anteroom, she hurried away and walked to the front door, trying to make it seem as if she had just come in.

Jorge marched out of his office, fists clenched at his sides and his face still tinged with the angry splotches of red and white. She noticed for the first time that there were strands of white salting his dark hair and he seemed thinner. He stopped short as he noticed her by the front door and relaxed his fists, but that was only a show.

Sauntering toward her, his gaze skipped over her face, as if trying to confirm she was really there. *Or possibly how long I've been here*, she worried.

"Mariela. What are you doing here?" he said as he stopped in front of her and continued his perusal.

She gestured toward the door. "I just came in," she said and nearly bit her lip at how defensive it sounded, as if she was desperate for him to think she hadn't been there long.

"Did you now?" he said and looked away from her down toward his office, his gaze narrowed. Assessing.

Trying to distract him, she gestured to the empty office. "Where is everyone?"

He grimaced, peered around the vacant office and said, "Things have been...slow."

"I'm sorry to hear that," she said truthfully, but not because she cared for Jorge. It was more about his staff, who had generally been a nice group of people and might be suffering from the downturn in the business.

He glanced at her again, gauging her sincerity and, seemingly satisfied, he said, "What can I do for you?"

"You can leave me alone, Jorge. I'm not coming back no matter how often you call or visit," she said and braced herself for the explosion that usually came when she asserted herself.

He clenched and unclenched his hands, and the color rose on his face once more, but to her surprise, he relaxed his hands again and sucked in a deep, controlling breath. "I'm a changed man, Mari. You have to believe that," he said and held his hands out in pleading.

Maybe he was. For now, she thought as she examined his features. He'd aged in the short year and change since she'd left him. Guilt slammed into her that she was maybe responsible for that until she reminded herself that he'd regularly made her feel guilty to justify why he punished her, either verbally or physically.

Grateful for that reminder, she told herself that she didn't care if he had somehow become a better man. She wasn't willing to take the risk to find out because whatever they'd once had was long gone.

"I'm sorry, Jorge, but what we had is over. You have to accept that because—"

"I can't accept that, Mari. What we had was special," he said and reached for her, but she jumped back, unable to stand his touch.

"I have to go. Please don't come again or I'll have no choice but to contact the authorities," she said and rushed out of his office before Jorge could say or do anything else.

As she waited for the elevator, she constantly checked over her shoulder, expecting him to rush out after her, to punish her, but he didn't.

Had he believed that I had only just arrived? That I didn't overhear his conversation? she wondered. And what would happen if he didn't? The phone call had seemed urgent and not entirely aboveboard.

She'd had her suspicions more than once that Jorge had pushed projects through in shady ways, but he'd always either smooth-talked away her concern or bullied past her misgivings. Because she'd never wanted to push and unleash the monster inside him, she'd let it go, telling herself that her survival outweighed what he was doing. Especially since nothing had ever happened over the years on any of his construction projects.

But this conversation had sounded like there was major trouble and danger. Too much for her to ignore, only…

As she stepped onto the elevator, she reached into her back jeans pocket, and removed the card Maggie had given her. *Elena Diaz-Gonzalez, Attorney at Law.*

The attorney's office was right nearby in another of the buildings on Brickell Avenue. She could walk the short distance to her office, but first she had to check out the attorney. As Maggie had said earlier, her ex-husband, Jorge, was wealthy and well-connected. Mariela needed to know Ms. Diaz-Gonzalez also had influential contacts in order to deal with whatever Jorge would do.

Whipping out her smartphone, she did an internet search on the lawyer and immediately found Diaz-Gonzalez's website and bio, but that was self-serving promotion. Digging deeper, she located several articles on high-profile cases the lawyer had won. She also discovered that Elena was related to the South Beach Security family. She recognized the Gonzalez family well and hadn't realized the attorney was connected to them. The family patriarch was the equivalent of a local hero to Miami Cubans since he'd been involved in the Bay of Pigs Invasion, and the family was a prominent one in Miami. Not to mention that SBS had recently been in the news because of a human trafficking ring they'd helped stop. But unfortunately, Elena was also the wife of Jose Gonzalez, who worked in the Miami District Attorney's office.

The same DA's office that had refused to charge Jorge when he'd beaten her so badly she'd had to be hospitalized.

That made her slow her headlong flight to Elena's nearby office. But as she walked, she considered what had happened at the halfway house earlier and what she'd just overheard in Jorge's office. They were both things she couldn't handle alone, and as Maggie had said, Ms. Diaz-Gonzalez might be someone who would have the connections to help.

Sucking in a deep breath, she pulled her shoulders back and dialed the law office hoping someone was still there even though it was after five.

When a receptionist cheerily answered, she said, "I'd like to make an appointment to see Ms. Diaz-Gonzalez. Tonight, if possible."

Chapter Two

Ricky sat on the couch in his aunt's office, sharing with her what he thought about the client she had sent him for a consult. "I think she's experienced abuse based on what we discussed. Her husband regularly bullied her verbally and made her beg for money and time away from the house. He normally only let her out to do household errands and insisted on tracking her every move. There are also her accounts of how her husband would physically attack her."

His aunt Elena nodded as she sat on the couch beside him. "We have a number of police reports about visits to the home. Neighbors called in because they were worried. She was also hospitalized a number of times because of his physical abuse."

"It sounds like you have enough to build a self defense argument against the murder charge," Ricky said, considering all the evidence his aunt had gathered.

"It does and I appreciate your help. Would you mind if I call in Dave Baker to confirm your analysis?" she asked.

He didn't mind at all. He'd only just finished getting his PhD and license while Baker was an experienced psychologist well-known for his handling of domestic abuse victims. "Baker is an excellent choice, *tia*. His opinion will carry a lot of weight with the court."

She leaned over and patted his knee. "Your opinion will

be helpful also, Ricky. I see how well you're doing with the members of your support group. In no time more people will be coming to you for help and for your opinion."

"I hope so," he said, but in the meantime, he was actively building his private practice, helping his aunt and the SBS when they needed it, as well as running his support group for people suffering from trauma.

His aunt's phone rang, and she reached over and picked up the extension sitting on a table beside the sofa.

"This young lady wants to see me tonight?" *Tia* Elena said and did a quick look at her watch. With a resigned sigh, she said, "If Maggie recommended her to me, I can't refuse. Please ask her to come over as soon as she can."

"Another late night, *tia*?" Ricky asked when his aunt hung up the phone.

"Sometimes it's unavoidable," she said, stood and held out her hand. "Thank you for helping me out."

He cupped her hand with both of his and squeezed tenderly. "Thank you for trusting me enough to give me the business. I truly appreciate it."

Tia Elena smiled indulgently. "The Gonzalez family sticks together."

"We do, but only if you think I can do the job," he said, not wanting the work if he wasn't up to it.

"Of course, Ricky. I wouldn't jeopardize my clients if I didn't think you could handle it," his aunt said and guided him toward the door to her office.

They exchanged a quick hug and a kiss on the cheek, and then he headed into the main space of the law firm where nearly a dozen attorneys and their staff worked on assorted cases.

As he neared the door, an extremely attractive young woman entered. Sun-streaked, caramel-colored hair fell in soft waves around her heart-shaped face, accenting stunning eyes of deep emerald. She was casually dressed in jeans that hugged nicely rounded hips and thighs, and a flowing tunic top that did nothing to hide her voluptuous breasts.

His gut tightened in appreciation of her natural beauty, but he reminded himself that if this was the young woman who had just called for an appointment, she was likely a survivor of domestic abuse if Maggie Alonso had given her his aunt's number.

Because of that, he gave her plenty of space as she hurried in, a wary look on her face as she saw him by the door. She was clearly leery of men, and it saddened him that she had experienced so much pain at such a young age. By his guesstimate, she couldn't be more than thirty, but then again, abuse knew no age limits.

"Mariela Hernandez," she said to the receptionist and shot a quick, suspicious look over her shoulder at him as he lingered by the entrance.

He raised his hands as if to say *We're cool* and hurried out the door, his one hope that his aunt would be able to help her.

WAY TO GO, MARI. You just chased off that poor man, her inner voice chastised, and quickly added, *And a very handsome one at that.*

Jorge is handsome, too, she reminded herself and shot another quick look over her shoulder to make sure the man had gone.

He had. She released a pent-up breath as a young woman walked up to the receptionist's desk.

"Ms. Hernandez? I'm Chelly, Ms. Diaz-Gonzalez's assistant. Would you follow me, please?" she said and gestured for her to walk down the hall. The young woman's pace was sedate and measured as they went to a large corner office at the far side of the floor.

Chelly motioned for Mariela to enter, and she did, taking a hesitant step while wringing her hands with worry.

An older woman who some might call handsome rose and held her hand out in welcome. She had dark mahogany hair with a few strands of gray, cut in a bob that accented her strong jaw. Chocolate brown eyes were filled with concern and seemed at odds with the very business-like black suit she wore.

"Please come in, Mariela. May I call you Mariela?"

"Yes, of course," she said, walked in and perched herself on the edge of a chair, prepared to run away if things got too intense.

With an elegant wave of her hand, the woman said, "I'm Elena. I understand Maggie Alonso recommended me."

Mariela nodded. "She did. I volunteer at her halfway house."

Elena leaned back in her chair and peered at her with her sharp, brown-eyed gaze. "Maggie's a good friend. I admire what she's done to help so many with her nonprofit."

Mariela admired her as well and had been the recipient of Maggie's help in the first few weeks after she'd made the decision to divorce her husband and fled her home to escape his abuse.

"She's helped many women...women like me. When I left my husband, I didn't know what to do or where to go and Maggie took me in," Mariela said and laid a hand on her chest in emphasis.

Elena nodded and dipped her head with understanding. "Is that why you're here? Are you still having issues with your husband?"

Mariela hesitated, uncertainty about Elena's husband driving her doubts. Which was why she didn't share the main reason that had pushed her to reach out to the attorney.

"My ex...he abused me. Physically and emotionally. We divorced a little over a year ago," she said, her speech halting as emotion nearly choked her throat tight. She pushed on to finish with, "He won't stop coming around. He thinks we can reconcile and stay together."

Elena shot away from her desk and came around to sit in the cushioned chair next to Mariela. She laid a comforting hand on Mariela's thigh. "Are you concerned he'll hurt you?"

Mariela had often worried that Jorge would grow violent with Maggie or anyone who got in his way. After what had happened barely an hour earlier when she'd been in his office, Mariela also worried that he'd kill her if he thought she'd overheard his conversation.

Shakily, she nodded and said, "Yes. Either me or anyone who helps me."

With another stroke and a pat of Mariela's knee, Elena said, "We won't let that happen." She paused for a long second and said, "Is there anything else you're worried about?"

Her mother had said that she always knew everything Mariela was thinking just from a look at her face. She wondered if Elena had that same gift and had seen that she was keeping something secret. Trying to guard against that, she looked away as she said, "No. *Nada.*"

Another protracted pause followed until Elena finally said, "We will help you, Mariela."

"We?" she croaked, confused by who else would be helping.

"Yes, we. My legal team and I will begin drafting a restraining order against your ex-husband. But we both know they're sometimes not worth the paper they're printed on, so I may call in members of SBS if I feel you're in danger."

"South Beach Security? I'm not sure I can afford them," she said, fear shooting through her at how much this all might cost. SBS usually protected the rich and famous and she was neither. Whatever money she had saved was earmarked for her dreams and taking care of her parents.

"Don't worry about the cost. South Beach Security is family and now you're family as well," Elena said, reassuring her until she continued. "There's just one thing."

Mariela clasped her hands tightly together, her palms wet with the sweat of fear. Elena reached out and covered her hands with hers. "Relax, Mariela. I think that it might be good for you to talk to someone about what you've experienced. It could help you deal with the trauma and any fears you must have. If there's anything else that's worrying you, sharing might ease your concerns."

Maggie had suggested the same thing more than once, but Mariela had always resisted, being a very private person. But as she met Elena's determined gaze, it was clear that refusing that request might not be an option. Plus, maybe it was time she shared her fears and shed the weight of them that dragged on her every day of her life. Not to mention possibly sharing what she'd just overheard about Jorge's business dealings with the proper authorities.

"I'll think about talking to someone," she said.

"Good," Elena replied, hopped out of her chair and returned to her side of the desk. She picked up her phone, dialed and a few seconds later she said, "Ricky. Are you still at the office?"

A short pause came before she said, "Yes, of course. I forgot tonight was your support group. Would you mind if someone new joined you today?"

Elena eyed Mariela with determination, and for a moment, Mariela felt like her life was spinning out of control again. But she told herself Elena was only trying to help and not just bully her.

"*Gracias.* I'll send her down in a few minutes." When she hung up, she continued to peer at Mariela, her gaze assessing. "I suspect you feel as if I'm being pushy."

It was apparently impossible to hide anything from the sharp-eyed attorney. "I do. Jorge—my ex—used to decide things 'for my own good' as well," she said, emphasizing the words with air quotes.

Elena nodded sharply. "I appreciate you being honest with me. I leave it up to you whether or not you go to Ricky's support group, but I think sharing with others might be a good way for you to get started on your healing."

Healing. A funny word to use, but maybe the right one. She may have escaped Jorge's abuse, but inside she was often that scared woman waiting for the next blow to come. Much like she had been at the front door when the handsome man had walked by. She'd braced herself, fearful as she often was among strangers. It made the simplest things scary, like her earlier ride with the car service. She'd been apprehensive the entire time she'd been in the vehicle.

It was no way to live and maybe Elena was right that it was time to heal emotionally as well.

"*Gracias.* I will go to… Ricky, was it?" she asked.

Elena reached to a business card holder on her desk, grabbed a card and handed it to her. "Ricardo Gonzalez. He's a psychologist and his office is just a few floors down."

Another Gonzalez family member, she thought. It occurred to her then that this was possibly the SBS office building given how many Gonzalez family members had their offices here. They were a family that stuck together, something she hadn't really experienced in her life. When she'd told her parents about the abuse and her intention to ask for a divorce, they'd worried more about losing the lifestyle they'd gained as Jorge's in-laws than about Mariela's safety and happiness.

"What else do you need from me?" Mariela asked.

"We'll need your permission to obtain any police or hospital records so we can build our case to ask for the restraining order. If you don't mind coming back in the morning, we'll draft all the paperwork tonight so you can sign off."

Mariela nodded. "I assume you'll need a retainer of some kind."

Elena waved her off. "We'll have an engagement letter for you in the morning, but don't worry about the money, Mariela. You're one of Maggie's women and we'll take care of you."

"*Gracias.* I genuinely appreciate that," she said and surged to her feet.

Elena likewise stood and shook Mariela's hand. "Don't worry about anything," she repeated.

With a nod, Mariela hurried from the office and to the elevator bank. When the elevator arrived, she hopped on for the short ride down a few floors. *Before Jorge* she would have taken the stairs to get in her steps, but *After Jorge* things like stairwells and even elevators sometimes freaked her out. Mostly because she felt like she couldn't escape them.

She counted numbers in her head as the elevator dropped, a coping mechanism that she'd found helped dampen her fear.

She'd barely reached ten when the elevator stopped.

Walking off, she searched for a sign designating the numbers on the floor and hurried toward the psychologist's office. She hesitated at the door, bracing herself for what waited for her inside, but then grabbed the knob and pushed through.

There were five people in the office, sitting around the reception area in comfy-looking sofas and chairs. It surprised her to see a man there, but then again, domestic violence wasn't limited to women.

A second later another man walked out of a door at the far end of the space.

The handsome man from earlier that night, she realized.

She muttered a curse and was about to turn around and leave when he called out, "Welcome, Mariela. We're very happy to have you here."

Chapter Three

She was going to bolt. Ricky was sure of that as the young woman took a hesitant step back, but at his welcome she stopped short and wrapped her arms around herself. He recognized the defensive gesture as well as the look of almost dread on her beautiful face.

"Please join us," he said, his tone calm, and gestured for her to take a seat, hoping she wouldn't run out.

She hesitated, but then with a stutter-step, she slowly walked to a wing chair and perched on the edge of it as if she would dash away at any moment. But then again, there were others in his group who had also started off like that. Wary. Distrustful.

To ease into that night's meeting, he sat in a chair next to another of the support group members and opposite Mariela and said, "How is everyone today?"

A murmur of responses greeted him and he eased his group into sharing how their days were going and what might be bothering them or what might be going well. Little by little the tension lessened for many of the group members, but not for Mariela, who still sat there anxiously, her body wound as tight as a violin string.

He didn't press. The release of the strain had to come naturally and only when she was ready. Too many abused women had lacked control in their lives, and it was important for her to be able to regain control again.

As the hour wore on, the others in the group shared some of what had happened to them in their daily lives and how they were coping. Or not. One of the younger women in their group, someone close in age to Mariela, explained how she had worked up the courage to leave her abusive husband. Much like he suspected Mariela had done.

With that young woman's story, he finally noticed a slight relaxation in Mariela's shoulders. He hoped that the release would continue, but Mariela's arms were still tightly wrapped around her body as if they were the only thing keeping her together. When it came time for Mariela to share, her gaze flitted around nervously and she sucked in a deep breath and held it before she blurted out, "My husband abused me, and I divorced him. He still won't let me be, but I'm not going to let him do that. I won't let him control me."

Determination filled her words, which earned commiseration and praise from the others in the group. But he sensed there were more secrets buried behind her pained gaze. More than what she had just shared.

"That's a difficult thing to do," he said, hoping she would continue the discussion and reveal whatever she was keeping private.

"It was," she said, but closed herself off again.

He didn't press even though he wanted to know more and not just on a professional level. Something about her had called his attention to her in his aunt's office. He had to admit it had been the physical at first. She was a beautiful woman. But as she'd sat there tonight, something else had intrigued him. Bothered him as well. She may have escaped her husband, but she was still hiding something. Still hurting.

Aware she wouldn't continue to share, he pressed on

with the support group meeting, finishing with the last member who wasn't much more open than Mariela despite months with the group. Like Mariela, he hoped that the older woman would one day find relief from the memories that plagued her.

With their time virtually over, he ended the session. "It's almost time for when we said we'd stop, and I know you all probably want to go home because it's late. But before we go, are there any last thoughts you want to share?"

He smiled and peered around the room, but no one had anything to add. "I'm glad you all came tonight. I think we discussed some important things and I hope you'll come back next month on the 16th. Same time if that's okay with all of you."

When they all nodded, except Mariela, he stood and waited for his support group to disband. Some liked to thank him while others, still traumatized by their pasts, kept to themselves. Much like Mariela as she ducked out after a murmured, "Good night."

After the rest of the group filed out of his office, he took a moment to jot down some notes about what had been discussed by the various members.

Satisfied he had captured the key details, he closed his journal, grabbed his keys from his desk drawer and hurried out of his office and down to street level. He wanted to grab some takeout from the Cuban restaurant on the corner before he went home.

As he exited the building, he noticed Mariela standing by the curb. Since it was late and most of the business crowd in the area had gone, making the street a little empty, he walked over to make sure she was okay.

"Waiting for a ride?" he asked, and she jumped, startled, when he came up to her.

"Y-yes," she stammered, glanced at her smartphone and grimaced. "They canceled my ride."

"If you're okay with it, I can drive you home," he said and held up his keys.

"I don't want to put you out," she said and peered down at the ground, avoiding his gaze.

"It's not a problem, but if you don't want to, at least let me keep you company while you wait for another ride." She'd probably had little say about what she could do in her marital relationship, and he wouldn't do the same with her.

She nodded and fiddled with her phone again, probably placing a new request for a ride, but then she shook her head and her lips tightened in disgust. Glancing up at him, she said, "I'm having trouble getting a car. Peak hours and it's too short a ride apparently."

He held his keys up again and she took the hint. "Are you sure it's not a problem? My house is in Little Havana."

"Not a problem at all. I have to head that way to go to my place," he said and, with a sweep of his hand, pointed her in the general direction of his car. He'd pick up some food once he got closer to home.

"*Gracias.* That's very nice of you," she said. They walked together, but not really together since they were a foot apart. His Audi A4 was in the parking lot beneath his family's building.

He tapped the fob to unlock the car and walked over to open the door for her. She slipped inside and he hurried to the driver's side and got in. "What's the address?" he asked.

After she gave it, he headed down Brickell Avenue to Southwest Eighth Avenue and her home, which was located not far from some of his favorite restaurants in Little Havana. He'd pop by one on the way home to pick up dinner.

Mariela was silent during the short ten-minute drive from his family's office building to her home. He pulled up in front of the small cinder-block home just a few houses away from *Calle Ocho*. It was well-kept with a manicured front lawn, low-lying beds of colorful flowers and crotons, with taller palm trees here and there.

"Very nice," he said, but she quickly offered up a terse explanation.

"It's my parents' home. I'm trying to save my money so I can finish college and help them," she explained, obviously worried that he might think badly of her family's home.

"It's very pretty. Do you do the gardening yourself?" he asked, hoping to get her to relax and open up more about her life.

A big unrestrained smile erupted on her face. "I do. I love the colors and feeling my fingers in the dirt."

"My *abuelo* is the same way. He's 87, but he can't keep his hands out of the soil," he said, smiling as he thought about his grandfather and the remarkable gardens he had at his home.

"He sounds amazing," she said with the first hint of a smile.

"He is. Let me walk you to your door," Ricky said and rushed out of the car. He wanted to be sure she got into her home safely. It was late and the area could be iffy at times.

"You don't have to do that," she said when he opened her door and offered her a hand to help her out of the car and onto the sidewalk.

"It's not a problem," Ricky insisted, released her hand and strolled with her to the front door. He glanced around, looking for signs of any kind of security precautions, but there were none, not even one of those simple video doorbells. Because of that, he waited as she unlocked the door and stepped inside.

The screen door closed behind her, but she turned to offer him a hesitant smile. *"Gracias,"* she said again, her face shadowed by the screen.

"*Buenas noches*, Mariela. I hope to see you again soon," Ricky said with a smile, hoping to build trust with her.

"*Buenas noches*," she said with a determined nod and closed the front door.

He started the walk back to his car, but suddenly heard something that sounded like a scream. A loud crash echoed from inside her home. The front door shook, as if hit by something. Maybe a body being slammed against it.

Ricky didn't hesitate.

He ran to the screen door and opened it. Grabbed the handle of the front door. Locked. Shouldering the door, he gave a hard shove but it held fast. He stepped back and rammed it with his shoulder, using all his strength, and it broke open, slamming against a far wall.

Glass shattered from somewhere inside the home and Mariela screamed again.

Ricky rushed deeper into her home and braced himself for an attack.

MARIELA STRUGGLED AGAINST the masked man who had assaulted her as soon as she had closed the door.

He had an arm wrapped around her waist and his gloved hand covered her mouth, muffling her screams and cutting off her air until black circles danced in her vision.

At the crash of someone breaking down the front door, the man reacted, loosening his grip slightly, and she bit down hard on his hand. The leather kept her from breaking skin, but her vicious bite made the man yelp and loosen his hold enough that she could elbow him in the stomach.

He let out a rough "Oomph" at the blow and released her. She rushed toward the front door and hopefully safety, but the man was on her again, tackling her to the ground. The weight of his body drove the air from her lungs, but a second later that weight lifted off her.

Rolling onto her side, she saw Ricky Gonzalez tossing

the masked man away from her. The man stumbled back, but then regained his footing and whirled to attack again.

Ricky faced him, standing between her and her attacker. Protecting her with his body.

The man rushed at Ricky, throwing punch after punch as he tried to reach Mariela. The blows landed with sickening thuds against Ricky's face, arms and occasionally his midsection.

Ricky took the brunt of the violence, defending against the wild, almost haymaker punches of her attacker. But when their assailant paused, Ricky fought back with almost surgical precision, landing a sharp blow to the man's face that snapped the man's head back. The man reeled from the jab, but then struck out again.

Mariela screamed, "I'm calling the police."

She dialed 911 but the attack didn't stop. Ricky blocked blow after blow until the assailant gave him an opening and Ricky once again struck out, punching the other man and driving him back. That gave Ricky the space to execute a roundhouse kick that sent the man reeling across the room. The man stood unsteadily and raised his fists to fight again until the sound of sirens coming closer made her attacker stop short.

Before either Ricky or she could react, the man raced toward the back of the home and disappeared through the open sliding glass doors into her backyard.

Ricky came to her side, his face bloodied. His one eye swelling shut from the masked man's blows.

"Are you okay?" he asked, apparently unconcerned about his own injuries.

"I am," she said, but suddenly her knees felt weak. She swayed, struggling to stay upright.

Ricky slipped an arm around her waist and helped her to a sofa. A second later two armed police officers rushed through the door, guns pointed and yelling, "Police." But as they saw Ricky and her sitting on the sofa, they lowered their weapons.

Ricky motioned toward the sliders and said, "He ran out the back."

One officer raced in that direction while the other holstered his gun and walked over to them. "Are you hurt?"

Mariela shook her head and glanced at Ricky, who said, "I'm fine. I need to make a call."

As Ricky walked off, the officer pulled out a pad and started asking Mariela questions about what had happened.

She answered as best she could, trying to remember everything from the moment the man had grabbed her when she'd walked in, to when Ricky had burst in to protect her.

It seemed like long minutes passed as she talked to the officer and the second policeman returned with Ricky and another man who looked so much like Ricky they had to be brothers. They had the same dark wavy hair, light eyes, straight noses and dimpled chins. But this man's body had heavier muscle, unlike Ricky's lean, almost elegant, build.

The man walked over and the police officer, who had been sitting in a nearby chair, popped to his feet. "Detective Gonzalez," he said, admiration obvious in his voice.

Ricky's brother smiled and clapped the officer on the back. "Just Trey Gonzalez now, Officer Walsh. I retired from the force last month."

Trey walked over to her, smiled and offered his hand in greeting. "I'm Ricky's older brother, Trey."

She hesitantly shook his hand. "Mariela Hernandez."

"Nice to meet you, Mariela. I'm not sure Officer Walsh has explained yet—"

"I haven't had a chance," the officer jumped in to confirm.

Trey nodded and continued. "This is a crime scene now, which means you won't be able to stay here for a few days. If you can pack up some things—"

"But where will I go?" she said, worried about not only the money if she had to stay in a hotel, but whether Jorge would come after her again. She had no doubt that Jorge had sent the man who had attacked her. And she had no doubt that if it hadn't been for Ricky, she'd be dead.

Ricky came over then, his one eye even more swollen than before. He sat on the coffee table in front of the sofa and said, "You're coming with us. We'll make sure you're safe."

Safe. It had been so long since she'd felt safe, but as she scrutinized Trey and Ricky, she realized that if anyone could keep her physically safe, it was these two men.

But she worried that Ricky presented a different danger. In the brief time she'd known him, there was something about him that fascinated her. That threatened her on another level, but she had no choice.

Her ex wouldn't stop until she was dead, but worse than that, if he succeeded with his plan, others might die also. She had no doubt about that after the conversation she'd heard earlier that night.

She couldn't let that happen.

Chapter Four

Ricky sat in the back seat beside Mariela as Trey drove to the South Beach Security building. His body was a little sore from the attack but he hadn't felt the need for a hospital visit and an ice pack had helped ease most of the swelling around his eye. Still, a deadly silence filled the air and tension radiated from every line of Mariela's body.

She had her arms wrapped around herself tightly as if to hold herself together. Her body trembled violently, and as much as he wanted to comfort her, he suspected she wouldn't welcome his touch at the moment.

Ricky understood how she was feeling. He felt much the same way. Although his father had insisted that Trey, his sister, Mia, and he all take marital arts lessons to be able to defend themselves, he had never imagined that he'd actually have to use those skills. But he'd been able to keep Mariela's attacker at bay, even if his body and face were now suffering a little from the blows the masked man had landed.

At the building, Trey pulled into one of their reserved spots in the parking lot and hurried to help Mariela out of the car, but she shied away from his touch, obviously still traumatized. Trey understood and stepped away so she could exit the car, but he remained close by both of them, seemingly vigilant for any signs of danger.

Ricky shot him a puzzled look and Trey said, "I wanted to make sure no one followed us."

That hadn't occurred to him, making him feel a little foolish, but then again, attempted murder and mayhem weren't usually his thing. It made him wonder what he'd gotten himself into, but as he glanced at Mariela's pale and strained face, he realized he'd had no choice.

He couldn't let Mariela deal with this danger on her own.

Mindful of her mental state, he barely rested his hand at her back to guide her inside and to the elevator. At his whisper touch on her back, she jumped and glanced at him, but then relaxed a bit and offered him a tentative smile.

That smile did something weird to his insides, like ice cream melting on a scorching hot Miami day. It made him feel all soft inside.

He smiled back to reassure her as they stepped into the elevator and Trey keyed open the penthouse suite floor, which was normally only used for guests, family who worked very late and situations where they had people they had to protect since the floor was as secure as Fort Knox.

Once they were in the penthouse suite, Ricky gestured for Mariela to make herself comfortable on the sofa. As she did so, Trey stepped to one side of the room, probably to round up the rest of the team members of South Beach Security.

"How are you feeling?" Ricky asked and sat across from Mariela on the coffee table.

Mariela met his gaze but darted it nervously to Trey, who had gone over to the kitchen area in the suite.

"Mariela?" he said softly, drawing her attention back to him.

"I'm…scared. Worried," she finally admitted and ran her hands up and down her arms, as if she were cold.

Trey strolled over with a tray with three glasses of

Scotch and an ice pack. He set the tray on the coffee table beside Ricky, handed him the ice pack and said, "Get that on your eye. It's swelling again and looks pretty bad."

"You should see the other guy," Ricky teased, trying to lighten the almost funereal mood. He applied the ice pack to his face, wincing at the cold and the tenderness of his cheekbone and brow.

"I wish I could. Did either of you notice anything about your attacker?" Trey asked, clearly in cop mode.

Mariela shook her head and Ricky said, "Nothing, really. About my height. Six-foot. Strong. White. I could see the area around his eyes. Hazel, I think." He circled a finger around that area on his face to show Trey how much had been visible beneath the mask.

Trey nodded, picked up a glass and handed it to Mariela. She accepted it with a shaky hand and took a tentative sip, grimacing at the strong taste of the liquor.

"Do you think your ex-husband sent this man?" Ricky asked, even though he was certain that her ex had. *But had it been to scare her into going back to him or to kill her because she'd refused him?* he wondered.

Mariela's gaze flitted from him to Trey. She took another sip, grimaced again and in a quavery voice she said, "I do."

But then she said nothing else, prompting Trey to say, "Because of your divorce?"

The ice rattled in the glass as Mariela's hands trembled violently. She avoided their gaze and in hushed tones said, "No. Because I overheard something in his office that I shouldn't have."

Ricky shared a shocked look with Trey, who continued to press. "What did you overhear?"

Her gaze locked with his and he sensed she was almost asking forgiveness, which made him reach out and lay his hand over hers. She didn't flinch or pull away, but it was impossible to miss the chill on her skin and the quiver of her muscles.

"Mariela. What did you overhear?" Ricky pressed, sure that this was what she had been keeping from him earlier.

"I'm sorry, Ricky. I never meant to bring danger to you or anyone in your family," she said, and tears leaked from her eyes and rolled down her face. She swiped at them and continued with her story. "Jorge, my ex, refused to believe our marriage was over. He kept on calling and texting me and then he came by the halfway house. It scared some of the women there."

"That's why you went to see our *tia* Elena?" Ricky said, his tone soothing and meant to encourage her to share what she had kept secret.

Mariela shook her head, surprising both him and Trey, and then she continued. "I went to see Jorge to try and talk some sense into him. But things were weird in his office. No one was there, which was unusual. When I went to Jorge's private office, I heard him talking to someone on the phone. Yelling at times because he was upset about what the other person wanted."

Trey slipped into the discussion and said, "What did that person want?"

Mariela shook her head, shrugged and took another sip of the Scotch. "If I had to guess, money. Jorge was paying them off for something. Something big."

"Something illegal?" Ricky pressed, surprised that Mariela had kept something like that from him and his aunt, but then again, maybe she hadn't felt comfortable enough to trust them with that kind of information.

MARIELA'S GUILT AT hiding her true reason had been weighing on her and she finally knew sharing it was the best thing for everyone involved. "I think so. I had worries about some of Jorge's other dealings, but he always had an excuse or made me feel like I was crazy or bullied me to stop asking. He also normally didn't involve me in his business like that."

"How did he involve you?" Trey asked, obviously wanting to get the whole picture of what the Gonzalez family had become pulled into.

Mariela shrugged and explained her role in her ex's company. "I did all the social events. I planned the parties and made sure Jorge's connections were treated right. I helped him build his network of possible investors for his various projects."

"But you had no idea of his day-to-day business dealings or projects?" Ricky asked.

She shook her head. "Not really. I mean, I knew when he was putting together another real estate deal or building a development because I had to plan the events, but nothing else. But like I said, I got the sense something wasn't right about some of them."

Trey looked at his brother and then jerked his head toward the far side of the room. Both men rose, walked away and spoke in hushed tones, glancing at her occasionally.

It struck her once again how similar and yet different they were. Both handsome, only Trey was dark and stormy while Ricky was all brightness and light. And it was clear that darkness and light were having a major battle.

When they returned, Ricky once again sat in front of her while Trey finally took a seat at the far end of the sofa, his sea-green eyes blazing with irritation.

"Is there anything else you need to tell us?" Ricky said, his tone encouraging her to share. His gaze compassionate, in total contrast to his brother's angry look.

"Jorge said it was dangerous, and he said he'd paid this person in the past. I think it has to do with one of his new developments and I worry that people might die if we don't stop him," Mariela admitted.

"We?" Trey said with the arch of a dark brow.

Guilt slammed into her again. She'd drawn them into this trouble and understood Trey's upset.

"I didn't share this with your aunt because I didn't know if I could trust her," Mariela confessed.

"You didn't think you could trust her? But you still went to her anyway?" Trey accused, his anger clearly escalating.

"Chill, Trey," Ricky said and laid a reassuring hand on her knee. "If you didn't trust *Tia* Elena, why did you go to her?"

She glanced from Ricky to Trey and then back to Ricky. "Because I had no one else I could trust. Nowhere else I could go."

Chapter Five

Ricky's heart hurt for her, but that still didn't change the fact that his family and he were now involved and in possible danger.

"You can trust us, and you can stay here until we figure out what's going on," he said.

Mariela shot a hesitant glance at Trey, who reluctantly nodded to confirm what Ricky had said. "We will help you, but you need to share everything with us, including why you don't trust our aunt."

"Your aunt's husband—"

"*Tio* Jose?" Ricky said, confused about why she'd know him.

Mariela nodded. "Jorge beat me up pretty badly one time. Broken ribs and wrist. He punched me so hard he knocked me out. One of the neighbors heard me screaming for him to stop and called the police. When they arrived and saw my condition, they took me to the hospital and arrested Jorge, but the DA's office refused to charge him."

"The DA's office where *Tio* Jose works," Trey said, connecting the dots in her story, and continued. "There are lots of reasons why they wouldn't prosecute, mainly if you wouldn't testify."

Mariela did a little dip of her head. "I was afraid about testifying, but I got the sense that Jorge's attorneys convinced the DA that it had been the first time and that he'd go to counseling."

"Did he?" Ricky interjected.

"He went a couple of times, but I also wondered if Jorge bought his way out of it, both at the DA's and with the psychologist, since he stopped going to the sessions."

"And you think your ex also paid off people in some of his business dealings?" Ricky pressed, wanting to understand her mindset and how that was going to impact how his family could help her.

"I do. I'm worried about what I overheard. That people could be killed," Mariela said and took another sip of her Scotch.

Ricky peered at Trey and his brother's concern and anger were obvious. Despite that, his brother nodded to confirm that South Beach Security would help find out what was happening. Because of that, Ricky said, "We will help, Mariela. Let me get you settled and then Trey and I can discuss what to do next and order up some food. I don't know about you, but I'm a little hungry."

Maybe sitting around the table sharing a meal would help her relax some more and also help her grow comfortable enough to be totally honest with them.

Mariela shot to her feet, grabbed her bag and followed Ricky to one of the bedrooms in the penthouse suite.

"Feel free to put your things in here. There's a bathroom at the far end and it should be stocked with toiletries," Ricky said.

"Gracias," Mariela said and entered the bedroom while Ricky returned to his brother's side, losing some of his earlier confidence.

"You okay?" Trey asked, his gaze inquiring.

Ricky let out a rough laugh. "I think that's normally my line."

Trey chuckled and nodded. "Yeah, I think it is. So are you? Okay?"

Ricky blew out a slow breath and shook his head, which only made it hurt from where the attacker had hit him. Wincing, he said, "This isn't normally my thing, Trey. You're the hero type, not me."

With a dip of his head, his brother said, "You probably saved her life today. Seems to me that's kind of heroic."

"I had no choice," he said with unexpected anger, surprising himself and Trey.

"You have a right to be angry. You could have been killed and now our family may be in danger as well, but we have no choice but to investigate."

Ricky nodded. "You going to call everybody in?"

"I'll call *papi* and let him know what's happening. Tonight, you can use some clothes I left in the main bedroom in case I was working late. I'll round up everyone in the morning and call you so you can come down to the office to begin our investigation," Trey advised.

"Thanks, I appreciate that. I'll order in some food—"

Trey raised his hand to stop him. "None for me, thanks. Roni is off tonight and has been holding dinner for me."

"Okay. Have a good night and thanks for everything," he said and bro-hugged Trey.

Trey returned the embrace heartily, making Ricky's body ache from the blows the attacker had landed. He was sure he'd have a gallery of colorful bruises all along his midsection and face come morning.

After he pulled away, his brother pointed at his eye and said, "Put the ice back on that. You know *mami* is going to freak when she sees that shiner."

Ricky escorted his brother to the elevator bank and said, "It's not like she hasn't seen one on you more than once."

Trey laughed and shook his head. "But I'm not her Little Ricky."

He wasn't sure he was that Little Ricky anymore either. The bookworm had been tested tonight and had somehow managed to survive.

"See you in the morning," Ricky said and heard a foot-fall behind him as Trey entered the elevator.

Mariela had come out of the bedroom wearing loose-fitting fleece. Her arms were wrapped tight around her body again and she had a fearful look on her face.

"You're okay here. No one can come up without the key card and there's 24-hour security in the building lobby," he said to reassure her.

"I know. It's just that… This place reminds me of Jorge's Indian Creek house."

Ricky glanced around the room. It was elegantly done in a modern minimalist style that said money and luxury. He could picture the expensive furnishings in a pricey Indian Creek location. He also found it revealing that she called it Jorge's house and not her home.

"I get that it makes you feel uncomfortable. We can see about staying somewhere else in the morning," he said, thinking that his home might not be secure enough. But his family's home was on Palm Island, which was a gated community, providing the security they might need.

"*Gracias.* I'd appreciate that," she said and visibly re-laxed.

"Great. Let's get some food. I was going to order from the Cuban restaurant on the corner if that's okay," he said, mindful to include her in the decision because she'd likely had little say in things during her abusive marriage.

She nodded and smiled. "I'd like that."

He pulled up a menu on his phone and they decided on what to eat. He placed the order and got some sodas out of the fridge they kept stocked for whoever was staying in the suite. While they waited for the food delivery, they chatted.

"You mentioned you were going back to school. What's your major?" Ricky asked.

Mariela hesitated as she set a fork on a napkin. "I had been premed, but I dropped out after I married Jorge. Now that I'm enrolled again, I decided to go into marketing. I did so much of it anyway for Jorge's business and I have the connections that might help me get a good-paying job."

Money being important apparently despite her divorce settlement. It made him recall her earlier comments about her parents. "You help your mom and dad, right?"

Her hand shook again as she finished setting the cutlery on the table. "I do. They're in an assisted living facility. Their health has declined in the last few years."

Something about the way she said it made him say, "That's a big responsibility."

A careless shrug was her answer. He didn't get to question her about it more since the lobby called to announce that their order had arrived.

"I'll be right back," he said and walked to the elevator to head to the lobby to get the delivery.

MARIELA HAD NO doubt that Ricky had picked up on her ambivalence about her parents. His training as a psychologist would assist him in seeing what she wasn't saying. But what she was feeling about her parents and how they'd made her feel in return was something she didn't want to discuss because it was too hurtful. After all, how was she supposed to feel about parents who'd been willing to keep her in an abusive relationship so they'd be taken care of?

She drove those thoughts out of her mind, hoping to keep them away from Ricky's keen eyes.

When he returned a few minutes later, she forced a smile to her face as he walked to the table with their order.

"It smells delicious," she said, hoping to keep the discussion from anything too personal.

Ricky lifted an eyebrow in question, clearly aware of what she was doing, but played along with it.

"It's a great restaurant. I often pick up a meal there on my way home," he said and laid the take-out containers on the table.

"I guess you don't like to cook?" she said and removed the cover from an order of rice.

Ricky shook his head. "I love to cook, but it seems silly to do it just for me. Especially when I work late."

She didn't need to be a psychologist to draw conclusions from what he'd said, and before she could stop herself, she said, "No girlfriend?"

He met her gaze directly and she noticed for the first time the shards of green and darker blue in his intense light blue eyes. She noticed the pain there as well.

"Not anymore. She couldn't handle my hours. Truthfully, I think we only stayed together so long because of my family," he admitted.

His Gonzalez family was well-known to most Miamians and quite successful. She'd even met his cousin Pepe on various occasions because he was an up-and-coming real estate agent who had often attended their functions.

"I imagine it can be hard for people to see you for you and not your family," she said as she uncovered the last dish for their meal.

A grunt was his only reply as he took a seat at the table and scooped roast pork, rice and beans onto his plate and then added some ripe plantains. He immediately dug into his meal, and she did the same, hunger rousing with the enticing smells wafting off the food. The citrus, cumin and garlic from the pork, earthiness of the beans and the enticing sweetness of the ripe plantains.

She devoured the food on her plate in no time, surprising herself because she hadn't expected to be hungry with all that had happened that night. When she finished, she reached for seconds at the same time he did. Their hands collided over the black beans and, at the touch, an unexpected feeling zapped through her: comfort.

They both pulled away slowly, and as she met his gaze, Ricky said, "It will be okay, Mariela."

"Will it?" she said, doubtful that even the powerful Gonzalez family could accomplish that. The anger that had been simmering in her over the years of her marriage and after her divorce finally erupted. "I told myself it would be okay when Jorge started with his nasty comments. But it only got worse. I told myself my parents would support me, only they didn't. And now… I can't even think about how this is all not okay," she said, her throat choking up with the release of the emotions she had kept bottled up for so long.

Ricky cupped her cheek, and to her surprise, she didn't jerk back as she so often did after the years of abuse. As it had before, that sense of comfort filled her and tamed the heat of the emotions that had swept over her.

BENEATH HIS PALM Ricky felt the tempering of the rage that had overtaken her just moments before. He stroked her cheek with his thumb to reassure her about his words.

"I can't imagine how hard it's been for you. But we are here for you, and we will make sure you're safe," he said and genuinely believed that his family could do just what he had promised.

"I know you believe that," she said, her voice breaking with worry.

"I do. I may not be like Trey—"

"You may not think you are, but I see it differently," she said, covered his hand with hers and drew it away from her face to twine her fingers with his. "I don't think I'd be alive right now if it wasn't for you."

He didn't think so either and, unfortunately, he was also

sure that they weren't done with being in danger. Who-ever had sent the masked man tonight was likely to keep on trying to silence Mariela. His one hope was that he'd be up for the challenge of keeping her safe.

With a gentle squeeze of her hand, he said, "It's late. You should go get some rest."

She nodded but said, "I'll help you clean up."

"No need. I can handle it myself," he said, imagining that in Mariela's life she'd had few people who'd taken care of her. Plus, he needed time alone to think about all that had happened and prepare himself for tomorrow.

A ghost of a smile finally drifted across her face. "*Gracias.* I appreciate that. I'm not used to…" Her voice choked up and she forced herself to finish. "It's been a long time since someone was nice to me."

He wanted to say that it was a shame that she'd lacked that in her life but bit it back. He didn't want her to think he was pitying her or making a play. She was too vulner-able for that.

"We'll meet with my family in the morning, and you'll need to be sharp so we can figure out what we need to do about your ex."

With a small nod, she slipped her hand from his. De-spite his earlier words, she grabbed her dirty plates and cutlery and walked them over to the sink before heading to her bedroom.

He likewise picked up his dirty dishes and brought them over to the kitchen. He threw out the take-out containers and loaded the dishwasher.

The simple, homey tasks made him stop short and lean on the counter heavily. There was nothing simple or homey about the situation he'd been pulled into. He needed to re-group and prepare himself for tomorrow and whatever else was coming their way. And he needed to get more ice on his face because his mother was going to freak for sure when she saw him in the morning.

He made himself a fresh ice pack and headed to what would be his bedroom for the night.

As he lay in bed in his brother's too-large sweats, he worried the challenge ahead would likewise be too large for him to handle. But he told himself he could handle it. That the same vein of strength that ran through his grandfather, father and Trey ran through him as well.

He was just a different kind of hero, not that he'd ever thought of himself in that role. But he intended to be ready for the challenge, he told himself over and over again as he lay in bed, hoping to convince himself of the truth of those words by morning.

JORGE HERNANDEZ PACED back and forth across his living room, worry and anger twined together in his gut like a viny weed as he waited for word from his man.

He'd tried calling the burner phone he'd given his old foreman a few times, but the man hadn't answered. Jorge didn't know whether that meant something had gone wrong, or if he was being as unreliable as he had been when he'd worked for him.

He should have gotten someone else to do the job, only he hadn't had time to find anyone else.

Cursing, he dialed again, hand fisted around the phone tightly as it rang and rang.

No one answered.

The pressure built in his head and the fire of rage kindled in his gut until it exploded like a volcano spewing lava.

He tossed the phone against the wall where it shattered and fell onto the cold marble floor in pieces that reminded him of the state of his life.

He'd once had everything. A successful business. A beautiful wife and home.

But now all that was left of his life were the broken pieces, never to be put back together again. He knew that now. There was no going back to his old life, and he had to make sure Mariela wouldn't talk and ruin his plans for the future.

Chapter Six

It is more than a little intimidating to be surrounded by some of Miami's most prominent and wealthy individuals, Mariela thought as she sat at the conference room table the following morning.

Tia Elena sat beside Ricky's father, Ramon, the current head of South Beach Security, and Ricky's mother, Samantha. It had been impossible to miss the worry on Samantha's classic features when she'd first seen Ricky's bruised face. Truth be told, Mariela had also been shocked by the kaleidoscope of purple and blue along his cheek and the deeper black beneath Ricky's eye.

An attractive woman with sun-streaked light brown hair sat beside Trey in a dark black suit that screamed cop. His fiancée, Roni, she guessed. She vaguely recalled seeing a photo of her in the news article about the human trafficking ring Trey and she had broken up just a couple of weeks ago.

Mia Gonzalez was next at the table together with her cousin Carolina Gonzalez. The Twins, as they were known to the family and many others in Miami, were social media influencers invited to all the top events and, as always, they were dressed to the nines in designer sundresses. She'd had them to Jorge's parties on a few occasions and they'd always been pleasant. She wondered how they could possibly help in this situation, but then again, SBS had its own way of getting things done.

The last two people at the table, a man and woman with the unmistakable Gonzalez looks, were twentysomethings with open laptops sitting before them. They were dressed casually, the man in a button-down Oxford shirt while the woman wore a simple, pale peach blouse.

Unlike last night when he'd been in a *guayabera* shirt and jeans, Trey wore a dark blue pinstriped suit with an electric white shirt and red tie. He rose from the table and formally introduced everyone seated at the table.

"I think you already know *Tia* Elena. My father, Ramon, is the head of the agency, and my mother, Samantha, is our Mama Bear," he said with sincere affection and continued.

"My fiancée, Roni. She's a detective with Miami Beach PD," he explained, his voice filled with pride and love.

He gestured to the Twins. "I think you've probably met Mia and Carolina. They know everyone who's anyone in Miami, which comes in handy a lot."

With another wave of his hand at the direction of the two twentysomethings, he said, "Sophie and Robert Whitaker, our cousins. They're top tech gurus and ethical hackers. If they can't find it or break into it, no one can."

Ricky laid his hand on hers as it rested on the tabletop. "This is the heart and soul of South Beach Security, Mariela. We will protect you," he said.

"Thank you, everyone. I appreciate all that you've done so far, but I'm not sure I can afford—"

Ramon held his hand up to stop her. "That's not how we work, Mariela. Besides, Ricky is involved in this now also and we always protect our family."

She shot a quick glance at Ricky, who nodded in confirmation. "I don't know how to thank you. This is all so… crazy. I mean, Jorge has been violent in the past, but this… it's a whole new level of crazy."

"People get that way when money is involved. Especially big money," Trey said.

"Do you have any idea what projects your ex-husband is currently developing?" Ramon asked.

Mariela shook her head. "I haven't been involved at all since our divorce."

"It makes sense to call in Pepe," Ricky said, but that prompted uneasy murmurs around the table since all of them knew Pepe didn't like to be involved in agency business.

"I'll call Pepe. He won't say no to me," Ramon said, ending the discussion.

"I'm sure Robbie and I can also get that information," Sophie said and shot a quick look at her brother, who confirmed it with a nod.

"All right," Ricky said and sat back as Trey assumed control of the meeting.

"Roni. Can you get us a copy of any evidence that Miami PD has about the attack last night?" Trey asked.

"It depends on which detectives are handling it, but hopefully I can," his fiancée replied.

"Good. Back to the new construction developments. My guess is that whoever your ex is paying off works as an inspector of some kind. Did you ever meet any of the inspectors on the various projects?" Trey asked.

With a shrug, she said, "Some of them occasionally attended Jorge's holiday parties. I may still have the invite lists on my laptop or in my old planner. The planner is still in my parents' house."

"Will Miami PD let us back into the house?" Ricky asked, concerned about being able to access the planner.

"We can call PD to request access to the crime scene," Roni said and then muttered a curse and apologized. "I'm sorry, Mariela. I didn't mean to be insensitive."

"It's okay, Roni. I'm not sure I'll be able to think of it

as my home for a long time," Mariela admitted. A chill filled her as she remembered being assaulted the second she walked into her family home.

IT WAS IMPOSSIBLE for Ricky to miss Mariela's upset. Her hand had tightened against his as he held it, mirroring the growing tension of her body.

He gave her hand a reassuring squeeze. "We will help you get through this."

She offered up a weak smile. "I can probably make a partial list if we can't get the planner or it's not on my laptop. Possibly the names of some of the special inspectors and structural engineers as well."

"We can check to see if any of the reports are available to the public," Robbie said and began tapping away on the laptop. With a small hoot and a laugh, he said, "Look at that. The inspection reports are all online. I just need the addresses."

"You were worried there was something shady going on with some of the projects. Do you remember which ones?" Ricky asked Mariela.

Mariela tightened her lips and did a little bobble with her head. "Maybe. I can think of at least two where I thought something was off."

"Great. Let's start with those. If you can give the addresses to Sophie and Robbie, we'll dig through the reports later and start making a list of suspects," Trey advised and clapped his hands as if to say *Let's get going.*

Sophie and Robbie closed their laptops and shot to their feet, eager to get to work.

Roni rose and walked over to Trey, who laid a possessive hand at her waist. She dropped a quick kiss on his lips. "See you later," she said.

"Stay safe," Trey said and swept his hand across her back lovingly.

"You, too," Roni said before she hurried out the door.

The obvious love between the two caused an ache in the middle of her chest. When she had first married Jorge, they'd had that kind of love. Or at least she thought they'd had. The illusion had disappeared like the wisps of smoke from a candle that had just been blown out.

Trey peered at Ricky. "If you two could make those lists, it'll give us more to work with," he said.

"Will do," Ricky agreed.

"I'll be in my office, getting settled," Trey advised and pointed a thumb to the door of the conference room.

As he walked there, his father met him and clapped him on the back. "You did well, Trey."

Trey smiled. *"Gracias, papi."*

After Trey had left, Ricky's dad looked at them and said, "Do you need anything else right now?"

Ricky peeked at her from the corner of his eye, did a little cough of discomfort and said, "I was hoping Mariela and I could stay with you. The penthouse is a little… intimidating."

"Of course, Ricardo. When do you want to come over?"

"I have to get my car. We left it at Mariela's since Trey drove us here last night," Ricky said.

His mother fluttered her hands to wave him off. "We'll arrange for someone to get the car. Do you need anything else?"

Ricky once again looked at Mariela and she shook her head. "I was able to pack some things last night and I guess we'll have to wait for the police to let us back in to get the planner."

"Trey lent me some clothes he had in the penthouse, but I'd like to get some clothing from my home," Ricky told his mom.

Samantha nodded. "We can run by your house on the way to our house so you can pick up whatever you need."

"Great," he said, and everyone left the table to get to work.

When they neared the door, Ricky's mother lightly cupped his bruised cheek and said, "This looks like it hurts."

"Only when I smile," he said and grinned, but then immediately winced, seemingly forgetful of his injury.

"Oh, Ricky. I never thought I'd see you look like this," his mom said with worry and a final stroke of his cheek.

Embarrassed color rushed across his face, and he shot a look at Mariela, obviously wishing he could crawl into a hole to avoid the babying.

She understood, but how she wished her parents would show her that kind of love now, the way they used to before worries about health had changed everything.

When Ricky's mother and father finally left the room, Mariela leaned close and whispered, "You're lucky to have that much love."

He chuckled, did a little half grin that had him wincing again and said, "I am."

With that, they headed off to his parents' car and did a quick side trip to a beautiful waterfront home in nearby Gables by the Sea. His father pulled his Jaguar sedan into the circular driveway of the sprawling ice white ranch house.

Low bushes lined the periphery of his home, their deep emerald color a contrast to the bright pink and white flowers in the planting beds and the brighter green of the lawn. Two large aqua-colored planters added yet more color as they stood sentry at either side of the patio by the front door.

Ricky was about to jump out of the car, but his father laid a hand on his arm to stop him.

"We'll go in with you," Ramon said, clearly worried that whoever had attacked her the night before might also know who had saved her and be waiting in Ricky's home.

But Ricky held his hand up and said, "I can handle this. There's no need to worry."

HE APPRECIATED HIS parents' concerns, but for far too long it had also made him feel as if he didn't quite measure up to the Gonzalez men standards.

Last night had given him his first inkling that his feelings might have been wrong. Not that he intended to be dead wrong by placing anyone in danger. He had a security system in place, and it hadn't been tripped. It was also highly unlikely that whoever had attacked Mariela last night had hung around to get his name. Still, if Mariela's husband had a connection in the DA's office or even the police, he might have been able to get that info.

Because of that, he entered his home with caution. The alarm was engaged, and nothing seemed out of place in the areas visible from the door. Disarming the security system, he waved to his father that all was clear, and his parents and Mariela walked into his home to wait for him to pack.

He hurried up the stairs to his bedroom and quickly filled a bag with what he'd need for at least a week. Not that he thought it would take that long for SBS to get to the bottom of what was happening with Mariela's ex-husband.

As a member of the agency's team, he intended to help in whatever way he could so that Mariela could get on with her life.

On a professional level, he wanted to help her heal from the abuse she had suffered at the hands of her ex. But as a professional, he wasn't supposed to become involved with a client. That was at odds with the instant attraction that he'd felt for her. Only was she really a client based on just one visit to his support group?

That conflict is one I'm going to have to work out for myself, he thought as he finished packing.

He rushed down to where his parents and Mariela sat in the living room, seemingly making small talk. But if he knew his parents, they were conducting their own kind of interrogation.

That was confirmed as he heard his mother say, "How long were you married?"

"Five years."

"How did you meet him?" his mother asked.

"I met Jorge when I was working part-time as a hostess at a local restaurant. Jorge was a regular customer. He was handsome and always charming. He treated me well at first."

Ricky had heard similar stories way too often from his patients and some of the people in his support group. Things usually started well, but then disintegrated as either stress or just time revealed the real nature of the abuser.

"Mami," Ricky said in a tone that warned his mother to cease her inquisition.

"Just getting to know Mariela, *mi'jo*," she said with an arch of a perfectly plucked brow.

"Give her a chance to breathe, *mami*," he warned, and with a slight dip of her head, his mother acquiesced, and Mariela released a relieved sigh.

They were about to step outside when Ricky caught sight of motion from the corner of his eye. A black BMW had pulled up in front of his home. A masked driver got out of the car, and some kind of internal warning system made him sweep his arm across his father, mother and Mariela as they were about to open the door.

"Get down," he shouted.

His father opened his arms wide and pulled the women to the ground. Ricky threw his body over all of them, trying to shield them from danger.

A second later a spray of gunfire shattered the glass in the front windows and plowed into the metal front door.

It seemed like forever that the shooting went on, destroying everything in the path of the bullets. Glass shattered on nearby picture frames. Ceramic lamps exploded from the gunshots. The duller thud of bullets smashing into the door, walls and books made his body jump as he imagined them slamming into their bodies.

Luckily, they were safely on the floor and behind the protective metal of the front door.

As quickly as it had begun, the gunfire stopped, and a squeal of tires signaled that the shooter had driven off. Barely a few minutes later, the wail of police sirens said that the cavalry had arrived.

Ricky stood and helped his father, mother and Mariela to their feet. As he made sure the women were okay, his father partially opened the door. Seeing the officer rushing toward the house, his father threw it open to let him in.

"Are you okay, *mami*?" he asked as his mother smoothed her blouse into place and ran a shaky hand through her hair.

"I am. Mariela?" his mother asked and glanced at the young woman.

"I'm good," she said and slowly spun to look all around.

"Your beautiful home. I'm so sorry, Ricky," Mariela murmured and covered her mouth with her hands. Tears shimmered in her gaze as she skipped it over the broken pieces of his belongings.

"It's just things," he said, even though it hurt to see the damage to the objects he had gathered so carefully to make the house his home.

"Is everyone okay?" the first officer asked and holstered his gun when he realized there was no threat from them. The officer's eyes widened as he realized who was inside. "Mr. Gonzalez. I didn't realize this was your home."

"It's my son's," Ramon said and gestured to Ricky.

"We're all fine," Ricky said and wished he could say the same about his living room and office, which had taken the brunt of the attack. The gunfire had broken a number of items in addition to the windows, and bullet holes peppered the walls, sofas and built-ins.

But what bothered him most was the very real possibility that either a cop or someone in the DA's office had revealed his name and address to Mariela's attacker. How else would someone have known where they might go?

As his gaze locked with his father's, it was clear he was thinking the same thing.

Chapter Seven

His father whipped out his cell phone and dialed. When someone answered, he said, "We have a leak, Trey. Someone just shot up Ricky's home."

The murmured sound of a few choice curses was audible before his father said, "We're all okay, *mi' jo*. As soon as we finish with the officers, we're heading home."

There was another curt response from Trey and his father nodded. "A security detail would be welcome. Can you call your contacts at PD and see what they have to say?"

A second later his father ended the call and faced the officer. "I know you have a job to do. How can we help?"

The officer nodded and took out his notepad. "Can you tell me what happened?"

Ricky motioned to the front window of his office. "I caught sight of a car pulling up and something about it worried me."

"Can you tell me what kind of car?" the officer asked.

"Late-model BMW. Black. Masked driver got out and I could see he had a rifle before we all hit the ground," Ricky said.

After jotting down the notes about the car and driver, the officer continued peppering them with questions, getting statements from each of them. When he was done, he called for a CSI unit to come and collect evidence and secured the scene with yellow police tape.

When they stepped outside, there was another police car with officers holding back a small crowd of neighbors who had come to see what had happened as well as two sets of security guards and Trey.

He rushed over as they cleared the police tape and examined them carefully, as if to reassure himself that they were all truly unharmed. Satisfied, he said, "I've got two guards to follow you back to the house. Since it's gated, you should be fine once you clear security there. The other two guards will sit here until the CSI folks are finished and then put up plywood until we can get some repairs done."

"Thanks, Trey," Ricky said and hugged him, but his brother held him just a little longer and squeezed just a little harder.

"You've got to stop scaring the life out of me," he whispered into his ear.

"Believe me, I wish I could," Ricky said and stepped back to stand beside Mariela, who had clearly retreated into herself with the violence of the attack. She'd gone back to wrapping her arms around herself tightly and worried her lower lip with her teeth. All traces of color were gone from her face, which was almost a sickly green color.

He swept his hand across her back. "It's going to be okay."

Mariela only nodded, as if she didn't trust herself to speak.

"We're going to be safe at my parents'. I promise," he said, and all she did was nod again, the action stiff.

"Let's get you there and then we can meet with Sophie and Robbie. They've gotten some info from Pepe and the building department website," Trey said.

Ricky nodded and applied gentle pressure on Mariela's back to direct her to his parents' car. Silence reigned during the short drive onto the highway, the McArthur Causeway, and finally the security gate for Palm Island. Trey was in the lead in his restored vintage Camaro while a Suburban with their security detail guarded their rear.

Once on the island they'd be safe from any land attack, but not from the air or water. An air attack seemed unlikely, but anyone could drive a boat through the canal that opened into Biscayne Bay behind the home.

As he got out of the car, he met Trey and gestured to the back of the house. "What about the dock?"

Trey nodded. "It's not likely, but there's no sense taking any chances. We'll have the guards take positions there. Good call."

"Learned from an expert," he said with a smile, fighting back a wince from his sore cheek.

THE OBVIOUS AFFECTION and respect between the two brothers helped ease some of Mariela's upset from the earlier attack. That and passing through the secured gate as well as the armed guards and the Gonzalez family. Since Trey was a retired police officer, she trusted that he was capable of arranging for the protection they needed. Ricky's father also, but what impressed her more was how Ricky was rising to the challenge.

He had been the first one to notice something was off and keep them from walking out into a hail of gunfire.

Ricky had saved her life. Again. His parents also, but they didn't seem fazed by all that had happened. Not even his mother. Maybe because as the Mama Bear of South Beach Security she was used to things like this.

As Mariela's gaze met Samantha's, his mother smiled gently and held her hand out to Mariela. "Let's get you settled while the men work out the details."

Mariela nodded, but at the door, she paused to look back at the men as they stood in the courtyard in front of the home. It was then she realized that a beautiful wrought-iron gate protected the mouth of the driveway, and a matching fence surrounded the property, providing security for the home. The floral motif in the gate and fence were mirrored in the wrought iron of the double doors at the entrance to the house.

The home was a bright white color against the myriad greens of the palms, grass and other plants in the surrounding landscape. Brightly hued flowers were interspersed here and there, helping to break up the austerity of the white of the house and black of all the wrought iron.

Samantha led her into a large foyer and hall done in brilliant white again. For a second it reminded her of Jorge's home once more, but as she walked in, the white and black of the wrought iron on the stairways and landing was warmed by the rich wood of what had to be antique Colonial Spanish furniture and a beautiful family portrait above a massive stone fireplace.

"Your home is lovely," she said, doing a slow twirl to take it all in.

"We're lucky to have it and lots of family to fill it," Samantha said and then quickly tacked on, "And friends like you."

She wasn't sure she could think of herself as Ricky's friend, but she hoped that might happen in the future once they got to know each other better. She ignored the little voice in her head that said Ricky was the kind of man who could become more. If she could ever get over what Jorge had done to her.

Samantha guided her up the stairs to a large central landing laid out with a comfortable seating area that overlooked the living room downstairs and had amazing views out windows facing the back of the house. A canal, the Port of Miami and Biscayne Bay were visible beyond just a short distance away. A large cruise ship sat in the port, waiting for people to board.

With a wave of her hand, Ricky's mother said, "Ricky and you will be over in this guest wing. Ramon and I are on the other side of the floor if you need anything."

"*Gracias.* I really appreciate you being kind enough to do this for me," Mariela said and followed Samantha into the one room. It was an immense space with large windows on one wall and French doors onto a small balcony that faced the backyard with its water views. She noticed the two guards policing the grounds at the edge of the property and a speedboat at a dock on the canal. From this side of the home a beautiful pool and patio were also visible on the grounds below.

"Anything for Ricky and his friends," Samantha said, but Mariela didn't fail to detect the notes of worry woven into her voice.

"I never meant to bring this danger to your home or your family," she said, tightening her hands on the handle of her overnight bag.

Samantha laid a hand on hers. "Sadly, we've faced danger before. It comes with running something like SBS."

Mariela relaxed beneath his mother's gentle touch, but it only assuaged her guilt a little bit. Not to mention that she couldn't imagine living with that kind of danger every day.

Samantha must have seen what she was thinking since she said, "Having family at your side makes it easier. I get the sense you haven't had that in some time."

Mariela couldn't disagree. "My parents haven't been well and that's changed a lot in our relationship."

"You have us now. We will get to the bottom of this," she said and quickly added, "I'll leave you to get comfortable."

"*Gracias,*" she said again, grateful for everything that this group of virtual strangers was doing for her. It made her feel like she had a family again, something that had been lacking in recent years due to her parents' illness and Jorge's abuse.

She quickly put away the few things she had packed, stepped out of the room and literally ran into Ricky, who was leaving the room across the way from her. He grabbed her as they collided to keep her from falling.

Her instincts took over and she instantly recoiled even though his touch was surprisingly gentle.

He released her immediately, obviously aware of her discomfort. "Are you okay?" he asked.

"I am. It's just that… I'm not used to a man being…caring," she admitted and a sudden wave of sadness washed over her.

He reached for her again, intending to comfort her, but then pulled back, clearly mindful of her issues. With a flip of his hand, he motioned toward the stairs and landing. "They're waiting for us downstairs. Sophie and Robbie have some info for us. Roni also."

She hurried down the stairs, but on the ground floor deferred to Ricky, who guided her to a study in a large wing at the front of the home. There was a small conference table off to one side of the room and an ornately carved wooden desk on the other. Two of the walls were lined with bookshelves packed with books and memorabilia while the third wall boasted an immense television, sound system and computer equipment. The final wall had numerous windows that faced the front courtyard of the property and the lush gardens along the edges of the property.

Trey and his father, Ramon, were already seated at the table and a young housekeeper was setting out a coffee service on a bar cart in one corner of the room.

Both men rose as she entered. Apparently, manners had not disappeared in the Gonzalez family.

Ramon said, "Please help yourself to some coffee or tea. If you'd like anything else, please let Josie know."

Josie grabbed a coffee cup and carafe, but Mariela waved her off. She was too edgy as it was, and the coffee would only make her even more jittery.

Ricky took a cup and Josie poured him some coffee. When he smiled and thanked her, the young woman blushed and grew awkward. Josie clearly had a crush on the youngest Gonzalez family member. Mariela understood. Ricky was handsome, intelligent, caring and brave.

Seemingly too good to be true and that scared her a little because Jorge had seemed that way at first also.

When Ramon sat down at the table, Mariela did as well. Once Trey and Ricky had joined them, their father quickly dipped his head in silent command. Trey video-called his cousins, who immediately answered, their faces filling the large television on the wall.

"Good to see you all in one piece," Robbie said, earning an elbow from Sophie.

"Ignore him. He spends too much time with the computers," Sophie said in apology.

Robbie did an eye roll. "Says the woman who named her PC Blanche after her favorite Golden Girl."

Sophie released an exasperated sigh and said, "We have some information that Pepe got from the Multiple Listing Service entries."

"Does that include new construction?" Trey asked.

Sophie nodded. "It does include new construction if the builder lists it. So there may be a new development that's not yet in the MLS," she explained.

"Do you know if your ex regularly listed new projects?" Ricky asked.

"He almost always did. It was a way to keep the cash flow stable," Mariela said, but then blurted out, "But Jorge told me last night that things have been slow."

Trey tapped his pen against a pad of paper. "How slow?"

With a shrug, Mariela said, "The office was empty last night. I'd never seen it like that. There always used to be someone in there working. But it could have been he didn't want anyone to overhear his conversation."

"Like you did," Ramon said.

"Like I did. I tried to make it seem like I'd just walked in, but I guess Jorge didn't buy it," she admitted.

"It must be pretty important to him to have you killed," Ricky said, his brow furrowed in concern.

Mariela ran some of the development numbers for past deals she remembered through her head. "A mid-rise building with about 200 units could make Jorge about 5 million. If it was a big high-rise project, he could make 10 million or more," she advised.

"Enough to kill for," Robbie chimed in with a low whistle.

Beside him Sophie flipped through a pile of papers; her lips pursed with frustration. "We have only one high-rise project on the MLS listing Pepe provided," she said.

Trey tapped his pad of paper again. "Can you send that list over for Mariela to review?"

"Sure thing," Robbie said and then continued. "If Mariela can identify any of the projects she thinks had issues, we can get the names of the inspectors so you can investigate them."

"*Gracias.* We will get to work on it as soon as we receive it. You had news for us as well, Trey," Ramon said and peered at his oldest son.

"Roni talked to the officers who had investigated when her ex put Mariela into the hospital. They seemed angry that the DA wouldn't press charges but said there was nothing they could do about it. They gave Roni a copy of the file and the name of the DA. The detectives had some choice words about how often they had issues with this DA letting people go."

"Even with violent crimes?" Ricky asked, clearly frustrated about what had happened to her.

"Even in cases where the perp was armed and dangerous, and then they wonder why the crime rate goes up," Trey said, even more frustrated than his younger brother.

"This DA who won't charge people is the one who let Jorge go?" she asked, wanting to be sure she was understanding what had happened.

Trey blew out an exasperated sigh and said, "Apparently it is. I guess we can ask *Tio* Jose about him. Maybe Sophie and Robbie can dig into his record as well."

Tio *Jose*, Tia *Elena's husband*, Mariela thought. He had been the reason she had hesitated to approach Elena at first. It relieved her worries that Elena's husband hadn't been the one to drop the charges, but it still angered her that the DA's office hadn't pursued the case.

Ricky tentatively laid a hand on her shoulder and gave a reassuring squeeze. "We will get to the bottom of why he wasn't charged."

She wanted to say it was water under the bridge, but it did matter. "I want to know why, so someone else doesn't suffer the way I did."

HER WORDS WERE a testament to the kind of person she was. Someone willing to sacrifice herself to help aging parents. Someone who cared more for others than herself. Someone brave enough not to shrink even in the face of the abuse as well as the attacks on her life.

"We will make sure of that," he said and meant it. Whatever it took, he would push to make sure violence against women wouldn't be ignored by that DA again.

Mariela's face reflected her concern, but with his words, a wave of release seemed to wash over her. But it was also clear she wanted to move on from that memory as she said, "I'll get to work on the MLS list as soon as we get it."

A bing on the laptop in front of Trey drew everyone's attention. After a few taps, Trey smiled and said, "I think you got your wish, Mariela."

Chapter Eight

"Great. Mariela and I will get to work," Ricky said, but then bit it back, remembering that Mariela might have control issues. Deferring to her, he said, "If that's okay with you."

She nodded. "It is."

Ramon peered around the table and said, "Trey and I will leave you to work on the list. We'll be at the office if you need us."

"We will work on it immediately," Mariela said, her determination obvious.

"Great. Like *papi* said, we'll be at the office," Trey said, a bit of annoyance in his tone, and it made Ricky wonder if his brother was finding it difficult to play second fiddle to their father. As a lead detective, Trey was used to calling his own shots, but then again, he'd had to answer to his chief on cases as well.

After the two men had left, Ricky walked to the printer to get the list and returned to the table with it. He placed it in front of Mariela and sat down beside her.

"You ready?"

MARIELA WASN'T SURE she was ready, but she had to help this investigation in any way she could, especially since she was responsible for drawing the Gonzalez family into this dangerous situation.

She grabbed a highlighter from an organizer in the center of the table and started her review of the MLS listings. The new construction projects were unfamiliar to her, but she drew a star next to a high-rise project.

"This one is 400 units right across from the beach. Luxury condos as well. If Jorge could get that to sell out it could easily make him 15 million or more," she said.

"It's a great neighborhood and oceanside. I can't imagine it wouldn't sell out," Ricky said as he leaned close to look at the entry.

Mariela screwed her eyes nearly closed as she tried to recall things she'd overheard on other projects when she'd helped Jorge with the events and marketing. "To build something like this he'd need lots of cash. Forty to 50 million is my guess."

"And you don't think he has that?" Ricky said and took another look at the MLS listing.

"When we divorced a year ago, Jorge was already pleading poverty. I thought it was just a ploy to reduce the settlement he'd have to pay me, but maybe it wasn't," she said with a shrug.

"What about presales of the units? Wouldn't they help?" Ricky wondered.

"With enough of them presold it would be easier to get the funding he needs from a bank," she said.

"I know who might be able to give us that info," Ricky said and whipped out his cell phone.

Mariela guessed that it was his cousin and that was confirmed as Pepe's voice came across the speaker.

"What can I do for you, *primo*?" Pepe said, but then quickly added, "As long as it doesn't get me shot at."

"I guess you heard about this morning," Ricky said with a grimace.

"I think most of Miami has heard. It was on the local news at lunchtime, and I suspect it'll be on the evening news as well," Pepe said.

"Great," Ricky muttered, but then pressed on. "I've got Mariela Hernandez with me. We were wondering if you knew how many units had sold on her ex's new condo development near Bal Harbour."

"Let me check," his cousin said, and Mariela heard the tap-tap of keys across the speaker.

"Hmm. The units are selling pretty fast. I can send you a link to the virtual tour so you can see for yourselves what the condos will look like when they're finished," Pepe said, and the sounds of the keys followed again and then a bing to confirm the email had arrived.

"Thanks, Pepe. I know you usually like to stay out of things—"

"I do. Stay safe," Pepe said and hung up.

Mariela had sensed the undertones as the men had finished the call. She narrowed her eyes to peer at Ricky as he opened the email and brought up the virtual tour on the large television screen on the far wall.

"I get the sense Pepe didn't want to be involved in this," Mariela said, once again feeling guilty about bringing yet another family member into the mess of her life.

Ricky did an uneasy shrug. "Pepe tries to shy away from South Beach Security. He's made his own success as a real estate agent."

"It must not be easy to be the next generation in a family like yours," she said, aware of some of the history of the family.

The shrug greeted her again, which she was learning meant he was uncomfortable with the discussion. "I don't mean to pry," she said and gestured toward the laptop as a way to shift the conversation away from the family dynamics.

Ricky met her gaze head-on, clearly aware of what she was trying to do. "How about I share if you share?"

Mariela opened her eyes wide and her voice almost squeaked as she said, "Share?"

Ricky nodded. "Yes, share. Like why it's hard for me and Pepe to be the next generation and why you dropped out of college."

A very visible gulp from Mariela warned it might be difficult for her to start the share, so he began. "My *abuelo*, *papi*, his brother Jose and Trey were all military. Heroes who came home and became even larger than life after. *Abuelo* started the agency and *papi* has kept it going."

"And now Trey is here to continue the legacy," Mariela finished for him.

Ricky dipped his head to confirm it. "Trey is the natural successor. I may help out on occasion, but my dream is to build my practice. What about you?"

Mariela hesitated and looked away, avoiding his gaze, and despite how open he'd been, he realized she wasn't quite ready to tell her life story. He didn't press. She'd share when she was ready.

"Let's take a look at the condo units," he said after her obvious hesitation and opened the link Pepe had sent.

Together they did a virtual walk-through of what the various condos would look like when they were finished.

As much as Ricky didn't like Jorge based on how he had abused Mariela, he had to admit that the condos looked great on the virtual tour. He could understand why the units were selling fast. But despite that, something niggled in the back of his brain.

"Do you think this is the place you overheard Jorge discussing?"

Mariela worried her lower lip as she considered his question. "Possibly. I mean, this is his biggest new project."

Big and costly, Ricky thought, but didn't want to jump to any conclusions because too much was at stake.

"Let's take a look at the other new construction and finish going through the list," he said.

They reviewed the other pending projects, a mid-rise condo of one hundred units near the beach and a subdevelopment of half a dozen custom homes farther inland. The first would certainly make Mariela's ex a few million. The homes less because of their size and the neighborhood.

After, they scrutinized the list of completed projects over the last few years, marking up those that Mariela remembered had had issues that suddenly went away.

Jorge had been quite busy until this year, Ricky thought, and Mariela had noticed the same thing.

"He hasn't done as many projects since the divorce, but then again, that high-rise is costly," Mariela said, but Ricky detected something in her tone.

"You shouldn't feel guilty," he said, imagining that she felt the divorce was somehow responsible for the issues Jorge might be having.

With a shrug of her shoulders, she said, "I shouldn't feel guilty, but I do. Maybe the settlement I got—"

"Which you deserved for all the work you did for him. Maybe his business isn't doing well because he's missing your wonderful events and marketing," Ricky said.

MARIELA CONSIDERED HIS words and they filled her with warmth. "I did do a lot of good work for him," she said with a determined nod.

"You did," he said and gestured to the list they had marked up. "We can wait until Sophie and Robbie look up the inspectors, but we can also get started ourselves," he said and immediately worked on the computer to create an account in the building inspection department's online portal to review the reports for the various projects she had identified.

They were about to search the records for the first location when Samantha sashayed into the room and over to the table. "How is it going?" she asked, laying a hand on Ricky's shoulder in a very maternal gesture.

"Good, but if you're here, I'm gathering you need us for something," Ricky said, totally in tune with his mother.

"I do, *mi' jo.* You obviously haven't noticed that it's time for dinner," she said. She stroked her hand across his back and winced again as Ricky looked up at her and she noticed the bruises on his face.

"*Gracias, mami.* We'll be there soon," Ricky said, obvious affection in his voice.

"Not too long. Your siblings, Roni and Carolina are already here. So are your *abuelos,*" she said and hurried away.

Mariela's stomach clenched with a sick feeling at the thought of meeting his grandparents as well as trying to be social with the other Gonzalez family members.

"It'll be okay. They don't bite, although Mia and Carolina can be a little over the top," Ricky said with a smile and a small grimace.

She didn't worry about the Twins since she knew them relatively well and had seen them the day before. But the reception from Ricky's grandparents was an unknown, especially considering all that had happened in the last twenty-four hours. If it were her family, she wouldn't be very pleased with the person who had brought danger to them.

Sucking in a deep, bracing breath, she accepted the hand Ricky offered and rose from the table. He didn't release her hand, gently guiding her toward the back of the home and a large outdoor dining area with an immense glass and wrought-iron table.

The rest of the family was already seated there and stood as Ricky and she walked in.

She tensed and Ricky squeezed her hand in reassurance. "Mariela, say hello to the family."

Chapter Nine

An older man walked over, followed by a small almost birdlike woman, and held out his hand. "Mariela. Ramon Gonzalez," he said and grasped her hand warmly in his two big hands. "My wife, Maria."

The woman also shook Mariela's hand with affection, relieving some of her apprehension about meeting them.

"Mis abuelos," Ricky said, although she had guessed that already. It was obvious the younger Gonzalez family members got their Roman noses and dimpled chins from their grandfather. The brilliant blues of their eyes had come from Maria. His grandparents had to be in their late eighties, but there was nothing about them that hinted at that age. They moved with grace and assurance.

His grandfather swept a hand in the direction of the family gathered around the table. "You've already met the rest of the family, I gather. *Ramoncito* and his wife, Samantha. My grandson Ramon the third. It's why we call him Trey. His fiancée, Roni. My granddaughters Mia and Carolina."

Mariela did an awkward little wave at the remaining family members before Ricky slipped a hand to her back and guided her to the two empty seats at the table.

A second later a woman who looked like an older version of Josie wheeled in a serving cart with several large platters and placed it off to one side of the covered dining area. Josie and another man followed with smaller platters, placed them on a side table and began serving the food.

As they did so, Ricky said, "This is Josie's mom, Alicia. The young man is Javier, their cousin."

A family affair, Mariela thought, and as the three served those at the table, it was apparent there was real affection between the two families despite their different stations in life.

The appetizer consisted of a play on a tamale, with a light and fluffy corn meal base topped with *picadillo* and *cotija* cheese.

Appreciative murmurs filled the air as everyone tried the dish and Mariela had to agree. The sharp taste of the *picadillo* with its tomato sauce and ground meat was balanced perfectly by the sweetness of the corn meal and saltiness of the cheese.

"You outdid yourself, Alicia," Ricky said after he'd finished his food and Alicia and her family prepped the dishes with the main meal.

To her surprise, Trey, Mia and Ricky got up from the table to help clear off the dishes while plates piled high with *arroz con pollo* and sweet plantains were served to everyone.

She hadn't been hungry at first, too worried and caught up in all that they were trying to investigate, but the delicious tamale pie as well as the feelings of warmth and friendliness around the table had awakened her appetite.

Once the siblings had sat again, the family started eating and chatting about everything except what had happened the night before and that morning. She appreciated their thoughtfulness and got so swept up in that sense of normal she almost forgot why she was sitting there at the table.

Almost being the operative word, especially as she

caught sight of the armed guards down at the waterfront, patrolling the dock area.

When tension crept into her body, Ricky immediately swept a hand up her back to offer a calming stroke. It surprised her that she didn't recoil the way she often did when a man came by, but then again Ricky had shown her he was anything but an ordinary man.

The siblings once again got up to help Alicia and her family clean up so that coffee and flan could be set out for dessert.

She had thought she was full, but it was impossible not to finish the wonderfully prepared flan Josie placed in front of her.

Once they'd finished, Ricky leaned close and said, "What about a walk?"

Mariela really wanted to get back to work on reviewing the lists and hesitated, but Ricky said, "It'll clear our minds so we can be more efficient."

He was hard to refuse, especially as he grinned, which made him look boyish despite the bruises on his face.

She nodded, and he rose and said, "If you'll excuse us. We're going to get some air."

"Of course. We'll have some more coffee," his grandfather said, but Mariela sensed the family would be doing more than just having coffee.

She forced those thoughts away to allow herself to enjoy the last rays of the sun as dusk fled and was replaced by night.

Ricky guided her toward the water's edge where the security guards had drifted away to either end of the property, giving them some privacy.

Water lapped up against the bulkhead at the edge of the yard and the hull of the speedboat docked there. Across the canal and causeway were the lights in the port and the skyline of Miami snapping to life at night. Even farther in the distance, the final kiss of sunlight bathed the waters of Biscayne Bay with shades of pink, purple and blue.

A light breeze swept off the water, rustling the fronds of the palms above them.

"Beautiful," she said, appreciating how the man-made elements blended with those of nature to create the stunning scene playing out before them.

"It is," Ricky said, a hint of something in his tone that dragged her attention to him.

He was gazing at her with the kind of interest she hadn't seen in a long time. Or maybe it was better to say what she had avoided for a long time. And which she wanted to avoid what with all that was going on.

"It's too soon," she said, and he smiled sadly and nodded.

"I understand."

They turned back toward the house, their pace slow. A calm silence settled over them as they enjoyed those last few moments of daylight and the peace before reality intruded again.

His family was huddled together at the table.

Ricky had no doubt what they were talking about. He tempered his anger that they hadn't included him because he knew they were only trying to do what they thought was best. Even Roni was in on the family discussion despite the fact that Trey and she had only recently become engaged.

Normally he was only tangentially involved in their investigations, offering his opinions on their possible suspects or counseling their clients.

But he thought he had proved in the last twenty-four hours that he could be more, do more, as part of South Beach Security.

As Mariela and he approached the table, Trey gestured

for them to join the discussion. "We didn't mean to exclude you," Trey said, as if reading his thoughts.

"I'm up for this," he said, determined to be in control of his fate during this investigation.

"We know," Mia and Carolina said, almost in unison.

"Please sit," his father suggested, but before he could, his grandparents rose from the table.

"You'll have to excuse us. We'd like to get home before it gets too late," his *abuelo* said and helped his grandmother stand, offering his arm in a gallant gesture.

Ricky walked over to hug them, grateful they had come to visit, although it had likely been to confirm that he was okay after all that had happened in the last day.

When his grandparents stepped away from the table, his grandfather faced Mariela. "It was very nice to meet you. I promise we'll take care of you," he said.

"I know you will," she said with a smile, but Ricky couldn't miss that her smile was stilted, and she had wrapped her arms around herself again, clearly in defensive mode.

His grandfather peered at the rest of the family. "You'll call if you need me," he said, and Ramon and Trey nodded.

"We will," Ricky's father said, and with that his grandparents slowly ambled off, arm in arm. Their heads bent together as they chatted while they walked.

It brought a little ache in his heart to see them so in love after over sixty years of marriage and because he had always hoped that he'd have the same kind of love one day. Which made him shoot a quick peek at Mariela, who still stood there uneasily.

Slipping his hand to her back, he urged her to the table so they could sit and discuss the investigation.

His butt had no sooner hit the seat when Trey said, "Roni was just telling us that she heard back from some other detectives who had experienced issues with Mariela's DA."

Mariela plucked at the tablecloth nervously. "What did they say?"

Roni did a little shake of her head and her lips tightened. "Mariela's case isn't unique, unfortunately. This DA supports no bail for offenders, even violent ones. He's also using extreme discretion as to what crimes to prosecute."

"If I understand you correctly, it's possible Jorge and his attorney had nothing to do with the DA not charging him," Mariela said with another, more violent tug at the tablecloth, which she then smoothed with shaky hands.

He laid an arm across her shoulders, and she did a little flinch but then relaxed with his touch.

"That's very possible," Roni said with a frustrated sigh. "It makes our jobs harder and decreases public safety, but what can you do?"

"How about speaking to Jose? He is one of the senior DAs," his mother said and glanced at her husband, who had a close relationship with his brother.

"I will. A prosecutor is responsible for protecting the community and people like Mariela. That didn't happen," Ramon said.

"It didn't. The detectives were also able to pull the video from Ricky's security system and from some of your neighbors' doorbell cameras. Hopefully they can get some useful photos of the suspect and the car," Roni advised.

"Did you two find anything useful?" Trey asked.

Ricky and Mariela shared a look. "We reviewed Hernandez's new construction projects. Two of them could generate a lot of money for him. We also have a list of his older construction jobs and were just going to start reviewing the inspection reports on those," he said.

"Do you need help?" Trey asked.

"Sophie and Robbie are going to help. Once we have a list of the inspectors, we can decide what to do," he said.

"I'll try to remember which of the inspectors are ones I remember from Jorge's work," Mariela added.

"Roni and I will stay on top of the detectives investigating your assault and the shooting. Hopefully they'll have something that will help us with what we're doing," Trey said and slapped the tabletop as if to signal that their discussion was done. That was confirmed as he stood and held out a hand to his fiancée.

Roni slipped her hand into his but glanced their way. "We will keep on top of this."

"We know you will," his mother said and likewise rose from the table.

Since it was obviously time to go, he stood and Mariela joined him, slipping her hand into his as they followed his family back into the house.

He took comfort from the fact that Mariela had made that first small move. It spoke of a growing trust between them and that she was possibly beginning to heal from the trauma of her abusive marriage.

Inside, the couples all shared goodbyes before Trey and Roni left to go home, and his parents went upstairs to their wing of the house.

"Are you game to keep on working?" Ricky asked, unsure of whether Mariela was up to it after all the events of the night before and that morning.

She nodded. "I am. I'd like to get to the bottom of this as soon as we can."

So she could be back to her regular life, he thought. *Hopefully one without fear.*

In his father's study they sat back at the table and split the list into three to speed their review. They sent one third to Sophie and Robbie so they could make their list of the inspectors on the projects. Mariela and he took the other sections and got to work.

As Mariela read through the inspection reports, she tried to recall some of the conversations she'd overheard over the years, and which had roused suspicions in her that Jorge might be doing something shady. When they'd first been married and she'd started helping him with the business, she'd asked him about what was happening.

That had been the first time she'd seen the monster emerge in Jorge and the memory actually made her stomach twist with fear.

She should have seen the signs then. The quick, explosive anger. The name-calling.

She'd written it off as Jorge being under pressure to build his business and possible money issues, but over time that monster would materialize more and more often. At first it had been verbal, and then it had become physical. A slap across the face. A punch to the stomach.

The beating that had landed her in the hospital when she'd asked him about some unusual expenses. One of the business's accountants had questioned why one of her events had been so costly, only she hadn't spent anything near that amount the accountant had mentioned.

Which made her say, "Jorge used to hide some expenses by charging them to things like the promotions he asked me to do."

Ricky looked up from his laptop. "You think he used that money to pay people off?"

Remembering his anger when she'd questioned him, she now had no doubt that's what he was doing. "I think so. I just don't know how to prove it."

Ricky leaned back in his chair, steepled his arms on the edges and tapped his mouth with his fingers as he considered what she'd said. "Did he give you any financial information when you were trying to get divorced?"

The financial settlement had been something they'd fought about repeatedly. As part of that process, her ex's attorneys had sent info, but her attorney and his experts had been the ones to look at it.

"My attorney has that info. I could ask him for it, only I don't know how detailed it is," she said. She logged into her email account and instantly sent a request for the information.

"If it is detailed, it may help us identify if and when bribes occurred," Ricky said and returned to the perusal of his list.

She did the same, but soon the reports were forming a jumble in her brain and her eyes were drifting closed.

Not good, she thought and shot a peek at Ricky. He leaned forward in his chair, his attention squarely on the information on the screen. Every now and then he'd jot something down on the list and on a pad of paper beside him, much like she had done as she reviewed her entries.

He seemed alert enough. Even though it was imperative that they get to the bottom of what was happening, she didn't want to possibly miss something important because she was tired.

Ricky must have sensed her distraction. He looked her way and said, "I can see you need to rest."

"I do. I'm a little tired," she admitted. In the past she would have kept something like that secret, afraid of the retribution if she didn't do what Jorge wanted.

"I am, too. Let's call it a night," he said and shut his laptop.

"Thanks," she said, appreciating his understanding.

He sighed, pushed out of the leather chair and stood before her. His gaze was intense as he looked at her and said, "You never have to hesitate with me, Mariela."

Inside she knew that somehow, but it didn't make it to her brain as she said, "I need time to learn to trust, Ricky."

"I KNOW. BELIEVE ME, I know," Ricky said. It was his job to understand as a professional, but even though their relationship had started that way, it had definitely morphed into something more personal with all that was happening.

But he didn't press.

He gave her space as she left the table, walked out into the living area and up the stairs to the guest wing. At her door, she laid a hand on the jamb and faced him. "I don't know how to thank you for everything you and your family are doing."

"It's what we do," he said and once again realized that he was as much a part of SBS as the three Ramons, his grandmother and mother, the Twins and his tech-savvy cousins.

She cupped his cheek, tenderly stroked her thumb across his evening stubble, mindful of the bruises, and smiled, a real smile that made her emerald-colored eyes sparkle with bits of lighter green and blue. "Good night."

He stroked his hand over hers and grinned. "Good night," he said and waited until she had closed her door behind her. But he didn't head to his bedroom right away.

Lightly treading down the stairs, he went to do a walk around the grounds to make sure all was in order.

Chapter Ten

It shouldn't have surprised him that he ran into his father by the front door.

"*Mi'jo*. There was no need for you to come down," his father said.

He smiled and clapped his father on the back. "I can say the same about you, *papi*."

"Let's walk," he said with a half smile, and they strolled out the door together and to the front gate, which was firmly locked.

As they did their tour of the grounds, his father said, "Mariela seems like an interesting woman."

He wasn't quite sure what to make of his father's use of "interesting."

"She's had a hard time in her life recently," he said in her defense.

His father raised his hand. "I understand she's been abused, *mi'jo*. I'm just concerned about what that means for our family, especially you."

"Because I'm not like *abuelo* or you or Trey," he said, feeling that insecurity that he had battled for so much of his life rise to the surface.

A rough laugh escaped his father. "We might be physically stronger, but what you have in here…" he said and tapped a spot in the center of Ricky's chest. "What you have there is as strong. Maybe stronger."

He was so shocked he didn't know what to say. Instead, he ambled beside his father in the quiet of the night, making sure their home was safe and secure. They strolled around the perimeter of the lot and down to the dock. Bright moonlight illuminated the waters of the bay and canal. A row of lights along the top edge of the bulkhead snapped to life and made the two guards at either end of the property visible.

At the wave of his father's hand, they walked over to join them.

"Everything okay, Esteban? Patrick?"

"All is in order, *jefe*," Esteban said and gestured toward the canal. "No one will get past us."

"Thank you," Ricky said and looked toward the canal. With the moonlight and the lights along the water's edge, any approach would be way too visible. But that morning's attack in broad daylight had been pretty brazen also.

When the guards returned to their positions and his father and he sauntered toward the house, he said, "I want to be ready to defend us."

His father stopped short and peered at him in the dim light beneath a stand of palm trees. A slight breeze shifted the palms, making the fronds crackle and snap.

"I know you're familiar with using a gun. I didn't think you liked them," his father said.

"I don't, but there's a time for everything and I think it's time," he admitted, trusting that the training he'd received over the years would serve him well. Certainly, the martial arts instruction had the night before.

His father laid an arm across his shoulders. "Come with me."

They hurried into the house where his father armed the security system and led him back into his study. At the far end of the room, his father reached into a panel on one of the built-ins and the section swung open like a door: the entrance to the gun range and the small armory beneath the first floor.

They entered the narrow staircase and Ricky closed the door behind them. It had been years since he'd been down in the basement. When they were younger his father would regularly take him and his siblings there so they could learn how to shoot and handle a weapon.

His father had always said that you needed to be prepared to defend your country. As he did so, he'd tell them stories of fleeing Cuba and how his father, their *abuelo*, had fought to make Cuba free. Often, he also shared his stories of being in the marines and serving overseas and then as a police officer.

Ricky had listened and watched. He had even taken his turns shooting when it was time, not that he enjoyed it. But as he'd just told his father, he understood there might be a time when you needed to use a gun.

He stood by his father as he used his palm to open the biometric lock on a large gun safe near the base of the hidden staircase.

Ricky helped him open the heavy doors to reveal half a dozen or so rifles, some of them semiautomatic. Two shotguns. Half a dozen pistols, both semis and revolvers.

He drifted his fingers over the weapons and picked up a nine-millimeter Glock. He checked to make sure there wasn't a bullet in the chamber, not that his father would store a weapon that way, but you always had to check.

"Do you want to reacquaint yourself with it?" his father asked and grabbed a smaller twenty-two-caliber Smith and Wesson from the safe.

The gun range was soundproofed. No one above them would hear a thing if he decided to shoot off a few rounds and test his skills.

He nodded. It had been a few years since he'd fired a weapon. If he needed to use the gun, he wanted to be prepared. Grabbing a magazine and box of ammo, he slipped on protective glasses and ear protection and walked to one of the lanes in the range.

There was a pad with paper targets hanging on one wall and he ripped one off and placed it on the target carrier. With the push of a button, he moved the target down the lane about twenty-five feet.

Carefully he loaded the magazine, slammed it into the grip of the gun, pulled back the slide and flipped the safety off.

His father came up behind him to watch as Ricky took aim and fired. He emptied the entire magazine and was pleased to see that most of the bullets had hit center mass on the target. He removed the magazine, engaged the safety, reloaded and fired off another round of bullets. This time he aimed for different areas on the target and, when he was finished, smiled in satisfaction at hitting his mark almost every time.

With a woot, his father heartily clapped his back. "You haven't lost your touch. You could give Mia a run for the money."

He slipped the magazine from the gun, flipped on the safety and laid the gun on the tabletop. Removing his ear protection, he said in a puzzled tone, "I could give *Mia* a run?"

"Your sister has become quite the shot. Better than Trey. By the way, I've kept your concealed carry permit in order if you want to take that one," he said and gestured to the Glock.

Ricky hesitated and looked from the gun to the target. With a nod, he said, "I'll take it. Are you going to use that one?"

His father shook his head. "No stopping power." He reached behind him, lifted the hem of his *guayabera* shirt and withdrew his gun to show to Ricky. It was an old-style Dirty Harry revolver and loaded. "Never jams."

"I'll keep that in mind," he said, but he'd bet on his fifteen bullets over his father's seven any day. He returned to the tabletop, loaded the magazine and slipped it into the gun. He made sure the safety was on, and when his father handed him a holster, he secured the gun in it and tucked the holster in his waistband against the small of his back.

The weight of it felt weird there. Totally foreign because it was out of his wheelhouse. But given all that had happened last night and this morning, he intended to be prepared for the next time even though he prayed there wouldn't be a next time.

He hoped that the detectives on the two cases would get some useful evidence from the crime scenes and the videos they had gathered to help identify their suspect.

Armed with that hope, he walked back up to the main floor with his father. They embraced in the foyer and his father tightened his hold and said, "I'm very proud of the man you've become."

The words meant more than his father could imagine. For too long he'd lived in the shadow of the three Ramons and even the Twins. All unique and amazing individuals, which was why he'd always felt more comfortable with his more subdued techie cousins and Pepe, who avoided South Beach Security involvement at all costs.

"Good night, *papi*. I love you," he said. His father had always been a good father. Kind. Patient. Supportive. Loving. The insecurities about who he was in the family dynamic had been ones he'd inserted into their relationship, he realized.

His father playfully ruffled his hair and smiled. "I love you, too, *mi'jo*. Get some rest. Tomorrow will be a busy day."

With a nod, he hurried up the stairs, taking them two

at a time in his rush to get to his bedroom, but he skidded to a halt at the sight of Mariela's closed door.

His heart told him to check in on her, but his brain said it was best to leave her alone.

It was much too soon for anyone to handle such new feelings and even harder for someone as fragile as Mariela. He had seen how defensive she'd been during her short stint in the support group as well as her initial reactions to his touch and nearness.

She needed the time alone to process what was happening and realize she wasn't alone anymore. She had the police, his family and him to watch her back.

Much like he'd risen to the challenges presented recently, now it was time for her to harness the inner strength he'd seen to overcome the hurt of the past and build her future.

With that in mind, he turned away from her door and went to his room to get some rest and prepare for tomorrow and the challenges it would bring.

"I PAID YOU to scare her off, not shoot up houses," Jorge shouted and ran a hand through his hair in frustration. "And why didn't you pick up last night? I must have called a dozen times."

"I was trying to lay low, and it wasn't me who shot at them," his former foreman said. He had fired the man for coming to work drunk one time too many, and it was obvious now that he shouldn't have relied on him to do any kind of job. He was sure the man was lying about trying to shoot Mariela.

He paced back and forth across his living room, his fist tight around his cell phone as he said, "All you had to do was warn her to keep her mouth shut."

"I didn't get a chance," the man whined. "She had some guy with her who came in like a ninja or something."

Ninja, Jorge thought and scoffed. His old foreman had probably been drunk again when he'd gone to Mariela's. Maybe even when he'd decided to shoot up the house in Gables by the Sea.

"You royally messed this up. I need you to disappear for a while," Jorge said, his gut twisting with fear at what would happen if anyone discovered he'd paid for the attack.

"What's a while? I can't afford to just up and take a vacation. I need more money," his foreman said.

With what he'd already paid the idiot he could take quite a lot of time off. But he had something different in mind for his former employee.

"Do you know where my new high-rise is going up?"

At the man's grunt, he said, "Meet me there at midnight tonight. I'll have more money for you."

"Thanks, *jefe*," the man said and hung up.

Jorge stopped pacing and paused by the wall of windows that faced the perfectly landscaped gardens surrounding his very expensive pool and spa. Turning, he scrutinized the modern and lavish furniture in the living room and, beyond that, the dream designer kitchen.

He didn't know any woman who wouldn't have wanted to live in such luxury.

Except Mariela, of course.

It hadn't been like that at first. They'd been happy. But Mariela hadn't understood the pressures he'd been under. Hadn't appreciated that everything he'd been doing had been for her.

Always for her, but no longer. Now he had to put himself first.

BY LATE MORNING the next day they had made a list of building inspectors who had handled the various projects Mariela had identified as being problematic. They had also noted a pattern in those projects and others where the two inspectors would reinspect items that had previously failed. Miraculously the buildings would then pass inspection.

Some of those second inspections happened to match up with some odd expenses in the financial statements her attorney had sent over earlier. Much like Mariela had thought, her ex had been hiding the payoffs by claiming them as the costs for marketing and other promotions.

"I remember that there were a few complaints about this building," Mariela said and ran a finger across the one entry on their list.

Ricky nodded. "Maybe there are more at these other buildings as well. Even lawsuits, if the situation is bad enough. We could do a search of the court records for those."

"There was at least one, I think," Mariela confirmed and screwed her eyes shut as she attempted to recall. She popped her eyes open when she remembered and jabbed at another entry on their list of suspect properties. "This one, I think."

"Good job. Let's call Sophie and Robbie to see what they have and if they can help us get the court records," Ricky said.

He speed-dialed his cousins, who immediately answered. "Good morning, Ricky. We were just about to send our analysis of the list you sent. Lots of hinky things there," Sophie said.

"I've got you on speaker, Soph. We've got suspicious things as well. We were hoping you could help us get information on any lawsuits filed against Hernandez's company," Ricky advised.

"We can. How about information on these building inspectors?" Robbie asked.

Ricky took a quick look at her, as if seeking confirmation, and she nodded. "It might help us decide if they're taking bribes," she said.

With a quick dip of his head, he said, "What kind of info can you get?"

"You'd be surprised what's available publicly and what people share," Sophie said with a husky laugh.

Mariela didn't doubt it. She was often shocked by the kind of information people posted on social media. "Whatever you can get would be great," she said.

"We'll touch base with you later. In the meantime, you might want to discuss this information with *Tia* Elena and see what she thinks," Robbie added and ended the call.

A ding immediately followed to advise that an email had arrived. Ricky opened it and printed out the list from his cousins. As they examined it, the same two names that were on their list kept popping up.

"Do you think your aunt can do something with this information?" Mariela asked, doubting that they had enough at the moment for any kind of criminal charges against the men.

"Maybe not, but if she thinks we're on to something, she probably knows who to contact," he said and dialed his aunt.

The conversation with her was short and hopeful since Elena felt there might be enough there to reach out to authorities who could decide whether to investigate the two men.

"That's great, *tia*. We'll get together everything we have and send it to you shortly," Ricky said and hung up.

"What do we do now?" Mariela worried that they had to do more so life could go back to normal. Whatever normal was. She hadn't had normal in a long time. Maybe it would be possible one day, and as she met Ricky's bright blue-eyed gaze, hope grew within her that it would happen soon.

Chapter Eleven

Ricky powered up the engines of the speedboat and pulled away from the dock, Mariela in the cockpit beside him. They'd left the security guards on land to protect his parents, although he was certain his father could handle the kind of trouble likely to come his way. Especially with the discussion he'd had with his father and Trey just a few minutes before while Mariela and his mother had been cleaning up from lunch.

Both his father and brother were certain that it was a one-man operation trying to take out Mariela and probably not a professional. If it had been a professional Mariela would have likely been killed during the first attack. As for the shooting, Trey had been told that the police had a partial license plate number from one of the neighbors' doorbell video feeds. A professional would have been more careful and blacked out the license plate.

Armed with that knowledge, it seemed reasonable to take the boat out to one of the building locations they had identified the night before. He hoped that a quick visual inspection might give them a clue if something was going on with it.

The high-rise condo under construction was located near Bal Harbour and it wouldn't take long to drive the boat to that area.

"Are you sure we'll be okay?" Mariela said, peering around the area as he turned out of the canal and into the waters of Biscayne Bay.

Guilt filled him that he hadn't shared that afternoon's report. "I'm sorry I didn't tell you before. There's been some progress on the case," he said and relayed the information he had discussed with Trey and his father.

"That's good news," she said, visibly relaxing in her seat.

"It is. Hopefully with that info and what we sent to *Tia* Elena, we'll be able to make more progress and keep you safe," he said, steering across the bay and toward the northern-most points on Miami Beach.

"Safe," she said with a harsh laugh.

From the corner of his eye, he could see her retreating again as she wrapped her arms around herself.

"I know it's hard for you to believe that. You haven't been safe in a long time," he said and laid his hand on the throttle, preparing to give the engines some speed. "You strapped in well?"

She pulled on the seat belt straps and, seemingly satisfied, nodded.

"Hold on," he said and pushed the throttle forward, increasing the speed slowly at first, but once they were safely between the mainland and Miami Beach, he pushed the boat to its top speed.

They flew over the surface, water splashing over the bow and windshield as they hit a small swell. The spray drenched them, and he laughed, feeling more carefree than he had in a long time. Her laughter drifted over to him as well and he was grateful that she was enjoying the ride.

He zigged and zagged, mindful of other boats in the area, sending more water up and over. Enjoying Mariela's delight with the ride until they got closer to the location of her ex's new development. He slowed the boat's speed until they neared the backside of the construction site where he killed the boat's engine and pulled out a pair of binoculars to examine the location.

As the boat rocked from a passing wake, Mariela bumped into him.

He slipped an arm around her waist to steady her and handed her the binoculars.

"I don't see anything out of the ordinary," he said as she took them and brought them up to her eyes.

"Not many people working today. Usually there's more activity on a project of this size," she said and gestured to the very bare bones of the building.

At his questioning gaze, she said, "You pick up a few things when you work on projects like this." She motioned to the location again. "Could you get a little closer?"

"Sure. Strap yourself in again," he said and, as soon as she was secured, he cut into the channel of water between Bay Harbour and Bal Harbour so they could get a close-up look at the structure. From what he could see, maybe two dozen men or so were ambling around the property doing a lot of nothing.

"Is that typical?" he asked, wondering how anything got built with so few men and such little labor going on.

Mariela raised the binoculars and surveyed the construction location. He was right that it was far from typical. She'd been on many a job site to show investors around and they'd always been a hub of activity. "It's not," she said and zoomed in to look at where a number of workers sat on a large pile of steel beams, playing a game of cards.

"It looks like they've driven the steel piles for securing the foundation. That usually means they'd be pouring concrete by now," she explained and handed Ricky the binoculars.

He was about to raise them when the windshield of the

speedboat suddenly cracked, and a Sea-Doo raced past them. The rider turned, his face mostly hidden by the cowl of the wetsuit he wore, and fired at them again, shattering another section on the windshield.

Mariela ducked down, but Ricky whipped out a gun and opened fire on the Sea-Doo. The rider must have thought better of attacking again and sped away from them, bouncing across the waves created by the wake of a passing boat.

"HANG ON," RICKY SAID, whipped their boat around and chased after the Sea-Doo, catching up to it easily with the greater power of the speedboat.

Ricky stayed on the tail of the Sea-Doo, trying to get a better look at the rider, but as the Sea-Doo turned toward land, Ricky had to slow down and then stop. The large outboard engines, which had given him the speed to catch up to their shooter, prevented him from entering the shallower waters.

He banged his hand in frustration against the steering wheel and cursed. "He got away. Are you okay?"

"Bounced around a little, but okay otherwise," she said.

"We need to head back, but first…" He whipped out his phone and dialed Trey. When his brother answered, he said, "We were attacked again. Rider on a Sea-Doo. He was headed toward the eastern side of Bal Harbour the last time I saw him."

"How do you know it's a 'him'?" Trey asked.

"Too big and bulky for a woman. He had the same build as the person who shot at us yesterday," he said, recalling what he'd seen of the watercraft rider and yesterday's attacker.

"I'll call some friends on the force there and have them ask around at the local marinas. He has to pull in somewhere," Trey said.

"Thanks. We're headed back to the house," he said,

but plopped into the captain's chair as his knees suddenly felt weak.

"Are you sure you're okay?" Mariela asked and laid a hand on his chest, directly above his heart.

He took hold of her hand and brought it to his lips. "I'm fine. Just a little shaken, as I imagine you are."

"I am. I'll be better once we're home," she said with a smile.

Home. The word sounded nice coming off her lips. Those full lips that he'd thought about last night as he'd finally drifted off to sleep. He found himself shifting toward her, closer and closer to those lips he wanted to taste until the rev of an engine reminded him they weren't safe out here on open water.

He stroked a hand across her cheek, trailing his thumb along the line of her lips. "Let's go home."

HIS MOTHER WAS waiting for them back at the house, nervously pacing back and forth along the length of the dock. Hands tucked beneath her arms. She stopped at the sight of the speedboat, hurried to the water's edge and grabbed hold of the line that Mariela tossed to her while he eased the boat closer.

One of the security guards rushed over to tie the line onto a cleat while the second man stood to secure the area and protect them.

He killed the engine as Mariela tossed out a second line and he rushed over to make sure the bumpers were in place. Once the boat was tied to the dock, he jumped out onto the wooden planks and helped Mariela from the boat.

His mother's blue-eyed gaze, so much like his own, mirrored his worry. He forced a smile to his lips, trying to dispel her fear. "I handled it."

She shook her head and tears glistened in her eyes. "I

know. It's just that I hoped… I was glad when you didn't join the agency because it meant you were safe. Now…"

"It will be fine. Trey is already working on getting more information for us," he said, reassuring his mother.

She nodded and abruptly rushed toward the house.

He sighed and Mariela slipped her arm around his waist. "She's just worried."

"Who isn't?" he said and mimicked Mariela's gesture, encircling her waist with his arm and drawing her close. "Let's get cleaned up. I'm sure Trey and *papi* will be here soon and want a report on what happened."

"Then let's get going," she said, and they walked arm in arm toward the house, hips bumping. They didn't separate once inside and went up the stairs together. In the small foyer before their bedrooms, they finally parted to stand there and stare at each other.

Ricky cupped her cheek and stepped close until her warm breath spilled against his lips. Soft and regular at first, but then harder, faster, when he laid a hand at her waist and closed the gap between them.

She inched up on tiptoes and met his lips with hers, the kiss gentle. Hesitant as if she hadn't kissed anyone in a long time.

He didn't press, aware of her past. Hoping to build trust for the future.

He let her end the kiss, giving her the control she'd lacked in her life for so long.

When she stepped away, he ran the back of his hand across her cheek. "I'll meet you downstairs when you're done."

MARIELA COULDN'T FIND her voice. Her throat was too choked up with the emotion of that so simple, but so pure, touch.

All she could do was nod and rush off to her bedroom

to wash off the sea spray from their ride and the fear that had gripped her yet again at the sound of the first bullet hitting the boat's windshield.

He had defended her again, risking his life. Again.

She had no doubt it was going to happen again. This time she intended to be prepared for it just like Ricky had been prepared. She'd been surprised when he'd pulled out a weapon to chase away their attacker, but he'd handled it with ease.

After their meeting with Trey and his father, she was going to ask Ricky to show her how to protect herself. She wouldn't be caught defenseless again.

"ARE YOU SURE you want to do this?" Ricky asked, worry slithering through him even as he slipped off his shoes and stepped onto the mat in the family gym.

"I want to be able to do something," Mariela said and toed off her sneakers. She grabbed the loose strands of her caramel-colored hair and did a little flip and twist with it that turned the longish strands into a top knot. An oversize T-shirt with the U of M logo hung loosely over her upper body and the leggings she had changed into after dinner and a short walk around the grounds. As they had strolled to the water's edge, she had asked him to teach her how to defend herself.

She stepped onto the mat, and he shook his head with doubt but began the lesson. "Okay. Let's start with what to do if someone grabs you from behind," he said and took a position at her back, his arm wrapped around her throat.

"First thing to do is to jam your elbow into their midsection," he said and instructed her to mimic the action. When she did, he play-acted the position he'd be in, doubled over slightly and said, "Now you can either use your elbow or the palm of your hand to hit them in the nose."

She tried to do it but couldn't quite come around because of their height difference. "I can't," she said, dejection in her voice.

"That's okay. If you can't, drive your foot into his instep, especially if you've got heels on," he instructed.

She made believe she had done that, and Ricky released her so that they were now facing one another. "Now that you're free, use your legs. Women's legs are their strongest feature. Kick him in the groin. The knee. Anywhere, really."

Mariela hesitated, clearly not wanting to hurt him. "I get it."

Ricky nodded. "Once he's doubled over, don't stop. Use the heel of your palm and smash his nose in or punch him in the throat."

"And after that?" she asked.

"Scream. Actually, start screaming the moment he grabs you. If that doesn't scare him off, someone may hear and call the police. If you have keys in your hand, put them between your fingers and jab at his eyes or throat. Anything to disable the person," he said and was about to show her another move when his cell phone started ringing.

"It's Trey," he said and put the phone on speaker.

"I have good news and bad news. Which do you want to hear first?" Trey said.

Ricky met Mariela's worry-filled gaze. "The bad news," she said.

"They tracked down the license plate on the BMW, but it appears to have been stolen."

Ricky muttered a curse and shook his head. "Is that all the bad news?"

"Yes. The good news is we have more video of the car from a marina in Bal Harbour. Probably stolen plates again, but we were able to confirm the make and model of the car. It's a late model black BMW 330 sedan."

With a low whistle, Ricky said, "There must be thousands of them in the Miami-Dade area."

"There are, but the vehicle had some distinguishing features—a custom spoiler and front bumper valance. There was also a decal on a side window that looks like it's from a local university."

"I guess that's good news," Mariela said, hesitation alive in her tone. "What about the driver?" she quickly tacked on.

"No visuals from the marina. Just what we have from your neighbor's doorbell camera. But the police have a BOLO out for the vehicle and a basic description of the driver. I've got Sophie and Robbie making a list of vehicle owners and trying to enhance the doorbell and marina videos the police finally released to us."

"How long will that take?" Ricky asked, worried that they had so little to go on when lives were at stake.

"Robbie says we'll have more from them by midafternoon tomorrow," Trey advised, and in the background he heard Roni call out to his brother.

"I have to go, but I'll keep you posted as soon as we have anything else. In the meantime, sit tight," Trey advised and ended the call.

Ricky stared at the silent phone, frustrated. "Sit tight. I guess he's right. I don't want anyone shooting at us again."

Mariela felt the waves of frustration pouring off Ricky's body. She laid a hand on his forearm as he stood there, still staring at the phone. "They're going to get the information, but…there must be something else we can do."

"I agree. You seemed to know a lot about what was happening at that building site," he said and took hold of her hand.

"You learn a lot when you're taking possible investors around. They would ask questions and I made a point of learning so I could answer," she explained and tugged on his hand. "Go ahead. Ask me."

A small smile inched across his lips. "Why do you think that they wouldn't be doing more work on that site today?"

With a shrug, she said, "It could be as simple as they're waiting on an inspection or found problems with the foundation."

Ricky wagged his head back and forth, considering what she'd said. "Who would know what's happening?"

"Lots of people," she said with another shrug. "Jorge, of course. The engineers on the project. Inspectors—"

"Think lower down the food chain. People who might be willing to speak to us," Ricky said and, with a tug on her hand, led her to the edge of the mat where they picked up their shoes and walked out into the main living space on the first floor. His parents had gone up to their wing shortly after dinner and the area was empty.

Soft light bathed the space from some table lamps on either side of the room, creating a welcoming feel.

They sat on a sofa that faced windows offering views of the stunning vista beyond. The pool and gardens. The canal, the skyline of Miami and the waters of Biscayne Bay.

Once she'd sat, she said, "Lower in the food chain? The foreman. Assistant foreman. Of course, the workers. They talk a lot about what's happening on the site because their jobs depend on it going well."

Ricky faced her on the couch and took hold of both of her hands. "Is there anyone who would speak to you? Who you trust? Like one of those workers?"

Trust? It had been so long since she'd thought she could trust anyone. She'd been too busy helping Jorge to build any real friendships. When she'd gone to her parents about her divorce, they hadn't understood why she would want to leave Jorge. In their minds he'd given her and them so much. So much that they stood to lose.

"Mariela?" Ricky pressed at her prolonged silence.

"Maybe one of the foremen. Rafael Lopez. We became friendly, especially once I recommended him to become the head foreman when Jorge had to fire the other one," she said, recalling how grateful Rafael had been that she'd spoken up for him.

Ricky nodded. "Do you think he'd talk to you? Tell you what's happening at the site?"

"Maybe," she said, possibly a little too quickly. Rafael had a wife and children. Talking to her might risk his job, but she hoped he was an honest man who would speak out if there was something wrong at the location.

"We can reach out to him. See what he says," she said, didn't wait for him to answer and pulled her cell phone out of her pocket.

"Or we could sit tight," Ricky said, repeating his brother's earlier instructions.

"Is that what you really want to do?" she asked, held up her cell phone and gestured to him with it.

"No. I want to get to the bottom of this. Too much is at stake."

Chapter Twelve

He'd missed them again and cursed himself for how he'd blundered. It had been silly to try and take them out on open water and he'd been careless when driving away from the marina where he'd ditched the stolen Sea-Doo.

The BOLO on the BMW had come across the police scanner, warning him that he had to be more careful. He had to wait for the right opportunity to strike out once more.

Being impatient would not do him any good. It wouldn't help him accomplish his goal.

Patience, he counseled himself, turned up the police scanner to see if they had any more info on him and poured himself a drink.

Taking a sip of the rum, he smiled when nothing else came across the scanner about him and the BMW and planned out his next steps.

RAFAEL LOPEZ HAD been hesitant to speak to her at first. When she'd called, it had almost been impossible to hear him over the excited laughter of his children in the background. She'd worried he'd hang up, until she'd mentioned her fears that someone might get hurt if he didn't help them. At that mention, he'd reluctantly agreed to meet with her the next morning and given her the name of a small café in South Beach.

Ricky and she sat in the café the next morning, waiting for Rafael to show up. She tapped her foot nervously, not sure that he would come as he had promised. Peering around the café, she didn't see any familiar faces or any workmen. The location was in the heart of South Beach on Collins and filled mostly with tourists and beachgoers picking up coffees and breakfast.

They had ordered breakfast also as they waited. *Cafés con leche* and toasted Cuban bread. Across from her Ricky dipped his bread into the coffee and ate, but it was almost mechanical, like something he had to do to keep patient as they waited and waited.

She looked around again, but there was no sign of Rafael. Peering at Ricky's phone, she said, "Any news?" They had given Rafael Ricky's phone number because at Sophie's suggestion earlier that morning, they'd disabled her phone, worried that Jorge had been tracking her.

It made sense because there was no other way anyone could know that they'd gone to Ricky's house and then to the new construction site.

She picked up her piece of toast and nibbled on it, not really hungry either. Nerves had killed her appetite and, like Ricky, she just needed something to do to keep from going crazy during their wait. She had finished her bread and *café con leche* and almost given up hope when Rafael hurried through the door.

He wore faded jeans and a denim work shirt tossed over a T-shirt. Heavy work boots clomped on the tile floor as he walked over to them.

She stood as he approached and introduced the two men. "Rafael Lopez. Meet Ricky Gonzalez. He and his family—"

"I know who his family is. But why are they involved?"

Rafael asked and slipped into a seat across from her at the table.

She worried about telling Rafael too much, but then again, he was risking a great deal to meet them. "Someone attacked me the other night."

"And shot up his house," Rafael jumped in and gestured with a work-roughened hand in Ricky's direction. "It was all over the news."

"It was," Ricky acknowledged with a curt nod. "We think someone did that because Mariela knows something major is wrong with one of Hernandez's latest projects."

"They want to keep her quiet?" Lopez said and pointed to his chest. "I have a family, *mano*. I can't be involved in anything that could hurt them."

"We understand. We won't betray your trust," Mariela said and covered the foreman's hand with her own. It trembled beneath her palm, and he withdrew it quickly, possibly afraid she'd sense his fear.

"And you could be saving lives, Rafael," Ricky urged, clearly trying to appeal to the man's humanity.

Rafael peered down at the tabletop and splayed his thick fingers on the wooden surface. They were workman's hands, nicked and cut in places. Calloused. He ran them back and forth across the surface, and then dipped his head before glancing at them.

"What do you need?"

RICKY HAD DOZENS of questions, but let Mariela take the lead since she understood more about the construction process than he did.

"No one seems to be working on the high-rise condo. Is there something wrong there?" she asked.

Rafael shrugged broad shoulders, stretching tight the fabric of his work shirt with his labor-hard muscles. "The structural engineer inspected and said he wanted the beams deeper, but the pile driver had already been moved to another location. We have to wait for it to come back."

"So nothing's wrong at that location?" Mariela asked.

Rafael dipped his head in confirmation. "*Nada, pero…* The mid-rise passed the inspection the other day, only… I noticed some cracks. That shouldn't be happening. I think they're coming back for more inspections soon."

"You think something was wrong with that first inspection?" Mariela asked while Ricky pulled out his smartphone, tapped in something and then held the phone up for both Rafael and her to see.

"These are the inspection reports. Do the inspectors' names seem familiar?" he asked.

Rafael peered at the names, squinting, and when the foreman sat back, she looked at the reports also, although she had already seen them the other morning.

"I know those two. Smith and Levy. They've inspected a number of our buildings," Rafael said and once again swiped his hands across the surface of the table as if he was clearing away dirt.

"Rafael?" Mariela pressed.

"Sometimes we had a problem and didn't pass. I'd get the men to work on fixing the issues, but sometimes before we did, I'd be told that we were good to go," Rafael admitted.

"Good to go as in you had passed the inspection?" Ricky asked, wanting to make sure he understood what the other man was saying.

"*Sí.* Like we had passed, only I don't remember any new inspections," the other man said and shot to his feet. "I have to go, or I'll be late for work."

He started to walk away, but Mariela stopped him with a gentle touch on his arm. "Do you remember which properties, Rafael?"

The man nodded. "I'll send you a list. Later. I have to get to work," he said and rushed off.

Ricky stared at his back as the foreman hurried from the café and walked down the block. "He seems like a good man."

"He is," Mariela said and sipped the last little bit of her coffee, which was lukewarm by now.

"Do you think he'll send us a list?" Ricky asked, worried that the other man might reconsider if he thought it might endanger his family to assist them.

Mariela's brow furrowed as she considered his question. But then she nodded and said, "I do. But he said later. What do we do in the meantime?"

As if in answer, his phone pinged. A message from Sophie and Robbie. Here's a list of lawsuits filed against the developer.

He held up the phone for Mariela to see the message. "Looks like we have some homework to do."

THE LIST OF lawsuits was longer than she had expected.

She had occasionally overheard Jorge talking to his attorney about one of the actions, but when she'd asked, he'd always blown her off, telling her it was nothing for her to worry about. Seeing the list made her wonder how Jorge had managed to keep it all from her and what would happen if he lost the lawsuits.

"There are so many," she said as she ran her finger down the list of well over a dozen legal actions against her ex's company.

"There are. Let's find out which properties are involved in the lawsuits and cross-reference that against the inspectors who worked on them," Ricky said as they sat beside each other at the table in his father's study.

Mariela grabbed a pad and pen from the center of the table while Ricky manned the laptop to get the addresses of the buildings involved in the legal actions. "Could you let me have the names of the people suing also? Maybe we can reach out to them for more information," she said.

"Got it." He worked off the list that Sophie and Robbie had produced. One by one he got the information for the addresses and plaintiffs and read them off to her.

It seemed like it took forever to organize the information. They had just finished when Ricky's mother came in together with Josie, who was wheeling a service cart that held several dishes, glasses and an assortment of sodas.

"We thought you might be hungry since it's lunch hour," she said as Josie whipped the tops off the plates to reveal Cuban sandwiches and plantain chips.

"That's so nice of you," Mariela said and rose to hug the other two women.

"Anytime. Besides, Ricky can be a bear if he's hungry," Samantha said with a laugh. "Will you be around for dinner?" she asked with an arch of a brow.

RICKY WAS WELL aware of what his mother was asking with that tone. She probably knew Trey had told them to sit tight and was worried that Ricky wouldn't listen and do something else that was risky. But as much as he always appreciated his mother's concern, he was a grown man who could take care of himself.

"I don't know, *mami*. We may have to step out to speak to some people," he said.

"Ricky—" she began.

But he cut her off with, "We'll be fine."

His mom's lips tightened into a knife-sharp line. "I understand," she said even though it was obvious she didn't.

After his mother and Josie had left, he hopped to his feet to grab them sodas while Mariela placed the plates with the sandwiches on the table. Once they had sat down to eat and continue working, Mariela said, "Your mom is very nice."

Much as he had heard the silent question in his mother's voice, what Mariela hadn't said was as clear to him. "But she worries too much."

"It must be hard to see her family in danger," Mariela said and nibbled on one of the halves of the Cuban sandwich.

"It is. It almost broke my heart to hear her crying if my dad was hurt and when Trey was shot several weeks ago," he said and took a bite of his sandwich. The roast pork had the overtones of a citrus marinade, the ham was sweet, the swiss cheese nutty and the final touches of yellow mustard and pickles just helped boost all the different flavors in the sandwich.

"It must be scary," she said and munched on a few of the crispy plantain chips.

"It's not as scary now that they're both with the agency."

Mariela chewed on the chips thoughtfully. "But you're with the agency also, right?"

Ricky did a hesitant shrug. "Yes and no."

Mariela's puzzled look pressed him for more and he said, "I assist them on cases with people who might have issues with trauma or abuse. Sometimes I help profile possible suspects, even though that's not really my thing."

A long pause followed, and Mariela bit her lower lip before she blurted out, "People like me. Clients like me."

Ricky sucked in a deep breath and trapped it before he released it slowly. "I don't think of you as a client. Not anymore," he admitted.

She did a little half smile, and as he met her gaze, her emerald eyes glittered with joy. "I'm glad you don't."

She was too much to resist. He cupped her cheek and leaned forward until their lips were barely an inch apart. But he hesitated and said, "Are you sure?"

Chapter Thirteen

"I am," Mariela said and closed the distance between them.

His lips were warm, soft at first, but as the kiss intensified, they became harder. More insistent, and something about that, about the force of it, sent a shiver of fear through her.

Sensing it, Ricky tempered his kiss and inched away, but he stroked his thumb across her cheek and then down across her lips. "I would never hurt you, Mariela."

"I know, it's just… I know," she repeated, reminding herself that Ricky was nothing like Jorge. He was thoughtful and caring. The kind of man a woman would want at her side as a partner. But she'd sensed he had his demons as well.

"Let's finish this up and see who the inspectors were," Ricky said and settled back into his chair, giving her needed space.

They went back to work, adding the names of the individuals who had inspected each of the projects to Mariela's list. Time and time again the same names came up.

"It's too much coincidence," Ricky said, leaned back and stroked his chin while reviewing the list.

"What do we do now?" she asked, skimming the names with a finger.

Ricky looked at his watch and then at the list again.

"Let's get phone numbers for these plaintiffs and call to see if they'll talk to us. If they won't, maybe their attorneys will."

"I'm Jorge's ex-wife. Do you actually think they'll talk to me?" Mariela said and pushed the pad toward Ricky.

"Good point. But you're not named in any of the lawsuits," Ricky said.

Mariela raked her hair back with her fingers. "Still, his ex. For all they know, I had something to do with whatever shady stuff went on."

Ricky nodded and blew out a rough sigh. "They may not think it was shady stuff, just bad construction."

Mariela hadn't thought there was anything underhanded at first either. By the time she'd had serious misgivings about Jorge's business dealings, she'd been too busy avoiding his barbed words and then his fists. Between that, school and her parents' illnesses, she hadn't been able to do anything but focus on how to get out of her abusive marriage.

"You can't blame yourself," Ricky said, clearly sensitive to what she was thinking.

In truth, she didn't blame herself. "I'm not. I was just trying to survive, but I want to make things right."

Ricky stroked his hand across her back, his touch reassuring. "We will. Together."

"Together," she said, grateful that she no longer had to bear the burden alone.

He held up the pad of paper and smiled. "Let's make those calls."

RICKY STOOD BY Trey as his brother poured Scotch into glasses for the men.

Roni, Mariela and their mom had stepped out for an after-dinner stroll in the garden.

"How's your part of the investigation going?" Trey asked and handed him a glass.

"Good. We've put together a list of problem properties and the building inspectors who worked on them. We have a few meetings lined up for tomorrow to chat with the condo owners and one of the lawyers," he said and walked to the living room sofa.

His father sat in one of the wing chairs across from the sofa and Trey detoured there to hand his father a glass before sitting beside Ricky. But instead of sitting, Trey stood there and sipped his Scotch, his face slightly downturned.

"Spit it out, Trey," Ricky said, well familiar with his brother's avoidance mode.

"The police haven't made a lot of progress on finding the BMW. Sophie, Robbie and me either. But there is some good news. They got some partial prints from Mariela's sliding door and they're running them through the system," Trey said, a glower on his face.

"It is good news. Why the face?" he asked, puzzled by his brother's upset.

Trey shook his head. "It just doesn't feel like enough to keep you safe," he said and took a big slug of his Scotch.

Ricky stared down at his glass and swirled around the ice and liquor. "We were careful to make sure no one was following us. Nothing happened today. Sophie was right that Hernandez must have had a tracker on Mariela's phone."

Trey pointed to him with the hand that held the glass. "I should have thought of that right off the bat."

Maybe he should have, but Trey had had a lot on his mind lately. Before he could point it out, their father did.

"*Mi'jo*, you've had a lot going on. Leaving the force. Your engagement to Roni. And I've put a lot of responsibility on you at the agency. I should have thought about the phone being tracked as well."

"I won't make a mistake like that again, Ricky. I promise," Trey said and finally plopped onto the sofa next to him.

The slight grate of the sliding French door warned that the women were coming in from their walk.

Mariela and his mother were strolling arm in arm like old friends. Roni had her head tucked close to Mariela's and all the women were smiling, like they didn't have a care in the world. It reminded him of how strong his mother had been no matter what had been going on in their lives. She had always put on a brave face for them. Always made them feel things would be okay no matter how hard it had been at times.

Much like the three women were doing right now.

When they neared, his mother slipped her arm from Mariela, who strolled over and sat to his right. His mother took the wing chair beside his father and Roni slipped in beside Trey on the large leather sofa.

The only thing that kept it from being a homey family scene was Mia's absence, but no sooner had he thought it than Mia came bounding in with Carolina. The Twins waltzed over, kissed everyone in welcome and hauled over two chairs from the nearby dining area table.

"Looks like you're heading to a party," he said, taking in the expensive dresses and heels the two were wearing.

"Going over to the Del Sol," Mia said and a blush worked across her cheeks.

"Going to see John Wilson? The millionaire gamer?" Trey said, and the color deepened even more.

"He's not what he seems, and he's given me some info on Hernandez," Mia said defensively and raised her chin a defiant inch.

"What kind of info?" Ricky asked, wondering what someone like Wilson would be doing with Mariela's husband.

"Apparently Hernandez had heard that Wilson was looking for a location for a new software company he's created. He offered to sell him one of the properties he's just starting to develop. John—"

"It's John now?" Trey teased with the arch of a dark brow.

Mia rolled her eyes and lifted her hand to ask Carolina to finish the story.

"John asked around to other real estate types. We did, too. Wives. Household staff. Rumor is that Hernandez is seriously in debt and may not have enough to complete his high-rise project unless he can offload the mid-rise development," Carolina said.

"We think there's something funky with that project," Ricky explained.

"Why is that, *mi'jo*?" his father asked.

Ricky shared a look with Mariela and, at her nod, he said, "A reliable source."

"How reliable?" Trey pushed.

"We're not at liberty to say," Ricky replied, honoring their promise to Rafael.

Trey waited a beat, but then nodded. "It's late, but I'll call Sophie and Robbie and have them get as much information as they can about that project. Blueprints and things like that."

"We've already reviewed the inspection reports. We have meetings with people suing about other projects to see what they have to say," Ricky advised the larger group, repeating what he'd told Trey and his father earlier.

Mariela jumped in with, "We think there may be problems with other buildings."

"You'll both keep us posted on what you find?" his father said.

"And you'll all be careful," his mother tacked on, ever the Mama Bear.

"We will," Trey and he said in almost unison, drawing chuckles from both parents.

"Well, we'd love to stay, but we've got to make our entrance at the Del Sol," Mia said, shot onto her three-inch heels and smoothed the black fabric of her dress over her generous curves. Carolina also stood and tugged the hem of her silver dress lower over her thighs.

"Say hello to John, for me," Roni said. She had met the reclusive millionaire while undercover on her last investigation.

"I will. By the way, he says you should come by and game with him again. You're the best so far," Mia said with a smile and wink at Trey, who wrapped a possessive arm around Roni. Payback for his earlier teasing.

"I'll think about it," Roni said with a chuckle.

The Twins waved goodbye and rushed out the door, laughing and teasing each other.

"Are they always that upbeat?" Mariela whispered in his ear.

"Mostly, but they can be serious when they need to," he said, remembering their worry when Trey had been shot just several weeks earlier.

"Time for us to go, too. I'm on the early shift tomorrow," Roni said, rose and extended a hand to her fiancé, coupled with a wink.

Ricky bit back any comment on the wink because he was very happy that Trey finally had more in his life than his old cop job.

The couple gave their goodbyes, leaving Ricky and Mariela alone with his parents. But not for long. Barely a minute had passed when his father stood and gestured for his wife to join him. His mother rose, slipped her hand into his father's and tucked herself into his side, the gesture heartwarming. So loving.

"It's time for us to give you some privacy," his father said.

Privacy? Ricky thought and peeked at Mariela.

Like Mia before her, hot color flooded Mariela's cheeks.

"Thank you, but we were just going to go back to work," he lied, wanting to dissuade his parents from any thoughts they might have about Mariela and him being together.

As much as he wanted it to happen, he didn't want to rush it.

His mother and father shared a look, clearly not believing him. But they didn't press the issue.

"We'll see you in the morning," his mother said and, with a wave, his parents walked up the stairs, hand in hand, heads bent together. At something his father said, his mother chuckled and dropped a kiss on his cheek.

"They're still so in love. Roni and Trey, too," Mariela said with a heartfelt sigh.

"They are. It gives me hope I can have the same thing one day," he said and gazed at her, but she looked away, clearly unsettled by his words.

"Hopefully. I guess we should go up, too, and get some rest. Tomorrow is going to be a busy day." She almost jumped to her feet and nervously slapped her thighs with her hands.

She wasn't wrong about tomorrow. With all the meetings they'd set up for the next day, they'd be very busy.

He stood and walked with her up the stairs, but not side by side, giving her some distance to make her feel more at ease. At her door, she stopped to look at him and it was obvious she needed space that night.

Because of that, he stuffed his hands into his jeans pockets to keep from touching her. "Have a good night."

"Good night and thank you for everything, Ricky." She rocked to-and-fro on her feet for a second before dropping a quick kiss on his cheek and rushing into her room.

He stood there for a long moment, staring at the closed door. But then he turned and hurried down to his father's study.

He was too wound up to sleep and intended to go over all the information they had gleaned that day. Hopefully he would find something else that would tell them what Jorge was doing that was important enough to kill for.

Chapter Fourteen

"I hope you understand why I'm reticent to discuss my client's lawsuit in the presence of Ms. Hernandez," the attorney said and leaned back in his chair. He placed his elbows on the arms, brought his fingers to his lips and stared from Ricky to her over and over.

Mariela leaned forward in her chair and said, "We're divorced, and it wasn't amicable, Mr. Angelo."

The attorney remained silent, glaring at them.

"We won't waste any more of your time," Ricky said and popped out of his chair.

Mariela was about to follow him when the attorney surged forward and opened the file that had been sitting on his desk when they had first walked in.

"Sit down, Mr. Gonzalez," he said and pulled a thick sheaf of papers from the file. He pushed them toward the edge of the desk. "I know your family quite well."

Ricky's lips tightened into a harsh slash. "We'd like your assistance because it's the right thing to do, not to earn brownie points with my family."

"Call it whatever you like. That's a structural engineer's report on the property. The building was constructed on reclaimed land," the attorney explained.

"But many buildings in Miami and in other coastal cities are built on reclaimed land," Mariela said.

"And most of the Netherlands," the attorney replied and continued. "The issue is that it was improperly constructed. Based on the state of the ground beneath the building, the support beams should have been driven deeper."

Just like the beams on the high-rise structure, Mariela thought.

"Is that what the other homeowners are alleging?" Ricky asked.

Mr. Angelo nodded. "They are. We tried to initiate the lawsuits as a class action, but we didn't have enough people to do that. It's why there are so many legal actions instead of one."

"May we make a copy?" Ricky asked and held up the report.

The attorney waved his hand at it. "That's a copy I made for you."

"We appreciate it," Mariela said and stood, sensing that their time with the attorney was up.

Ricky did the same, but as they headed for the door, the attorney stopped them. "Just another thing. When the condo board first suggested that the residents sue, people were harassed. Little things at first, like flat car tires and elevators that went out of order and took a lot of time to fix."

Mariela didn't miss where he was going. "You said 'at first.'"

The attorney nodded and rose from his chair to join them at the door. "One of the board members got mugged in the parking lot. Another one's car was broken into and trashed. You didn't hear this from me, but a lot of people thought Hernandez was behind it all."

"Thank you for the warning, Mr. Angelo," Ricky said and glanced at her over his shoulder.

"Thanks again for chatting with us," she said and slipped her hand into Ricky's as they left the attorney's office, walked past his assistant and out into the corridor where Ricky stopped to look at her again.

"Maybe we should rethink the visit to the condo owners. We don't want to cause them any more trouble," he said.

"I agree. We can probably get the answers we need over the phone." Answers but not an in-person view of the problems they had sued over.

"Let's head back home and make those calls."

Home. She had to admit his parents' place felt like a home. Maybe because it was filled with family that loved and cared for each other so much.

As they neared Ricky's car, his phone rang, and he answered. "*Hola, mano...* That's good to hear. We'll meet you there." He paused to look at his watch. "We can be there in about fifteen minutes."

When he finished, he said, "The police have released both our houses. Trey is meeting us at my house so I can see what I need to do to make it habitable. If there's anything you need, we can run by your house afterward."

She held her hands up to shut that down because she still couldn't face going into her home. Being alone again. "I'm good."

He did a little nod. "Let's go. We can phone the condo owners on the way and explain our concerns about meeting with them in person."

After he pulled out of the parking lot, they contacted everyone who had agreed to talk to them and, surprisingly, most were still agreeable to having them come by in person as planned.

"My daddy always told me there's only one way to deal with a bully—you have to stand up to them," the last owner had said before hanging up.

"Are you up for the visit?" Ricky asked and shot her a quick look from the corner of his eye as he drove.

"I'm not going to let him scare me away," she said,

determined to be in control of her own life. Determined not to be bullied anymore.

RICKY RISKED ANOTHER look at her and the determination was clear in the set of her face and body.

"I'm proud of you, Mariela," he said, truly admiring her for the strength she had shown in standing up for herself by divorcing Jorge and by continuing to take part in this investigation. Someone else might have hidden out to stay safe instead of trying to get to the truth.

"Thank you," she said, and he could tell that it had been a long time since she'd heard those words from someone.

When he turned onto his street just over ten minutes later, Trey's car was parked to one side of the circular drive. Ricky pulled up opposite him, killed the engine and gripped the steering wheel tightly as he stared at his home.

Plywood covered what had once been big picture windows in his living room and office. Bits of glass from the windows and front door littered the ground and bullet holes marred the normally smooth stucco exterior.

"I'm so sorry," Mariela said and hugged him hard, surprising him with the affection.

"Thank you," he said, returned the embrace and held her for long seconds.

A knock on the driver's side glass jerked them apart and Trey bent to peer through the window.

Heat filled his cheeks, but he ignored his brother's knowing grin and shoved the door open, driving Trey away from the car.

He stepped out and his brother walked beside him to the front door, Mariela trailing slightly behind them. "The detectives locked up," Trey said as they stepped onto the small patio at the entrance. A bullet had hit one of the aqua-colored planters flanking the patio and it had broken in two. Dirt and wilted impatiens littered the ground around it.

Ricky took a deep breath, preparing himself for what he would find inside. He slipped in his key, unlocked the door and walked in.

The bulk of the glass from the windows and doors carpeted the hardwood floors of the foyer, living room and his office. Intermixed with the glass were shards from lamps, picture frames and mementos shattered by the fusillade of gunfire.

His brother clapped his back while Mariela slipped an arm around his waist.

"We will fix this, *mano*," Trey said, grasped his shoulder and squeezed.

A soft sob came from beside him and he looked at Mariela. Tears streamed down her face.

He wrapped her in his arms, kissed the top of her head and murmured, "They're just things. They're not what's important."

That quieted her crying, but only a little. He held her, soothing her by running his hand up and down her back as he once again surveyed the damage to his home.

"*Papi* gave me the name of a contractor and I can call him if you want. Hang out here and get some estimates for you," Trey said, his hands tucked into his pants pockets. He rocked on his heels, clearly also upset by what he was seeing.

"That would be great. Mariela and I were supposed to meet with some people this afternoon," Ricky said and quickly tacked on, "That is if you still feel up to it."

SHE WASN'T UP to it, but she owed him for all that he'd done and for what Jorge or his henchman had done to Ricky's home.

"I'm up to it. I want to find out who did this," she said,

waving her arm around at the destruction in the rooms. "I want Jorge to pay for all this."

"Between South Beach Security and the police, we will find out who did this and make them pay," Trey replied.

"Like he did when he beat me bad enough to put me in the hospital?" she shot back, eyebrows raised in challenge.

"My uncle is dealing with that. He's pulled that DA's case files and is reviewing them with the head DA," Trey said.

That caught her off guard because she hadn't thought there was anything they could do about the DA's prosecution decisions.

"I didn't realize… Thank you. Again," she said, feeling as if she would never be able to thank them enough for all that they were doing on her behalf.

"You two should get going," Trey said and tipped his head in a go-ahead gesture.

"Thank you for helping out," Ricky said and hugged Trey. He reached over with a hand, inviting her to join him, and she slipped her hand into his.

They hurried out of the house, and as they did so, Ricky took a long look over his shoulder at his home. His face was stern, lips tight, and a hard glitter darkened his blue eyes.

"We will fix this," she said and gently squeezed his hand.

Is it a we? Ricky wondered, worried that there were so many emotions at play with both of them that anything they might be feeling was not trustworthy.

Ignoring that worry, he helped her into the car, got in and drove to the building that was the subject of the lawsuits. Pulling in front of the condos there was nothing in-your-face obvious to say there were structural issues. But when they walked to the front door, he noticed some hairline cracks at the upper corners of the glass doors, and it took a hard pull to open them.

Inside, they went to the elevator. A big Out of Order sign was taped to the metal door.

"I guess he's still punishing them," Mariela said.

"Seems that way. It's the stairs for us," Ricky said and peered up and down the corridor, searching for the entrance to the stairs. It was at the end of the hall, and they hurried there and up the three stories to the first condo unit on their list of interviews.

To their surprise, there were multiple owners present inside.

"We thought it might be easier for you to meet with us all at once. It'll probably avoid repetition," the one man said. He was an older gentleman, probably in his seventies, and he invited them into his unit with a wave of his hand. Once they had stepped in, he took a spot beside a gray-haired woman who Ricky assumed was his wife.

There were two other couples there as well. He guessed the men sitting together on a white wicker sofa were in their thirties and partners, while the other duo was a fortysomething man and woman. The fortysomethings sat in a pair of wing chairs leaving a white wicker love seat for Mariela and him.

The gentleman who had let them in introduced everyone gathered there. "I'm Russ Smith. This is my wife, Betty," he said and laid a hand on his spouse's shoulder. "Tim and Bob are in unit 400. Elaine and Jerry are above them in unit 500."

"Thank you for the introductions. I'm Ricardo Gonzalez and this is Mariela Hernandez," he said, which caused a ripple of surprise and worry to rush over the owners.

Tim stammered, "H-Hernandez, as in—"

"He's my ex. We divorced a year ago because…he abused me. Physically and mentally," she said, her voice wavering with upset but the truth of her words resonated with the owners.

Bob reached over and grasped Mariela's hand. "It's okay, Mariela. I was once in a similar relationship until I got out. Now I'm incredibly happy with Tim."

"Thank you," she said, and with that awkwardness done, Ricky and Mariela questioned the owners about the problems they had encountered and what Mariela's ex had done in retribution for the lawsuits.

Ricky listened, mentally taking notes. At one point Russ stood, stalked over to the windows to point out the small cracks near the frames and then to a corner of the room where there was a very visible separation between the walls. "Since we're all in the corner condos, we're seeing the settling of the building more visibly than those in the center," he explained.

"And Hernandez can fix the problem," Tim said with an annoyed huff.

"The structural engineer we hired said it would cost a great deal of money," Elaine said and shook her head in frustration.

"He'd rather bully us into forgetting about it, but we won't," Jerry said and patted his wife's hand in a show of unity.

Ricky wouldn't forget about it either, especially with other tragic building collapses they could never forget.

"Is the elevator being out of order more bullying?" he asked.

Russ shook his head. "Not this time. Mrs. Wilson from 320 somehow broke the door with her shopping cart."

Ricky did another quick look around the condo, taking in some other cracks here and there. Satisfied they had the information they needed, he glanced at Mariela. "I think we're good. How about you?"

She nodded and faced the owners. "Thanks so much for

chatting with us. I'm sorry for everything and hope things will work out for you."

"They will. We have a good lawyer and we're sure they'll get this fixed," Russ said, rose and walked them to the door.

Mariela and Ricky exited into the hallway, down the stairs, and when they reached the main floor, they noticed two men working on the elevator while another man in a suit leaned over them, watching what they were doing.

Mariela stopped short and grabbed his arm to stop him. "It's Jorge."

Sensing their arrival, Mariela's ex stood upright and glanced their way. His body tensed and he reached down and grabbed a large wrench from the one workman's tool bag. He walked toward them slowly, slapping the wrench against his one hand in a menacing gesture.

Ricky stepped slightly in front of Mariela and urged her to move with a tug of his hand.

But Jorge blocked their way down the hall. "Mariela. Who's your little boy toy?"

Mariela's ex was a well-built man with a waist starting to thicken a little. He had at least forty or more pounds and a few inches of height on him and the wrench, but Ricky didn't back down.

"Please step aside," Ricky said, voice steady. His gaze even steadier.

Jorge laughed and leaned forward until he was nose-to-nose with Ricky. "Say pretty please."

"Step aside," Ricky repeated and didn't waver in his stance. As one of the owners had said earlier that morning, you had to stand up to bullies.

Jorge hesitated, his glance skipping to where Mariela stood behind Ricky. But then he slowly stepped to the side to let them pass. Despite that, he continued to tap the wrench threateningly and Ricky was sure to keep Mariela's ex in his line of sight, ready to defend them as necessary.

Outside, Mariela wrapped her arm around his waist and urged him to face her. She cradled his face with her hands and said, "Thank you. I'm not sure I could have handled him alone."

With a grin, he said, "You're stronger than you think."

She offered him a sad smile, rose on tiptoes and kissed him. With the barest whisper before she retreated, she said, "I could love you."

I could love you, too, he thought, wanting to hold her close and show her just how much he could care for her, but the insistent ring of his phone interrupted the moment.

He jerked the phone from his pocket. It was Trey and he answered.

"What's up?" he asked.

"The police have a match on the fingerprints."

Chapter Fifteen

Since Trey, Sophie and Robbie were at work at the South Beach Security offices in downtown Miami, Ricky and she headed there to hear their report on the identity of the person who had attacked her in her home.

Inside the offices dozens of people were hard at work as Trey came out of his office and walked them to one of the conference rooms. Sophie and Robbie were sitting there with their laptops, but rose to greet them when they came in.

Mariela was struck once more by the similarities in the Gonzalez family members, even with the Whitaker cousin tech gurus. The Gonzalez genes were clearly strong.

Once they were seated, Trey went to the head of the table and motioned for the cousins to begin with the report.

A picture snapped on the screen and Mariela gasped as she stared at the face.

"You know this man?" Ricky asked.

Mariela's heart knocked against her ribs, and she nodded. "I do. His name is Hector Ramirez. He was Jorge's foreman for a few years."

"We pulled up his history, but it didn't reflect that," Sophie said and engaged a second screen with Ramirez's rap sheet and employment records.

"Maybe he was working off the books," Mariela said

in explanation and shook her head. "Jorge promised me he'd stop that when I called him on it."

"But in the meantime, Ramirez was collecting unemployment and public assistance, stealing money from the people who really need it," Ricky said in disgust.

"He was lucky your ex hired him at all. Look at that rap sheet. Shoplifting escalated into breaking and entering. Two assault and battery cases, but he only served time for one of them due to a plea deal," Trey said, walked up to the monitor and pointed out the entries on Ramirez's criminal record.

"Is it possible Jorge found that out about his criminal past and fired him?" Ricky asked.

Mariela shook her head. "Jorge fired him because he came to work drunk on a number of occasions. It caused problems on the work site, so Jorge finally had to let him go."

"Your ex knew Ramirez and he has a violent past. That's a perfect recipe for the assault that happened, but I just need to confirm. I assume Ramirez was never at your parents' house for any reason," Trey said.

Mariela racked her brain and shook her head. "Never. There was no reason for him to go there."

Trey dipped his head and said, "We can relay that info to the detectives on the case. They already have a BOLO out for Ramirez. Hopefully they'll be able to track him down shortly."

Mariela smiled, feeling relief that they had the identity of her attacker and that he would hopefully be behind bars soon.

"That's good news," she said.

"We have more to share," Robbie said and with several taps on his keys he switched out the images on the screen to bring up photos of two different men.

"Do they look familiar to you?" Trey asked.

"I don't think so," Mariela said.

"When Robbie and I compared all the lists of the inspectors and the inspections, these two names kept popping up—James Smith and Elliot Levy."

Ricky nodded and said, "Those were the same names that popped with us."

"But they weren't names I remembered from Jorge's holiday parties," Mariela added and stared at the screens again, but the men's faces still didn't register. "I've never seen these men," she confirmed once more.

The screens flipped to show salary information for the two individuals as Sophie said, "Salaries for public employees are accessible online. Smith and Levy are both senior building inspectors earning roughly $110,000 per year."

The images on the screen were replaced with ones of upscale homes in some of Miami's more desirable neighborhoods. "Assuming their wives made similar salaries and if this wasn't a first home purchase, they could easily afford between one and one and a half million."

Ricky gestured to the screen. "Those are not one-million-dollar homes."

"You're right," Robbie said, and numbers popped up over the images. "Here are a real estate site's estimates for these home values. Both are roughly between five and six million. Way out of the league for anyone with those building inspector salaries."

"They're on the take. That's the only explanation," Mariela said.

"Or they inherited money from a dead relative," Trey scoffed.

"Is there any way we can legally get their credit reports for more info?" Ricky asked.

Sophie shook her head. "If a person has a 'permissible purpose' they could, but we don't fall into any of those legal purposes."

"What about the police? Or the DA? Isn't there enough here to do something?" Mariela asked, starting to feel frustrated that her ex-husband and these men had been subverting the system for so long and possibly putting people's lives at risk.

"We've already given what we have to *Tia* Elena. We're preparing everything else we have to give to her and *Tio* Jose. But I think we need more info on these newer projects," Trey said and gestured to his cousins, who put up images of the two condo developments on the screens.

Trey walked to the screens and flipped a hand in their direction. "Whoever tried to hurt you did it because of one of these," he said.

"Probably the mid-rise," Ricky said and pointed to that image.

"Why do you say that?" Trey asked.

Ricky locked his gaze with hers and said, "As I mentioned the other day, we spoke to a reliable source who wishes to remain anonymous. They advised that everything seems aboveboard at the high-rise project."

"But not this mid-rise," Trey said and motioned to that image.

"Not that project," Mariela confirmed and repeated what Rafael had told them. "Our source said he noticed cracks in the building that shouldn't be happening already. He was also supposed to send us a list of other projects where he thought something was off with the inspections."

"But you don't have the list yet?" Trey pushed.

Ricky shrugged and said, "Our source was very worried about what might happen to his loved ones if Hernandez found out that he'd talked."

Trey nodded and glanced at his cousins. "You've already gotten some info online, but is there any way to get more detailed inspection reports, building plans, things like that?"

"We can check it out and try to have something for you by tomorrow," Sophie advised.

"So close and yet still so far away from stopping Hernandez," Ricky said, his frustration obvious.

"But it's so much more than what we started with," Mariela said, filled with optimism that the nightmare would soon be over.

Ricky offered up a strained smile. "You're right. We have a lot and hopefully it will be enough to let *Tio* Jose take action."

"In the meantime, why don't you go home and let us get to work?" Trey said, his tone conciliatory, hoping to calm his brother's worry.

"Good idea. We'll let you get to work and go home. I'm sure *mami* will be busy making dinner for everyone," Ricky said.

"Have her save some for Roni and me. We'll be over later. How about you two?" Trey asked his cousins.

"We can take a short break," Robbie said, but Mariela could tell that his sister would have preferred to just work through the night.

Ricky must have sensed it as well, since he said, "You can't be all work all the time, Soph. A break may help you think more clearly."

"Sure," she said, but her tone was unconvincing.

"We'll see you all later," Ricky said, and they hurried out of the SBS offices and down to the parking lot and Ricky's car.

It wasn't long before they were traveling along Brickell Avenue up to Biscayne Boulevard and onto the highway to the causeway and Palm Island.

THE TRACKER *I installed on Gonzalez's car is working perfectly*, he thought.

He patiently watched the blip on the tablet as it neared where he waited.

In his side view mirror, he caught sight of the Audi as it approached and let another car or two pass before he slipped from his parking spot and discreetly followed.

He had to time the attack perfectly. He'd already checked the traffic situation and luckily it was normal, with no accidents or construction to interfere.

Patience, he told himself as they hit the first part of the causeway heading toward Watson Island. He shifted out of his lane to make his move. Once they were past Jungle Island and the children's museum on the island, he had to act.

Luckily Mr. Ricky Responsible was following the speed limit in the right lane, giving him a perfect target for what he intended.

As the causeway swept down to sea level, he hit the accelerator and surged forward.

MARIELA WAS HAPPILY enjoying the sight of Biscayne Bay glittering in the late-afternoon sun, buoyed by her earlier optimism that they would soon have enough info to arrest Jorge and anyone else involved with his crimes.

A sudden jolt ripped her from that happiness.

Someone had hit them from behind. She turned to look and saw the black BMW with the masked driver. Another jolt on the left rear quarter panel sent the car lurching to the right. Ricky battled to keep the car under control, but the BMW sped forward and with another broadside swipe the nose of the Audi pointed toward the edge of the causeway and the waters of Biscayne Bay.

Mariela screamed, but Ricky somehow managed to right the wheel.

The driver of the BMW slammed his car against them again, trying to drive them into the water.

Ricky fought the wheel, turning into the other car, and

it was like two rams charging at each other. Metal grated against metal, crunched and groaned as the drivers battled for control.

And then, suddenly, Ricky stomped on the brake and the BMW shot forward toward Biscayne Bay until the driver righted the wheel and sped off.

COLD SWEAT BATHED Ricky's body and every inch of him shook as adrenaline raced across his nerve endings. He brought the car to a halt just feet away from the water.

Somehow instinct took over and he flipped on the hazard lights as he asked, "Are you okay?"

Mariela did a shaky nod. "I'm okay."

"I have to call 911," he said and was about to dial when two police cars pulled up. One slipped behind them while the other took a spot in front of his car.

As an officer stepped up to the window, hand on the gun in his holster, Ricky kept his hands on the wheel until the officer was beside them and bending over to look into the car.

"Ricky? Is that you, *mano*?" the officer asked and leaned an arm on the roof of the car.

Ricky took a longer look at the cop and smiled as he recognized one of Trey's high school friends. "Danny? You're looking good," he managed to say as the earlier fear dissipated.

Danny eyeballed the car. "Sorry you can't say the same. What happened?"

"Someone tried to run us off the road. Black BMW. Driver was masked," Ricky said and looked at Mariela for confirmation.

"That's what I saw," she said with a nod.

"The BOLO we have in place?" Danny asked and Ricky bobbed his head.

"Probably one and the same," he confirmed.

Danny held up a finger in a "wait" gesture and walked toward the vehicle in front of them, radioing someone as he went. When he reached that vehicle, he and the other officer stood there, listening to what he assumed were instructions.

"What's happening?" Mariela asked, leaning forward to get a better look at the officers.

"They're probably going to have to take the car in as evidence," Ricky said, recalling Trey's many tales over the years of what had happened on his assorted cases.

Sure enough, when Danny returned, he said, "Sorry to do this to you, but we have to secure this scene until the CSI team can process it. If you don't mind stepping from the car, I have a few more questions for you before we let you go."

Ricky gestured to the car and said, "And how will we go, Danny?"

"Trey is on his way, but I'm sure he'll want to stay and make sure we're doing everything by the book," Danny advised with a roll of his eyes and gestured to the other vehicle. "As soon as we're done, I can have Officer Duran take you home. It's not that far to your parents'."

"Thanks." Danny skewered him with cop's eyes, all earlier traces of friendliness gone.

He answered Danny's questions, trying to recall what he could from the moment of the first impact to that second when he'd thought they'd go flying into the waters of Biscayne Bay. It was only something instinctual that had made him stomp on the brake to stop the attack.

"Is that what you remember?" Danny asked Mariela.

She glanced at the car and then back up the road. Jabbing with her finger, she said, "He first hit us as we got near the end of Watson Island."

"And toward the flat part of the causeway?" Danny asked with a raised eyebrow.

She nodded. "It was hit after hit after that. Just like Ricky told you."

Danny jotted some notes down in his pad, slipped the pen into the holder and closed it. "I think I've got what I need for now."

A honk drew their attention and Ricky watched as Trey drove by in his vintage Camaro and parked beyond the police cruiser in front of them. A second later, the CSI unit pulled up behind Danny's cruiser.

"Cavalry has arrived," Danny said and walked away to coordinate with the CSI officers and Trey.

Ricky cupped her cheek and stroked a thumb across the pale color there. "Are you really okay?"

She reached up to take his hand with hers. "I am. I just don't understand how Jorge's old foreman found us."

"I don't either, but I'm sure Trey and the cops will find out how," Ricky said as he watched his brother work with his old colleagues before he walked over to them.

"Let me take you home," Trey said when he joined them.

"Will everything be okay?" Ricky asked and shot his chin up toward the officers and CSI on the scene.

"They sent their best when they saw your name. I have no doubt they'll do a thorough investigation," he said and added, "Let's go. I'm sure the adrenaline is racing through you now, but when you crash…it'll be better to be home."

Chapter Sixteen

Trey hadn't been wrong, Mariela thought. It had been good to be home because her knees had given out just after they'd reached the house. Samantha had pressed a Scotch into her hand and urged her to sit.

She'd fallen onto the sofa, the ice rattling in the glass until she braced her wobbly hand on the padded arm. Taking a little sip, she let the warmth of it travel down her throat.

Ricky sat beside her, wrapped an arm around her shoulders and drew her close. The heat of his body chased away the last remnants of the chill in her core.

"I don't get how they knew where we were, Trey. We shut down Mariela's phone days ago," Ricky said.

"I know, *mano*. They could have been watching you. It's possible they slipped a tracker on your car as well," Trey said and took a long drag on his Scotch. "CSI should be finished with their initial review of the car. If there's a tracker, we should know soon."

"In the meantime, let's sit down for some supper. Josie and I spent the better part of the day making *ropa vieja* for you," Samantha said, rose and smoothed the fabric of the linen tunic blouse she wore. The telltale gesture gave away how nervous she was despite her outwardly calm actions.

"I love *ropa vieja*. My *mami* and I always made it for

my father's birthday," Mariela said, popped to her feet and walked to Samantha's side.

Ricky's mother slipped an arm through hers and they strolled to the dining area of the open concept space, but as Samantha went to go into the kitchen, Mariela said, "Let me help."

"With pleasure," Samantha said, smiling.

RICKY WATCHED HIS mother and Mariela walk away and his heart did a little clench at just how natural it seemed when nothing around him was close to natural.

Someone had just tried to kill them. Again.

And despite all the progress they'd made on what Hernandez was doing, they still didn't have enough to shut down the threat to Mariela and him.

"*Vamos, mi'jo.* You've got to let go of it, if only for a little while," his father said.

"Is that what you did, *papi*? Let go of it?" he asked even though he already knew the answer.

When he thought back to his childhood, it had been about as normal as it could be while his father had been a marine and then a police officer. Of course, the demands of those jobs had been buffeted by the support of his grandparents and the growing success of South Beach Security, especially after his father had left the police force to join his grandfather at the agency. They'd had more stability then, both in terms of a home life and financially.

"It's what you do for your family and for yourself," his father said and urged him to go with him to the dining table across the way.

As he sat, he could hear the gentle murmur of voices from inside the kitchen as Mariela, Josie and his mom worked to prepare dinner. It was a comforting sound, making everything seem almost normal. It made him imagine the moment when every day would be like this and restored some calm to his soul.

Short moments later the women came into the room with plates piled with mounds of rice covered with the shredded beef in tomato sauce. *Ropa vieja* was one of his favorites and his stomach rumbled at the thought of eating.

Mariela placed a plate in front of him. "Thank you," he said.

"You're welcome," she said and walked back to the kitchen. Seconds later she returned with plates with ripe plantains and placed one at either end of the table. When she was done, she sat beside him and Trey, and once his mother took a spot beside his father, they ate.

The meal passed companionably with everyone eating and chatting. Time passed quickly but as the meal was ending, his brother pulled out his cell phone and took a look. His face went from easygoing to all hard sharp lines at whatever he read.

Ricky's earlier calm fled, replaced by worry as he waited to hear what his brother had to say.

"Ricky? Something wrong?" Mariela said from beside him.

"Nothing, *mi amor*," he said, the endearment slipping from his lips unintentionally.

She jumped, startled by it, but then nodded and smiled. "Whatever it is, *mi amor*, we will handle it together," she said, reached beneath the table and took hold of his hand.

Once they were finished, his mother and Mariela rose to clear off the table and Josie came in to help. He noticed that his brother leaned over to say something to his father, who looked his way and jerked his head in the direction of the living room area.

He rose, walked over with them, and they sat on the sofa. Trey took out his phone and flipped to an image. "My CSI contact sent me this," he said.

Ricky peered at the image, puzzled. "Is that a tracker?"

Trey nodded. "It is. Someone planted it beneath the wheel well of your car."

"Any idea when?" his father asked.

Trey shrugged. "The techs are going to try and access its logs. Maybe we'll know then."

"Did Hernandez do this?" Ricky asked.

"Either Hernandez or whoever he hired," Trey suggested. He peered at him, ran a hand through his hair in frustration and said, "I don't like this, Ricky. My gut tells me something else is going on here. Maybe even something that has nothing to do with Mariela."

"Like what?" Ricky asked.

"Something more personal," Trey said and his gaze bounced between them. "What if this is about Ricky? Or the family?"

"That makes no sense, Trey. What would anyone have against me or the family? We help people," Ricky said, unable to believe that it would be some kind of vendetta against the Gonzalez clan.

"We do, but for everyone we help there may be someone who hates us for what we do," his father said and sat back heavily against the sofa cushions.

Ricky's mind whirled with the possibility that maybe he was the one who had brought danger to Mariela.

"I need some air," he said and jumped to his feet.

Mariela had entered the living room with his mother, and he held out a hand to her. "Want to go for a walk?"

RICKY'S DISTRESS WAS there for her to see in the hard lines of his face. In the tension in his body and his hand as she held it. She squeezed it gently, trying to offer comfort as they hurried to the French doors and out onto the grounds.

They strolled around the pool and to the water's edge

in silence. They stopped on the dock where Ricky leaned on one of the posts and drew her close to lean against him.

"What's wrong? Did something else happen?" she asked, worried at about how upset he was—almost lost, it seemed to her.

He avoided her gaze and said, "There was a tracker on the car. Trey isn't sure that Jorge is the one responsible for the attack."

She turned in his arms to face him. "That can't be. Who else would do it?" she said and stroked a hand across his chest to soothe him.

"That's what I said," Ricky said with a shake of his head.

"This all started with me visiting your aunt. With someone attacking me," she said and tapped her chest in emphasis.

Ricky looked away and in a soft voice he said, "*Sí*, it did and yet… The shootings and this latest attack. It has to be something really, really big for your ex or his foreman to try that."

Mariela recalled what she had overheard in Jorge's office, and she had no doubt that it was something big. "I think it is, Ricky. Jorge sounded almost frantic that night. I think he would do anything to protect what he's doing. Especially if it could cost him millions."

Ricky nailed her with his gaze. "Let's hope you're right and we can end this danger."

"We will," she said and rose on tiptoes to kiss him. To offer him the same support he had given her.

He returned the kiss, tenderly at first, but as desire grew, he drew her tighter, their bodies pressed together.

Against her belly he hardened, and she shifted against him, needing him in a way she had never thought would be possible again.

"Mariela," he said and encircled her waist in his hands to urge her to stop.

"I want this, Ricky. What I feel with you… It's not anything I ever felt before," she said and cupped his face in her hands, reassuring him that she knew what she wanted.

"It's the same for me, *mi amor*." With a tender smile, he said, "Maybe it's time we go back in."

She grinned. "I'd like that."

They held hands and strolled toward the house, but as they neared, she realized Trey was standing on the back patio, hands on his hips. His face had that stony hard look that she already recognized meant trouble.

That Ricky understood it as well was evident from the way his hand tightened on hers.

They stopped before him and he glanced between them, uneasy.

"Just spit it out," Ricky said, tugged her closer and wrapped an arm around her shoulders to hold her close, as if preparing for a blow.

"The police found Hector Ramirez," Trey said.

Chapter Seventeen

"Where?" Mariela asked and braced for his reply.

"He washed up by the Collins Bridge near Haulover Park," Trey said.

Ricky immediately put two and two together. "Which is right near Hernandez's high-rise condo."

Trey's lips twisted with chagrin. "*Sí*, it is, and I know where you're going with this. There's one big problem. It appears Ramirez was murdered sometime last night."

"That doesn't mean that Hernandez wasn't behind the wheel this afternoon," Ricky pushed because he couldn't get on board with Trey's theory that it might not have to do with Mariela.

Reluctantly, Trey nodded. "You're right. Just call it my cop's instinct that I feel this isn't as cut and dry as you think."

"Are the police going to call Jorge in for questioning about his old foreman?" Mariela asked.

"My contact says that once the ME is finished with the autopsy and they know more, they'll call me and let me know what's up," Trey said and looked back toward the house when someone called his name.

Roni strolled through the house and up to Trey. She kissed him and hugged him hard before greeting them. "How are you handling the news?" she asked.

Ricky shot a quick glance at Mariela, who said, "We're dealing with it."

Roni blew out a harsh breath. "I know how frustrating it can be. Believe me, it's how I feel when I can't get a handle on a case, even when it involved Trey and me."

"I am frustrated, but I know you're all doing your best," Ricky said in resignation.

"We are. Trey and I will keep pressuring the detectives on the case and let you know once we have more," Roni promised and shot a look up at Trey, who nodded to confirm it.

"And Sophie and Robbie will have more info for us in the morning that we'll work on as well," Trey reminded.

"Seems like there's nothing else for us to do tonight," Mariela said.

Roni nodded. "You should get some rest. It could take up to four hours for the ME to finish the autopsy on Ramirez, but we may not have preliminary results for possibly twenty-four hours."

"Like Roni said, we'll keep you posted if anything does happen," Trey added, clearly sensing that Ricky had had enough of the discussion.

"Thanks. You two get some rest as well," Ricky said and leaned in to hug his future sister-in-law and his brother.

Mariela followed his lead to embrace Roni and Trey before taking hold of his hand and walking with him into the house and up the stairs.

In the foyer tucked between the two bedrooms in the wing, he faced her, unsure of whether she'd want to spend some more time with him.

He inched his head in the direction of his room. "Do you feel like having a drink?"

It surprised her yet again that she wanted more than just a drink with him, but for now, she'd take that and his company, which she enjoyed immensely.

She wanted to understand him better. What made him tick.

"I'd like that," she said and, at his playful tug, followed him into the room.

There was a large king-size bed as they entered and, at the far end, a small sitting area in the corner, which had a view of the backyard and the waters beyond that.

She sat on the love seat and the cushions enveloped her in their comfiness.

Ricky walked over to a dry bar at one side of the sitting area, poured them a Scotch and joined her on the love seat.

They sat there in comfortable silence, sipping their drinks, and savoring the sight of downtown Miami and Biscayne Bay. But as she recalled that they had almost ended up in those beautiful waters, she shivered and gulped down a healthy portion of the drink.

Wanting to drive those thoughts from her mind, she said, "How did you decide to become a psychologist?"

Ricky did a little noncommittal shrug. "I'm not really sure, to be honest. I was a book nerd but social also. People just seemed to like telling me their problems and I was good at listening."

"Like you do with the support group," she said, recalling her visit to his office.

"Like that and in the therapy sessions," he admitted and slipped his arm across her shoulders.

"But you work with your family's agency, too," she said, recalling what he'd said before.

"I do. But like my cousin Pepe, I didn't want to be involved. I couldn't see how I could help, but little by little I got drawn in and, truth be told, I don't hate working with my family at SBS," he confessed.

"Your family seems very nice," she said because in all the time that she'd been in contact with them they'd treated her well.

"They're the best even if a little too overprotective at

times. Especially my mom, even with everyone at the office. She is our Mama Bear," he said with a laugh.

"Must be nice," Mariela said with a forced smile, but Ricky immediately saw past that to the sadness in her tone.

"It's been a while since someone was nice to you," he said, but it was a statement, not a question.

She mimicked his earlier shrug, slightly uneasy about sharing. With a shaky breath, she said, "It's been a few hard years since my *mami* and *papi* got sick."

"What's wrong with them?" he asked and stroked his hand back and forth her upper arm in a calming gesture.

"*Papi* has the beginning stages of dementia. He could probably still live at home, but *mami* broke her hip and still can't move around all that well."

"You've been taking care of them by yourself? No siblings?" he asked.

"I'm an only child so it's been up to me to pay for the assisted living and keep their house up, hoping that maybe one day they can come home and be with me. That it could be a little bit more like it was when I was younger and they were so full of life and we were happy," she said, trying to hold on to those joyful memories rather than the pain of the present.

"I hope that can happen," he said and sipped the last of his Scotch. He set the glass on the coffee table in front of him and shifted in the seat slightly to see her better.

"I hope I can, too," she said with a determined dip of her head, trying to convince herself that she'd be able to make that wish come true.

He tucked his hand beneath her chin, applied gentle pressure to urge her to face him and tenderly stroked his thumb across her cheek.

"YOU'RE A GOOD DAUGHTER. A good person," Ricky said, sensing that she had some doubt about her dream of bringing her family back together again.

Her lips twisted up in a half smile and she did a little laugh. "Jorge didn't think so."

"Jorge is an ass," he said and brushed a whisper-soft kiss across her cheek and then down to lightly trace the edges of her lips.

It was a kiss of promise, of invite. He wanted her to accept him and what might be possible between them.

She leaned into him, opening herself to him. Her lips on his, tentative at first, but growing more mobile, more intense, as they kept on kissing until he needed her closer. Needed to feel her, her heartbeat against his, racing as his was.

He leaned back onto the arm of the sofa, urged her to come with him, and she crawled into his lap, her center over him. Over the growing hardness at the feel of her against him.

Breaking apart from her only long enough to say her name, almost as a prayer, he cradled her back in his hands as they kissed over and over.

He opened his mouth and accepted the slide of her tongue, tasting her, a mix of the Scotch and sweetness. *Mariela's sweetness*, he thought with a groan as she shook in his arms.

He didn't want to misread the signals so he shifted away the slightest bit, and husked, "We can stop whenever you want."

"I don't want to stop," she said and stroked her hand across his cheek before tunneling her fingers into his hair and urging him into the kiss again.

IT HAD BEEN too long, maybe never, since she had been treasured this way. As if she was someone special. Someone who deserved to be loved. Someone who could love someone else, love Ricky, with all her heart.

She drifted against him, against the hard planes of his

body, relishing the feel of him. The gentle way he clasped her to him, his hands splayed across her back. His body beneath her, between her legs as she straddled him. Hard and growing harder until she had to move on him. Had to have his hands on her.

"Touch me, Ricky. Please, touch me," she said, unafraid because she knew Ricky would never hurt her.

He groaned and his body shook beneath hers, but he did as she asked, slipping his hand around to cup her breast. Rub his thumb across her hard nipple before tweaking it between his thumb and forefinger.

The action dragged a rough moan from her, and damp flooded her center. When he tempered his touch, she whispered against his lips, "Don't stop. It feels so good."

A harsh breath escaped him along with a needy moan. "You feel so good," he said and brought his other hand around to caress her other breast.

She watched, loving the sight of his hands on her. He had an artist's hands, long and elegant. Strong and yet amazingly tender. Her heart tightened in her chest, and she sucked in a ragged breath. When he bent his head and teethed one hard nipple, she jumped, and her insides clenched with need. The need for him not to stop. The need to feel his mouth on her skin. His hardness buried deep inside her.

Reaching down, she grabbed the hem of the loose blouse she wore and ripped it up and over her head, and as she did so, he reached around and undid the clasp of her bra. Her breasts spilled free, and he immediately kissed her breasts, shifting from one to the other as he loved her with his mouth.

"*Dios*, you are so beautiful," he whispered against her breasts.

His mouth was so warm, so moist, against her. She clasped his head to her, loving his touch. His care and patience that was driving her to move on him, passion building. Her body tightening as she climbed ever higher.

His hands came down to still her hips and he whispered, "I don't know if I can hold back anymore."

"I don't want you to hold back."

"DIOS," RICKY MUTTERED, his body shaking from the desire rushing through him.

Somehow, he didn't know how, he was on his feet with her in his arms, hurrying to the bed on the other side of the room. He let her slip down his body until she was on her feet, slightly wobbly. Laying his hands on her waist, he steadied her while she undid the buttons on his *guayabera* shirt and bared him to her gaze.

Barely a second passed before her hands were on him, smoothing across the muscles of his chest. She shifted them down, the backs of *her* hands skimming his defined abs and lower to cover his erection. Stroke him over the fabric of his jeans, her touch tentative. Hesitant, but he tempered his need, aware of what a big decision this was for her. What a major step considering the nightmare she had suffered during her marriage.

He let her take her time exploring him and she moved her hands all across his body, learning the shape of him, but when she reached for the button on his jeans, he stilled the motion of her hands.

"Let me," he said and instead undid the button and zipper on her jeans and helped her step out of them, leaving her in nothing but a tiny scrap of black cotton around her lush hips.

"So, so beautiful," he said again.

She smiled, a sexy little grin, ran her hands across his chest and said, "So are you."

That smile undid what was left of his restraint. He toed

off his shoes and socks, and yanked off his jeans and briefs, hopping from foot to foot in his haste to be with her.

He urged her down onto the bed, shifting with her until they were in the center of the large mattress, side by side. He still wanted to give her space because of her past.

They lay there, touching. Exploring and kissing. Breaths growing ever more hurried as desire climbed ever higher until she slipped her hands to his shoulders and urged him over her, inviting him to join with her.

"Just a second," he said. He rushed off the bed and searched his pants for his wallet. When he found it, he pulled out a condom and hoped that it hadn't expired.

As he climbed back toward her, she reached out and took the condom from his hand, tore the foil wrapper and removed it with shaky hands.

He held his hand out for it, but she shook her head. "No. I want to do it."

He nodded, understanding her need to be in control. To be the one to decide how and when. He was the lucky man who had earned her trust and he didn't intend to shatter that trust.

He sat back against the pillows and headboard, and she straddled him, slowly unrolled the condom down his length. It was all he could do not to lose it and he gritted his teeth to hold on until she rose above him.

With hands slightly unsteady from the force of his passion, he guided her down and she took him in, the heat and tightness of her surrounding him.

"Ricky," she said, voice husky, her emerald gaze almost black with desire.

"Whatever you want, *mi amor*. I'm here for you," he said and swept his hand up to tenderly cup her jaw.

She worried her lower lip and shot a quick glance down at her breasts, silently communicating her request.

He leaned forward and kissed the hard tip, lightly teethed it while caressing her other breast with his fingers.

She moaned, held his head to her and moved, shifting her hips on him. Heightening passion that was already seriously on the edge.

When he sucked her nipple a touch harder, tweaked the other tight tip with his fingers, a rough gasp escaped her and she ground down on him, seeking her release.

"Let go, *mi amor*. I'm here to catch you when you fall," he said and splayed his hands across her back.

She bent and tucked her head against his, her breath ragged, almost wild, as she rode him.

His own breath grew more erratic as he battled to maintain control, wanting her to have her release before he lost it.

"Ricky, please," she pleaded and held on to his shoulders as she rolled onto her back and took him with her. "Please," she said again, her gaze locked on his.

He let go of his tenuous grasp and drove into her, his thrusts coming harder and faster as her soft cries urged him on. Inside him the pressure built until he couldn't hold back any longer.

With one last powerful thrust, he came, but as he did so she arched upward and dug her fingers into his back, calling his name.

His arms shook as he held his weight off her body until she stroked her hands up his arms and urged him down onto her.

"I'm too heavy," he said, and in response, she tightened her arms around him.

"You're just right," she said, a satisfied smile on her face. She stroked her hands up and down his back, and he let himself enjoy the aftermath of their lovemaking.

As her breathing slowed, he finally slipped to her side. "I'll be back," he said, needing to clean up.

"I'm not going anywhere," she teased, her tone light-hearted and a smile on her face that made her remarkable emerald eyes glitter brightly.

He took her words to heart, knowing just how much courage it had taken for her to trust him with her body and hopefully with her heart.

Rushing to the bathroom, he quickly washed up and returned to bed. She was already fast asleep, one hand tucked under cheek, her other hand resting on his spot in the bed, as if reaching out for him.

He slipped into bed and beneath her arm. At the contact, she stirred and shifted toward him, pressing her body to his, a smile still on her face.

Grinning, he wrapped an arm around her waist, and closed his eyes, but his mind whirled with all that had happened that day and thoughts of what they might encounter in the days to come.

No matter how hard it might be, he hoped they would continue on the journey they had just begun that night.

Chapter Eighteen

The thoughts that had chased Ricky to sleep jerked him from the bed early the next morning.

He tucked the covers in around Mariela and tossed on some clothes to go get himself a cup of coffee before calling Trey to see if he had any news on the Ramirez homicide or from Sophie and Robbie.

To his surprise, Trey was sitting at the dining area table with their father, having coffee and a huge mound of eggs, bacon and Cuban toast. His brother had just forked up a large portion of eggs when he spotted Ricky.

With a knowing grin, Trey said, "You look like you had a good night."

"Don't you have a home?" Ricky teased back and went to a serving cart to make himself a *café con leche* with the carafe of Cuban coffee and scalded milk on the cart.

After Trey swallowed, he grinned and said, "I do, but Roni had to go in early and Josie knows what I like for breakfast."

"It was meant to be rhetorical, *mano*," he said, not ready to deal with any comments from either Trey or his father, who had arched a brow at Trey's earlier comment and was clearly wondering what was going on between his two sons.

"Is everything…okay with Mariela?" his father asked, raising one thick salt-and-pepper brow in question.

"Everything is more than okay, *papi*. The only thing that would make it better would be for us to finish this investigation so Mariela can get on with her life," he said, took a sip of his coffee and added more sugar to his cup.

"And you with yours?" his father said, worry and disapproval twined together in his tone.

"Mariela is a good woman," he shot back, and his brother held up one hand in a stop gesture.

"No one is implying she isn't. It's just a little bit sudden," Trey said and set his fork down, his appetite apparently gone.

"Like you and Roni aren't?" he challenged, but guilt immediately swamped him with the realization that they were just worrying about him the way he'd worried about Trey.

"I'm sorry. I get it. Family worries about family," he said and sat down in between his brother and his father, who was at the head of the table.

Silence reigned for a moment until Trey picked up his fork and said, "The detectives on the Ramirez case have preliminary info from the ME. Time of death for Ramirez is around midnight the night before."

"Which confirms he couldn't have been the person driving the BMW that attacked us yesterday," Ricky said.

"It does, *mi'jo*," his father said with a nod and continued. "Hernandez must have had a falling-out with his old foreman and killed him. It's possible he either did the attack himself or found someone else to help him."

Trey made a face, prompting Ricky to ask, "But you think otherwise."

"Possibly. Like I said yesterday, something is rubbing me the wrong way about the last three attacks," Trey said and picked up his cup of coffee.

Trey had been an excellent cop with great instincts

about the cases he worked on, but Ricky couldn't understand why his brother seemed so hesitant about this one.

"If it isn't Hernandez behind these attacks, who is it?" he asked.

Trey's lips thinned into a harsh line. "I don't know, but we will find out. The detectives are sending over the preliminary report shortly. As soon as we have it, we can review it and decide what our next steps should be."

SUNLIGHT FILTERED BETWEEN her semiclosed lashes, and Mariela screwed them shut. She didn't want to get out of bed. She just wanted to lay there with Ricky and enjoy the morning, but as she reached out, she realized he was already gone.

She stretched to work out a morning kink and as she did so the slight soreness between her legs reminded her of what they had done last night. How they'd made love and then woken again in the middle of the night to pleasure each other when Ricky hadn't been able to locate another condom.

Her insides clenched with the memory of how he'd satisfied her over and over again and how she'd made him quake and shout her name.

She'd never expected to be intimate with a man again quite so soon. Then again, Ricky wasn't just any man.

And despite last night's very satisfying lovemaking, if they were to consider anything remotely permanent in a relationship, they had to get rid of the specter of Jorge and the danger he brought to them first.

Filled with that concern, she hurried from bed to take a shower and prepare for what she guessed would be another challenging day. Hopefully the police and Ricky's cousins would have information that moved along the investigation.

Although she wanted to luxuriate beneath the spray of hot water and memories of the night before, she rushed through the shower, got dressed and went into the bedroom she'd been using to make it seem as if she'd slept there. The last thing she needed was household gossip about her and Ricky.

She was about to head down when she ran into Samantha at the top of the stairs. As the older woman narrowed her gaze to peer at her, a rush of heat swept up from Mariela's neck to her face at the thought that Ricky's mom might have guessed what had happened with her son last night.

"How are you feeling? You look a little flushed," Samantha said as they walked down the wide flight of stairs to the ground floor.

"My room was a little warm," she lied.

"I'll have someone check the thermostat," Samantha said, but Mariela waved her hands.

"No, it's okay. I was actually quite comfortable," she said.

Samantha glanced toward the dining area table where Ricky had turned and was watching Mariela intently. With a wry grin, Samantha said, "I'm sure you were."

Mariela muttered a silent curse and bit her lip, sure that his mother was aware of what had gone on last night.

As they neared the table, the men rose and gestured for them to sit. Ricky's father kissed his wife on the cheek and said, "We were just going into my study to review the ME report Trey received."

"I guess Mariela and I will take our coffee there," Samantha said.

"No need, *mi amor*. We can handle this," Ramon said, but his wife held up a hand to stop him.

"If it involves my family's safety, I intend to be a part of it and I'm sure Mariela wants to know what's planned as well," Samantha said, steel in her voice. Then she turned to Mariela and said, "How do you like your coffee and would you like anything else for breakfast?"

"Just coffee, thanks. Light and sweet," she said and walked over to take the coffee and wait for Samantha as she prepared her own mug.

When his mother finished, she said, "We're ready now."

Ramon did a little bow and, with a flourish, waved his hand in the direction of his study. "After you, *mi amor.*"

"Thank you," Samantha said, and together they walked into her husband's study and took seats at the table.

The three men joined them just seconds later, but as Trey grabbed a laptop, he glanced at them and said, "The photos may be graphic."

"Are you okay with that, Mariela?" Ricky asked, concern evident in his voice.

"I can handle it." After all, she'd seen Jorge's violence firsthand.

With a nod, Trey popped the report onto the large monitor on the one wall of the office and recited pertinent facts from it while they followed along. "As I told Ricky and *papi* earlier, time of death was around midnight the night before, which rules him out of the road attack. Cause of death was strangulation using a thin nylon rope."

Trey shifted from the written report to a photo of a length of bright purple nylon rope and her stomach roiled at the sight of it. A chill sweat washed over her body and Ricky's arm was immediately around her shoulders.

"What's wrong?" he asked, seeing her upset response to the photo.

Memories pummeled her but somehow she wrestled them back, and with a shaky breath, she said, "Jorge had rope just like that. He used it to tie me up and rape me."

"MARIELA, *DIOS,*" RICKY said and waved at Trey to flip away from the photo.

His brother did as he was asked and in a sympathetic voice said, "Are you sure?"

Mariela was looking away at first, but then she slowly, almost regally, lifted her face and said, "I'm sure. He used to keep the rope in the garage to tie down things if a storm was coming."

To tie down things he didn't want to lose, Mariela being just another of his things, Ricky thought. Rage filled him at what she'd suffered, but he had to keep a level head for all their sakes.

"Will that info help in getting a search warrant?" he asked.

Trey shrugged. "Possibly. I can pass that info on to the detectives handling the case. If Hernandez consents to them looking around, he might be cocky enough not to have hidden it."

"You said Ramirez washed up around the Collins Bridge and Haulover Park. Any chance of any CCTVs in the area catching something?" Ricky asked.

"Detectives are already trying to get that info," Trey advised.

His father drummed his fingers on the tabletop and said, "Does your ex have a security system with cameras?"

Mariela nodded. "He does. Both at the house and the office. The Equinox Security Group installed it and monitors it."

"Equinox. That's our provider as well, isn't it?" his father said.

"It is. I'll see if they can do us a favor. Sophie and Robbie can also get to work on checking webcams in the area," Trey said, snatched the speakerphone from the tabletop and called their cousins.

"Good morning. How's the info on those inspectors going?" Trey asked.

"Just finishing up but I can tell you that almost every time one of Hernandez's buildings had a failed inspection, either Smith or Levy would show up and make it right somehow," Sophie said.

Robbie chimed in with, "Not that there's anything minor when you're talking about construction projects, but some were for minor electrical issues. Others were for plumbing. The ones that really stick out are when foundation issues were suddenly cleared."

Ricky shared a look with Mariela and said, "We have a source who says he noticed unusual cracks and issues on Hernandez's new mid-rise project."

"Smith worked on that one and approved it, but for some reason another inspection was requested. The second inspection has been outstanding for some time," Sophie said.

"And if Levy gets it, he'll just approve it," Mariela said with an exasperated sigh.

"He probably will," Robbie agreed.

"If that foundation is compromised, couldn't the whole structure collapse?" Samantha asked.

"It could if it's very compromised. There's no way to know for sure how bad it is without an independent inspection of the foundation and the ground beneath it," Sophie advised.

"Is that because the project is on reclaimed land?" Ricky asked, recalling the discussion they'd had about the issues with the one condo where they'd visited with the owners.

"It is. If the land beneath isn't properly compacted, it could cause all kinds of problems including the influx of water that would weaken the area even more," Sophie said.

"Thanks, Sophie. We need your help with something else," Trey said and provided their cousins with the information about the areas and times where they needed them to check for webcam footage.

"I'll get on it right away while Sophie finishes up the report on the inspectors," Robbie said and ended the call.

"We need to take a look at that mid-rise location," Ricky said and peered around the table at everyone gathered there.

"Didn't Mia mention that Hernandez was trying to offload one of those properties to John Wilson?" his mother said.

"She did," Ricky confirmed.

"Maybe Wilson can help us out and take a look," Mariela suggested, and everyone around the table nodded.

"It looks like we have our work cut out for us. I'll coordinate with the detectives on all the cases," Trey said and looked at him.

"Mariela and I can review the new reports on the inspectors and see why that foundation was scheduled for a reinspection," Ricky said.

"I'll speak to Mia about her friend and see if she thinks he'll assist us," Samantha said, stood and walked away from the table, already phoning Mia with their request.

"I'm heading to the office to see where we stand on our other cases," his father said and likewise rushed away from the room.

"I guess the rest of us should get to work as well. I'll keep you posted if I hear anything," Trey said and stood to leave.

"Stay safe, *mano*," Ricky said, and Mariela echoed his concern.

Trey jabbed a finger in their direction. "You, too. Just read the reports and leave the rest up to us," he said and left.

Once he had gone, he faced Mariela, cupped her cheek and said, "You know I can't just do that. We need to nail that bastard for all that he's done."

She offered him a pained smile. "I know. I want to see him behind bars as well."

"I'm glad we agree," he said just as his phone pinged. He snuck a peek and said, "The report is here."

Mariela's smile broadened. "Let's get to work."

Chapter Nineteen

Mariela raked her fingers through her hair in frustration and anger at herself as they finished reviewing the report Sophie and Robbie had sent over. "I always had a niggling worry that Jorge was doing something wrong. I should have said something."

"What would he have done to you if he found out you had talked to someone? At least you have us in your corner now," Ricky said, understanding her frustration but obviously concerned about how risky it would have been for her to go it alone.

She smiled and grasped his hand as it rested on the table. "I do have you and your family helping me. You don't know how grateful I am for that."

He held her hand and gave a gentle squeeze. "You have us, and we have connections. *Tia* Elena's law office also does real estate work. Let's call her and see if she can't get us the name of someone we can speak to in the building inspection department."

He made the call and his aunt said she would check with her colleagues in that department for the name of a friendly contact.

"Thank you, *tia*," he said, stood and rubbed his flat stomach. "I don't know about you, but I'm hungry."

She'd only had the coffee earlier that morning and her

stomach warned her with a rumble that it made sense to get something to eat. Especially if they were probably going to leave to chat with someone once his aunt provided a name.

"I am hungry. Do you want to go make some lunch?" she said, pushed to her feet and stretched to work out the kinks from sitting for so long.

Josie and Samantha were in the kitchen going over a grocery list and menus when they arrived.

"I can make you something for lunch, *Señor* Ricky," Josie said with an adoring smile. The young girl obviously had a crush on the handsome younger Gonzalez brother and Mariela was struck with jealousy.

"It's okay. We can make something ourselves," Ricky said and jerked open the door on one of the large Sub-Zero refrigerators.

Mariela peered inside at the fridge packed with all kinds of fresh vegetables, meats and cheeses. "I make a mean frittata," she said and didn't wait for him to haul out a red pepper, container of mushrooms and a bar of Swiss cheese.

Ricky assisted by grabbing the carton with the eggs and a container of half-and-half. At her questioning look, he said, "Makes the eggs creamier." He passed by one counter and snagged an onion from a woven basket.

They worked at one counter and as they did so Ricky called out, "Do you ladies want to join us for lunch?"

Josie laughed nervously and said, "I have to go to class."

Ricky's mother said, "I'm meeting your father at the office for lunch but thank you for the invitation."

With that they chopped and sautéed the vegetables in a large cast-iron skillet, whipped up the half-and-half and eggs to add to them and topped it with slices of Swiss cheese before popping everything beneath the broiler in the oven.

The cooking smells were making her even hungrier

while she kept an eye on the frittata to make sure it wouldn't burn.

Ricky took that time to set the table for two and pour them big glasses of iced tea.

Several minutes later Mariela was slicing pieces of the frittata and plating them. She took them inside to the dining area and Ricky joined her.

Silence filled the air as they filled their bellies, but once that initial hunger had been slaked, Ricky said, "Thank you. This is delicious."

Mariela smiled and dipped her head to acknowledge the compliment. "Thank you as well. You did help, after all, and that half-in-half did make the eggs creamier."

"A trick I learned from one of our other cooks," he said with a grin and forked up the last of the slice on his plate.

She immediately got him another slice and said, "Have you and your family always had cooks and servants?"

Ricky shook his head, so forcefully it sent the longish strands of hair at the top of his head shifting with the motion. "Not at all. In fact, when we were little, my mother really had to work to put food on the table. My dad was in the military and my *abuelo* had just started SBS. It got a little better once my dad finished his service and went to work as a cop. The worries about food stopped but other worries remained."

She understood. "Like if your dad would come home from work."

Ricky nodded and ate some more of his frittata. "Definitely that. It's always been a dangerous job, but even more so now. I'm glad Trey left the force and hope Roni does as well. We could use someone as bright as her in the agency."

Mariela considered his words as she finished her food. With a shrug, she said, "I don't really know Roni, but she strikes me as someone who really loves her job."

"She does, but she surprised us all when she went into

the academy after college. She and the Twins had been friends forever and we never suspected she wanted to be a cop," he admitted and gobbled down the rest of his second slice.

"I never thought I'd go into marketing, but I liked working with people and it seemed to make more sense since I did so well when I was helping Jorge," she admitted and helped Ricky clear off the table and load the dishes into the dishwasher.

They had just finished cleaning when his aunt called.

"I have a phone number for someone you can contact. I was given the number in confidence because this person has seen the news and is very worried," his aunt said.

RICKY UNDERSTOOD THE individual's concerns given that there had been several attempts on their lives so far. "I understand. Thanks for getting the number."

"I'll text it to you," she said and then quickly tacked on, "Stay safe, Ricky. I'm worried about you both."

"We'll be okay," he said and checked the text message once she'd hung up.

"Let's make this call on the patio. I'm a little tired of being cooped up in the house all day," he said.

They walked to the doors leading to the patio, only Ricky hesitated there to search for the security guards patrolling the grounds. Long moments passed, but he didn't see either of the two men.

Fear filled him at the possibility the guards had been neutralized. Besides the two of them, Josie's mom, Alicia, and her cousin Javier were both probably working somewhere either in the house or on the grounds. If a professional had taken out the guards, he wouldn't think twice about hurting them as well.

He handed Mariela his phone and said, "Lock up after me. If I'm not back in five minutes, call 911."

Her eyes widened in surprise as he reached to the small of his back and pulled out the Glock. "Stay here and lock up," he commanded again and cautiously stepped onto the patio.

He waited until she locked the sliders and crept to the far edge of the property past the pool. Peering up and down the side gardens, he didn't see either of the two guards. Luckily his mom's Jaguar was gone as well as Josie's little Mini-Cooper. It eased his mind that he didn't have to worry about them.

He raced up the side yard to the front of the house. The front gate was secure, and nothing seemed out of the ordinary. Rushing down the other side of the property, he finally caught sight of the guards down by the dock in an area that wasn't visible from the patio sliding doors.

Someone had pulled up close to their dock, and while one of the guards seemed to be providing directions to an apparently lost boater, the other guard stood a few feet back, monitoring the situation and ready to act.

As the boat pulled away from the dock and the two guards resumed their positions on either end of the waterfront area, Ricky slipped the gun back into the holster and returned to the patio doors.

"Everything's okay," he said, and Mariela ripped open the door and threw her arms around him.

"I was so worried," she said, her head buried against his chest.

He wrapped his arms around her, offering comfort until the trembling in her body stopped. "I overreacted when I didn't see the guards."

"You did the right thing. I didn't realize you were armed." When she stepped away, she motioned to his back.

"You asked me to teach you some self-defense the other night. I asked my dad for help. We decided it made sense for me to be able to protect us," he said and flipped a hand in the direction of the outdoor dining area.

"Let's make that call."

He dialed the number and a man answered. "Is this Gonzalez?"

"Ricky Gonzalez. Can I put you on speaker so my partner can hear?" he asked.

A long hesitation followed. "Sure, but no recording. Hernandez will know who I am if he hears my voice."

A good fact to know. The two men were apparently quite familiar. It surprised him that the man didn't ask who his partner was, and he didn't offer it up. Especially as Mariela grabbed her phone and tapped out a message.

His voice is familiar.

He nodded to confirm he'd seen what she'd written and said, "No problem. Thanks for talking to me. I understand you know Smith and Levy. What are they like?"

"Used to be regular guys like the rest of us. About four or five years back things started to change. First it was just a fancy vacation that none of us could ever have afforded. Then it was other things and most of us wondered what was up, but none of us had any proof," the man said, his voice suddenly hushed as if he was somewhere he feared being overheard.

The sounds of other voices and machinery filtered into the background and Ricky sensed he didn't have much time to get some answers. "But you have proof now?" he asked.

"No proof, not yet anyway," the man said.

"Does it have to do with Hernandez's mid-rise condo building?" Ricky pressed.

"Smith approved the foundation and it all seemed fine until one of the senior building inspectors got a call. Someone warned us that things weren't right."

"In what way?" Ricky pushed.

The muted noises of people and machinery in the background came again as the man called out to someone, "I'll be there in a sec."

Then he said to Ricky, "I have to go. All I can say is you need to check that foundation and the ground underneath."

That wasn't enough for Ricky since they already had their suspicions about both. "Why hasn't a new inspection been scheduled?" he hounded.

"I don't really know," the man said, and before Ricky could ask another question, the man hung up.

He peered at the phone and then at Mariela. "You said he sounded familiar."

She nodded. "We sometimes had inspectors at our holiday parties. I think he was one of the people who we invited. I should have those lists on my laptop," she said and, without waiting for him, she raced away to get her computer.

He sat at the table, considering what the man had said. That it had only been four or five years since Smith and Levy had apparently gone on the take. The condo embroiled in many of the lawsuits had been built nearly seven years earlier, presumably before the two inspectors had started taking bribes.

Which meant that the issues there could have been caused by normal settling, or worse, that another inspector was also accepting money.

When Mariela returned with her laptop, she brought up the invitation list. "This was the last party I did for Jorge. I filed for divorce just a few months after that."

He wondered what had finally pushed her over the edge to ask for a divorce and why a man like Jorge had even agreed to it. Had it possibly been the rape she'd mentioned earlier? Had she used the possibility of filing a criminal complaint as leverage? As much as he wanted to know more about that, he wouldn't push. He wanted her to be able to share it with him in her own time.

She had been tap-tap-tapping away to pull up the list, but when she looked up from her screen, she seemed to know what he'd been thinking. She immediately avoided his gaze, focused on the screen and said, "There were four inspectors at that party. Williams and Randall, who had come to other parties. Cook, who the other men called Cookie. He was a new hire. The fourth man was Livan Dillon, the 'Old Man.'"

"Do you think that's who was talking to us?" Ricky asked.

Mariela peered upward, as if searching the sky for answers, and then grudgingly nodded. "I think it was Dillon."

Something bugged him again along the edges of his brain. "Do you know why they called him 'Old Man'?"

Mariela pursed her lips and did a little shrug. "I got the sense he'd been with the department for a lot longer than they had."

Which meant he might have been around when the inspections had been done on the condo with all the problems. "I need to check something in those inspection reports," he said and held his hand out to invite her to join him inside.

Once they were back in the study, he pulled up the reports and searched them to confirm what he'd thought after chatting with the man and hearing Mariela's idea as to his identity.

"What is it, Ricky?" Mariela asked as she sat beside him and scanned the documents he was bringing up.

"Dillon, if that's who it was, says that it was four or five years ago when Smith and Levy seemed to start taking bribes, but that condo we visited was built almost seven years ago and neither of them did any inspections there. Smith wasn't even employed by the department at that time," he said and ran his index finger over the pertinent data in the report.

Mariela's opened her eyes wide. "Maybe Dillon didn't want us to know who he was because he took a bribe on that project."

Ricky nodded and displayed the detailed reports on the condo inspections. Dillon's name wasn't listed on any of the inspections. He muttered a curse and said, "Are you sure it was his voice?"

"There's one way to find out. May I?" she asked and took over the laptop.

MARIELA SEARCHED THE online inspection system and pulled up the address for a recent inspection Dillon had done. She opened another window and located the phone number for the building inspection department.

Since Dillon might recognize Ricky's number if he had caller ID and also might not answer an unknown number, she used her phone to call his office. "Miami Building Inspections," answered a cheery female voice.

"Livan Dillon, please," she said.

"I'm sorry, but Mr. Dillon is out in the field at the moment," the receptionist advised.

"Oh, no. I really need to speak to him. He just did an inspection at my house in Indian Creek and my contractor has some questions for him. Is there any way to reach him?"

"I'm sorry—"

"Please. My husband will be so angry if we can't get this finished today," she pleaded, hoping it would strike a chord with the woman on the other end of the line.

It did. "Let me see if I can't get him on his cell phone."

Mariela turned on her speaker and held her breath, waiting for Dillon to answer.

"Hello. Hello," he said, and Ricky did a little jump at the sound of his voice, recognizing it immediately.

"Livan Dillon?" she asked, just to confirm.

"Yes, this is he. Who is this?" he said, growing impatient.

"It's Mariela Hernandez and Ricky Gonzalez. I think it's time the three of us met face-to-face," she said.

Chapter Twenty

Livan "Old Man" Dillon wasn't really old, Ricky thought. He just had that kind of look that said he'd seen too much of the world. Suffered too much.

"You're going to get us all killed," Dillon hissed and looked around the Little Havana restaurant where they'd agreed to meet. With it being late afternoon, there were only a few people grabbing afternoon coffees from an outside counter. Locals from the prevalence of the *guayabera* shirts and panama hats on the older men.

"You need to tell us what you know about this development," Ricky said and pushed a sheet of paper with the condo building's photo and address in front of the man.

Dillon took one look at it, leaned back in his chair and laid thickly muscled arms across his lean chest. "I didn't have anything to do with these inspections."

"But you know something you're not saying," Mariela said and jabbed a finger at the address. "This may be where it all starts. Where all our problems, and yours, begin."

The muscles in his arms clenched at her words and Ricky pushed him to answer. "Whatever you tell us may help keep all of us safe."

An unforgiving laugh escaped Dillon, but then he shook his head, and leaned toward them again. Smoothing his hands over the piece of paper, almost like a caress, he said,

"My wife had cancer and the treatments weren't covered by our insurance. I didn't know what to do, but I knew that taking a bribe from Hernandez wasn't the answer."

Ricky didn't quite know what to think about his admission. "Hernandez offered you a bribe and you didn't take it?" he asked just to confirm he had understood Dillon's statement correctly.

"I didn't, but a few days later I saw Hernandez handing an envelope to one of our senior inspectors. I didn't need to be a genius to figure out what was going on," he said with a tired shrug of defeated shoulders.

"Why didn't you say something?" Mariela asked.

That shrug came again. "I hadn't been on the job that long and he had a lot of connections. I couldn't afford to lose my job and my medical insurance. Then he offered me money for my wife's treatments, and I broke. I didn't want to lose her."

"What's his name?" Ricky asked, wishing that with each new revelation it didn't get more and more complicated. Maybe even more and more dangerous.

At Dillon's prolonged silence, he asked again, "What's his name?"

Dillon didn't answer. He just shook his head and looked away until Mariela laid a hand on his arm.

"Your wife, is she okay?" Mariela asked, her voice filled with understanding and compassion.

Tears erupted in his eyes and spilled down his cheeks, but then the first glimmer of joy crept onto his features. "She is. She's been cancer free six years now. It would kill her to know what I did."

Mariela shook her head. "I don't think so. I think she would understand that you loved her so much you'd do anything to help her get better."

Dillon brushed away the tears and did a little bob of

his head. "His name is Billy Rooney. He's also the senior building inspector on your ex's mid-rise project."

THE GROUP GATHERED for dinner that night was even larger since Mia had brought John Wilson with her and his tech guru cousins had also come by.

As Ricky watched Mia and John during the meal, he didn't fail to miss the spark of something there, which surprised him. Mia hadn't really been seriously involved with any man since a sudden breakup with a college boyfriend years earlier. Like the social butterfly that she was, she'd flitted from one man to the other, but never for more than a date or two. By his count, she'd had more dates than that with the tech millionaire.

Carolina seemed to sense it as well, judging from the almost sad look on her face. If Mia did get serious with a man, she probably worried that the Twins would be no more. It wasn't an unreasonable assumption since he'd seen more than one woman's relationship change once a man came into the mix.

After coffee and dessert had been served, Wilson said, "Thank you so much for such a lovely meal, *Señora* Gonzalez."

"We should be thanking you for agreeing to assist us with this case, Mr. Wilson," his mother said.

With a little dip of his head, Wilson said, "If you don't mind, I'd like to hear more about what you need from me."

It was Trey who spoke up rather than his father, hinting at the fact that his father was slowly handing over the reins to his oldest son. "I hope you understand that everything we tell you tonight has to remain confidential."

Wilson chuckled, shook his head and peered at Roni as she sat beside her fiancé. "I guess he doesn't remember that I didn't out you during your last investigation."

"He remembers, John. It's just that this one is very close

to our hearts since it strikes at our family," Roni said and laid a hand on Trey's shoulder in a show of solidarity.

Wilson peered at Mia from the corner of his eye and nodded. "It's why I keep my people out of the limelight. What can I do to help you?"

"Thank you," Trey said and did a quick rundown on everything they'd learned so far. As he neared the end, he gestured for Ricky to provide the latest information on the corruption of the building inspectors.

"We know of at least three individuals that Hernandez has bribed," he said, omitting mention of Dillon since he empathized with the man's desire to help his sick wife. "One of the projects is already involved in various lawsuits but the issues don't seem life-threatening."

Wilson inched up an eyebrow. "You think one of the other projects is?"

"We have concerns that the mid-size condo development will be structurally unsound and if it is…it could result in a building collapse," Ricky advised.

"Hmm," Wilson said and leaned back in his chair before shooting forward again. He laced his fingers together and said, "These attacks on your family. You think Hernandez is behind them."

"Jorge is my ex. I overheard him talking to someone about a project. He said it was dangerous and a big risk but if the other person did it he'd get his 'blood money.' A lot of money from what I could tell," Mariela explained.

Wilson bounced his hands on the tabletop and remained silent, mulling over the information. "Have you made any progress in confirming Hernandez is behind the attacks?"

"No," Trey admitted, but quickly added, "But a recent homicide was Hernandez's old foreman, and we were able to confirm the foreman was responsible for the first attack on Mariela."

"But not the shootings or road rage?" Wilson challenged.

"We have CCTV footage from various areas but nothing definitive. The BMW visible at the various crime scenes had stolen plates each and every time," Trey explained.

Sophie jumped in with, "We're trying to secure additional footage from a security company that monitors Hernandez's properties."

Wilson remained silent once again, prompting Mia to say, "It's okay if you don't want to help, John. We'd understand."

Wilson shook his head and peered at Mia as he said, "I wasn't lucky enough to have family growing up." He ripped his gaze from hers and glanced at everyone gathered around the table. "But I see how much you all care for each other and for others," he said, finally settling his gaze on Mariela.

"So, you will help, after all?" Mia said, clearly surprised given what had seemed like his earlier reticence.

"I will, although I warn you, he might not fall for it. I already turned him down when he approached me about buying one of his projects and converting it to office space," Wilson said and reached for his nearly empty coffee mug.

"Let me freshen that for you," his mother said, but Wilson raised his hand to stop her.

"No, thanks. Although a Scotch might hit the spot right about now," he confessed.

Trey smiled. "I think we can make that happen."

AFTER THE SCOTCH and detailed plans on their next steps in the investigation, the family had scattered to go home, and Mia had left with Wilson.

"He seemed like a nice man," Mariela said as Ricky and she strolled around the gardens behind his family home.

"I guess," Ricky said with shrug, only she could tell he was less than happy with his sister's involvement with the other man.

"What don't you like about him?" she asked, wondering about his protectiveness. She'd never had the benefit of a sibling to care about her since she was an only child.

Ricky laughed and did a little wag of his head. "She's my sister, and as my *abuela* always told the Twins, 'Men are dogs.'"

Mariela did a little stutter-step and faced him. "Really. Does that include you, Ricardo Gonzalez? Should I worry about you?"

He had a wry grin on his lips as he cupped her cheek. "Point taken, only I'm not an eccentric millionaire—"

"Just a millionaire," she teased with a roll of her eyes.

"A very eccentric millionaire who keeps a pied-à-terre in the Del Sol for female-only parties," he said, continuing his earlier tirade.

Even she'd heard rumors about Wilson's weirdness from an assortment of internet news sites as well as the local television news channel when it covered one of his parties. But that didn't make them true or harmful.

"You've got to trust Mia's judgment. Roni's as well, apparently," she said, recalling what the other man had said at dinner about not outing Roni during a prior investigation.

"I guess I do. Let's hope he can get access to that construction site," he said, slipped an arm around her waist and gently urged her back into their stroll.

The night couldn't be more perfect, she thought, inhaling the fragrance from a nearby bush of night-blooming jasmine, but a slightly chilly breeze had a damp feel, warning that rain might be on its way. A new moon barely cast light across the lawn, leaving them in intimate shadows. As they neared a small stand of palms that hid them from the guards and anyone in the house, Ricky tugged her there, leaned against a tree and urged her close.

She went willingly, loving the feel of his hard body

against her softness and the way his hands swept up to cup her breasts.

"Is this you being a dog?" she teased and rose on tip-toes to brush a quick kiss on his lips.

"Woof," he kidded, his smile bright even in the dim moonlight.

She kissed that smile, exalting in the joy of it that kindled hope in her heart. His hands moving on her, caressing the sensitive tips of her breasts, kindled passion until she moaned into his mouth.

"Let's go in," Ricky said, and they hurried back to the house and up to his room. But unlike the night before, they didn't dawdle with drinks or conversation. By the time they reached the bed in the center of the room they were naked, and Ricky was reaching into the nightstand to whip out a strip of condoms he'd had a local pharmacy discreetly deliver earlier that day.

She raised her eyebrows at the length of the strip. "Feeling very lucky?"

IT DAWNED ON Ricky then that she often used humor as a defense mechanism when she might be feeling uncomfortable. Like now. He could have joked right back at her, only he wanted to chip away at those defenses to know more about her.

"No, it's not that. This isn't just about getting you into bed. It's about…more."

His words had a totally unexpected result: she shut down as if someone had tossed a bucket of cold water on her.

Rushing to her clothes scattered around the room, she hugged them to her body as if they were a shield.

He chased after her and grabbed her arm when she would have run.

"Don't," she shouted and jerked out of his grasp.

"Tell me what's wrong, Mariela? Tell me why you're running," he said, hands outstretched in pleading.

"You think this is something serious, but what do you really know about me?" she shot back.

"I know you're bright. Intelligent. Brave," he said, recalling what she'd said earlier about how her ex had raped her.

Tears glistened in her eyes and teetered precariously on her thick eyelashes. "How can you even look at me like that when you know what he did to me? That I'm damaged goods."

Her words explained so much. As the tears finally spilled down her cheeks, he swiped them away with the back of his hand. "No one is perfect and sometimes it's those imperfections that make something special. Like you."

MARIELA WANTED TO say that he was perfect, but she'd seen his cracks. "Like the way you worry you aren't as strong as the rest of the men in your family."

His lips thinned to knife-sharp slash and he tipped his head. "Like that. We're two imperfect people, but together...we're a hell of a team."

She didn't try to deny that. Dropping the clothes she'd had in a stranglehold, she took hold of his hand and guided him to the bed. Together they crawled in and beneath the covers. Embracing him, she said, "I want to tell you everything."

HE PACED BACK and forth in his workshop, angry that he hadn't been able to run them into the waters of Biscayne Bay. Now they were holed up even more tightly at the Gonzalez family compound.

Since it would be impossible to get past the security gate off the causeway, he'd tried to sneak in via the canal only to find two armed guards patrolling the waterfront. They'd chased him away quickly, not buying his story that he'd gotten lost on his way to a friend's home on the island.

He was going to have to bide his time to try to hit at them again. In the meantime, he'd keep a close eye on them, although he suspected that they would try and find a way to visit one of the new developments.

He'd be waiting for them when they did.

Chapter Twenty-One

They'd stayed up for hours as she'd shared more about what had happened during her marriage. He'd listened, but as a lover and not a psychologist. When she'd emptied her heart of so many fears and doubts, he'd shared his own and found togetherness with that giving.

Exhausted, they'd fallen to sleep but woken to make love.

As the first fingers of dawn had crept into the room, she'd roused him with her caresses and kisses and they'd made love again, welcoming a new day and maybe even a new beginning between them.

They'd taken a quick shower—together—and rushed down for breakfast. Ricky's mother was already there, reading the morning paper. Trey as well, devouring a large plate of pancakes and bacon.

"You keep eating like that and you'll never fit in your tux for the wedding," Ricky teased.

"Don't worry. I'm going to work it off," Trey said with a knowing glance between the two of them.

"Whatever you do with Roni is TMI, *mano*," Ricky parried to deflect from them.

"It is. Apologies," his older brother said and clearly meant it.

"Can I get you a *café con leche*?" his mother asked.

"I'd love some. Thanks," Mariela said, and luckily Josie came in a second later with two plates piled high with pancakes and bacon. She placed them in front of their seats and said, "I'll bring some hot maple syrup in a second."

"Thank you," she said just as Samantha handed her a mug and returned to her seat.

"Your father went in early to work on some things. What's on your list for today?" Ricky's mother asked Trey.

His brother stopped slicing up his pancakes and said, "Hounding the detectives to see if they have anything new on the attacks and talk to the ME to see if he has anything else. I'm hoping that rope had some DNA on it that will lead us to Hernandez."

Trey forked up some of his pancake and paused with it halfway to his mouth. "You two are going to stay in touch with Wilson and Mia, right?"

Ricky nodded. "We are. Hopefully Hernandez will agree to Wilson visiting the site."

"But will Wilson see anything more than just the cracks we've heard about?" Mariela asked as Josie returned with the promised maple syrup. She smiled at the young woman and thanked her.

"I don't know Wilson well, but I suspect he'll do a thorough visual inspection. I should get going," Trey said and took a final bite of his breakfast.

He was about to walk out when his phone rang. "What's up, Soph?"

Listening for just a few minutes, Trey said, "Hold on and let me put you on speaker."

Sophie's voice burst through the line. "Robbie and I know Wilson is hoping to visit the site today, but we had an idea."

"Go ahead, Josefina," Samantha said, using Sophie's given name.

"It seems as if there's worry about the ground settling

where it shouldn't be. We could use lidar to map the topography at the site and see just how much it's settled. Even do projections of what might happen when it does," she said.

"How does that work?" Trey asked and sat back down.

"We'd have to send up a drone to get some information and then analyze it with software," Robbie explained.

"Wouldn't the construction crew see a drone flying over them?" Mariela said, thinking that she'd seen one flying over more than once to get photos and video for their marketing.

"We'd send it up at night. It can actually be better for the laser at night and there's generally less air traffic as well," Sophie said.

Trey looked around the table, gauging their reactions before he said, "Please get ready to do it."

"Will do. In the meantime, we'll finish up what we can on the CCTV and webcam images," Robbie advised, and the line went dead as he hung up.

"It sounds like a great idea," Ricky said, grateful for his techie cousins and their skills.

"I guess we just wait for their report and Wilson," Mariela said, slightly disheartened that there wasn't more that she could do to help.

"You've done a lot, Mariela. All your connections helped us get to this point," Ricky said, reading her like the proverbial open book.

"He's right. We know as much as we do thanks to you," Trey agreed.

"Thank you," she said, but despite their words, guilt lingered that they were at risk because of what she'd overheard and her psycho husband.

It made her lose her appetite despite how wonderful the pancakes had tasted. "I think I need some air."

When Ricky rose to go with her, she stopped him with an upraised hand and nearly ran from the room.

"SHE FEELS RESPONSIBLE," his mother said as she stared at Mariela fleeing the room.

"If she hadn't overheard and been brave enough to do something about it, people might have died," Ricky said.

"Even if you do the right thing, you still feel the guilt," Trey said and leaned heavily on his chair.

His brother had always been the strong silent type, but for the first time Ricky was seeing a crack in that tough exterior. "You still feel responsible about your partner's death."

Trey gripped the top rung of the chair so hard his fingers went white with the pressure. "We did the right thing to investigate. I did all I could to get to him. To save him, only…"

It hadn't been enough, Ricky thought as Trey rushed from the room.

"I'm an idiot." His job was to read people and yet with two people he cared about he hadn't been able to see what was right in front of his face.

"Love can blind you sometimes," his mother said, as intuitive as ever.

"I'm not sure I'm in love with her." There was so much happening, and he worried that it was too soon.

His mother gave an exasperated sigh and rose to clear off the table. While she did so, she said, "You've always been my planner, my responsible one. You can't plan love, Ricardo. It just kind of happens."

She didn't wait for him to respond and left him sitting there, staring at the empty table and the remnants of his breakfast. Pieces of pancake drowned in a gloppy mess of melted butter and maple syrup.

In a way, he was drowning a little, too. Much like his mother had pointed out, he'd always been the one who'd needed structure and safety. If he had to psychoanalyze himself, it was possibly because of his family's unsettled years when he'd been little. He'd never wanted a life like his father's. He'd wanted stability, and yet here he was, embroiled in a situation as dangerous as any that his father or brother had ever been in.

"Ricky?" Mariela said as she returned to the table, her emerald gaze dark with worry.

"I was just thinking about all we had to do today," he lied, not wanting to add to her guilt.

If she saw through his fib, she didn't say. "Maybe we should see what we can find out about Rooney?" she said, referring to the senior inspector that Dillon had mentioned.

"That's a good idea. I don't think I could just sit here and wait," he said, hopped up from the table and grabbed his dish to take it into the kitchen.

At his action, a flicker of a smile flashed across her lips.

Puzzled, he narrowed his gaze in question and she gestured to the plates in his hands. "Your mom taught you well."

He grinned and nodded. His very perceptive mom had taught him that and more. "She most certainly did." As he placed the plates near the sink where his mother was rinsing the dishes, he dropped a kiss on her cheek.

"Just because," he said at her quizzical look and returned to the dining area where Mariela waited, still smiling.

She held her hand out to him and he twined his fingers with hers and walked with her into the other room. They'd been pulled into this situation together and together they would find a way out of it.

MARIELA WATCHED AS RICKY, Trey and their cousins tested the drone in the backyard.

Sophie was operating the controls while Robbie monitored the path of the drone on his laptop. Trey and Robbie stood across the way from them, heads bent together as they chatted.

"We used satellite views of this property and the construction site to program the drone's route," Sophie explained to her as the drone took flight. It hovered in the air directly above them and she said, "You can run the program now, Robbie."

Sophie's brother tapped a few keys and the drone started flying back and forth across the property for the family home, gathering information.

The drone had something that looked like a small camera in the middle, facing downward. Mariela pointed to it and asked, "Is that the laser thing?"

Sophie nodded and smiled. "It is. The laser will take measurements, and once we have that, we'll use software to map the ground. We can even strip away any vegetation and man-made structures to see what it looks like."

"Amazing," Mariela said, watching the drone zip back and forth across the sky.

"What's amazing is what they're discovering with lidar, like whole Mayan cities and Egyptian pyramids," Robbie added from beside them as he kept an eye on the computer.

Trey and Ricky had been watching as well from across the yard, but seeing that the drone was working just fine, they joined Mariela and the cousins.

"Looks like it's working great," Ricky said.

"You've got the construction site programmed the same way?" Trey asked as he leaned over Robbie to view the laptop screen.

"We do. We got a satellite view of the site and programmed it. We can launch from the parking lot of the condo building next to it," Sophie advised.

"Great work. The three of us will go once it's totally dark," Trey said, but Ricky and she immediately protested.

"We're going as well," she said.

Ricky agreed. "We're in this because of us so we're going."

Trey jammed his hands on his hips and his shoulders shifted with his very visible harrumph. But then they drooped with resignation as he said, "I get it. I don't have to like it, but I get it."

His mother stepped out from the house and called out, "Come in and get something to eat."

"Because nothing gets you ready for an assignment like a full stomach," Trey teased with a chuckle.

"It's a sign of love, *mano*," Ricky said and clapped his brother on the back.

Robbie hopped to his feet, inhaled deeply and wrung his hands together in anticipation. "It smells like *picadillo*. Your mom makes a mean *picadillo*."

He rushed off toward the house, leaving them all chuckling and following at a slower pace.

Inside, Robbie had already plopped himself at the table and his mother and Josie were bringing out big platters with rice and the *picadillo* Robbie had salivated over.

Mariela smiled and sat, relishing the comfort that came from sharing a meal with family.

There was genial teasing as Robbie piled his plate high with rice and the meat flavored with tomato sauce, onions, peppers, garlic and olives. "You make the best *picadillo*, *tia*," he said.

"Thank you, Robbie. That's high praise because your mom is quite a cook," Samantha said.

"When she isn't busy cooking up some weird program," Trey said around a mouthful of food.

The comment puzzled Mariela. "Your mom is a programmer?"

Sophie shook her head and swallowed. "Kind of. She and my dad work for the NSA."

"Wow, the NSA? Like supersecret spy types?" Mariela said, eyes wide in surprise.

"Kind of," Sophie said again with a little lift of her shoulders.

"If we told you what they really did we'd have to kill you," Robbie teased, but Mariela suspected that maybe it wasn't all that far from the truth.

"*Tia* Mercedes is my dad's sister. He always says she's the smartest Gonzalez," Ricky said with a grin.

Considering how impressive all the Gonzalez family members were, Mercedes had to be a genius, but then again, she probably was a genius since she was working for the NSA.

The family continued chatting, explaining how Mercedes had met her husband as well as how Samantha and Ramon had met. Which left her wondering about Carolina's connection and Ricky explained.

"Carolina and Pepe, whose real name is Jose, are my *tio* Jose's kids. He's my dad's younger brother. Mercedes is the baby sister."

"So many family members," she said, her mind whirling with all the names.

Ricky patted her hand in understanding. "Don't worry. You'll get to meet them all eventually."

"I'm looking forward to it," she said, optimistic that whatever was happening with Ricky would continue after the conclusion of the investigation.

They were halfway through the meal when Ricky's father finally showed up, looking a little tired and worn.

"Everything okay?" Samantha asked as she rose and dropped a kiss on his cheek.

"Fine, just a small problem," he said, slipped off his suit jacket and took his spot at the head of the table.

"Anything I can help with?" Trey immediately asked, bringing a smile to his father's face.

"In time, *mi'jo*," his father said and dug into the plate that his wife placed in front of him.

Dinner resumed at a leisurely pace, especially since they had to wait for full night to fall in order to fly the drone. They had just finished the meal with coffee and flan when Trey peered out the window to the darkness beyond.

"It's time," he said.

Chapter Twenty-Two

They had no issue pulling into the parking lot for the condo building next to Hernandez's construction site and Sophie and Robbie had the drone up in no time.

Ricky tracked the small flashing red and white lights as it ran his cousin's program to map the topography of the ground. Mariela stood next to him, but her gaze was fixed not on the drone, but on the building behind them.

"I don't see any cracks on this building," she said, and both Trey and he turned to scrutinize the structure.

After a long inspection, Ricky said, "I don't either, but maybe it's possible the ground here is more stable."

"Or they did remedial work to stabilize it," Trey said, which reminded Ricky of something the condo owners involved in the lawsuit had said.

"Those condo owners said Hernandez didn't want to do that because it was too expensive," he repeated.

"And we've heard that he's strapped for cash," Mariela added.

"We'll see just how bad the situation is once we have the footage and can analyze it," Sophie said over her shoulder, but her gaze was fixed on the drone.

From what Ricky could see, the drone was halfway over the property, and it hadn't been all that long, maybe fifteen minutes. Which made him wonder aloud, "How long will it take to analyze the data you get?"

Sophie made a face. "That's the rub. It could take up to twenty-four hours to process on our computers."

"What about on Wilson's computers?" Trey asked.

"He's probably got some kind of supercomputer to run all his programs. I'm thinking a few hours?" Sophie said.

"You're going to ask him for another favor?" Ricky said, worried by what all those favors were going to do to his sister's budding relationship with the wealthy tech mogul.

Trey did a little shrug. "Yeah, I get where you're going. We can wait. Wilson isn't going to inspect the property until tomorrow anyway. Hernandez is apparently playing it cool and making it seem like there's no rush to sell it off."

"Almost done," Robbie said, but a second later a series of gunshots rang out in the night.

"Damn. They're shooting at the drone," Trey said.

"Just a few more passes," Sophie said and focused on Robbie's laptop, watching the progress.

Trey shot his arm out in the direction of their SUV. "Load up any loose gear and get in the car," he instructed and raced over to grab the case for the drone.

He joined his brother to lift the large carrying case for the device into the back of the SUV while Mariela picked up a smaller duffel with supplies the cousins had also brought with them.

Voices called out in the dark, the words muted until someone shouted out, "Take down that drone."

A volley of gunfire erupted, shooting up at the drone.

"I'm bringing it home," Sophie said as Robbie stood and started walking toward the SUV with the laptop. "I've got the data," he confirmed.

In a few seconds Sophie had landed the drone and they were lifting it into the back of the SUV.

The heavy pounding of footsteps getting closer sounded

from the other side of the fence, but by then they were all in the car and pulling away.

As Ricky peered over his shoulder toward the fence, a head popped over for the barest second, but not long enough for him to see much of anything.

"I think you made a clean getaway," he said, but as they were about to pull out of the entrance to the condo, a black SUV blocked their path and armed guards jumped out.

Trey immediately put the car in reverse and drove backward until with a sharp turn that sent all of them flying side to side in their seats he whipped out of a service entrance for the building.

As he did so Ricky looked back, hoping they weren't being followed. Luckily, a trio of police cruisers had boxed in the black SUV and the security guards stood there, hands raised above their heads.

Trey took a quick look at the rearview mirror. "Someone must have called in the gunshots."

"Thank God," Mariela said from beside them. "They were going to shoot us."

Trey shook his head. "I don't think so. They probably only wanted the drone."

"We still would have had the data. It was feeding to a cloud account," Robbie said.

"But they would have guessed that we knew something was wrong with that property. And Hernandez was willing to kill Mariela for just that reason," Ricky pointed out, and beside him Mariela shook with fear.

"I'm sorry I got you all involved in this," she said again.

"Stop apologizing. You did the right thing. You could be saving lives," Trey said, rising anger in his voice.

"Chill, Trey," Ricky warned as Mariela's body trembled beside his and he slipped his arm to pull her close and comfort her.

"Sorry. I'm just frustrated at how long it's taking. I

want you all to be safe and I know we'll make it happen," he said, hands tight on the steering wheel.

"We'll start processing the data immediately and let you know as soon as we have the info," Sophie said, trying to ease Trey's frustration.

"I know you will, Soph. You guys have been amazing through all this," Trey said and glanced at them in the rearview mirror. "You and Mariela also. It's thanks to all of you that we're this close to nailing Hernandez," he said and held one hand up with his index finger and thumb just an inch apart to emphasize his words.

Ricky knew part of his frustration was also that the detectives handling the cases had found little evidence at any of the scenes. "Did you hear anything from the ME yet?" he asked, hoping there was a least some motion on that front.

"He has some DNA off the rope, but no match against any databases," Trey said.

"But it could be Jorge's, right?" Mariela asked, likewise beginning to show some frustration.

"It could. The detectives asked him for a sample when they went to question him about Ramirez, but he lawyered up and we don't really have enough for a warrant," Trey said as he pulled onto the highway for the ride back to their family home.

"What about a genealogy site? Jorge did one of those a few years ago," Mariela said.

"Also need a warrant," Trey confirmed.

"Any family who's pissed off at him?" Ricky asked, thinking they might be able to at least do a familial match.

"He's an only child," Mariela offered up.

"I guess we have to wait on that until we have more," Ricky said and didn't miss how his brother's hands tightened on the wheel of the car.

Sophie reached over to squeeze Trey's shoulder in re-assurance. "We'll have more soon," she said.

"We will," Trey said, but it was almost as if to convince himself.

Mariela slipped her hand into Ricky's, looked up at him and mouthed, *It'll be okay.*

He smiled, bent and dropped a kiss on her lips, whispering, "It will."

The rest of the drive passed in silence, everyone lost in their thoughts. When they opened the gate and pulled into the courtyard in front of the house, a bright red Lamborghini was parked off to one side.

"Sweet Lord, do you know what that is? It's a Veneno," Robbie said in awe when they pulled up beside the supercar. "It costs a few million," he said and hopped out to inspect the Lamborghini.

"I guess Wilson's here," Trey said in amusement.

"I guess so," Ricky said and climbed out of the SUV to examine the über-pricey automobile.

Trey jammed his hands on his hips and scoffed as he looked at the car. "Overcompensating much."

Sophie barely shot a glance at the car and said, "Boys and their toys."

Mariela grabbed hold of his hand and playfully pulled him away from the shiny red toy. "Let's go see why Mia and John are here."

Reluctantly, he said, "You're right."

Inside Mia and John were sitting at the dining area table with his mother and father, having coffee.

His father rose, worry etching deep lines on his face. "The police scanner said there was gunfire at your location."

"The guards shot at the drone and then came after us, but Trey was able to get us away," Ricky said and tossed a hand in the direction of his brother and cousins, who had just come through the door.

"Armed guards seem a little extreme at a construction site," Wilson said with the lift of a light brown brow.

"It does and it might make it harder for you to inspect the location," Ricky said.

"You said they shot at a drone. With lidar, I assume," Wilson said and glanced toward Sophie and Robbie.

Sophie nodded and took a spot at the table. "We plan to map the topography of the site to see if there is sinking going on."

"We'll also strip away the building and any other structures or vegetation to see what's happening there," Robbie added.

"Impressive. You must need a lot of computing power for that," Wilson said with a quick dip of his head.

The cousins shared a look that the tech millionaire immediately understood. "If it would help, I have a supercomputer that we've put together for a new venture. I'd be more than happy to help out."

"That would really speed things up," Sophie said with a grateful sigh.

Wilson reached into the pocket of his white linen shirt, extracted a business card and handed it to them. "This is my number and also one for Miles, my half brother. He's my business partner. Let him know you're sending the data and we'll process it immediately."

"Thank you, John," Mia said. She was sitting beside him, but judging from her body language, Ricky sensed all was not right with her and Wilson. In truth, Ricky was wondering why the man was being so accommodating when he barely knew the family.

Trey must have also been getting those vibes since he said, "We're really grateful, but—"

Wilson raised a hand to stop him. "It's too much. I get

it. Most people would believe I want something in return," he said and shot a look at Mia from the corner of his eye.

His sister tensed even more, and the lines of her beautiful face grew hard.

"I don't, but if one day I need help, I hope you'd do the same," he said.

An uneasy silence filled the air until Trey said, "We would. You just have to ask."

Wilson smiled, his hazel eyes bright and without deception if Ricky was a good judge.

"I hope I won't have to ask," he said without hesitation.

"Are you ready for your visit tomorrow?" his father asked, worry still sitting heavily on his face and in the tightness of his body. It concerned Ricky because his father rarely wore his emotions on his sleeve, but since his arrival last night, something had clearly been troubling him. He'd have to get him aside and ask, not that he thought his father would share.

"I am, only I'm not so sure that a visual inspection will tell you much. What you really need, besides what Sophie and Robbie are doing, is to see what's underground," Wilson said.

"You mean ground penetrating radar?" Sophie said, her mind clearly racing with ideas.

Wilson nodded, but Trey immediately said, "I doubt Hernandez will let you do that if he knows there's an issue."

"You're right. He seemed eager for me to take the property as is, no questions asked. That alone is a red flag," Wilson said, and everyone around the table nodded in agreement.

MARIELA PROCESSED ALL that Wilson had said, but something just didn't seem right to her. "Jorge was willing to bribe someone to let that building go up. Now he's selling it? Why? To avoid paying the bribe?"

"Or to avoid something that even he thinks is too dangerous to do," Ricky offered.

With all that she knew about her husband, and the way he'd treated her, she found that altruism too hard to believe. "Maybe, only that's not the Jorge I know."

"There's only one way to find out. After I take a look around, I'll tell him I'm not interested in the property," Wilson said.

Chapter Twenty-Three

"I thought he'd stroke out. Red face, eyes bulging," Wilson said and emphasized it with his hands the following day.

"Jorge has a temper," Mariela added as the team sat at the outside dining area to shade themselves from the midday sun.

"He does, but we have some really good news," his father said, looking a little more relieved than he had last night. "I gave *Tio* Jose all the information we'd gathered. It wasn't easy, but I convinced him to open an investigation into the building inspection department."

"That is good news," Ricky said, guessing that the tension he'd sensed had been caused by conflict between the two brothers. Even though he was relieved about his father, he wondered why Mia hadn't come with Wilson to share what had happened that morning at the construction site.

"But will they be watching Jorge in time to catch him paying the bribe?" Mariela said and raked her fingers through the waves of her caramel-colored hair.

His father pursed his lips and said, "I'm not sure."

So close and yet still so very far, Mariela thought, her gut tightening with worry that, despite everything, her ex was going to get away with what he had done and what he planned to do.

"We have to do more," she said softly, that worry driving her to speak out. "What about that radar John mentioned?"

"The problem is getting on-site because of those armed guards," Trey said, but she could tell ideas were already spinning around in his brain on how to do it.

"A decoy," Ricky said, almost as if reading his brother's brain.

"The drone," Sophie added, totally in sync with her cousins.

"We can send it up and pull the guards away from the site so we can use the radar to do some testing," Robbie said.

"I can ask around and see if we can get the radar," Wilson said, but Trey was quick to shut him down.

"We appreciate everything you've done, John, but I can't ask you to do something that risky."

With a shrug, Wilson relented. "I understand. I'll send over that lidar data ASAP. It should be ready soon," he said and rose from the table.

Trey, Ricky and their dad stood as well and shook the other man's hand. "We really do appreciate it," Ricky said, and the others echoed his words.

"*No problema.* I guess I'll see you around," Wilson said and walked away, leaving Mariela to wonder if things with him and Mia hadn't worked out. Especially since she hadn't come with him, and Mariela had sensed tension the night before.

Once he was gone, everyone sat back down around the table and started planning. She sat back, listening. It was like watching generals mapping out a military campaign as Trey and his father laid out the primary objective while Ricky, Sophie and Robbie tossed out suggestions.

She was impressed as Ricky held his own with the others because this really wasn't his thing. Even though he occasionally helped the agency, he was a psychologist with his own work and life.

She felt a little useless just sitting there, but there wasn't any more that she could add to the conversation. But as they started laying out the responsibilities for all that they would have to do that night, she piped in with, "I'm going as well. I have no intention of just sitting here, waiting and worrying."

Trey raised his hands to quiet her, but Ricky said, "She's as much a part of this as the family, maybe more."

"I am," she said, appreciating his support.

With that, they worked together to complete the plans for breaking into the site that night.

HE LOOKS DANGEROUSLY sexy in all black, Mariela thought as Ricky finished dressing. It made his chestnut brown hair look even darker and his light blue eyes pop. His black eye and the bruises around his face were finally fading and the first hints of evening stubble shaded his cheeks and chin, making him look even sexier.

She walked up to him and cradled his cheek, rubbing her hands across the sandpapery stubble. He laid a hand on her waist and drew her close. "You don't have to do this," he said and leaned his forehead against hers.

"I have to. I have to make sure he gets the justice he deserves," she said and tilted her head to drop a butterfly-light kiss on his lips.

When she pulled away, he tightened his hand at her waist and kissed her hard, deepening the kiss until they were straining against each other despite making love just an hour earlier.

A cough jerked them apart.

Trey stood at the door, eyeing them with concern. "It's time to go. Are you sure you want to do this?"

Mariela met Ricky's gaze and he said, "We're sure."

"Then let's roll," Trey said and tapped the doorjamb in emphasis before whirling to hurry down the stairs.

Ricky slipped his arm around her waist, and they followed Trey to the dining area where Sophie had placed several printouts on the table. Robbie stood beside the table with his laptop in hand. Ricky's mother and father sat tensely, a radio and laptop in front of them.

"These are the renderings that we were able to create from the lidar data we got from the drone," Sophie explained and ran her fingers along what looked like topographical maps.

"There is unusual unsettling all along this area and beneath the building," Robbie said as Sophie pointed out the areas on the maps. "We were also able to calculate the rate at which the building was settling and what might happen," he added and flipped open his computer to run the simulation.

They watched as the simulation showed the gradual lean of one side of the building until it got so severe that half of the structure completely sheered off the rest of the building and collapsed onto the ground.

"That could kill a lot of people," Ricky said with a low whistle.

"I know Jorge is desperate, but to do something like this…" Mariela said, anger and disgust in her tone.

"It's why we have to stop him," Ricky said and hugged her to his side.

Trey gestured to the maps. "We want to use the GPR on those areas in the simulation to see what's happening underground. Ricky and I will run the radar. Mariela will be our lookout."

He peered from Sophie to Robbie. "Are you two sure you can use the drone to draw away the security guards?"

"As long as you got us a good driver, we can lure them away," Sophie said, no hesitation in her voice.

Mariela wished she could be as certain. "Will we have a driver as well?"

"You will. I've pulled in two of the best drivers from the South Beach Security pool. Roni will also be available in case we need help," Trey confirmed and gestured to the radio and laptop in front of his parents. "*Mami* and *papi* will be tracking the cars and communications in case we need to call in Roni and her police colleagues."

Murmurs drifted around the table from everyone and then Ricky asked, "What do we do next?"

"Let me get you all wired up with the coms so we can stay in touch," Trey said and walked over with a large black suitcase that he laid on the table. He opened it, pulled out communications equipment and got everyone prepared. Once they'd confirmed that everyone could communicate, including with Ricky and Trey's parents, they flew into action.

Trey almost jogged down the few stairs from the front door to the courtyard where two SUVs waited along with the two drivers Trey had mentioned earlier. In a flurry of activity, Mariela piled into the vehicle with Ricky and Trey, and they drove off, the other SUV trailing behind them.

He watched them pull away from the Gonzalez family compound in the two black SUVs. From what he could see through the gate, two of the heirs to the agency were in the SUV in the lead, heading to the construction site, he guessed.

He was ready for them. More than ready thanks to a guard who was willing to look the other way for a nice wad of money.

He smiled as he imagined tripping the surprise he had in the building. Watching it all come down around the Gonzalez family members.

Putting down the binoculars, he wheeled his car around

and onto the causeway to head to the site, careful to keep a discreet distance from the two SUVs.

Minutes later, one of the SUVs peeled away, but he kept his eyes on the prize: the SUV carrying the Gonzalez heirs.

It traveled to within a few blocks of the site and pulled over.

He doubled back toward the construction location and parked, gleefully anticipating the moment when he'd teach them all a lesson.

"WHENEVER YOU'RE READY, SOPHIE," Trey said from the front passenger seat.

Ricky tightened his hold on Mariela's hand, anxious about the plan they had all agreed on. It seemed like there were too many things that had to fall into place for them to accomplish their mission.

Across the earpiece he wore, Sophie said, "I'm sending the drone up over the site now. Robbie has hacked their CCTV to confirm if any guards are left on the site."

"Roger that. Let us know when we can go in," Trey instructed.

"Will do," Sophie said, and Ricky sucked in a breath, his heart pounding as he waited for the moment they'd have to head onto the location.

Long minutes passed and he tapped his foot nervously until Mariela laid a hand on his knee. "*Mi amor*, I think I can hear your knees knocking."

"Nervous," he admitted and twined his fingers with hers.

"Me, too. It feels like the wait is forever—"

"It's time to go. Robbie says all the guards have gone to follow them," Trey said, and with a tap on the dashboard, the driver shot the SUV forward and down the few blocks to the entrance to the construction site.

The security guards had left the gate open in their haste to chase after the drone and whoever was controlling it.

As Ricky exited the SUV, he caught sight of the red and white lights on the drone flying away from the construction lot. Sophie and Robbie had done their part; now they had to do theirs.

He rushed to the rear of the SUV where Trey and he muscled the radar device out of the back of the vehicle. The GPR was larger than a lawn mower and a lot heavier, but still manageable between them. Once it was on the ground, Trey called out to the driver, "Turn the car around so we can make a fast exit."

Mariela stood beside them, hands wrapped around the binoculars they'd given her to use.

Ricky looked at the shell of the building that had already been constructed. "You should be able to be a lookout from the third floor."

He bent to give her a quick kiss and she was off, rushing toward the structure.

"Let's move this into place," Trey said, and together they pushed the GPR device toward the edge of the building, which the lidar had identified as having the most settling.

Once they had it in place, his brother said, "I hope I remember how to get this working."

The contact who had lent them the device had provided them a quick lesson earlier that afternoon and Ricky was sure of how to get it running. "Let me," he said and urged his brother aside.

With the press of a few buttons, the device jumped to life and Ricky slowly pushed it along the edge, collecting the data they would need to know whether what was happening belowground could cause the collapse of the building that Sophie and Robbie had predicted in their simulation.

His hands were damp on the handles, his heartbeat racing as he focused on the task. Run the GPR device too fast and they wouldn't get accurate data. But with every second that passed they ran the risk of the armed security guards returning and it was anyone's guess what would happen then.

Steadying his breath and his pace, he pushed on, intent on finishing the task.

MARIELA HAD ENTERED the shell of the building and found a staircase that she used to race up to the third floor of the partially constructed structure. There was only one other floor above, but the plans she remembered seeing on the real estate listing had shown at least two more floors. As she ran up the stairs, her flashlight providing light, she looked for signs of damage to the structure, but couldn't see any since the staircase was on the side of the building farthest from the area where the settling was occurring.

When she reached the third floor, she shut off the flashlight, pulled out the binoculars and searched for the drone and the SUV with Sophie and Robbie as well as the other black SUV with the guards from the building site. Neither was in sight, giving her some peace of mind that they'd have more than enough time to finish their testing of the ground before having to make an escape.

She walked to the opposite side of the building and flipped on the flashlight, careful to shield its light with her body while she inspected the areas around the support columns. Sure enough, there were small hairline cracks already developing just as her ex's foreman had warned.

She hurried to the next column and noted the same kind of damage. She was about to shut off the flashlight when from the corner of her eye something caught her attention. Training the flashlight on the column near the stairs, she noticed a blob plastered to the base of the column. Inching closer, she realized there were several blobs pressed against all the columns in that row. Wires ran from one to the other and as she tracked them down she realized they all led to a small box with a red LED indicator.

2:58, the LED said.

2:57.

2:56.

Her heart stopped dead. A bomb. And there was only a little less than three minutes before it would go off.

"Trey. Ricky. There's a bomb on the third floor. We only have a little over two and a half minutes to get out of here before it blows," she said and raced toward the staircase.

FOR A MOMENT, Ricky imagined that he hadn't just heard what Mariela had said.

"Repeat, Mariela. Did you say a bomb?" Trey asked as Ricky finished a pass along the building's edge and turned to do another.

"Bomb. Two minutes. Boom," Mariela said, her breath short and choppy across the line.

Trey called to the driver. "Get ready to roll," he commanded, and the SUV's engine roared to life.

"Come on, Ricky. Shut that thing down," Trey said, but Ricky had to finish the pass, worried that if they didn't they wouldn't have enough data to confirm their fears.

"I have to finish," he said, maintaining his pace even though his flight response was saying to get the hell out of there.

Trey peered at his watch. "We've only got a little more than a minute," he warned just as Mariela rushed over to them.

"We've got to go," she urged Ricky, but he didn't waver, taking the last almost painfully slow steps to finish the pass.

"Let's go," he shouted and shut down the radar. Together

the three of them picked up the GPR device, hauled it over to the SUV and almost tossed it into the back.

They jumped into the vehicle and the driver sped away just as the first boom sounded and was followed by three other blasts.

The ground shook beneath them, but the driver steadied the car, and they flew out of the construction lot and into the street as a loud rumble filled the air.

As they drove a safe distance away, Trey, Ricky and Mariela turned in their seats to see the one side of the building coming down and crashing onto the ground, the force of the blasts and the collapse strong enough to shake their SUV and trip the car alarms of several vehicles in the area.

It took only seconds for the sounds of sirens to join the wail of the car alarms and Roni's voice shot across their earpieces.

"Trey, are you all okay?"

"We are, but you need to get here. Someone set off a bomb," he said.

THE POLICE HAD questioned them at the site and then taken them over to the nearest precinct where Roni, *Tio* Jose and *Tia* Elena had come to help them during the interviews the detectives assigned to the investigation had wanted to conduct.

They had provided all the details they had about the bribes and the attacks on their lives, only omitting the names of Hernandez's current foreman and Dillon. His uncle had confirmed to the police that his office already had all the details and were commencing their own investigation of the building inspectors and Hernandez.

Seemingly satisfied, the detectives were about to release them when they received a call from the police officers investigating the other earlier attacks.

"Let me put you on speakerphone," the one officer said and peered around the room at the various Gonzalez members gathered around the interview table.

"Please give us your report," the detective requested.

"We went to Hernandez's home to advise him about the incident at his construction site, but no one answered. When we did a quick inspection, we noticed that someone was in a front room and attempted to get a response again. When there wasn't one, we entered."

Ricky's gut clenched as he waited and wrapped an arm around Mariela, expecting the worst.

In a forced, almost clinical monotone, the detective said, "We found a male inside with a gunshot wound to the head. We identified him as Jorge Hernandez, but we'll need someone to come and identify him at the ME's."

Mariela sucked in a shocked breath and whispered, "I'll go ID but it can't be Jorge. He would never do something like that."

The detective on the line continued with his report. "We searched the home for any signs of forced entry, but there weren't any, so we have to assume this is a suicide."

"Don't make any assumptions, Pete," Roni warned her fellow detective.

"Got it, Roni, but it all points to that. Also, we found a BMW in the garage. Judging from the body damage and plates, we think it's the car used to try and run Ricky Gonzalez off the road."

Roni and Trey shared a look that Ricky didn't quite know how to read.

"Can you please get the CSI team to sweep that car for prints and the like? We need to confirm that it was Hernandez who was driving it," Roni said.

"Who else would it have been?" Mariela asked, clearly as puzzled as he by the question.

"I have to trust my gut," Trey said, repeating what he'd said days before about his concerns on the case.

Ricky wasn't about to argue with his brother, even though from everything he could see the case was about as cut and dry as it could be.

When the other detective hung up, they headed to the ME's office.

She was shaking as she viewed her dead ex, but stiffened her spine and identified him. Once she did that, they were free to go and returned to his parents' home. Only once he got there, it occurred to him that there was no reason for Mariela and him to stay there any longer. Whatever threat had existed from Hernandez was over.

That Mariela felt the same way was evident as they climbed the stairs, each step they took feeling the way a death row inmate might on their way to the electric chair.

They paused in the foyer before the two bedrooms, and she said, "I guess I can go home in the morning. Go visit my parents at the assisted living center and let them know what's happening."

"I guess, only…" He took hold of her hand and drew her near. "Stay with me and we can go see your parents together."

She worried her lower lip, obviously hesitant. "That's a big step when we don't know this is real. That it wasn't just because of everything that was happening," she said and pointed to the two of them.

It was a fair enough question and he answered in the only way he could think of.

"Let me prove to you this is real. Tonight, and every other night of our lives together," he said, knowing in his heart that it was what he wanted. That he wanted her in his life forever.

The faint glimmer of a smile broadened and reached

up into her eyes, lighting them with joy. "I'd like that, Ricky. I love you."

"I love you, too, Mariela," he said, slipped his hand into hers and led her into his bedroom.

There was no rush, no worry, as they undressed each other and climbed into bed, sealing the promise they'd made each other with their kisses and loving.

As they cuddled close after making love, the rose-colored rays of dawn filtered into the room.

It had been a long and tiring night, but their nightmare was finally over and hope filled Ricky as he thought about his future life together with Mariela.

MARIELA HAD ALWAYS liked rising to see the light of day chasing away the darkness.

She had seen so much of that darkness in her life, but lying there next to Ricky, she knew that her life now would be filled with the light of his love.

Slipping her body over his, she whispered against his lips, "I love you, Ricky. I can't imagine spending the rest of my life without you."

He smiled and rolled, trapping her beneath him, and she experienced a moment of panic, remembering another man and his abuse. But as she met Ricky's clear blue gaze, filled with such light and love, she knew that she'd only ever experience joy in his arms and gave herself over to his loving.

DAYS LATER, IT DIDN'T take a psychologist to see that his brother wasn't accepting the results of the investigations the detectives had conducted into Hernandez's suicide and the BMW they had located in his garage.

"But it wasn't there the first time they checked out his place," Trey argued with his wife as they sat at the dining area table in his parents' home.

"Hernandez could have had it elsewhere. He could have hidden it in one of the warehouses where he kept his construction equipment," Roni said and added, "They didn't see the purple nylon rope the first time either, but it was there in one of the drawers."

"GSR on his gun hand was a little off," Trey said.

"But still consistent with the kind of gunshot residue you'd get with a suicide," Roni advised.

It was like watching a tennis match since for everything that Trey brought up Roni went right back at him with an answer until there were no more questions from Trey.

Roni laid her hand on his arm and squeezed reassuringly. "I trust your gut, Trey. Only this time I think it's a little off. There's no need for us to worry anymore."

With a rough sigh and heave of his broad shoulders, Trey finally agreed. "You're right. It's just that ever since I was shot, I seem to see bogeymen everywhere," he admitted.

Ricky understood. He'd worried that his brother was suffering from PTSD ever since he'd nearly been killed during his last investigation and that could certainly explain how he was feeling. Add to that his leaving the force to join SBS and his upcoming marriage to Roni, things were bound to be off with Trey.

"I can recommend someone you can see—"

"I'm good," Trey said with a flip of his hand, committed to staying the alpha male, but Ricky intended to be there for him and for Mariela, he thought and gazed at her as she sat beside him.

It seemed as good a time as any to share with his brother the news that Mariela and he had shared with his parents the night before.

"I know this might seem sudden, but Mariela and I are going to get married," he said and waited for his brother's admonishments that it was, as Ricky had said, sudden and way too soon.

To his surprise, Trey grinned and clapped his hands with delight. "Congratulations. I was worried at first, but my gut tells me this is right for both of you."

"Wow, really?" he asked as his brother, and Roni rose to hug them.

"Really, *mano*. I know the real thing when I see it," his brother said, filling Ricky with relief.

Everything was right in his world and Mariela's. They had visited her parent to share the news and they'd been happy that Mariela had found someone who loved and respected her. After, they'd talked to his parents about staying until the repairs were finished at his home, and once that was done, they'd move in there and begin the rest of their lives together.

Nothing could be better, he thought, leaned over and kissed Mariela to celebrate the news he'd just shared with Trey and Roni.

HE WATCHED THROUGH the binoculars and wanted to throw up as the family members shared hugs and goodbyes in the courtyard of the family home.

So much happiness and joy while his family had been suffering. While they'd been ignored and the Gonzalez family had become like Miami royalty.

He hated that he'd failed so many times to finish off Ricky, the baby of the family.

The bomb was supposed to have taken him out and maybe some of the others as well, only Ricky's new girl had been too observant.

Next time they might not be so lucky, he thought and drove away.

His family needed him, and he never disappointed family.

* * * * *

COMING SOON!

We really hope you enjoyed reading this book.
If you're looking for more romance, be sure to
head to the shops when new books are
available on

Thursday 5th January

To see which titles are coming soon, please visit
millsandboon.co.uk/nextmonth

MILLS & BOON

THE HEART OF ROMANCE

A ROMANCE FOR EVERY READER

MODERN

Prepare to be swept off your feet by sophisticated, sexy and seductive heroes, in some of the world's most glamourous and romantic locations, where power and passion collide.

HISTORICAL

Escape with historical heroes from time gone by. Whether your passion is for wicked Regency Rakes, muscled Vikings or rugged Highlanders, await the romance of the past.

MEDICAL

Set your pulse racing with dedicated, delectable doctors in the high-pressure world of medicine, where emotions run high and passion, comfort and love are the best medicine.

True Love

Celebrate true love with tender stories of heartfelt romance, from the rush of falling in love to the joy a new baby can bring, and a focus on the emotional heart of a relationship.

Desire

Indulge in secrets and scandal, intense drama and plenty of sizzling hot action with powerful and passionate heroes who have it all: wealth, status, good looks…everything but the right woman.

HEROES

Experience all the excitement of a gripping thriller, with an intense romance at its heart. Resourceful, true-to-life women and strong, fearless men face danger and desire - a killer combination!

To see which titles are coming soon, please visit

millsandboon.co.uk/nextmonth

LET'S TALK

Romance

For exclusive extracts, competitions
and special offers, find us online:

JOIN US ON SOCIAL MEDIA!

Stay up to date with our latest releases, author news and gossip, special offers and discounts, and all the behind-the-scenes action from Mills & Boon...

 @millsandboon

 @millsandboonuk

 facebook.com/millsandboon

 @millsandboonuk

It might just be true love...

GET YOUR ROMANCE FIX!

Get the latest romance news,
exclusive author interviews, story
extracts and much more!

blog.millsandboon.co.uk

MILLS & BOON

Desire

Indulge in secrets and scandal, intense drama and plenty of sizzling hot action with powerful and passionate heroes who have it all: wealth, status, good looks…everything but the right woman.

MILLS & BOON

MODERN

Power and Passion

Prepare to be swept off your feet by sophisticated, sexy and seductive heroes, in some of the world's most glamourous and romantic locations, where power and passion collide.

MILLS & BOON
MEDICAL
Pulse-Racing Passion

Set your pulse racing with dedicated, delectable doctors in the high-pressure world of medicine, where emotions run high and passion, comfort and love are the best medicine.

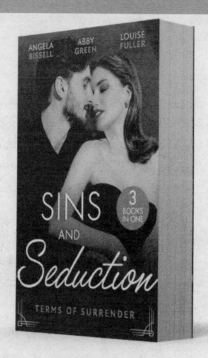